Kenneth Rayner

Life and Times of Andrew Johnson, Seventeenth President of the United States

Written from a national stand-point. Vol. 2

Kenneth Rayner

Life and Times of Andrew Johnson, Seventeenth President of the United States
Written from a national stand-point. Vol. 2

ISBN/EAN: 9783337402730

Printed in Europe, USA, Canada, Australia, Japan

Cover: Foto ©Raphael Reischuk / pixelio.de

More available books at **www.hansebooks.com**

LIFE AND TIMES

OF

ANDREW JOHNSON,

SEVENTEENTH PRESIDENT OF THE UNITED STATES.

WRITTEN FROM A NATIONAL STAND-POINT.

BY A NATIONAL MAN.

A man's first care should be, to avoid the reproaches of his own Heart; his next, to escape the censures of the World. If the latter interferes with the former, it should be entirely disregarded; but otherwise, there cannot be a greater satisfaction to an honest mind, than to see those approbations which it gives itself, seconded by the applauses of the public.—*Addison.*

NEW YORK:
D. APPLETON AND COMPANY,
443 & 445 BROADWAY
1866.

PREFACE.

The author of the following pages throws himself on the generous forbearance of the reader, so far as any shortcomings of style, or of systematic arrangement, may be involved. Having thought much, and feeling very deeply as he does, in regard to the present state of the country, the author considers it a matter of very great importance that President Johnson's position, his relations to the parties engaged in the late unfortunate struggle, and his views and opinions in reference to the proper policy of the Government for the future, should be thoroughly understood and appreciated by the public. The author has waited, to see if some more competent pen would not undertake the task. Every one must admit that President Johnson's position is one of transcendent importance at the present time. From the very necessity of the case, the task devolves on him of having to readjust the component parts of a great empire shaken by the conflict of four years of war, without precedent to guide him, and with the public mind yet in a state of effervescence and anxiety. It is indispensable to the success of the Government, and the advancement of the public good, that the popular judgment should be enabled to decide fairly and impartially in regard to him. If his policy is the correct one, then it is all-important that public opinion should sustain him. There never has been, in the history of our Government, so great a necessity for harmonizing the public opinion of the country, as exists at the present time. War has had its triumphs, and now is the time for aiding peace in achieving *its* triumphs, also. If, on examination, it should appear that Mr. Johnson is the *representative man* to restore harmony, and the mutual dependence of the interests of the different sections of the country, then it is the patriotic duty of every good man to sustain him. The public mind is confused, agitated, disturbed, anxious. Every one is more or less nervous in regard to the future. All eyes are turned toward Mr. Johnson. Every one is solicitous of information concerning him. Confidence in his unselfish patriotism, his moderation, his conservatism, his nationality, would do more toward quieting all apprehensions as to the future, than any thing else. The object of the author is to present Mr. Johnson to the public mind *just as he is*—to convey a correct impression as to his character—and to enable popular opinion to judge of his future course by an investigation of his conduct in the past.

Mr. Johnson is a man who, in the history of his political life, has evidently acted on a regular system. His course has not been one of versatility—of mere expedients. The public appetite is hungry for information in regard to him. In endeavoring to impart this information, the author has been conscientious in his desire to promote the public good. If it is to the interest of the people of this country to support, and aid, and strengthen Mr. Johnson, then he who may be instrumental in convincing them of this, and of removing any erroneous impressions concerning him, will have done his country a service.

The author has been actuated with a desire to do justice to Mr. Johnson, as well as serve the public interests in conveying correct information. He admits his high admiration of Mr. Johnson's character—an admiration founded on a close study and rigid scrutiny of his political life. No matter how pure and patriotic his character may be—no matter how blameless and upright his administration of public affairs, yet he cannot expect to escape that censure and fault-finding which are the common lot of all men who reach such high eminence of position by their own force of character. Old party issues have disappeared, but new ones will take their places. They will be made for the occasion, if they do not necessarily arise. In a country like ours, where thought is untrammelled, and the press is free, parties must exist. We may expect to see new issues presented, and new combinations formed; and as reflections, growing out of the war and its consequences, have superseded all other questions in the public mind, we may reasonably suppose that these new issues and combinations will have reference to the events of, and the results produced by, the late unhappy war. We have already foreshadowings of this; and since the assemblage of Congress in December, 1865, we have already seen the elements of opposition assuming regular shape and form. His friends are already forewarned; they owe it to Mr. Johnson, to justice, and to truth, that they should be forearmed also.

In order to properly appreciate the author's purpose in

this humble effort, the reader must have in view the object and design aimed at. It is not to narrate startling adventures, nor to describe amusing and entertaining incidents in human affairs, nor to inculcate any peculiar views of government or politics. His object is to inform the public in regard to the character, morally, intellectually, and politically—of the man who now holds the highest executive position in the Government. His purpose is to calm and compose any anxiety or apprehension, in either section, as to the difficulties which beset the future, by affording an assurance that in Mr. Johnson we have a man for President whose whole public life has been uniform and consistent in sustaining and upholding the great principles of constitutional liberty, based, as they are, on THE RIGHTS OF THE PEOPLE. His further purpose is to warn Mr. Johnson's friends to be on their guard against the machinations of faction ; to avoid all conflicts, except in self-defence ; but still to be prepared to defend him when unjustly assailed, and, in defending him, to defend the cause of free government and a restored Union, with which his name will be identified to the latest posterity.

CONTENTS.

CHAPTER IV.

CHAPTER V.

CHAPTER VI.

CHAPTER VII.

CHAPTER VIII.

CHAPTER XIII.

CHAPTER XIV.

CHAPTER XV

CHAPTER XVI.

CHAPTER XVII.

CHAPTER XVIII.

CHAPTER XIX.

CHAPTER·XX.

CHAPTER XXI.

CHAPTER XXII.

CHAPTER XXIII.

LIFE OF ANDREW JOHNSON.

CHAPTER I.

Practical working of our Free Institutions—Birth of Andrew Johnson—Parents —Jacob Johnson—His character and pursuits—Orphanage of Andrew Johnson—Apprenticed to a tailor—His studious habits—Goes to Laurens Court House, S. C.—Moves to Greenville, Tenn.—In business—Marriage —Industry—Learning the alphabet—Chosen a Town Commissioner— Elected Mayor—Trustee of Rhea Academy—Chosen Member of the Tennessee Legislature—State of feeling in that body—Candidate for Presidential Elector—Elected State Senator—Chosen Representative in Congress.

THERE has not been, in our history, a more striking exemplification of the spirit and practical working of our free institutions, than that presented in the life, character, and elevation to the highest position in the Government, of Andrew Johnson, now President of the United States. The history of this distinguished man's life presents as forcible a commentary as could be written, on the peculiar structure of our Government and the influence and operation of constitutional liberty, in the great American Republic.

The great philosophical principle, which underlies the whole framework of our Republican system, is, that in the possession and enjoyment of rights and privileges— whether by birthright or under the law of the land—all men are on an equality. The reader must not suppose that this is advocating any doctrine of radical agrarianism. It is not meant to be said that the vicious and bad man is the equal of the virtuous and good man—that the stupidly ignorant man is the equal of the man of high intellectual culture—that the rude and unmannerly clown is the equal of the civil, polite, and benevolent man. The meaning of the author is, that every man, both naturally and under the law, is the equal of every other man, under similar conditions and circumstances. Our institutions ignore every thing like monarchy, and—what is still more objectionable, in the estimation of the author—of aristocracy also. In our country, the road to distinction, to honor, to fame, is open and free to all alike. Merit, capacity, usefulness, are the only criteria for fitness for the highest honors and the most elevated positions. The stand-point of our whole free government and liberty is to be found in two simple lines, that are indelibly impressed on our memories, from the earliest associations of our school-boy days :

"Honor and fame from no condition rise;
Act well your part—there all the honor lies."

ANDREW JOHNSON, the seventeenth President of the United States, is a native of North Carolina, and of the city of Raleigh. He was born on the 29th day of December, 1808, and is consequently in the fifty-eighth year of his age. His family, though not persons of wealth or pretension, were worthy and respectable people. His father, Jacob Johnson, lived and died in the city of Raleigh. In regard to Jacob Johnson, the information of the author, derived from reliable sources, is, that he was an honest, upright, and worthy man. He was a *poor* man, but a man of probity and honor. Information, derived from aged persons in Raleigh, now living, states that he was a favorite with the prominent and leading men of Raleigh in his day, and that he possessed their confidence and respect. In an old volume of the "Raleigh Star," in the State Library at Raleigh, the number dated January 12, 1812, has the following obituary notice of Jacob Johnson :

"Died, in this city, on Saturday last, Jacob Johnson, who had, for many years, occupied an humble, but useful station in society. He was city constable, sexton, and porter of the State Bank. In his last illness he was visited by the principal inhabitants of the city, by all of whom he was esteemed for his honesty, sobriety, industry, and humane, friendly disposition. Among all by whom he was known and esteemed, none lament him more (except, perhaps, his relatives) than the publisher of this paper, for he owes his life, on a particular occasion, to the boldness and humanity of Johnson."

The "Raleigh Standard," of August 28, 1865, in copying the above, states as follows :

" The occasion referred to in the concluding lines of the above obituary notice, was this: Thomas Henderson was upset in a canoe, and was so near being drowned, that life was nearly extinct when he was recovered. Jacob Johnson was on the bank, safe and secure. But he saw *his friend* drowning before his face. Thoughtless of self, he plunged in, at the hazard of his own life. He did finally succeed in saving his friend, but both were nearly exhausted when they reached the shore. The statement, in regard to Jacob Johnson being ' esteemed for his honesty, sobriety, industry, and humane, friendly disposition,' is concurred in by the old inhabitants now living in this city. This grateful and generous tribute to his worth and goodness of heart is more to be valued and esteemed than ' storied urn or animated bust.' "

There was no man of that day who possessed more character and influence, or who was more highly esteemed and regarded in the community where he lived, than Colonel

William Polk. He had been a revolutionary officer of distinction and merit. He was a man of wonderful energy, sagacity, and business habits. He was the intimate and close friend of General Jackson. By his industry and enterprise he amassed a large fortune, and was charitable to the poor and a patron and friend of honest worth. As president of the institution, he appointed Jacob Johnson porter of the State Bank, entertained for him the kindest feelings, and treated him with friendly regard. In a communication to the " Raleigh Standard," of September 8, 1865, it is stated, in reference to this appointment of Jacob Johnson as porter in the bank, that " Colonel Polk was shrewd, sagacious, energetic, and industrious. No idler, no spendthrift, no drunkard, could have won his confidence, or eluded his vigilance."

Andrew Johnson, being thus left fatherless, without fortune, and without influential friends to aid him, had no means of acquiring an education; and, at ten years of age, he was apprenticed to a tailor in Raleigh. He had had no schooling whatever. He did not know the alphabet even. But, at that early age, the prompting of his native genius displayed itself in an aspiration for knowledge. His youthful mind hungered for instruction. There was, at that time, a gentleman living in Raleigh who was in the habit of reading to the young workingmen of the town, during the hours of relaxation from labor. Through the kind invitation of a boyish friend, young Johnson availed himself of this opportunity of listening to the speeches of the eminent English statesmen, whose immortal productions, in advocacy of the great principles of English liberty, no doubt, sank deep into his heart at that period of his life; for, strange as it may seem, it was from a volume of that kind, that the gentleman alluded to was in the habit of reading. Young Johnson resolved that, in defiance of all obstacles, he *would* learn to read, and that the great store-house of knowledge, contained in books, should no longer remain closed to him. The gentleman alluded to, seeing the deep interest he manifested in it, made him a present of the book; and from that book he learned the alphabet, and also how to spell and to read. He devoted his nights, after the labors of the day were over, in poring over its pages. From his eager anxiety to learn, it may readily be supposed that his proficiency was very rapid. There are men now living in the town of Raleigh who recollect him well as a youth of strong, physical vigor, fond of the exciting sports of hunting and fishing in the neighboring forests and streams, during the periods of relaxation from labor—of kind and genial social qualities, and of unquestioned pluck and spirit, whenever he felt his rights or self-respect to be infringed upon.

In 1824, at the age of sixteen, he left Raleigh, and went to Laurens Court House, South Carolina, where he continued to work as a journeyman tailor for two years, when he again returned to Raleigh, in 1826. He remained in Raleigh, however, only about five months, when he again left, to try his fortunes elsewhere. His main object was to look after and provide for his widowed and destitute mother. Like an affectionate and dutiful son, he resolved to share his destiny and fortunes with that mother who had loved and nursed him in his infancy. He took his mother with him to Greenville, a village in East Tennessee, where he obtained employment in his line of business, and where he concluded to locate himself. Soon after settling in Greenville, he was married to Miss Eliza McCardell, a lady of considerable attainments and most estimable character, which have not been without their influence on his future destiny. Soon after his marriage, with a view to better his condition, he left Greenville, and went farther west to Rutledge, in Grainger Co., Tenn. But he remained there only a few months, and then returned, resolving to make Greenville his permanent home. There he settled himself, there he continued to work faithfully and laboriously at his trade. He earned his bread for the support of himself and his family by the sweat of his brow. His thrift, in acquiring a competency, was slow, but sure. For years, he thus pursued the quiet and even tenor of his way. Of industrious and sober habits, of modest and unobtrusive deportment, fond of domestic quiet, and devoted to his wife and children, he looked calmly on the great and stirring events that were transpiring in the world.

The author has taken some pains to find out whether there was any truth in the rumor, that has long been talked about, of his wife having aided him, in early life, in acquiring an education. The report is founded in truth. Mrs. Johnson, being a lady of fine native intellect, and of considerable cultivation, devoted herself to the welcome and affectionate task of aiding her husband in laying the foundations of a course of instruction, which has continued to enlarge in scope and efficiency, from the ordinary rudiments of learning to the highest elements of statesmanship. What tranquil happiness, what consoling reflections, must be hers in witnessing such a harvest of honor, of usefulness and fame, from seeds sown in part by her own hands!

In 1828, at only twenty years of age, Andrew Johnson was chosen one of the commissioners of the town of Greenville, by the voters of the place. This, though an inconsiderable position, yet, under the circumstances, was a very high compliment. It afforded the strongest evidence of the high appreciation in which he was held by his fellow-townsmen. It is a very rare thing, even in the smallest villages in our country, for a young mechanic, under lawful age, to be chosen a member of their legislative councils. But in two years afterwards, in 1830, he was elected Mayor of the town—thus affording the most incontestable proof that he had so demeaned himself in his place as Commissioner, as to have acquired the confidence and respect of his countrymen. Soon after he was appointed by the County Court one of the trustees of "Rhea Academy." When it is taken into consideration that only a few years before he did not even know the alphabet, it is evident that he must have been regarded as a special friend and advocate of education; as indeed he was, and has ever continued to be. Well he might have been. No man had more keenly felt the need of it—no man had sacrificed more devotedly at its altars—no man more cordially appreciated its blessings.

From this time forth Mr. Johnson's advancement in public favor and confidence was regular and rapid. He had established a character for strong practical common sense, of sobriety and industry, and for his jealous interest in the welfare of the substantial working-classes. In 1835 he was elected a member of the House of Representatives of the Legislature of Tennessee, from the counties of Greene and Washington. At the ensuing session of the Tennessee Legislature he acquired the character of a useful, business, working-man. He then exhibited that same trait of rigid economy in public expenditures that has marked his course as a public man throughout his political life. Mr. Johnson has always opposed extravagance in the expenditure of the public money, on high grounds of *principle;* that generally extravagant and reckless appropriations entailed heavy burdens on the people, whilst the benefits accrued to monopolies and corporations, and that a still greater evil consisted in the demoralization, both of the representative and constituent bodies, by the frauds,

peculations, jobs, and contracts attendant on the appropriations, collections, and disbursements of these large sums of
public money. The period of Mr. Johnson's first service
in the Legislature of Tennessee was at the time when
there was a *furor* pervading the whole country in regard
to a general system of internal improvement by the States.
It was about this time that such enormous amounts were
expended, and such heavy debts incurred, by many of the
States, under the "log-rolling system;" by which many
works were constructed that proved to be useless and bur-
densome, merely for the purpose of obtaining for other
works the votes of the sections through which they ran.
Andrew Johnson strongly opposed this log-rolling system
of extravagance and heavy debts. Hence it was, for the
time being, he was charged with being the opponent of all
internal improvements by the States. In this, great injustice was done him. He was not opposed, but friendly to
such works of improvement as the public wants and ne-
cessities required, and as were compatible with the ability
of the people to sustain the burdens of. So overwhelming
was the feeling, however, in favor of a grand system of internal improvement, at the time, that at the succeeding
election in 1837 Mr. Johnson was defeated for the Legislature. If he had been the demagogue his enemies have
sometimes charged him with being, he would have gone
with the current of public opinion. But he resisted public sentiment, believing it to be in error. He preferred defeat, sustained by his convictions of duty, in preference
to success by abandoning them. Time brought about reaction in the popular mind. In 1839 Mr. Johnson's constituents again elected him to the Legislature.

In 1840, in the memorable contest between General
Harrison and Mr. Van Buren, Mr. Johnson was selected
by the Democratic party of Tennessee as a candidate for

elector, for the State at large, on the Van Buren ticket. He canvassed the State with great assiduity and ability, but without success. The State voted for Gen. Harrison. His selection for this position shows how much character he had made by his service in the Legislature, and the very high estimate his party must have put upon his powers and talents as a popular orator. To have been chosen for this important task, at the age of thirty-two, when he had to meet the many able champions of the Whig party, in a State remarkable for the number of its great popular orators, and in which each party has been in the habit of putting forth its ablest men, is the strongest proof that can be offered of the rapid progress he had made in public opinion and the hold he had secured on public confidence—at a time, too, when his party had assigned to him the leading of a forlorn hope in the advocacy of Mr. Van Buren.

In 1841 Mr. Johnson was elected a State Senator in the Legislature of Tennessee, from the district composed of Greene and Hawkins Counties. After serving one session in that capacity, with his usual industry and attention to the practical details of legislative business, in 1843 he was nominated for the House of Representatives of the United States, from the First District, composed of seven counties in East Tennessee. His opponent was Col. John A. Aiken, a gentleman of high character and ability ; and after a spirited canvass, conducted with courtesy and decorum, Mr. Johnson was elected by a handsome majority. He took his seat at Washington City in December, 1843.

CHAPTER II.

The first occasion on which Mr. Johnson addressed the House was in the course of an exciting debate, in which the everlasting slavery agitation was the great element. Mr. J. then deprecated it, in its unhappy tendency to sever the kind feelings between the two sections, and thus to threaten the destruction of the Union. Young member as he was, he did not hesitate to enter the lists with the veteran debater and statesman, J. Quincy Adams. At that early day he foresaw and predicted danger to the Union, from the constant agitation of the question of slavery. In a bold and forcible style he rebuked several prominent members of the House, whom he regarded as pandering to this agitation. On that occasion he managed to get the ear of the House—a fortunate thing for a young member in the delivery of his first speech. The author has been informed by one who was a member of Congress at the time, that on the occasion of Mr. Johnson's delivering the speech alluded to, the late Charles J. Ingersoll, who was a very observant man, and a severe critic in his estimate of human character, and who was also a member at the same time, after listening to Mr. J. for a while, inquired of the said informant, "Who is that man now speaking?" On being told it was Mr. Johnson, of Tennessee, "Well," said Mr. Ingersoll, "he is a man of mind, and my word for it, he will make his mark in the world." It appears that, during the debate, some reference had been made to the direct exertion of Divine power in the control of human affairs. Mr. Johnson, in reply, took the position that whilst the Almighty in former times had manifested His power, by *special* interposition, in opposition to Nature's laws, yet ever since the days of miracles had past, He left no one in doubt as to His omnipotent authority, who observed the phenomena of Nature in the material world. Warming up with the subject, he gave utterance to the following outburst of eloquence:

"I might go on multiplying cases from the sacred volume, in aid of those already referred to. We may consult our own observation and senses: sometimes we see the power of God displayed in the agitation of the winds, in the heaving and contending billows of the mighty deep; sometimes we hear the mutterings of His discontent in the threatening peal of thunder; sometimes He exhibits the brilliancy and awful grandeur of His countenance in the forked lightning's glare; sometimes He lets loose the baleful comet, passing from one extremity of the universe to the other, emitting from its fiery tail pestilence and death. This idea is more forcibly carried out, in the lines of the poet, that these are

> ' Signs sent by God, to mark the will of heaven,
> Signs which bid nations weep, and be forgiven.' "

Let those who may feel inclined to a rigid criticism, reflect that the author of the above was not able, eighteen years before their delivery, to read and write. Let them further reflect, that this was his first speech, only about seven weeks after he had taken his seat. The foregoing extract was about the conclusion of a long speech, exhibiting strong argumentative powers.

The next question of great national concern on which Mr. Johnson addressed the House, was at the succeeding session, in January, 1845, on the question of annexing Texas to the Union. Parts of this speech are marked by great argumentative power, and other parts by the most pathetic eloquence. Mr. Johnson urged annexation, not on any sectional ground, or with a view to the promotion of any sectional interest. He placed it on the high ground of an enlarged national policy, addressing itself to the patriotic feelings of all sections and interests of the country alike. In one respect he presents the argument in a way which seems to have been original with himself, viz. : that the United States were bound by treaty stipulations with France, in the treaty of 1803 (at a time when Louisiana comprehended within its limits the Territory of Texas), to protect the people therein in the free enjoyment of their liberty, property, religion, etc., and to admit them into the Union as soon as possible, etc. That the United States, in ceding the Texas portion of Louisiana to Spain, by the treaty of 1819, could not thereby divest themselves of the obligation they had assumed in the treaty with France in 1803. After quoting "Vattel's Laws of Nations," page 166, section 165, he goes on to say :

"The treaty made in 1803 with France, is the most ancient treaty; the treaty made with Spain, sixteen years after, is the posterior treaty. The treaty of 1819 is in direct conflict with the third article of the treaty of 1803, and, to that extent, is void from the beginning—never vesting Spain with the shadow of title to the territory and people of Texas. Notwithstanding the United States have slept upon, or permitted, her right, which she obtained from France in 1803, to be latent from 1819 up to this time, this Government has never been divested of it, according to the laws of nations. And it can be resumed or exercised at any time, the people and Government of Texas assenting thereto, without violating the rights of Mexico or Spain. Admit, for the sake of the argument, the fact, that the title set up by Texas, to herself, is not clear beyond dispute; admit, also, the fact of her passing voluntarily under the jurisdiction of the United States, thereby putting this Government in possession of the whole country. Once in possession, this Government is not merely bound to rely on the possessory title, but is cast back upon her more ancient right, acquired by treaty from France in 1803, which is beyond dispute, and good against the world, and places this Government in a position that will enable her to do justice to a brave and patriotic people, by incorporating them into the Union, and thereby redeem its plighted faith. The title to the whole country was legally and constitutionally acquired from France in 1803. In 1819 it had been surrendered, or ceded, to Spain, contrary to the consent of the inhabitants, in disregard of national law, and by trampling under foot treaty stipulations, solemnly made and entered into.   *   *   *   *   *   *   *

"If the premises be correctly laid, and the conclusions be lawfully drawn, the whole question resolves itself into a plain, simple proposition of admitting a new State into the Union—a power which no one doubts or denies; and all that remains for Congress now to do is, to prescribe the mode and manner of admission. I think the great error the committee has fallen into in the discussion of this subject is, the confounding of two separate and distinct things; the one, to acquire territory under the treaty-making power; the other, the admission of new States into the Union. It has been contended by some, since this discussion commenced, that the Government must first acquire the territory by treaty, and then, I suppose, keep it in a kind of political probation for a certain length of time, and then admit the territory so acquired into the Union as a sovereign State. The acquisition of territory under the treaty-making power is wholly incidental. There is nowhere to be found in the Constitution the power expressly conferred on the General Government to acquire territory. If the admission of new States into the Union be made dependent upon the exercise of an incidental power, flowing from the treaty-making power to acquire territory, the express grant of power becomes the inferior and subordinate to the incidental power, which is an absurdity in itself. The admission of a sovereign State into the Union, is not an acquisition of territory in the sense that territory is or can be acquired under the treaty-making power. They are wholly different. When territory is acquired by this Government, under the treaty-making power, the entire jurisdiction and right inure to this Government; or, in other words, the territory so acquired becomes the property and creature of the States composing the Union at the time of such acquisition. Not so when a State is admitted into the Union. She then comes in as an integral, clothed with all the attributes of the other sovereignties, retaining the entire control and disposition of her own territory. The admission of Georgia and North Carolina into the Union, after the adoption of the Federal Constitution by the other States, did not vest the right of territory in the Federal Government. For long after their admission into the Union as States, they made deeds of cession of their territory to the General Government."

The foregoing extract from Mr. Johnson's speech on Texas annexation, is here given to the reader to enable him to see that he urged it upon high considerations of national policy and national duty; and also to present a specimen of his close ratiocinative style of argument. There are other portions of the same speech that are highly eloquent. In speaking of the people of Texas, then eagerly waiting for the action of our Government, he used the following language:

"They have gone out from their mother-country as the twelve spies in olden times. They have succeeded in exploring and possessing themselves of the only remaining portion of Canaan, destined by God for His American Israel. Having accomplished the great object of their mission, they now return, not as prodigals, whose estates have been wasted in riotous living, or with even specimens of the production of their delightful country; but with the country itself, sufficient in itself to make an empire; and this country they are willing to lay down at our feet. Shall we refuse them admission into our family of States? * * * For myself, I am willing (when I take a glance at the historic page, giving an account of their rise and progress; the privations and hardships they have undergone; the money and toil they have expended; the valor and patriotism they have displayed in the hour of danger; their magnanimity and forbearance in the hour of triumph over a captive foe, whose garments were red with their brothers' blood; the battles they have fought and fields of carnage through which they have passed; the brilliant and unsurpassed victories they have won, on their grand and glorious march to freedom and independence), to extend to them the right hand of fellowship, and welcome them into our glorious sisterhood of States."

Such language as this could have proceeded from the lips only of one who was *sincere*, and the judgment of whose head was sustained by the feelings of his heart. There is one passage in the speech quoted from, of significant—may it not be of almost prophetic—import. It is this: Speaking of the advantages, both present and prospective, to be derived from the annexation of Texas, Mr. Johnson mentioned:

"The profitable employment it would give to slave-labor, thereby enabling the master to clothe and feed that portion of our population, softening and alleviating their condition; and in the end, when it shall please Him who works out all great events by general laws, prove to be the gateway out of which the sable sons of Africa are to pass from bondage to freedom; where they can become merged in a population congenial with themselves, who know and feel no distinction in consequence of the various hues of skin or crosses of blood."

Here is a suggestion, incidentally made, at a time when the present state of affairs could not have been dreamed of by any one, which may possibly contain the germ of our future national policy in regard to the colored race. Up to the present time, all is doubt and uncertainty as to what time and experience may prove to be our true policy in reference to the status of the African race. It is a question, however, which from its vast importance will soon become the predominant one, in the philosophy of national as well as of Southern politics. One thing is certain : the idea of colonizing them to themselves, so that the problem of their capacity for civilization and social elevation may be fairly tested, is growing in favor, and gaining proselytes daily. This plan of colonization is gaining ground constantly, as involving the best interests of both races. The author knows the fact, that many of the most sagacious and philanthropic officers of the Federal army, including general officers of distinction, have become convinced, from their observation and experience in the South, that the two races never can prosperously and happily coexist in the same country, where their relative numbers approximate as nearly as they do in the Southern States. These men leave the South, decided converts to, and advocates of, colonization of the blacks to themselves. The most perplexing question is, *Where?* May it not be that Mr. Johnson prefigured the solution of this difficulty ? If, as he said in the foregoing extract from his speech, Almighty Power "works out all great events by general laws," may it not be that through the gateway of Texas may be the exodus of the African race to a land of their own, hereafter to be acquired ? May not the working out of the Monroe doctrine to its natural and logical consequences, involve one of those " general laws," from which the " great event " of African colonization is to be eliminated? Thus far, President Johnson has not committed himself on this question. The probability is, he regards it the part of duty and of wisdom to wait, and see what the developments of the future may suggest as the most advisable course. When he does speak out on that subject, it will not be in the language of equivocation.

In the first session of the Twenty-ninth Congress, 1845–'46, the question of giving notice to Great Britain of our purpose to terminate the joint occupancy of Oregon by the two countries, was the great and exciting subject of the session. It was discussed at great length, with great ability, eloquence, and deep feeling. It was regarded by many of the ablest and most discreet men in both Houses as involving in its decision war with England. At that time the feeling of hostility to Great Britain was very strong. It does not seem to have been a party question; and on reading the debates it seems that neither those who advocated a termination of the joint occupancy, nor those who opposed it, were actuated by any common motive or object. Some who advocated it contended for it as a *peace* measure, whilst others did not hesitate to avow that their purpose was *war*.

The reader will understand that, up to this time, the real title to Oregon, and also the proper limits of the territory, were matters of dispute. The United States claimed the country, first, under prior discovery and settlement, and secondly, under the treaty of cession from Spain, in 1819. Great Britain claimed not the exclusive title, but the right of "joint occupancy" with Spain, under the "Nootka Sound Convention," subject to which right by Great Britain the United States purchased from Spain. This "joint occupation" consisted in securing to the citizens of both countries the right of entering, trading, etc., for the space of ten years. Several attempts to settle the question and nature of title having failed, in 1827 the convention for joint occupation was indefinitely renewed, a provision being inserted that either party might terminate it by giving to the other twelve months' notice of the intention to do so. At the session of 1845–'46, the Committee on Foreign Affairs, in the House of Representatives, reported resolutions for giving notice to Great Britain for the termination of the joint occupation by the two countries. The question was, whether we should continue the joint occupation, which the British Government seemed to be willing to—whether we should compromise the difficulty by dividing the territory between the two powers—or whether the United States should rigidly contend for the whole, up to the line of 54° 40'.

Mr. Johnson took the position last mentioned. It was a question on which he seems to have felt deeply. He urged the propriety of terminating the joint occupation. That he insisted on as a *peace* measure. The value of the country was beginning to be appreciated. Settlers, both British and American, were pouring into it. Collisions were threatening, growing out of rival jurisdictions. Mr. Johnson saw and urged the difficulties that must arise from two peoples being governed by two rival authorities on the same soil—that then was the time to settle the matter definitely—that as the settlers on both sides increased, and the country came to be regarded as of more importance, the greater would be the difficulty of an amicable settlement. Mr. Johnson contended strenuously for the whole of Oregon, up to 54° 40'. He seems not to have regarded the British claim south of that line as worth any thing; that her right under the Nootka Convention to navigate the waters, and to trade with the inhabitants of the territory, did not and could not affect the title of domain existing in the United States. Some extracts are given below from Mr. Johnson's speech, explanatory of his position on this question, so important and exciting at that time:

" When discussing a question so important as the one now presented to the House and the country, it should be in a spirit of calm deliberation; and we should consider well the consequences that are to follow from the action that is to be taken by this House upon it. I know that since this discussion commenced we have heard much of wars and rumors of wars; and that the passions and feelings of the country have been addressed to a very great extent. So far as I am concerned, if I know the feelings of my own bosom, I am for peace, if peace can be continued on honorable terms. But if, in adopting the means which we believe best calculated to secure peace, war is to be the result, I am prepared for the consequences. No member of this House desires peace more earnestly than I do. Yes, in the language of high authority, I desire the day speedily to come when we shall have ' peace on earth, and good will among men ' throughout the world. I wish I could hope that the beginning of that glorious era would commence in my day and generation. If I could believe there was a reasonable prospect, I should now stand on tiptoe, as it were, stretching my ken to its utmost tension, to discover the streaks of the dawn of that glorious morning. But, as ardently as I desire peace for my country, I must take that view of this subject, and that stand upon the question under consideration, which I believe my position and the rights, the interests, and the honor of my country demand.   *   *   *   *

" I am for giving the notice as recommended by the President of the United States, as the surest means of preserving peace between the two nations which is so much desired by every lover of his kind. I believe that Great Britain will treat upon more favorable terms after the notice is given to terminate the joint occupancy, than she would before. The giving the notice cannot be construed by the English Government into a hostile move on the part of the United States. The. giving of the notice is expressly provided for in the Convention of 1827. It is one of the stipulations agreed upon by the high contracting parties, to be exercised by either at any time, without any just cause of offence to the other. I further contend that the giving the twelve months' notice will increase the chances of settling this question without war; without the notice, sooner or later war is inevitable. The idea of two governments—the laws, institutions, manners, and customs of whose peoples are different from each other—exercising jurisdiction, criminal and civil, at the same time, over the same territory, but upon the subjects of the respective governments living promiscuously together, would never do in practice, however plausible in theory. A policy of this kind would most assuredly lead to war; conflicts would take place between the two jurisdictions; jealousy among the people claiming protection under different governments, would finally result in outbreaks and violence. The certain result of each government continuing to protect its own citizens in Oregon, would be war. I shall vote for the 'notice' as a peace measure. I look upon the notice as holding out the olive-branch of peace in time to prevent war in future. I believe it would be so construed by the Christian world. But, if in taking steps to attain so desirable an end as peace, war should be the consequence, why the nation must be prepared for the worst. Let the notice be given."

From the foregoing extract it may be seen what are Mr. Johnson's views and feelings in regard to *peace*, as the proper policy of nations, as long as it can be preserved without compromising national honor. In this the people of the country have an earnest of what they may rely on, as President Johnson's policy, in case of complications with foreign powers. They have an assurance that he will anxiously cultivate relations of peace with the nations of the earth, whilst at the same time he will scrupulously insist on maintaining our country's rights and character, even at the hazard of war.

Mr. Johnson contended for the whole of Oregon. He

was unwilling to *compromise* where the title to the whole was so clear to his own mind. Mr. Johnson is a genuine Anglo-Saxon in his fond desire for the acquisition of land. He seems to regard the settling, the cultivating, the improving and adorning our vast public domain, and the extension of republican institutions, civil and religious liberty, and well-regulated law and order over the Continent, to be the great mission of American civilization. Hence it is he pertinaciously adheres to every foot of our soil which he considers to be ours. The following extract from the same speech will show to the reader the direct and summary method of thought and argument by which he arrived at his conclusion that our title to the whole territory was clear and valid:

" I have no doubt but that our title to the whole of Oregon is 'clear and unquestionable.' On examining the subject, we find that Spain made the first discovery in 1528. That was followed up by a discovery in 1775, three years before Great Britain's discovery; and this was followed up again by landing at the mouth of the Columbia River in 1792, the year of Captain Gray's first discovery. Then came the exploration of Lewis and Clarke in 1806, then the settlement of Astoria in 1810, and in 1819 the purchase by this Government of all the title Spain had to this Oregon territory (Great Britain stood by, and did not dispute that purchase being made); and in 1824 the United States transferred a portion of this territory to Russia, fixing the line of 54° 40' as the boundary between the two Governments. In 1825 Great Britain negotiated with Russia for a portion of the same territory; and now, upon the north of that line, she holds absolute possession, derived from Russia, which latter power had derived her power from the United States, the United States having purchased from Spain all her title in 1819. I consider Great Britain as estopped from objecting to our title. She holds the territory north of 54° 40', under the same title that we hold the territory south of it."

In the course of the debate, many members had spoken of the difficulties and dangers of a war with England. They had dwelt on the great power of that country, the unprepared condition of the United States to engage in a war with her, and the terrible consequences to the American people likely to ensue. Mr. Johnson, who is known to be very sensitive in regard to the honor, power, and glory of our country—although a decided advocate for peace, in reply to these war arguments, warmed up, and said:

"A great deal has been said in this debate about the British lion and the American eagle. Let the British lion growl, let him assume a menacing attitude, if he is so inclined. He will be closely watched in the distance, from Oregon's lofty peak of Mount St. Helen's, which lifts its proud and majestic form fifteen thousand feet above the ocean-level, by the American eagle, with talons more terrible than the glittering spear of Mars; with an eye that does not wince, though coming in contact with the sun's brightest rays. If that same British lion shall approach, if he shall dare make a hostile foot-print on our shore, then will the armor-bearer of Jove descend from his lofty position, and uttering a scream of bolder defiance than ever was heard from him before, he will strike terror to the heart of the forest-monarch, and force him, cowering and roaring, dastardly to retreat, with blood dripping from his mane, from a soil he has dared to pollute by his impious tread. We will not 'track him around the globe,' in the language of the gentleman from Virginia (Mr. Hunter), but we will drive him forever from this continent."

As the reader knows, this troublesome question of so many years' standing, was afterwards settled by a treaty, making the 49th parallel of latitude the permanent boundary between the American and British possessions.

CHAPTER III.

In August, 1848, Mr. Johnson addressed the House on
the *veto* power of the President—a subject then very much
agitated, both in Congress and out of it. It was a question on which, at several times, propositions had been offered in Congress, looking to an amendment of the Constitution in that particular. It was discussed at great length
before the people, particularly in the Presidential canvass
of 1848. Any one acquainted with Mr. Johnson's political
life and opinions, might readily suppose what would be
his position on the question of the veto power. There are
associations connected with its origin, among the old Romans, nearly five centuries before Christ, well calculated
to enlist his feelings and sympathies in its favor. It was a
popular institution. The people of Rome, when in a state
of revolt against what they regarded as intolerable oppression on the part of the *patrician* Senate, extorted from the
latter a decree allowing them (the people) to elect tribunes
annually—each one of whom could arrest the passage of a
decree of the Senate by the use of the word *veto* (I forbid).
It was designed as a protection of the rights of the *ple-*

beian order against oppression by the patricians. In other words, it was intended for the protection of the *people* against the *aristocracy.*

In his speech on this question, Mr. Johnson traced the history of this veto power, from its first origin in Rome, down through the English Constitution and that of France, in 1789, until its incorporation into the Constitution of the United States, exhibiting a minute research and investigation on his part, which shows that he had studied the subject well. In reply to the argument which had been advanced—that the monarch of Great Britain dare not now exercise the veto power—Mr. J. said:

"'Tis true the veto has not been exercised in England since 1692, one hundred and sixty-six years ago, and from this an argument has been drawn to prove that even the King of England is afraid to exercise this power, and therefore it is dangerous, and should never be exercised in a democracy or a republic. The King of England is not immediately responsible to the people for the exercise of this power, or responsible to them for the position he holds. He ascends the throne in the course of hereditary succession, and when the power is exercised by him, in most instances, it is to resist popular will, instead of carrying it out; hence the great fear of exercising the veto power in England, lest the popular will should become so strong that it might overturn the throne. Consequently, the King resorts to the liberal bestowment of immense patronage at his disposal to defeat those measures on their passage which would require the exercise of the veto power, as necessary to protect the other prerogatives of the crown.

"I do not look upon the veto power as a 'snag' in the Mississippi [referring to a figure of Mr. Schenck, of Ohio, who compared the veto power to a snag in the Mississippi], to obstruct the navigation to our commerce, but as a breakwater—to use a figure—placed in the Constitution to arrest the mighty current, heavily setting in, of Federal power, or to break the dashing waves of encroachment upon the liberty and interests of the people. The veto, as exercised by our Executive, is conservative, and enables the people, through their *tribunitian* officer, the President, to arrest or suspend, for the time being, unconstitutional, hasty, or improvident legislation, until the people—the sovereigns in this country—have time and opportunity to consider of its propriety.   *   *   *   For myself, I will take the instrument, as handed down by Washington and his compeers, and if it is tyranny to exercise this power, as it has been by every republican President, from Washinton's inauguration down to the present time, I am willing to abide by it, and await the ultimate decision of the people on the subject. If the gentleman from Ohio could succeed, with his Federal snag-boat, in extracting the people's power, the veto, from the Constitution, the harmony of our beautiful, though complex, form of government would be lost, the equilibrium would be gone, and some two of the Departments would absorb the other. The result would be the concentration of all power in one Department."

From the foregoing remarks it will be seen that upon this, as on all other great questions, Mr. Johnson acted upon a high principle of political philosophy. In his view, the *rationale* of the veto is the protection of the people's rights. He regards the President as a great national *tribune*, representing the people of the Union in their aggregate capacity. He considers that the veto power was intrusted to the President in this his representative character. Such being his view, it is not probable that he is likely to agree to having the veto power impaired during his administration. And it may be fairly assumed that he will not hesitate to exercise it, whenever he regards the rights of the people as assailed by the legislative department.

In 1850, in the Thirty-first Congress, the House of Representatives had under consideration the President's message transmitting the constitution of California. Congress having failed to provide a territorial government for California—owing to difficulties growing out of the agitation of slavery—the people of California, acting under the protection and encouragement of the military commanders stationed there, selected delegates, who met in convention, framed a constitution, and forwarded it to the President, to be laid before Congress. The people of California were driven to this course by the pressure of necessity. The country was very rapidly being settled—all the conservative elements of social life were left to take care of themselves without regulation by lawful authority. The admission of California as a State, under her new constitution, was resisted with great zeal and vehemence.

The admission of California, with her antislavery constitution, would, it was urged by some, destroy the equilibrium between the slave and antislave States, making one more of the latter than of the former. Mr. Johnson had previously introduced a series of resolutions, looking to a compromise of the disturbing questions connected with slavery. One of his propositions was for the admission of California. He hoped that the moral strength of that question might carry with it the settlement of other mooted points. And, in his speech on the subject, he seems to have been looking more to the pacification of the country, and the compromise of conflicting opinions between the North and the South, than to the isolated question of admitting California alone. The following extract from his speech on the occasion breathes the most deep and earnest anxiety for the restoration of kind feelings between the North and the South. They also show the disfavor with which he looked on the perpetual agitation of the question of slavery, and his fears of the effect of such agitation upon the Union :

" If Congress keeps up the agitation" (of slavery), " and commences legislation on this momentous question, the friction will be so great, the excitement will become so intense, diffusing itself from the centre along the great arteries of the nation, until the whole body politic will wax so hot, that this mighty Union will melt in twain. Is there one in this House—is there one throughout the length and breadth of this broad Confederacy, while standing in full view of the grand arch of human liberty, so gracefully and beautifully composed of thirty sovereign States—is there one so lost to patriotism, so vile in his nature, so diabolical in spirit, as to lay impious hands upon the magnificent structure and topple it to the ground, crushing all beneath the only hope and last experiment of man's capability for self-government ?   *   *   * Let me make an appeal to the North and to the South, to the East and to the West—to Whigs and to Democrats—*to all*—to come forward and join in one fraternal band, and make one solemn resolve that we will stand by the Constitution of the country and all its compromises as our only ark of safety—as the palladium of our civil and religious liberty; that we will cling to it as the mariner clings to the last plank when night and the tempest close around him."

Those who have observed Mr. Johnson's course in in Congress, and who have attentively read his speeches, cannot reasonably entertain any fears for the rights of the States, under his administration. On many occasions his published speeches represent him as most earnestly urging vigilance on the part of the States, in guarding their rights against Federal encroachment. It is a subject on which he seems to have felt deeply, and to have entertained the strongest convictions. He seems to have had a great fear of the usurpation of power by the General Government, and on many occasions expressed his apprehension that the danger to our system was in the centripetal, rather than the centrifugal force. When Mr. Fillmore, in 1850, proposed to use military force to dispossess Texas of a portion of territory which she had occupied, claiming it to be within her boundaries, but which the General Government claimed to be in New Mexico, the most intense excitement prevailed both in Congress and throughout the country. At one time a collision of arms between the United States and Texas was thought to be inevitable. In his speech on the subject, Mr. Johnson seems to have felt much more deeply concerned about the question of the "rights of the States," which he regarded as threatened with overthrow by Federal power, than about the merits of the controversy as to the right to the territory in dispute. In his speech he said :

"To preserve the harmony and unity of all the parts, this Government must be kept moving within its proper sphere. I want to see no great central power created, like the sun in our solar system, with its satellites revolving around the great central body. I do not look on this Government as the centre of a system, imparting its light, its heat, its motion, to the sovereign States, as so many distant satellites. And wherever this Government attempts to encroach upon the powers of the State, the duty of every man who loves the Union, who is faithful to that Government which was formed by the wisdom of the fathers of the Revolution, is to step forward, and enter his protest against such encroachment.

"I have felt it to be my duty to protest against these enormous and extraordinary doctrines, put forth by the Executive in his message recently submitted to the House, upon the Texas boundary. These doctrines, if carried out, must result in the overshadowing of State rights, and the consolidation of this Government. It is time the States began to look to the encroachments that are being made upon their reserved rights, and thereby preserve the Constitution as it is, with all its compromises.

"I consider it to be the imperative duty of all the States to enter their protest against so unprecedented and dangerous a usurpation of power. When the Executive usurps a power so far beyond the limits assigned to him by the Constitution, it is time he should be met and checked in his course by a solemn protest from all the States. I am no advocate of disunion. I am for the settlement and harmonious adjustment of this difficulty with all my heart, but I desire to see the Constitution preserved. I wish to see each. branch of the Government moving in its legitimate sphere."

The views of Mr. Johnson, as herein set forth, concerning the rights of the States, are significant, and at the present time they are important as foreshadowing what may be his course whenever the constitutional rights of the States may be involved. The theory of State rights has received a severe shock in the results produced by the conclusion of the war. But because they were perverted into an attempt to destroy the Union, they do not therefore exist in any less force and power than they did before the late conflict of arms. The Constitution is unchanged in that provision which " reserves to the States respectively, or to the people, the powers not delegated to the United States, nor prohibited by it to the States." At this time, when great anxiety is felt even by many of the best and truest loyal men in the country, lest from the very force of circumstances the tendency of our Government may be toward consolidation, it is consoling to reflect that the chief executive officer of the Government entertains the views he does, as set forth in the preceding extracts, of the constitutional relations between the General Government and the States. .The public mind may rest secure, and rely with confidence, that he will scrupulously respect the rights of the States, and that he will not encourage any violation of the same. His language on the subject, in expressing his views, is plain, direct, and unmistakable.

In January, 1852, a most exciting and interesting discussion took place in the House of Representatives on the bill for appropriating $3,180,000, the instalment and interest due in May, 1852, under the twelfth article of the treaty of peace between the United States and Mexico, known as the treaty of Guadalupe Hidalgo, made and concluded in February, 1848. The debate was marked with great ability and with considerable feeling. The position was assumed and earnestly enforced by many members, that in case of a treaty stipulation for the payment of money, Congress was bound to make the appropriation unconditionally, without inquiry into the merits, and had no right to go behind the record and regulate the details as to the manner of payment. The previous instalment due Mexico under the treaty had been appropriated fourteen months in advance of the day of payment; the contractors for paying over the same in the city of Mexico had realized three and a half per cent. on the operation, and the payment had been made under the direction of the Secretary of State. Public rumor and the public press had indulged in many surmises and strictures upon the manner of the payment of the previous instalment; that the Government of the United States had lost materially by anticipating the appropriation, and thus allowing the contractors the use of the money in the mean time; that the Secretary of State (Mr. Webster), under whose direction the instalment had been paid, had used his official influence in behalf of favorite contractors, and the insinuation had been freely indulged in that he had consulted his own personal interests in the transaction. Mr. Johnson, by way of quieting any apprehension on that score for the future, whilst disclaiming even the remotest idea of countenancing any suspicion of Mr. Webster's integrity, introduced an amendment to the bill, providing—

"That said sum be paid over to the proper authorities of Mexico, by the Secretary of the Treasury, under the supervision of the President."

Mr. Johnson's speech on this question was marked with great earnestness and great ability. In it he exhibits the same watchful jealousy over the public Treasury, which is a peculiar trait in his public life. The money in the Treasury he seems to have ever considered as belonging *to the people.* The voice of warning has always been heard from him when he thought it was in danger of being perverted to the advancement of private interests. His views in regard to the binding obligations of treaties (so far as the appropriation of money is involved), now that he is President, are significant and important. He said:

"There are reasons, conclusive in my mind, why we shall designate in this act the party who is to have the direction of the payment of this money. There is a power authorized under the Constitution of the United States to make treaties; and in conformity with this power, in 1848 there was a treaty made with the Mexican Government. The twelfth article of that treaty provides, that we shall pay to the Mexican authorities, at specified times, certain amounts of money. Fifteen millions was the whole amount stipulated. A certain portion thereof was to be paid at the conclusion of the treaty, and the balance in annual instalments at times fixed by the treaty. Now, this is the treaty, and we have agreed, so far as the treaty-making power is concerned, to pay money at certain times. What has the treaty-making power to do with it here? Is the treaty-making power conclusive and binding? I put this question to the House, and, humble as I am, to the country also. Suppose, in the exercise of this treaty-making power, great abuses were to grow out of it; that treaties were made and money stipulated to be paid over, which was wrong, and which would result in oppression and in heavy taxation. So far as the payment of the money is concerned, I ask this House and the country—is there no conservative power, is there no point at which the abuses of the treaty-making power may be resisted? I know that the Constitution says, that a treaty made in pursuance of the Constitution, shall be the supreme law of the land; and it is conclusive so far as the judiciary is concerned. But how are the abuses of this power to be resisted? When a treaty provides that money shall be paid, I say that money cannot be paid until an appropriation is made by Congress. For the Constitution says expressly, that no money shall be drawn from the Treasury, except in pursuance of an appropriation made by lay. Hence all treaties providing for the payment of money are subjected to the appropriating power. Has not this House—the Representatives of the people—the authority and power; and, moreover, would it not be their sworn duty, if they believed a treaty was wrong and oppressive, to withhold the appropriation, and thereby defeat the compliance with, and the consummation of, the abuses of the treaty? Where is the check, where the limit to the abuses of the treaty-making power? It must exist somewhere; if not, every thing so far as this Government is concerned, can be absorbed and swallowed up by the improper and dangerous exercise of this treaty-making power. We find, in 1820, that the great statesman from Kentucky, in the discussion of the Florida treaty, introduced a resolution in which this doctrine was boldly proclaimed; and he went so far as to say that the treaty made at that time should be set aside if Spain faltered in her course, and refused to do us justice, and adopt the means necessary to maintain the treaty. Well, some gentlemen may think this is a little foreign, and has no direct bearing on this subject. But I will show the application I wish to make of it. Here is a treaty made, and money promised to be paid under it at certain times, but subject to other provisions of the Constitution, and subject to this conservative power. Then comes up another question. Here, in the absence of law, in the absence of an appropriation by Congress, the Secretary of State (I mean before the appropriation is made), before the treaty is consummated, makes a contract with British and American bankers to pay over money which has not been appropriated by the laws of the country. After the contract is made, after the agreement has been entered into, that they are to give a certain per cent. before the money is appropriated; then what is the result presented to the House? It is this: the contract is made, and the gentlemen are ready to consummate it—ready to pay over the money—and hence you are bound to appropriate it; and the Secretary of State, with the great influence he is able to bring to bear upon this Hall, says, Pass the bill, let us make the contract fourteen months before the instalment is due. Such was the case during the last Congress, to enable certain bankers—British bankers—to speculate upon this Government and the Mexican Government. But pass the law, appropriate the money to enable certain bankers to have three millions of dollars out of the Treasury, to operate upon fourteen months in advance. When we see how this thing is, when we see the appliances that are brought to bear, when we see the speculation in every phase of the act, when we see some or all parties have to be operated upon, it calls upon us to assert our prerogative, and to say to the Secretary of State, You shall not act in advance of appropriations by Congress, or assume to exercise such a power. You shall not dictate to the Representatives of the people as to who shall pay the money, but we will specify in our act who shall pay it."

The above being Mr. Johnson's views in regard to the obligations of the Congress of the United States in making appropriations to carry out the stipulations of treaties, now that he is President, they are of great importance. Upon this, as upon all other questions of great public concern, he regards the interests of the people and their wishes, as reflected through their Representatives, to be of paramount consideration. The country may herein feel an assurance that Mr. Johnson will not, even in negotiating treaties, feel himself at liberty to disregard the popular feeling. He will never consult his mere arbitrary will, esteeming it, as he does, to be the right and the duty of the representatives of the people to impose a limit and a restraint upon what might be the abuses of the treaty-making power. In this he is entirely consistent. His

views on this subject are in accord with the moving
principle of his whole public life, namely, the rights
and interests and welfare of the popular *many*, in contradistinction to the power and authority of the official
few.

CHAPTER IV.

In July, 1850, Mr. Johnson made a speech on the great question with which his name has become, and ever will remain, identified, the " HOMESTEAD LAW." This he seems to have regarded as *the* great purpose it was the mission of his political life to accomplish. There never has been, in the history of legislation, a more striking instance of what determination, perseverance, and tenacity of purpose—backed up and sustained by boldness and ability—may accomplish, than has been afforded by the course of Mr. Johnson on this question. He may be regarded as the author, originator, and father of this great feature in our public land system—the HOMESTEAD LAW. He first introduced the measure in 1845. At first, it found but few supporters. It was regarded as a rather wild and visionary plan, and was denounced as an extravagant and wasteful project to squander the whole public domain, without any remuneration to the Government, and without any reason to sustain it. Mr. Johnson's speeches on the subject exhibit a degree of research and information, which show that he had studied it deeply, and thoroughly understood it. The earnestness and zeal and deep feeling he manifested in support of the scheme, show that his heart was thoroughly enlisted in its support. Although foiled again and again, he still persevered. Session after session he brought forward his favorite measure for the ten long years, from 1843 to 1853, he was in the House of Representatives. His last great speech in that House was in its advocacy and support. There never was, perhaps, in any country, a great source of public wealth so perverted to carry out the projects of political agitators, and to foster the purposes of peculation and corruption, as the great land domain of the United States. The struggle, in every State where the lands lay, among political aspirants, was in rival schemes to squander the lands in promoting private and sectional and corporation interests. Systems of preëmption, graduation, cession to the States, and distribution, entered into the political agitation of the hustings at every election, year after year, and kept up the fever of party excitement to the highest pitch. The public lands were a great corruption-field, indeed. The malpractices and peculations of land offices were proverbial. The combinations of speculators rendered the public land sales a ridiculous farce. The forcing large quantities of land into market, at inauspicious times, merely to influence local elections, or to benefit speculating friends, was again and again charged upon the public authorities—and with too much show of truth, in many instances. The benefits accrued to the favored few, and not to the people at large.

Mr. Johnson saw all this, and his determined purpose seems to have been to break down the barriers with which a complicated land system had hedged in this great inheritance of the people, and to throw wide open the gateway through which the teeming millions might pass, to the settlement and improvement of this wilderness-empire. His speeches on this subject are among the greatest of his life. They constitute the superstructure of his fame, his ability, and his usefulness as a legislator and debater. In the discussion of the question he seems to disregard and ignore the mere incidental and ephemeral relations it may bear toward temporary political and partisan complications. He raises himself up to the high philosophical contemplation of its influences upon our national development and prosperity, for ages to come. Portions of his speeches, where he discusses the measure in its relations to, and bearings on, the development and progress of American civilization, power, and glory, will compare favorably with those master-pieces of philosophical eloquence, by Edmund Burke, that have made his name immortal. The following extracts from his speeches, though copious, could not well be curtailed, and will amply repay the reader for the time spent in their perusal. The object of the measure, as explained by its title, was—

"A bill to encourage agriculture, commerce, manufactures, and all other branches of industry, by granting to every man, who is the head of a family, and a citizen of the United States, a homestead of one hundred and sixty acres of land, out of the public domain, upon condition of occupancy and cultivation of the same, for the period therein specified."

July 25, 1850, Mr. Johnson said:

"I contend that the Government has no authority, neither under the Constitution, nor in compliance with the *four great elementary principles* (fire, air, *earth*, and water) indispensable to the existence of man, to withhold the usufruct of the soil from its citizens. Man cannot live without the use of the soil, and Government cannot, in compliance with first principles, withhold the essentials of life from the people. The Government, whose legislation is directed against these first principles, is making war upon the great scheme of the Deity himself, and reduces its operations to practical infidelity.   *   *   *   Go to any country, where the soil has passed into the hands of a few, and where the mass of the people have become mere tenants and cultivators of the soil for an inflated and heartless landed aristocracy. When famine comes on such a land, the first that suffer for bread are those whose very hands produce it ; hence we see that the withholding the use of the soil from the actual cultivator, is violative of one of those principles essential to human existence ; and when the violation reaches that point at which it can no longer be borne, revolution begins."

After going on to show how this measure would bring money into the Treasury, instead of keeping it out, he proceeded as follows :

"Independently of realizing more to the Government in dollars and cents, you make the settler a better citizen of the community. He becomes the better qualified to discharge the duties of a freeman. He comes to the ballot-box and votes without the restraint or fear of some landlord. He is, in fact, the representative of his own homestead, and is a man in the enlarged and proper sense of the term. After the interchange of opinions, and the hurry and bustle of the election day is over, he mounts his own horse and returns to his own domicil, where all his cares and his affections centre. He then goes to his own hay-mow, to his own barn, to his own stable, and feeds his own stock. His wife, the partner of his bosom, on the other hand, turns out and milks their own cows, churns their own butter, and when the rural repast is ready, he and his wife and their children sit down at the same table together, to enjoy the sweet product of their own hands, with hearts thankful to God for having cast their lots in this country, where the land is made free under the protecting and fostering care of such a Government.

"To see every man in the United States domiciled, is an object that has long been near to my heart ; and if this bill shall not be passed into a law during the present session of Congress, I most ardently desire to see this great scheme of philanthropy, as begun, *pressed* on to its final consummation. Once accomplished, it would create the strongest tie between the citizen and the Government. What a great incentive it would afford to the citizen to obey every call of duty! At the first summons of the note of war, you would find him leaving his plough in the half-finished furrow, taking his only horse and converting him into a war-steed; his scythe and sickle would be thrown aside, and his rustic armor buckled on, and, with a heart full of valor and patriotism, he would rush with alacrity to his country's standard. If he should fall on the battle-field, how consoling would be his reflection, 'I perish in defending my country's right and a Government that has provided a home for my wife and my children!'

"I confess that my attachments are strong for the people; I believe them to be better and purer than their rulers; it is their interest to do right, and they have no motive to do wrong in government affairs. I feel bound to the people by the strongest ties that can bind man to his kind; they have made me all that I am, let that be much or little; and by the people I intend to stand as long as I have a vote to give or a tongue to speak in vindication of their rights, regardless of the taunts and jeers of those who forget that they have constituents, and those who feel contempt for the masses. I believe that this scheme is connected with, and calculated to advance, the very principles of Christianity itself. For there is much in man being placed in a condition to do right, and with no inducement to do wrong. While a man is oppressed, surrounded with adverse circumstances, and poverty staring him in the face, the strong restraints of morality and religion are apt to give way, and he condescends to acts and means which, under more favored circumstances, he would spurn and lift himself above.

"Pass this bill, or some one containing its principles, and you will make many a poor man's heart rejoice. Pass this bill, and the wives and children of the poor and needy will invoke blessings on your heads. Pass this bill, and millions now unborn will look back with wonder and admiration upon the age in which it was done. Pass this bill, and you strengthen the basis of Christianity, and enlarge the sphere of true philanthropy. Pass this bill, and every member, when he returns to his constituents, can announce to them the glad tidings of great joy—that the way is made open and the day of deliverance is at hand. Pass this bill, and, as regards my humble self, I shall feel that I have filled the full object of my mission here, and I can return home to my constituents in quiet and peace."

During this, the Thirty-first Congress, no vote was reached on the bill, in either House. It was perceptible, however, that it was daily gaining strength. At the next Congress, the Thirty-second, the question again came forward in a report from the Committee on Agriculture, and underwent a long debate in the House. On all hands, by every one, Mr. Johnson was regarded as the father of the measure. His name was identified with it.

April 29, 1852, Mr. Johnson said :

" The opponents of this measure seem to think that they have erected a rampart that is impregnable, and over which none can pass. This rampart, thus erected, they try to sustain by three main barriers : first, that it is *unconstitutional ;* second, that it will *diminish the revenue ;* third, that it smacks of *demagoguism* and *agrarianism.*

" There is a provision in the Constitution on which I wish to address myself to the intellect and thinking powers of this House. It is this : 'The President, by and with the consent of the Senate, can make treaties.' By the exercise of the treaty-making power territory can be acquired, and that without the payment of a dollar. Suppose that in the acquisition of the territory of California, we had acquired it without the payment of any thing whatever. What was the object of the acquisition ? It was for settlement and cultivation. It is one of the highest objects of government, whether democratic or monarchical, in the acquisition of territory, to have it peopled. Our territory was acquired for the purpose of settlement and cultivation. Now we have the territory acquired by the treaty-making power. Then there comes in another provision of the Constitution which bears immediately on such acquisition. What is it? That 'Congress shall have power to dispose of, and make all needful rules and regulations, respecting the territory, or other property, of the United States.' Is not the passage of a law, to induce settlement and cultivation, carrying out one of the highest objects contemplated by the Constitution in regard to the acquisition of territory? Certainly. Is there any encroachment, any infringement, of the Constitution in this? Is it not in strict compliance with the objects of the Constitution—the settlement and cultivation of the territory? What, then, becomes of this Virginia abstraction? What becomes of the arguments of the men who march through the Constitution, who make an opening through which they pass with a hundred millions of acres, and yet cannot see the power, in the Constitution, to appropriate lands to settlers for cultivation?"

[Mr. Johnson here had reference to the votes, at a previous session, of those gentlemen who opposed the Homestead bill, on the ground of unconstitutionality, who had then supported bills for giving nearly one hundred millions of acres of public lands in the way of bounties to soldiers, gratuities to the new States, etc.]

Mr. AVERITT.—"I will respectfully inquire of my friend from Tennessee what he means by 'this Virginia abstraction?'"

Mr. JOHNSON.—"It means any thing or nothing, just as it suits the whims and caprices of individuals who wish to talk about it. I have shown how we can acquire territory, and if the great object of the acquisition of territory is settlement and cultivation, to give power and potency to the country, is it not strange that under that other provision of the Constitution, 'to dispose' of the territory, you cannot dispose of it so as to accomplish and carry out the very object for which you acquired it? We fail to perform a constitutional duty if, after the acquisition of territory, we do not adopt the means which induce settlement.

"What, then, is the proposition? We have acquired territory by the exercise of the treaty-making power. Where does the fee pass ? The fee passed, upon its acquisition, into the Government, as the trustee; the equity passed to the people in the aggregate; and this is merely a proposition to distribute, in severalty, the fee where the equity already resides. That is what it proposes, and gentlemen who can spin distinctions down to a fifteen hundredth, can certainly understand a plain, common-sense proposition like this. Oh, say they, but you gave money for it, and you must have money back for it. Is money the only consideration you paid for it ? Where are those gallant sons that now sleep in Mexico ? Where are the ten thousand graves containing the bones of many of your best citizens ? You owe it to the gallant dead, who now sleep in your own and in a foreign land, who sacrificed their all in the acquisition of the territory, to dispose of it in that way best calculated to promote the interest and happiness of those left behind.   *   *   *   *

"Let us now examine the second objection—that the result will be a diminution of the revenue. I say it is a revenue measure. I say it will increase the receipts into the Treasury. How ? By the enhancement of the value of the remainder of your public domain. Let us take a case by way of illustration : Take the laborer in society who has no profession, no trade, who has no fixed employment, and how much tax does he pay to the support of the Government under the present system ? Scarcely any thing. But take such a man, transplant him in the West upon one hundred and sixty acres of its fat virgin soil, and in a few years, when he clears a few acres around him, gets a horse and a mule or two, and some fat thrifty hogs, which come grunting up to his log-cabin through the bushes, and a few milch cows, lowing at the barn-yard, with their udders distended with rich milk—at once you have increased his ability to do what ? To purchase one hundred dollars' worth of foreign imports, or goods of domestic manufacture, when previously he could have bought little or nothing. I beg your attention while I take a single case to illustrate this principle. You have nine millions of quarter sections of land, and you have three millions of qualified voters. Take one qualified voter who is the head of a family—say, a family of seven; you transplant him from the position where he is making hardly any thing, and consequently buying but little, to a possession in the West of one hundred and sixty acres of land. Suppose you increase his ability, by bringing his labor in contact with the productive soil, to buy one dollar more than he bought before for each head of his family. That would be seven dollars more than he was able to purchase before, or two dollars and ten cents revenue to the Government."

[Here Mr. Johnson evidently based his calculation on thirty per cent. as the average duty on the imported articles consumed.]

" Let us take a case more perceptible in its effects, and which would be felt in the Treasury of the United States. Suppose you take a million of families of seven each, and transfer them to positions such as I have described—making seven millions of persons—one dollar increased ability to purchase per head will make seven millions. *   *   * Thirty per cent. on seven millions amounts to two million, one hundred thousand dollars—so much gain to the Treasury. How much do you get for your public lands now? A little over two million dollars. By giving away—by *wasting*, as some say—only one-ninth part of the lands, you bring into the Treasury an increased revenue of two million, one hundred thousand dollars, an amount greater than you now receive from the entire sales of your public lands, or *will* receive for the next sixteen years, as we are informed by the Secretary of the Treasury. Does not every one see that is only the miniature view of the operation of the system? Is it not plain, that when a man is placed in the position supposed, and he begins to thrive, when his sons and daughters grow up around him, a school-house and meeting-house will be erected in his neighborhood, and the first year after he gets under *head-way*, he will spend more than fifty-six dollars in purchasing dresses and other comforts for his family? Suppose you average it at fifty-six dollars per family of seven, only eight dollars per head. One million of families would consume fifty-six million dollars' worth more, thirty per cent. duty on which would amount to sixteen million, eight hundred thousand dollars. Does the operation stop there? Not at all. The Secretary of the Treasury tells us, that for every six dollars' worth of imports consumed in the United States, there are ninety-four dollars' worth of home-manufactured articles consumed, embracing furniture, agricultural products, etc. Suppose we reduce it down to one-half of what the Secretary makes it, fifty millions. Then, while you have increased the ability to consume fifty-six million dollars' worth of foreign imports, you have correspondingly increased his ability to buy fifty million dollars' worth of home manufactures. If time would allow me, I could show how much the Government will lose under the present system, and the length of time it will require to bring this public domain into cultivation, considering the time it has already been in operation. It would be some seven hundred years at the present rate of disposition. I could show, upon the principle of time operating on value, what a great advantage it would be to the Government to give the land away, and thereby induce its settlement and cultivation.

"It ought to be readily seen what immense advantage the Government would derive from giving the land to the cultivators, instead of keeping it on hand such a great length of time. We find by this process, the Government would derive from each quarter section, in six hundred years (throwing off the excess of nearly one hundred years), seventeen thousand dollars. This, then, shows on the one hand what the Government would gain by giving the land away. Now let us see what it will lose by retaining the land on hand this length of time. Time operates on value, as distance does on magnitude. A ball of very large size, when close to the eye, is seen in its fullest extent, but when removed to a certain distance, dwindles to the human vision, or disappears altogether. So with the largest heavenly bodies, removed from the eye to the positions they occupy in space, they dwindle to a mere point. To the business, practical world, a hundred dollars at the present time is worth just a hundred dollars. A hundred dollars just twelve months hence is worth just six per cent. less, so on every twelve months, until the expiration of sixteen years and eight months, when it has lost an amount equal to the principal. So it will be perceived that in every sixteen years and eight months, the Government loses an amount equal to the price asked for each quarter section, which is two hundred dollars, by keeping it on hand. Sixteen will go into six hundred thirty-seven times, which would make seven thousand four hundred dollars the Government will lose.

"As to the third objection urged against this bill—that it is demagoguism and agrarianism—I would ask, Is it demagoguism to comply with the requirements of the Constitution? Is it agrarianism to permit a man to take that which is his own? Agrarianism consists, as I had supposed, in taking that which belongs to one man, and giving it to another. Such is not the principle of this bill. We have nine million quarter sections of land, and three million qualified voters. If we were to make a *pro rata* distribution, there would be three quarter sections for each qualified voter. * * * By permitting a man to take part of what belongs to him, injustice is done to no one else. There is no agrarianism in that. Agrarianism means, as I understand it, that property which has been accumulated by the labor, the industry, by the sweat of the brow, of you, or me, or any one else, should be taken and divided out with those who have not used a corresponding industry. Agrarianism is the division of property among those who did not participate in, or contribute to its accumulation. This proposition does no such thing. * * * * It pulls none down, but elevates all. It takes the poor by the hand, and lifts them up, taking nothing from the rich.

"Then we have the Constitution, sound morality, and an increase of revenue all combined in this bill. There is no conflict, no incongruity, no disagreement in its parts. We see that these great and essential principles do not move off in diverging or parallel lines, but they all travel in converging lines, concentrating in the accomplishment of a great national good, to carry out the purposes of the Constitution and the highest behest that man owes to his kind. This is the harmony presented by this great measure, consonant with the Constitution, based on the eternal principle of justice and right, and sustained by another great principle of charity and religion. Thus we have the three great principles on which this measure is based, bound together by the silken cords of charity and religion.

"Pass this bill, and you inspire the people of your country with faith in their Government, and at the same time you inspire their bosoms with the hope of doing better hereafter.   *   * I confess that my sympathies are strong for the laboring and toiling thousands of our country. I know something about the privations and hardships that an individual has to undergo in this or any other country, where gaunt poverty is staring him in the face. I know how to appreciate his sufferings, and consequently my sympathies are strong for those who have to toil. I admit it. Gentlemen may call it prejudice, or mistaken sympathy, but so long as I have a tongue to speak or a vote to give, regardless of the menaces, threats, or intimidations of men here or elsewhere, I intend to stand up and vindicate the rights and interests of the laboring men, for without them we are nothing.

"As to the objection—that the passage of this bill will take away the population from the old States—where is the man who has a heart that beats for love to his kind, and patriotism for his country, that could say to the poor laboring man of the old States, Do not go away; stay here in your poverty; do not go and settle on the new and fertile lands of the West, but remain where you are; linger, wither, and die in want, where the only inheritance you can leave to your children is your poverty. I care not where a man lives—whether in my district, or another district, whether in my State or another—if he can do better elsewhere, I say go, better your condition, make yourself a better citizen, and promote the welfare of your kind. I care not where he goes, so he confines himself to the great area of freedom, where he can look up to, and receive protection from your brilliant stars and broad stripes. Wherever he places himself, he is still my brother and still an American citizen."

After a very long and able, and exciting discussion, on

May 12, 1852, the House of Representatives came to a vote on this great measure; and the bill passed by the large majority of 107 to 56. Although the friends of the measure in the Senate made an effort to get a vote on it in that body, yet they failed in getting action on it. At the succeeding short session, beginning in December, 1852, there was such a press of business before Congress, that the bill was not considered in either house. With the expiration of this, the Thirty-second Congress, Mr. Johnson's ten years' services in the House of Representatives terminated. It is true he did not have the pleasure of seeing his favorite measure become the law of the land; but he had the proud consolation of seeing it pass the House of which he was a member, by a large majority. Further reference to Mr. Johnson's efforts in its behalf will be postponed till his senatorial career is explained and commented on.

CHAPTER V.

THE Legislature of Tennessee was charged with having
gerrymandered the State in the arrangement of the Congressional districts, with a view of getting out of Congress
certain members who were obnoxious to the majority then
in power, Mr. Johnson among others. In alluding to it
in his speech in Congress, he said:

"As motives may be impugned, so far as I am concerned, I
look from them to no future political advancement. My humble
political career will close with the present Congress. The decree
has gone forth, and been registered, not by my constituents, but
by those who think they occupy a higher place. Then, I have
no political future to which I can look, as my district has been
arranged to subserve certain purposes; and that, too, without respect either to Whigs or Democrats. I must be permitted to say here,
in this connection, that I believe it was the intention not only to
destroy me, but to destroy my colleague who lives in the ad-
joining district, who differs with me in politics generally, but who
agrees with me on this great question. Our places were wanted;
our political garments have been divided; and, hereafter, they
will cast lots upon our vesture—but there is much in the future."

What a prophetic remark! " There is much in the future." And how rapidly were the events with which that future was pregnant, about to crowd each other on the great theatre of American history, astounding the world with their magnitude, and shaking to its centre the fabric of American power and glory!

Having lost his chances of a further election to the Congress of the United States, owing to the rearrangement of the Congressional districts, Mr. Johnson was brought out by the Democratic party of Tennessee as a candidate for Governor of the State. The Whig candidate was Gustavus A. Henry, an able lawyer, and one of the most eloquent men of the South. He had been a prominent and influential member of the preceding Legislature, and had taken a leading part in the rearrangement of the districts. An arrangement of the Congressional districts, with a view to political results, had long gone by the name of " Gerrymandering," ever since the days of Elbridge Gerry, of Massachusetts, who, in the early days of the Republic, had been charged with altering or " Gerrymandering " the districts in his State, for the purpose of getting rid of certain members of Congress who were objectionable to him. Mr. Johnson charged Mr. Henry throughout the State with having *Henry*-mandered him out of Congress. That, and the question of Mr. Johnson's great favorite measure, the Homestead bill, and a proposition which Mr. Johnson had offered in the Legislature of Tennessee in 1842, for basing the representation on white population, were the leading issues in the election. After a laborious and exciting canvass, Mr. Johnson was elected by a handsome majority. In 1855 the Whigs and Americans, or Know-Nothings, of Tennessee, brought out as a candidate for Governor, against Mr. Johnson, Hon. Meredith P. Gentry. Mr. Gentry had acquired a national

3

reputation in Congress, was a man of great eloquence, with a clear, musical voice, of fine personal appearance, and of engaging manners and bearing. With Colonel Gentry the Whigs and Americans felt confident of success. The election excited considerable interest in other States. Governor Johnson was looked on as a rising politician of great promise, who was likely to give to his political opponents considerable trouble. It was confidently predicted by his enemies, that his political race was run ; that in a conflict with his able and eloquent opponent, his fall was certain. Political excitement and anxiety never ran higher in the State. The friends of Governor Johnson were not without their misgivings as to the result, so high was Colonel Gentry's reputation for talents, eloquence, private worth, and personal popularity. Still they had full confidence in their champion. The main issues discussed were the principles and doctrines of " Americanism," and the merits of the Kansas-Nebraska bill.

The author has received the following account of a discussion that took place between Governor Johnson and Colonel Gentry, at ——————, soon after the canvass opened. The narrator having been a warm supporter of Colonel Gentry, his statement cannot be considered as tinged with any bias or prejudice. Notice had been for some time given of the meeting, and at an early hour people began to pour in from every direction. The weather was fine, and, owing to the immense crowd, the speaking was in the open air, from a rostrum erected for the occasion in a large grove. The friends of the respective candidates were seen collected in groups, with anxious countenances, and in excited tones discussing the relative merits of their favorites, and the probable result of the contest. It was evident, however, that the Whigs and Americans were the more jubilant. At twelve o'clock the speaking commenced,

Colonel Gentry making the opening speech. "His speech," said the narrator, "was one of great power and surpassing eloquence. We thought we had Johnson, at last," said he. "Gentry's friends shouted and hurrahed. Johnson's friends felt it, and looked anxiously. Johnson himself sat quietly listening to Gentry, now and then taking notes of what he said. Gentry finally concluded, in a burst of eloquence. Johnson rose, and after calmly looking over the audience of two thousand persons, he commenced his reply. Not possessing the advantage of a fine musical voice to the extent of Colonel Gentry's, and being somewhat slow and hesitating in manner (till warmed up by excitement), Gentry's friends showed additional signs of triumph, and Johnson's friends looked a little worried. Johnson saw it, and it seemed to act upon him like inspiration. Elevating his voice, and raising himself, as it seemed to me, several inches in height, he hurled back Gentry's charges against him with a power and indignation I never saw equalled. He would not stand on the defensive. He disposed of the objections to him in a few sentences, and then assailed Gentry in turn. And although a warm friend of Gentry, yet I must confess I never witnessed a more perfect triumph than Johnson obtained over him. Johnson's friends gathered around him from all parts of the grove. It was now *their* time to shout, and shout they did. Johnson was perfectly armed at all points on the political affairs of the country, even in the most minute particulars. I then saw Gentry was doomed to defeat." This account, let it be recollected, was from a political and personal friend of Colonel Gentry. As he predicted, it so turned out. Governor Johnson was elected. Gentry was awkwardly situated in that contest. Hon. John Bell, the great favorite and leader of the Whig and American party in Tennessee, and their candidate in expectancy for the Presidency, had voted against the Kansas-Nebraska bill, whilst the members of the same party in the House of Representatives had voted for it. If Colonel Gentry defended Mr. Bell's vote, he thus threw himself in opposition to the former; if he sustained them, he was thrown in opposition to Mr. Bell. He tried to evade the dilemma by ignoring the question. But his competitor saw this weak point in his line, and, like a shrewd and able general, he there made his most furious assault, and carried every thing before him.

During the four years Mr. Johnson served as civil Governor of Tennessee, from 1853 to 1857, the political questions which were agitated in that State, relating as they did to matters of domestic local concern, have no great interest for the general reader. He was the ardent friend and advocate of education in the State. No one could appreciate the blessings of education more than he. No one had experienced the difficulties arising from a want of education, in early life, more than he. He deeply sympathized with the poor children of the State, who had not the means of acquiring an education, and was anxious to see its blessings extended to all. He was in favor of reforming and improving the banking system of the State —of holding the banks to a strict adherence to the terms of their charters, and a rigid accountability for a departure from the same. He required them to conform to what the policy of the law intended—that they should be so conducted as to promote the interest and convenience of the public at large, and not to advance the fortunes of monopolists and speculators. He was ready to favor and coöperate in such works of internal improvement, in the State, as were of general practical utility, but never would agree to impose burdens on the people for the purpose of aiding works for the benefit of private interests or of local concern.

Mr. Johnson was elected to the Senate of the United States, by the Tennessee Legislature at its session of 1856, and took his seat in the Senate at the extra session of March 4, 1857, with the commencement of Mr. Buchanan's administration. His *début* in the Senate was on the 18th of February, 1858, in which he suddenly took rank among the first debaters in that body. His speeches on that, and on the succeeding day, were marked with the same boldness, composure, and self-possession which he had exhibited in the House of Representatives. In was on a bill, reported from the military committee, to add to the force of the regular army, with a view to meet the exigencies of the service in the proposed expedition to Utah, to reduce the Mormons to submission. Mr. Johnson offered an amendment, proposing to raise, not exceeding four thousand volunteers, to serve during the pending difficulties with the Mormons; to be accepted by the President, in companies, battalions, or regiments, and that they should be authorized to elect their own officers, to be commissioned by the President. This speech, one of Mr. Johnson's ablest efforts, is of importance now, as containing his views on the policy of large standing armies, and also in reference to the great importance of retrenchment and economy in the expenditures of the Government.

The suggestion had been made, in the discussion, that the bill was an Administration measure. Mr. Johnson boldly expressed his views of the independence of the Senatorial character, in these words :

"I do not wish to be understood as being very squeamish and particular in the support of every measure that may come before the Senate as an Administration measure. If I support any measures that come before this body, I do so because I believe them to be right in principle and right in policy. I shall not support them on the mere dictum or recommendation of the Executive, without regard to their being right in themselves and correct in principle."

In opposing the original bill, as reported, Mr. Johnson argued against the additional expenditure it would entail on the Government by a permanent increase of the regular army, at a time when, he insisted, the expenses of the Government should be curtailed. He said:

"Let us go into the unnecessary and extraordinary expenditures of this Government, and reduce them down to what is reasonable and right. Is there no place at which we can begin this work? When we talk about retrenching on this bill, it is said, 'This is not the place—this is not the bill.' Then, if war happens to exist, and we talk about retrenching the expenditures, the answer is, 'Oh, you cannot do it now; the public mind is occupied about something else; the country is engaged in carrying on the war.' When will the time come? When are the foul, reeking corruptions of the Government to be arrested? What do these corruptions grow out of? They grow out of the unnecessary and improper expenditures of the Government.

"I know it is against the taste, the refined and peculiar notions of some men who get into high places, to talk about curtailing or reducing the expenditures of the Government. With them it is all cant; it is all 'for buncombe;' that it amounts to nothing. Some may talk about it in that light, and some may act on that principle, if it is a principle, but I intend to act in good faith, if I know myself. It may be said of me that I am a pence-calculating politician, and consequently not to be regarded as a statesman expanded in his views and liberal in his feelings. Edmund Burke, the distinguished British statesman, said: 'The revenue of the State is the State in effect; all depends upon it, whether for support or reformation.' Mr. Burke was one of your pence-calculating politicians. He was one of those demagogues who talk about the interests and the rights of the people. Lord Bacon has said: 'Above all things, good policy is to be used, that the treasure and moneys in a State be not gathered into a few hands; money is like muck, of no good, unless it is spread.' The meaning of which is, that the industrious and producing classes should be entitled to spend their money in their own way, and that the appropriations by the Government should be in such way as will best promote their interests, prosperity, and happiness. But we have reversed the proposition. We go on gathering muck from, instead of for, the barn-yards of the nation; we go on gathering revenue from the industry of the whole people, and we collect it here and squander it in appropriations wholly unnecessary, as I believe, so far as the interests and happiness of the people are concerned.

"Go to the governments that have risen and fallen before us, and what has been the cause of their decline and downfall? It is the influence of armies and navies, standing armies and navies, sustained by money drawn from the people; these are the two great arteries through which the nations that have gone before us have been bled to death. They are the two arteries through which the people of this country are now bleeding most freely. Shall we not profit by the experience of the past—shall we not stop and consider?

"Our Federal and State Constitutions were made by our fathers, who had studied the oppressions of the old world; who had witnessed the encroachments and dangers of standing armies in those governments. Hence we find in all our bills of rights— if not in all, certainly in most of them—that standing armies are dangerous and should not be allowed; and we see that the Constitution of the United States relies upon, and provides for, calling forth the militia to suppress rebellion or insurrection against the Government. This contemplates, most clearly, that the great military power of this Government is to reside in its citizen-soldiery. I am for confiding in, and relying upon, the volunteers of the country, who *go*, when war comes, and who *come*, when war goes; who are not willing to enter the army for a livelihood, and thus rely upon the army for a support.

"What is the material of which standing armies are composed in European countries? There you find a broken-down and brainless-headed aristocracy, members of decaying families, that have no energy by which they can elevate themselves, relying on ancestral honors and their connection with the Government. On the other hand, you find a rabble, in the proper acceptation of the term—a miserable lazzaroni, lingering and wallowing about their cities, who have no employment. They are ready, at any time, to enter the army for a few shillings to buy their grog and slight clothing to hide their nudity. Such is the material of which their armies are composed—the rabble composing the rank and file, on the one hand, and a broken-down and decaying aristocracy composing the officers, on the other. Where does the middle man stand? What is the position of the industrious bee that makes the honey—from whose labor all is drawn? He is placed between the upper and the nether mill-stone, and is ground to death by the office-hunter above him and the miserable rabble-soldiery below him. We want nothing like this, here in our country. Let us carry out those great principles of government and philanthropy which are calculated to elevate the masses, and dispense with all useless offices.

"A standing army is an incubus, a fungus, on the body politic. When you call for volunteers, the lowest man in the company does not start out with the feelings or subdued spirit of a common soldier; but each man that goes, goes as a hero. He goes with the expectation of distinguishing himself, even as a private, before he returns to his home. *   *   *   Those men who enter the service as volunteers, are cheered on to the discharge of their duty by knowing that they have mothers and sisters and fathers and brothers to care about them. And then, again, they have somebody to *care for*, too. They have, moreover, their country, that they love and are willing to defend, and in whose cause they are willing to perish. We do not want your 'cheap' men, who have none to care for or shed a tear over them when they fall. I do not wish to see a standing army composed of a rabble who have no country, no friends, no relatives, but who are mere machines to obey the orders of their commanders, *whatever* *they may be!* I want it composed of men who feel that they have a country that is worth defending.

"If I had time to set forth the many gallant achievements of the brave volunteers in the wars we have had, and to describe them, in regular order, before the gentleman from Georgia (Mr. Iverson), I think he would be almost horror-stricken with regret at what he said to-day in reference to the volunteer service of the country. In the war of 1812 where was there a battle-field in which volunteer prowess and ability were not displayed, and volunteer blood poured out like water? Go from Maine to Louisiana—go from the Atlantic coast to the golden shores of California —and where can you find a battle-field on which our volunteer citizen-soldiers have not afforded the highest evidence of love and devotion to their country? Are these men, who are ever ready to rally to your country's standard in all her perilous conflicts, and whose efforts have been so often crowned with victory, to be regarded as occupying an inferior position to the regular soldiery composed of this lower, 'cheaper material,' of which many seem to wish to have our army composed?"

These views of President Johnson, in regard to large standing armies, are important, and worthy of consideration at the present time. Many of our most reflecting men feel anxious about the future policy of the Government, concerning a large standing army, and the heavy expense to be incurred by it. Many entertain serious fears on the subject. That a large standing army, in time of peace, is opposed to the genius and theory of our Government, is a cardinal maxim that has been recognized as true from the beginning of our national existence. A large army necessarily involves a heavy expense, and a heavy expense involves heavy taxation. From Mr. Johnson's well-known consistency in the maintenance of his political opinions, we may suppose he entertains the same views which he did when this speech was delivered in 1858. The public mind may rest secure in the hope that, so far as his influence and wishes may go, he will, at the earliest practicable moment, reduce the army to the lowest possible point compatible with the public safety. His policy, in harmonizing our domestic troubles, is operating so successfully that we may hope there will be no necessity for a large army in preserving order at home. And if, contrary to all expectation, there should be any serious outbreak, volunteers may be relied on as they were during the war. Mr. Johnson has cause to feel gratified on witnessing the fulfilment of his predictions in regard to "volunteers," in the prosecution of the war. Who would have supposed that half a million of volunteers would have sprung forward, with the alacrity that they did, for the purpose of sustaining the Union? Andrew Johnson, in predicting that they would do it, has only proven that he knew well the temper and character of our people. The surviving volunteers of our several wars—whether of the war of 1812, the Mexican war, our many Indian wars, or the late civil war—cannot and will not forget, or fail to appreciate, Mr. Johnson's complimentary and eloquent allusions to them, or the graphic picture he drew of their services and sacrifices in their country's behalf. They will not forget their friend who indignantly repelled the idea of their being placed on an equality with the rabble-soldiery of the regular standing armies of Europe. At the proper time they will sustain him at the ballot-box against the assaults of faction with the same vigor and determination with which they defended their country's flag.

There is something beautiful and touching in the manner in which Mr. Johnson always alludes to his native State (North Carolina), and his adopted State (Tennessee). His grateful affection to that State and people that had received him in early life, and that have honored, sustained, and promoted him, is a prominent trait in his character. It proves the warmth and kindliness of his nature, and that he possesses the virtue of gratitude. During the debate alluded to, something had been said which Mr. Johnson regarded as an unkind allusion to the State of Tennessee, and her being generally called the "Volunteer State." He said:

"Not content with that invidious comparison between regular and volunteer troops, the Senator from Georgia must needs arraign the State I represent. It is true I am not her native son, but I am her adopted son. She took me by the hand, and that generous, that brave, that patriotic people, have made me all that I am, be that much or little. Having placed me here, I intend to stand by her through evil and through good report. Come weal or come woe, I shall be found standing by her interests, her honor —her sacred honor—let the consequences be what they may. Yes, I love her. The tenderest sympathies of my soul are entwined with her interests and her welfare. There is where I live, there is where I hope to die, and beneath the clods of some of her valleys I hope my remains will be deposited. It is the home of my children, it is a home that is sacred to me."

On a previous occasion, when in the House of Representatives, in a speech delivered on his favorite measure— the Homestead bill—he thus spoke of North Carolina:

"Some object to this measure, as calculated to take away the population from the old States. Let me ask the Old Dominion— let me ask North Carolina—*God bless her!* for although she is not, as the Romans would call it, my *alma mater*, yet she is my mother! Although Poverty, gaunt and haggard monster—expatriated me from her limits, to seek a home in my adopted State, where every fibre, every tendril of my heart is entwined with the interests of her people—*yet, still North Carolina is my native State, and in my heart I respect and love her.*"

Such sentiments, uttered in such warm and glowing language, could not have come from a cold and selfish man.   They show a warmth of heart, a tender recollection of past associations, that are invariably accompanied by sincerity, generosity, and truthfulness.   No man who is a sincere votary at the altars of his household gods, can be a mean or bad man.   Any man who loves sincerely the place where his children first saw the light, or who reveres the spot where sleep the ashes of his parents, although he may have infirmities, yet he *may be trusted*.   And so in regard to the place of his nativity or the place of his adopted home.   Patriotism, love of country, is only a more enlarged sentiment of that attachment, reverence, and devotion the heart feels for the home of childhood, or the adopted home, where the social relations and the domestic affections expand into full bloom.   No man ever betrayed his country, over whose heart crept a feeling of melancholy tenderness when he thought of the old homestead where he spent the halcyon days of his youth, or whose eyes were involuntarily moistened when recurring to the scenes and events associated with the budding and blooming of his domestic affections.   Whilst we admire and honor President Johnson for the manly and intellectual traits of his character—for the private and social virtues alluded to, we are bound to respect and love him.

CHAPTER VI.

In February, 1858, a most warm and exciting discussion took place in the Senate, running through the best part of three days, between Mr. Johnson and his colleague, Hon. John Bell. It grew out of the introduction of certain resolutions passed by the Legislature of Tennessee, instructing the Senators from that State to vote for the admission of Kansas as a State, etc. Inasmuch as the discussion related almost exclusively to the local politics of Tennessee, and to crimination and recrimination between the parties, it is not deemed necessary to give extracts from Mr. Johnson's speeches on the occasion. Mr. Johnson never showed himself more powerful in debate. Many of his replies were *impromptu*. And when it is recollected that his adversary was the Hon. John Bell, one of the ablest men and most adroit debaters in this country —when it is further borne in mind that it was Mr. Johnson's first session in the Senate, to say that he fully sustained himself, that he met Mr. Bell on every point, and came out of the discussion with largely increased reputation for intellectual and oratorical power, is the highest praise that can be awarded to him. The reader is referred to this debate, as reported in Vol. 36 of the "Congressional Globe," as one of the finest specimens of dialectical skill and oratorical dexterity in our Congressional annals. Mr. Bell showed himself unusually great. Each found in the other a foeman worthy of his steel. There is one short extract the author is disposed to give from Mr. Johnson's reply, in order to prove that he has had injustice done him in the charge, from certain quarters, that his party feelings were so bitter as to amount to prejudice. The passage alluded to is where Mr. Johnson refers incidentally to Mr. Clay, the great leader of the Whig party, to which Mr. Johnson had been uniformly opposed. Mr. Johnson said:

"We all remember the part taken by the distinguished statesman of Kentucky on that occasion—(the compromise measures of 1850). Notwithstanding it had been part of my teaching and education to oppose that distinguished man, yet I always looked on him as a gallant, talented, and daring leader. In 1850, when I witnessed his efforts here in the Senate, when he was struggling for what he believed to be for the peace and harmony of the country, when he threw himself into the breach, when he was standing here receiving assaults from all quarters, I came here to listen to him with delight and pleasure every day. The gallant bearing and the noble sentiments uttered by that great man during that contest, brought me up nearer to him, and removed many of the prejudices I had contracted in early life in reference to him."

In March, 1858, the bill for the admission of Minnesota as a State into the Union was before the Senate. During the debate on this bill, Mr. Johnson said:

"While I am up, I desire to enter my protest against a doctrine which may be supposed to be advanced here, in reference to the qualification of the voters of a State. This Government has no power, under the Constitution of the United States, to fix the qualification of voters in any sovereign State of the Confederacy. I wish to enter my protest against the doctrine being indulged in, or cultivated to any extent, that this Government has power to go inside a sovereign State, and prescribe the qualification of her voters at the ballot-box. It is for the State and not for the Government to do that. If the doctrine be once conceded, that the Federal Government has the power to fix the qualification of voters in a a State, the idea of State sovereignty is Utopian. There is no such thing as State sovereignty, if the Government can fix the qualification for voters. We have no right to inquire into it. There are simply two things to be ascertained here : First, have we evidence that a State has been formed ? Second, have we evidence that its constitution is republican in its character ? These two things being ascertained, every thing else is for the State that applies for admission into the Union."

These opinions of Mr. Johnson are of great importance, in reference to the bearing they may have on the readjustment now going on.   The author is not disposed to discuss the question, as to whether the foregoing position is right or wrong. It is enough that they were Mr. Johnson's views in 1858. His position is assumed, fairly, squarely, unequivocally, and unconditionally. It is expressed in language forcible and decided. It is an opinion expressed, not as a mere question of expedient policy, which may vary in its application according to circumstances; but it is laid down as a *principle*—a principle involved in the very structure of our system of government. Principles are lasting, they are permanent, they *cannot* change with the shifting blasts of opinion. How, then, can any one who is a friend of Mr. Johnson, wish him to abjure a deliberately expressed opinion upon an abstract principle of constitutional right ? Did those who are preparing to assail him, in reference to the qualifications of voters in the Southern states, expect him to renounce his opinions, as of record in the debates of the Senate? Did they expect to *drive* him to it? If so, they little know the man with whom they are dealing. Did they expect to wheedle and persuade him to it? If they could succeed in that, would they then have any respect for him? And, moreover, what hopes could they have for a Government that was in the hands of so unstable a man? Or was it, that having resolved on a breach with him, and knowing his firmness and consistency, they selected for an issue a question on which he had committed himself of record, and involving a *principle* on which they knew he would not retreat?

At this time, when the public mind is so anxious in regard to our heavy indebtedness, and the high taxes that we may have to meet, it is comforting to know that in Mr. Johnson we have a President whose influence will be exerted against extravagance in the appropriation and expenditure of the public money. On this subject, his uniform course in the Senate was in accord with his position when in the House of Representatives. In May, 1858, he made a speech in the Senate against the proposition to appropriate money from the public Treasury for the establishment of schools in the District of Columbia. He said, in referring to the constantly increasing expenses of the Government:

"It is in the power of Congress to prevent these enormous expenditures, and, if we do not interpose, we are responsible for them. This Government, but sixty-nine years of age, scarcely out of its swaddling-clothes, is making more corrupt uses of money, in proportion to the amount collected from the people, as I honestly believe, than any other Government on the face of the habitable globe. Just in proportion as you increase the amount collected and expended by the Federal Government, in the same proportion corruption goes along with it; and when you run the expenditures of the Government up to one hundred or one hundred and fifty millions a year, the Treasury of the United States will control the whole nation, and the people of the respective States will have very little part in the Government, except to foot its bills in the shape of taxes."

In May, 1858, Mr. Johnson delivered, in the Senate, the greatest of his many great speeches on his favorite measure, the " Homestead Bill." Having heretofore given very copious extracts from his speeches on this question in the House of Representatives, it is not deemed necessary to quote further from his arguments in favor of the proposition. The following extract, however, is given to show the brightness and prosperity of that future for his country, which he foresaw and predicted would result from the inauguration of the " homestead " policy :

" Let me here make the inquiry, where, in the history of mankind, in the progress of nations, was there any nation that ever reached the point we now occupy ? When was there a nation, in its settlement, its progress, and its achievement of all that constitutes national greatness, that occupied the position we now do ? When was there any nation that could look to the East, and behold the tide of emigration coming, and, at the same time, turn around and look to the mighty West, and behold the tide of emigration rolling from that direction too? The waves of emigration have usually been found running in one direction, but we find the tides of emigration approaching from opposite directions, so that we are occupying the central position on the globe. And when our vacant territory shall be filled up, and our population shall reach a hundred or a hundred and fifty millions, who can conceive what will be our destiny?

" We may look forward to the time when our railroad system shall be perfected, extending from one extreme of the country to the other, like so many arteries ; when our telegraphic wires shall be stretched alongside them, as the nerves in the human arms, running in parallel lines, and crossing each other, until this great centre of the globe shall be covered with a network of these arteries and nerves, when the whole face of our country shall flash intelligence like the face of man. Then this great central position on the globe, instead of receiving other nations from abroad, will be the great censorium from which our system of government, religion, and human advancement, morally and materially, shall radiate in every direction, and ultimately revolutionize the world.

"So far as I am concerned, if this bill could be passed, and the system which it inaugurates fully carried out—of furnishing to every man a home, and thus attaching him to the soil, and identifying his interests with the interests of his country—when I look into the distant future, and contemplate the results, I feel that my little mission would be accomplished. All that I desire is the honor and the credit of being one of the American Congress to consummate this great scheme, that is to elevate our race, and to make our institutions more permanent.

"I can go back to that period in my own history, when I could not say I had a home. This being so, when I cast my eyes from one extreme of the United States to the other, and behold the great numbers that are homeless, I feel for them. This bill, if passed, would give them homes, and I wish to see them realizing this sweet conception, when each and all can exclaim, 'I have a home, an abiding place for my wife and children.' Yes, Mr. President, if I should never be heard of again on earth, the proud and conscious satisfaction of having contributed my humble aid to the consummation of this great measure, is all the reward I desire."

Notwithstanding the earnest efforts of Mr. Johnson and the other friends of the measure, they were unable to get a vote on it during this session of 1857–'58, and consequently it had to go over to the next session. The next session being a short session, for want of time it again failed to reach a decisive vote.

At the session of 1858–'59, President Buchanan having, in his annual message, recommended retrenchment in the expenditures of the Government, Mr. Johnson devoted his main efforts toward carrying out that policy, and in support of his great favorite measure, the Homestead bill. On this question of retrenchment and economy in the public expenditures, he has always exhibited such a deep-seated conviction of its importance as to show that he regards the tendency of our Government to wasteful extravagance so strong, as to threaten our liberties as a people. On this subject, at this session, he displayed his usual tenacity of purpose and determination of character. At four different times during the session he brought this question before the Senate, by introducing resolutions instructing the Committee on Finance to confer with the heads of departments, and report a general system of reduction of the expenses of the Government. He urged his proposition in the most earnest and forcible appeals to the sense of duty, and consistency with their professions, on the part of Senators. Though foiled in his purpose, again and again, he did not desist. On January 4, 1859, Mr. Johnson said:

"I have been waiting a long time, and looking for a favorable opportunity to commence the work of retrenchment. I have long been satisfied, in my own mind, that it cannot be done, unless the movement be headed by the Administration of the country. One member may come into the Senate-chamber, and a few others into the House of Representatives, and they may talk about retrenchment, and introduce resolutions, and offer propositions, but it results in nothing. The effort fails; there is no retrenchment commenced, and there is no reform brought about. But now we have a favorable opportunity. It is a time of peace. A Democratic President now proposes, in his annual message, to lead in this work of retrenchment. The President proposes to lead, and why shall we not join him in the effort? It never will be done until this or some other Administration places itself in the lead of this great work.

"In 1790 the population of the United States was a fraction less than four millions, and the expenditures in 1791 were two million dollars. In 1858 the population was twenty-eight millions, and the expenditures of the Government for the last year were about seventy-five millions of dollars. From 1790 up to the present time, the population has increased seven-fold, whilst the expenditures of the Government have increased thirty-five fold. Thus it appears that from 1790 to the present time, the expenditures of the Government have gone twenty-eight hundred per cent. in advance of the population. With that ratio going on in the future, how long will it be before the expenditures of the Government go beyond the ability of the people to pay the same?

"I know, so far as I am concerned—and I say it in no spirit of egotism—that my acts, my votes, and my speeches in the Congress of the United States, for a number of years, correspond with my professions; and I am willing now to reduce my professions to practice. I am satisfied that the expenditures of this Government are too great, and satisfied that they are unnecessary and profligate. I do honestly believe that millions of the public money are collected, and squandered here for improper purposes. If we are earnest in this matter, if we are sincere, let us give the public some evidence of our sincerity. Let us not continue to talk about extravagance and expenditures, but let us reduce our professions and our theories to practice."

On this subject, as on all others which Mr. Johnson touches, he speaks so plainly and unequivocally, that the reader is at no loss to understand him. The people of this country know exactly what is his position in regard to Government expenditures. And from his firmness and consistency of character, they may rely upon his practice as President, conforming to his professions when Senator. His objections to heavy expenditures are based not only on his opposition to extravagance, as involving heavy taxation, but still more on the corruption and peculation they are likely to produce and foster.

In January, 1859, the proposition was before the Senate for building a railroad across the continent to the Pacific Ocean. The debate on it was a very able one, many of the most prominent men in the Senate participated in it. Mr. Johnson's speech on the subject was of extraordinary power and ability. That speech alone would have established his character as a deep thinker, as an able and eloquent debater, and as a legislator of an eminently practical cast of mind. The whole speech should be read, in order to a proper appreciation of its merits. Mr. Johnson objected to it on account of the latitudinous construction of the Constitution, under the power "to declare war," which its advocates had to resort to, in order to justify its constitutionality. In the extracts given from this great speech, the author has not selected those marked by most ability, or exhibiting the most oratorical talent, but those best calculated to afford information in reference to Mr. Johnson's fixed views and opinions on practical questions that may arise hereafter. He said:

"It is somewhat difficult to determine what character of improvement is clearly within the Constitution, or, in other words, to determine what particular character of improvement is national, and what is local. I know the distinction is hard to draw, in many instances, for local works approach national works so closely that the line of division is scarcely within reach of the human intellect; but there are some things that are certain. We cannot tell exactly when the light of day terminates and the shades of night begin, but we can tell when it is mid-day, when the sun is at meridian, and when midnight darkness is upon us. So we can determine the character of *some* of the works of internal improvement, we can tell when they are glaringly unconstitutional. I have been taught, and it is my settled conviction, that in all questions of doubt as to the constitutional power of Congress, in reference to internal improvements, Congress should desist from the exercise of a doubtful power, and, before its exercise, should look to the source of all our power, in order to specially define the extent of the authority to be exercised by the legislative body. I also believe in the fundamental principle laid down by Mr. Jefferson: that in all doubtful questions we should pursue principle, and that in the pursuit of a correct principle you cannot reach a wrong conclusion. What is the principle involved in this proposition? We assume, putting it on the best ground on which it can be placed, that it is of doubtful power, at least. Then, falling back on the rule laid down by Mr. Jefferson, what is the principle? It is to call upon the source of all power before you exercise a doubtful authority.

"The President, in his message, disclaims the power as existing in the Constitution, unless it is derived from the war power. This is an honest difference of opinion. I do not believe it can be derived from that power. There are others who claim the power as arising from the power in the Constitution to regulate commerce. I do not think that provision in the Constitution which provides for the regulation of commerce, confers power on Congress to make or create commerce. Some derive the power from that provision of the Constitution which authorizes Congress to establish post-offices and post-roads. I do not believe the language employed in the Constitution to be so meant. The debates in the Convention do not show that Congress was to make and construct roads through the country. The Constitution means, I think, simply and plainly, that where there are lines of communication, Congress may establish them as the Government channels through which communications of this kind may go, but not to construct roads."

It had been urged, during the discussion on this measure, that the Democratic Convention at Cincinnati which nominated Mr. Buchanan, had passed a resolution in favor of the policy of constructing a railroad to the Pacific. Mr. Johnson boldly repelled the idea of his being trammelled in the discharge of his senatorial duty by the action of such a body.   Referring to the Cincinnati Convention, he said :

" I think of that convention, as I have thought about all conventions, from my earliest advent into public life to the present time. We know how these conventions are gotten up. Experience and observation have satisfied my mind that the old Congressional caucus system was infinitely preferable to your recent national convention system. In the one case, the members of Congress, who made the nomination, felt that they had some responsibility resting upon them, and when they went to their Congressional districts, they were responsible for the nominee whom they had put upon the country as a candidate for the Presidency. I do not say it from any disrespect, but I refer to it as an historical fact, that a large proportion of the persons who attend national conventions go there without representing any body.

" I most sincerely hope the time will come when the people of the United States will have the constitutional right to elect their own President. Do they elect him now? They do not. Packed conventions are gotten up, and they, by the means to which I refer, make a nomination on one side or the other. Although our people are, in theory, a free people, and are supposed to elect their President, the fact is that, in practice, the conventions have made the choice before the people are called on to vote. After these conventions, on the one side and the other, have chosen a President, the freemen of this country are brought up to the ballot-box and taken through the ridiculous mockery of voting for electors. I have supported the nominees of conventions, and I have been in conventions, but need I stultify myself, or deceive myself? Do I not see their tendency—their alarming, corrupting, and dangerous tendency?"

Let it be recollected this language was uttered in high party times. What a remarkable degree of bold and manly courage does it not bespeak, in any man, who could thus assail a system to which all parties were committed, and by which he ran the risk of arousing the opposition of the legion of professional politicians throughout the country? In this Mr. Johnson was true to the great leading element of his character as a public man—devotion to the RIGHTS OF THE PEOPLE. He saw that the system of nominating conventions practically deprived the people of the great privilege intended to be secured to them—that of electing their own Chief Magistrate.

He next proceeded to expose the enormous cost of this road to the Government, by the gratuities to the contractors, in the first instance—$25,000,000 in five per cent. Government bonds, 25,000,000 acres of land lying on each side of the road, and a remission of the duty on all the railroad iron—costing the Government, according to his (Mr. Johnson's) estimates, certainly $100,000,000, and more probably $200,000,000.

The following views, in regard to the difficulties of such a work, show the practical character of Mr. Johnson's mind. Although living in the mountain region of Tennessee, where he had but little opportunity of observing the practical operations on the great channels of trade and intercourse, yet he had evidently studied and reflected deeply on such subjects. He said:

"If this road were constructed now, if it were completed in the course of a night by enchantment—so that it would cost the Government nothing—yet it would cost more than the entire expenses of the War Department to run the road. Why, you cannot protect the road when built. Suppose you put five men per mile on the road, for two thousand miles, and it will require ten thousand men. In the manner in which we have been raising regiments by this Government, it has cost us one million dollars for each thousand men. That was the estimate at the last session. Then you must take into the account the interest on the money expended, and the other expenses of keeping up the road without way-travel or way-freight. You must rely on through travel to sustain the line along such a trunk of railroad as that will be, if ever constructed, and all the railroad statistics of the country prove that railroads must rely on way-travel and way-freight to be sustained. You must have people, you must have country, you must have commerce, to sustain the road, and not arid and sterile deserts."

The argument had been used that the construction of this railroad to the Pacific would strengthen the bonds of union among the States. In reply to this suggestion, Mr. Johnson said:

"I have never considered the Union yet in danger. I do not believe all the factionists of this Government can pull it to pieces. They cannot dissolve the bonds that unite us—the bonds of mutual interest and patriotism, strengthened by the associations of a common suffering in the past, and a common prosperity for the future. * * * My great apprehensions—and I think they are well founded, when I look at the tendency of our whole policy—are, that every thing is tending to the centre; and just in proportion as you increase the amount of money collected and disbursed by this Government, in the very same proportion you increase the centralizing power here.

"The great fault and difficulty is, that we legislate too much, and one-half of our legislation is an impediment, an obstruction, thrown in the way of the laws of Nature, preventing our people from conforming their action and conduct to great fundamental laws. Let your Government take as little from the people as possible; permit them to enjoy their own industry; protect them in their pursuits; let the people become rich, and let your Treasury remain poor. I am glad the Treasury is empty. I am not sure that I shall vote to borrow a dollar. I think it is a fortunate thing for the country that it is reduced, and even drained, for the idea has got to be predominant here—I was going to say irrespective of party—that the way to get power, and to become popular, is by the expenditure of large sums of money."

4

The last extracts above quoted contain the true philosophy of Mr. Johnson's political creed. They are full of meaning. They comprise the science of government simplified—that the great aim and object of Government, are the prosperity and happiness of the people—the whole people; that the normal occupation and pursuit of man, is in the advancement of his happiness and moral elevation, by his own industry and labor; that the purpose of government is to protect and encourage him in these pursuits; that legislation should be confined and restrained within these limits; that the schemes and projects of peculiar classes, interests, and monopolies, tend to complicate and amplify legislation; that consequently *too much* legislation is to be guarded against, as tending to corruption, and as antagonistic to the rights and interests of the great masses of the people. It is cheering and consoling, at this time of difficulty and derangement of our political affairs and sectional relations, to reflect that we have for our Chief Magistrate a man who had the rare moral courage to hold up to public reprobation the tendency to corruption and class favoritism in our legislation. It is comforting to know that in this great POPULAR TRIBUNE, Andrew Johnson, we have a President, who, to the extent of his power and influence, will rear up again the old landmarks of principle erected by the fathers, and will bring back the administration of the Government to the intent and purpose of its immortal founders.

CHAPTER VII.

In December, 1859, Mr. Johnson delivered in the Senate a speech of great ability and eloquence on a resolution offered by Mr. Mason, of Virginia, for inquiring into all the facts connected with the foray at Harper's Ferry by John Brown. This speech should be read through and through, in order to an appreciation of the oratorical talent exhibited by Mr. Johnson, and also to a proper understanding of his position on the points so long at issue between the North and South. That was a time of most intense excitement, of bitterness and acrimony, between the two sections. The South was enraged on account of the scenes perpetrated at Harper's Ferry—the North was enraged at the outrages in Kansas, which the Northern members insisted had instigated Brown in his raid. Mr. Johnson's speech was in earnest advocacy of the constitutional rights of the South, but it was in good temper, and free from violent and intemperate denunciation. It was a serious, an able, and ardent appeal to all men and all sections, in favor of harmony and conciliation. It was the speech of a statesman who felt apprehensions of coming trouble.

Mr. Johnson then stated the ground on which he stood, and which he consistently maintained to the last. That was, that the South must contend for its rights, and do battle for its constitutional privileges, under the Constitution and *in the Union*. He never did concur with those who were for seeking redress by dissolving the Union. He needs no stronger vindication of his course, even with the most ultra advocates of Southern rights, than is to be found in that speech. He had the sagacity to see that the only ægis for the protection of slavery in the States, was the Constitution of the United States. He had warned his Southern brethren that they must fight the battle under that instrument, and that a resort to disunion would only be playing into the hands of the radical disunion factionists of the North. Time has proven his wisdom and foresight. How much better had it been for the South, if his counsels had been followed! Mr. Johnson had been, from his first taking his seat in Congress, an earnest, consistent, bold, and able advocate of the rights of the Southern people under the Constitution. But he had also ever declared his determination to maintain the Union at all hazards. No one, therefore, had a right to complain, or to charge him with inconsistency, when, on the issue being made, he clung to the Union.

Mr. Johnson said:

" For myself, I am no disunionist; I am no madcap on that subject. Because we cannot get our constitutional rights, I do not intend to be one of those who will violate the Constitution. When the time comes, if ever it does come, when it shall be necessary—and God forbid that it ever should come—I intend to place myself on the Constitution which I have sworn to support, and to stand there and battle for all its guarantees; and if the Constitution is to be violated, if the Union is to be broken up, it shall be done by those who are stealthily and insidiously making encroachments on its very foundation. I intend to stand upon the Constitution to the very last. * * * God forbid that the time should ever come when this country shall be involved in a servile or a civil war! I trust that that day may be postponed to some far-distant future, and I hope, in the sincerity of my heart, that that future may never arrive. I would rather see this people involved in hostility against every power on the civilized globe, than to see it involved in civil and servile war. If blood is to be shed, be it so; but let it not be the blood of the people of these Confederated States fighting against each other. So far as I am concerned, I intend to stand by the Constitution and its guarantees, as the palladium of our civil and religious liberty. When the time shall come, if ever it does come, for dividing this Union, I ask my friends, North and South, where is the line to be drawn?"

On May 10th, 1860, the Senate came to a vote on Mr. Johnson's great measure, the Homestead bill, and it passed by the large vote of 44 to 8. It had previously passed the House of Representatives by a vote of 112 to 51. On the 23d of June following, Mr. President Buchanan sent in his *veto* upon the passage of the bill. The Senate proceeded to a vote on the reconsideration; and it was lost on a vote of yeas 27, nays 18—two-thirds not voting for it. Mr. Johnson made a very earnest and able speech on the veto message, in which he displayed his great power as an off-hand and *impromptu* debater. Of course, he could have had no time for preparation. Yet he took up the various points of objection in the veto message, *seriatim;* dissected them, exposed their fallacies; and exposed Mr. Buchanan's inconsistencies and prevarications, in a most effective manner. The freedom with which he spoke of Mr. Buchanan, and his sophistical positions, proved that Andrew Johnson was no time-serving partisan. He evidently felt deeply and indignantly at seeing his long-cherished measure, after passing both Houses by a more than two-thirds vote in each House, thus summarily defeated by the Executive veto. He said :

"The President's argument against the bill, on the ground of unconstitutionality, is simply absurd, not to say ridiculous, after the long-established usage of the Government—receiving the sanction of nearly every President of the United States. The policy of granting lands to individuals, by the Government, as homesteads, was approved by Washington, sanctioned by Jefferson, and cherished by Jackson ; whose names and memories will compare, in my opinion, most favorably with that of the present Administration. Whether considerations so national, so humane, so Christian, have ever penetrated the brain of one whose bosom has never yet swelled with emotions for wife or children, is for an enlightened public to determine.

"I always have respect for a man who fills the office of President of the United States, irrespective of party ; and it would be very natural for me to have more respect for a President of my own party, than for any one of opposite politics. But does the fact of the President's objecting change the nature and character of great principles and truths ? If there is a great fundamental principle in this measure, involving the welfare of the Government and the great cause of humanity, the fact that the President withholds his approval does not change my opinion. If there were forty Presidents, with forty assistants to write out vetoes, I would still stand by this bill, and give it the sanction of my vote and my support.

"In these revolutionary times, it is hard to tell where we are going ; and it is, perhaps, difficult for each individual to know his precise locality. I started for this bill on principle, I supported it upon principle, I voted for it upon principle, and I intend to follow it to its conclusion, let it carry me wheresoever it may. For, in the pursuit of a correct principle, I feel well assured that I can never reach a wrong conclusion. Whether the President differs from me, or concurs with me, I do not intend to

veer either to the right or to the left. My course is onward and
direct."

As a member of Congress, Mr. Johnson rarely disturbed himself with local questions with which he had no
concern—nor did he make himself odious to his fellow-
members by interfering in their private legislation, unless
when he saw the public interest was likely to suffer. But
there was scarcely any *great* measure agitated in which he
did not participate in the debate. In this, he avoided the
rock on which many promising young men, who possess
oratorical powers, are apt to founder: that is, the frittering
away their talents and their usefulness by constantly talk-
ing on any and every question. When great and exciting
subjects came up for discussion, he evidently informed himself in regard to them; and hence it was that he rarely
failed to present some new and striking views in debating
them. He exhibited that sort of common sense—not too
common among public debaters—to know when to speak,
and to know when to stop speaking. The great extent of
his information in regard to the political history of the
country, is really surprising, and cannot fail to strike any
one on reading his speeches. There is one peculiarity in
all his great speeches—after examining a subject upon its
merits as affecting the governmental policy of the country,
he invariably applies to it the touchstone, by which he
tests all public measures, viz., its bearing and influence
upon the rights, the prosperity, and welfare *of the people.*
No matter how specious, how plausible, how captivating
may be the garb in which a practised debater might adorn
any favorite scheme, yet if Mr. Johnson saw in it any
thing which ignored the wishes and disregarded the interests of the great mass of the people, no one was at a loss
to know where he would be found.

Whilst Mr. Johnson was not a common talker on small

and immaterial questions, yet the journals of Congress will show that he paid strict attention to the details of business in all practical matters involving the general good. In his views he inclined to the practical and the useful, rather than to the grand and the imposing. In regard to the "Smithsonian Institution," which has been a sort of *pet* of the Government, he seems to have thought that the intention of the donor—the founding an institution "for the increase and diffusion of knowledge among men "—would be much better consulted by establishing a University, whence the blessings of education could be generally diffused, than by such an institution as Congress had endowed with the fund bequeathed by Mr. Smithson. According to his practical view, mere grandeur and imposing appearance, in their appeals to the senses, were much less likely to confer blessings on the country and the community at large, than an institution where learning and education might be disseminated among the rising generation. He accordingly introduced a resolution in January, 1848, proposing to raise a committee, who shall "take into consideration the propriety of so changing and remodelling the present design of the Smithsonian Institution, as to convert it into a University, in the extended sense of the term, including the manual labor feature—embracing agriculture, horticulture, and all the various branches of mechanism, or as many of them as may be deemed practicable and useful to the country."

The minutest details of legislation did not escape Mr. Johnson's notice, especially where the interests and happiness of *numbers* were concerned. No more striking instance can be presented than in a resolution offered by him in January, 1848, as follows:

" *Resolved*, That the Committee on Military Affairs be instructed to inquire into the expediency of providing a new and complete tent for the army, which shall protect the men from the water and the weather, be easily and quickly pitched and struck, and combine size, lightness, durability, and strength, with compactness of packing and facility of transportation."

The introduction of the above is at once a key to Mr. Johnson's character as a public man. It shows that the practical and the useful was his aim as a legislator. The peculiar phraseology and minute particularity of the resolution show the earnestness of purpose by which he was actuated. His thoughts and sympathies were for the *men* —the common soldiers of the army. He knew that, so far as the officers were concerned, *their* comfort would be sure to be provided for. If Mr. Johnson had been on the Committee on Military Affairs, then there might have been nothing remarkable in his offering such a proposition. But he did not belong to that committee. He was not particularly called on to attend to matters of that sort. If he had been a representative from some one of the large cities, or some great commercial thoroughfare, where the wants and requirements of the army were matters of public discussion, there would have been nothing peculiar in it. But he was from the mountain region of East Tennessee, where a soldier was hardly ever seen. The author, in presenting so earnestly this incident in Mr. Johnson's legislative experience, is aware that most persons would regard it as a very trivial, commonplace affair. The object is to show the entire consistency of the man upon any and all subjects, under any and all circumstances—that the philosophical principle which governs and directs his political life is the development of the practical and the useful for the welfare of the many. In looking at the army, Mr. Johnson saw that the common soldiery, the rank and file, constituted an important—the most important— element in its construction; in the same way that, in observing the Government of the country, he regards *the people* as the greater element than their official representatives. Mr. Johnson is a thorough disciple and advocate of the Baconian system of philosophy. Practical experience he considers to be the only test of truth and safety in all temporal and material things. The elevation of the masses, and the advancement of their prosperity and happiness, he regards as the great end and aim of all knowledge, all science, all government.

It was in pursuance of these principles—that the advantages, the benfits, and emoluments of the Government belong to all alike—that Mr. Johnson introduced a series of resolutions, in March, 1848, which provided for the distribution of the official patronage of the Government among the different Congressional districts, so as to give to " each district its fair ratio of offices under the Federal Government."

This proposition is eminently right and proper in itself, and it is strange that some legislation on the subject has not heretofore regulated the matter. From the foundation of the Government three-fourths of the offices have been monopolized by a few States contiguous to Washington. Not only was there rank injustice in this, but those Congressional districts, represented by members who were not political friends of the Administration, were cut off from all hope of any official patronage under the Government. The proposition was a very liberal one indeed, coming from one whose party had, with the exception of a few years, been in power for twenty years. If Mr. Johnson's proposition had been passed into a law, every Congressional district, no matter how much its people or its representatives might have been opposed to the party in power, would have received its due share of official patronage. It would have struck a blow at corruption in the appointing power, when it might have been considered necessary to appoint certain men, to effect certain party objects, in any certain district. It is important now to refer to Mr. Johnson's course on the subject in 1848. Possessing, as he now does, the entire appointing power, the country may feel assured that he will, in the distribution of office, consult the rights, the wishes, and the interests of every section. Upon this, as upon all other subjects, he is opposed to monopolies, whether of classes, of pursuits, or of sections.

There is one great abuse which has long prevailed at Washington, a reform of which the country may confidently rely upon, judging from Mr. Johnson's recorded opinions on the subject. The abuse alluded to is the multiplication of the number of clerks and employés at Washington whenever there is a *temporary* excess of labor to be performed in any of the departments. Many of them, whilst receiving pay from the Government for doing but little, are the pensioned correspondents of newspapers all over the Union, who deal in sensational letters, and who write this man up and that man down, according to their partialities or their prejudices. This class of men have become to be an *institution*, as it were. They are the manufacturers of a factitious public opinion in regard to men and to measures. They have become to be a power in the State, and their pens are wielded *in terrorem*. Mr. Johnson seems to understand them thoroughly. In some remarks by him, in the Thirtieth Congress, on a proposition for an increase of clerical force in the pension office, Mr. Johnson said:

"In some offices there are too many clerks; deploy them, concentrate your forces on some other point, and you can have the business of the country performed without augmenting the number of offices, that are constantly increasing and preying on the vitals of the country. I know that in this particular atmosphere it is a little dangerous to talk about office-holders. Many of them have nothing to do but to write letters to puff particular individuals, and he who dares raise his voice against this interested clique, this set of political vampires, who are fixed upon the Government and who care nothing for the interests of the people, is, I know, treading on dangerous ground. They write letters to the newspapers in various sections of the country, and misrepresent and vilify any one who dares to expose abuses of this sort. I had almost as soon set my foot in a nest of electric eels as to come in contact with this class of pensioners upon the public Treasury. Go along Pennsylvania Avenue of an evening, and whom do you find there? Why, this class of men, lounging about the hotels and places of public resort—some of them with pencil and paper in hand, collecting and noting down facts for a letter. A most enlightened set of gentlemen ! "

Mr. Johnson exhibited great vigilance and boldness and independence (for it required no small amount of these last-named traits) in maintaining the dignity of Congress and the personal reputation of its members. It is well known that much had been said, and many scandalous insinuations indulged in, in regard to the corrupt practices of members of Congress—of their urging measures through, in which they were personally interested—their receiving fees for their influence in the prosecution of claims, etc. Mr. Johnson seems to have been particularly shocked at any intimations of this sort, and he never failed to speak out boldly and in the most unqualified terms of denunciation at even the remotest grounds for suspicion. On a proposition to distribute the appointments of midshipmen in the navy among the Congressional districts—assimilating the appointments to those of cadets at West Point— Mr. Johnson moved an amendment—

" *Provided* that a member of Congress making a nomination, shall not nominate his own son, nor the son of any other member."

When the bill for establishing the Court of Claims was under consideration, Mr. Johnson moved as an amendment—

"That if any member of Congress shall appear as counsel or attorney, or otherwise aid any claimant in establishing any claim or claims against the United States before said Board of Commissioners, the seat of such member shall be vacated, and the member rendered ineligible for the remainder of the term for which he was elected."

Mr. Johnson said he "thought members of Congress should be kept out of this business; if they are not, they will monopolize all the business of this new court. It is opening the door to corruption—it is offering an opportunity to members of Congress to receive bribes in the shape of fees. As an evidence of the propriety of some such restriction, we see notices put in the newspapers by members of Congress, proposing to prosecute claims against the Government of the United States. If this court is established, it will be merely transferring the business of the Committee on Claims to the Board of Commissioners, and gentlemen know that these considerations must exercise an influence over the minds of members, when the cases are brought up here."

Mr. Johnson was equally severe in his strictures upon the custom, for many years past prevailing, of members of Congress voting to themselves heavy *douceurs*, in the shape of very valuable books. This had become to be regarded as a great outrage, even among members of Congress themselves, and throughout the country. The only decent pretence ever put forth in its mitigation was, that it had been long sanctioned by custom, and that every Congress, in voting to themselves these books, only did what others before them had done. In the Twenty-eighth Congress, on a proposition to purchase Greenhow's " History of Oregon and California," Mr. Johnson moved an amendment to rescind the resolution of 1844, which directed the Clerk to furnish to each member of the House such books as were furnished to the members of the Twenty-sixth and Twenty-seventh Congresses. Mr. Johnson said :

"I think it is time, as expressed in my amendment, that this matter should be put an end to. There is no difference between members voting themselves five or six hundred dollars additional pay, and voting the amount in books. I know an instance in which a member got the books ordered, and then sold them for one hundred and fifty dollars. The Government pays this enormous price (five hundred to six hundred dollars), members then sell them at this greatly reduced price (one hundred and fifty dollars), and put the money into their pockets. The next Congress orders them for *its* members, and pays this same excessive price to those booksellers that thus buy them of the members, who do not care enough for them to take them home. No public benefit results from these purchases of books by Congress for members ; for when not sold by them, they are taken home and deposited in their private libraries. If this practice is to continue, what an immense expense will it entail on the Government! I am informed, by a gentleman who has investigated the subject, that it has already cost the Government nearly a million of dollars."

In the cases thus referred to, Mr. Johnson's purpose evidently was, to guard the character of Congress against any grounds for suspicion. He regarded legislation as designed for the protection of the people's rights, and the advancement of their prosperity. He knew that the public treasure and popular freedom must suffer if the representative was unfaithful, and hence his anxiety to guard the latter against temptation even. It also shows what a high estimate he placed on the position of a Representative of the people. Some members looked upon these practices of procuring warrants for their own sons in the army and navy, or of swapping influence with fellow-members in regard to the promotion of *their* sons, as small matters, not involving any stigma whatever. Others regarded the taking of fees, for prosecuting claims against the Government, as mere professional transactions. Not so Andrew Johnson. He wished to preserve immaculate the character of the Representatives of the people. He thought of them as Cæsar did of his wife—that they must be not only pure, but unsuspected.

CHAPTER VIII.

IT is well known to the reader that, for many years past, the *prestige* of Congressional character has become materially impaired by the thousands of rumors that go out from Washington, in regard to the demoralization of the members, in perverting the influence of their official station to their own interests and to the advancement and promotion of friends, etc. Whether true or not, these charges have greatly affected public opinion; and, to a considerable extent, the popular respect and admiration for the legislative department of the Government have become lessened. This is much to be regretted. For in order to make a people proud of their Government, and proud of themselves as being the citizens of a Government which they admire and respect, they must have confidence in its purity and in its faithfulness to the great principles on which it is founded. The people of the country have much to hope from President Johnson, on this subject. His stern and uncompromising opinions in regard to the purity and integrity which should mark the character of the Representatives of the people are well known. The public mind may rest secure that he will not only never tamper with their integrity in his high executive capacity, but that he will exercise his executive power and influence, whenever necessary, in resisting every tendency to corruption in the legislative branch of the Government.

The fraud and peculation exposed in the celebrated "Gardiner claim" aroused in Mr. Johnson the most intense indignation. His speech on the subject is marked with the eloquence of indignant wrath, and reminds the reader of those forensic displays of the old Roman orators, in which they exposed the peculations and abuses of their times, which followed in the wake of the conquest of Roman arms. It is probably known to the reader that Gardiner was an itinerant adventurer in Mexico, a man of great shrewdness and energy, who preferred a claim against the Mexican Government for $500,000, under the treaty of 1831 with that Government. By the treaty of peace with Mexico in 1848, our Government reserved $3,250,000 of the $15,000,000 to be paid to Mexico, for the payment of the claims of our citizens against Mexico under the treaty of 1831, and a commission was appointed to adjudicate the claims. Under this claim the commission awarded to Gardiner $427,000. It leaked out, after a while, that this claim was improperly allowed, having no merits to sustain it. Mr. Johnson thus boldly and fearlessly denounced it in the House of Representatives in January, 1853 :

"One thing has been ascertained since this claim was allowed, and that is, that it is a fraudulent one, based only on perjury and forgery. We know that perjury and forgery were the means by and through which the amount of money I have specified as being awarded to Dr. Gardiner was taken out of the Treasury. This fact no one will controvert. The committee were unanimous in the opinion that it was a naked fraud upon the Treasury."

Many hard things were said, and many severe censures indulged, against the two distinguished men who were Gardiner's counsel in the prosecution of the claim, and who were understood to have received very heavy contingent fees. The subject had been referred to a committee, that reported a bill " to prevent frauds on the Treasury of the United States." In the debate on this bill, Mr. Johnson refused to be drawn into the discussion of the culpability of the counsel—as to whether they were, or were not, cognizant of its being a fraud on the Treasury. The position he assumed and maintained with great earnestness and ability—the stand-point of his argument—was this: that the connection of high functionaries of the Government with the prosecution of such claims involved an *impropriety*, according to his views, of political morality. Consequently, he was in favor of passing the law, so as to stamp such conduct with the disapprobation of the Government *legally*. He thus exposes the inconsistency of those who contended there was no *impropriety* on the part of the counsel who urged this claim before the commission, and who yet expressed an intention to vote for the bill to prevent such frauds on the Treasury in the future:

" Those who vote for this bill thereby admit that this thing should be made an offence legally, as it is morally; proceeding on the idea, that to have any thing like a perfect system of jurisprudence, law must be the perfection of reason—and, I will add, of *sound morals* also. The morals must precede the law, and the law should be made to sustain the morals. If it is not morally wrong to do this thing, I say it is wrong to pass a law making it a legal offence. If it is morally wrong, pass the law, and make it legally wrong. If it is not morally wrong, pass no such law; for if you do, you make law and morals antagonists; you have them running counter to each other. The gentleman from Ohio (Mr. Barrere) seems willing to justify Mr. ——'s connection with the claim *morally*, yet he is willing to make it an offence *legally*. I cannot reconcile that sort of argument. It reminds me of a position assumed at one period of time by Professor Hoffman. He wrote as long ago as 1598—just two hundred years before the passage of the Virginia resolutions—that philosophy was the mortal enemy of religion; and that truth was divisible into two branches, one philosophical and the other theological; and that what was true in philosophy was false in theology, and *vice versâ*. The gentleman from Ohio seems to assume the same position as to the antagonism between law and morals. It seems to me that morals should constitute the basis of all law.

"I cannot conclude without making an earnest appeal to the House to come forward and sustain this bill, as one step toward arresting and condemning the system of high-handed plundering and swindling which has been and is being carried on about Congress and the various departments of Government. Sound morality, common honesty, justice, an eviscerated Treasury—all demand that something should be done to separate these vampires from the body politic. There must be something done to restore public confidence; for it is going very fast, if not already gone. The Government, and the functionaries of Government, are beginning to be offensive in the very nostrils of the nation; many of the parts are already decayed, whilst the disease is working its way into others less accessible. The putrid stench is sent forth on every wind, and is arresting the attention of the voracious vultures throughout the land. They have gathered and are still gathering around the carcass, ready to begin their foul work:

> "They come from the mountain-tops; with hideous cry
> And clattering wings, the filthy harpies fly;
> Monsters more fierce offended Heaven ne'er sent
> From hell's abyss for human punishment."

As a mere question of dialectics, it is a matter of but little moment whether Mr. Johnson's views as to the inseparable dependence between law and morals be logically true to the extent laid down by him or not. But so far as regards practical results, his views are, at this time, of most significant importance. They prove that he contends for, and will maintain to the extent of his power, the highest standard of purity, integrity, and responsibility, on the part of all functionaries of the Government. It is well known that of late years very queer notions of political morality have been making progress in the public mind. The hackneyed and false adage—that " all is fair in politics "—though often quoted in derision, has yet, to a certain extent, taken root in *official soil.* There are many things which, if done in a political character, are tolerated, if not approved, yet which would be condemned as morally wrong if done in a private relation of life. The country may congratulate itself that such is not Mr. Johnson's opinion. His record upon that point is beyond cavil or doubt. Upon no subject has he exhibited more indignation, more uncompromising hostility, than that of the perversion of official power and influence to the advancement of private interests.

There is a striking trait of character which Mr. Johnson exhibited throughout his whole legislative life—that is, his watchful vigilance over the Treasury—his uniform opposition to all extravagance in the expenditure of the public money—his earnest advocacy of economy and retrenchment where practicable in the administration of the Government. Hence it is he was generally found opposing the various devices resorted to, session after session, for obtaining heavy appropriations, either under the pretext of claims upon the Government or of the temporary requirements of the public service. Propositions for increase of clerical force in the departments—for erecting gorgeous additions to the public buildings—for the purchase, at unreasonable prices, of the manuscript papers of distinguished men, found but little favor with him. These things are referred to here, not because of their intrinsic importance, for they are matters on which the most conscientious men might reasonably differ in opinion, but they are alluded to by way of showing the bias and tenor of Mr. Johnson's character in regard to the true purposes of free government—that the useful, and not the imposing, is the proper policy. A thorough examination of his public life will show that he was not governed by any niggard parsimony. Where the great vital interests of the public required it, no man was more liberal in voting money from the Treasury. But on any and all questions, whether in the appropriation of money or any other legislation affecting any class or interest, he was as true as the needle to the pole in his regard for the rights and interests of the laboring-man. Hence, on a proposition offered in the Thirty-second Congress to increase the pay of the employés in the legislative and executive departments of the Government, in the city of Washington, from ten to twenty per cent., Mr. Johnson moved as an amendment:

"That twenty per cent. be added to the *per diem* or monthly pay now received by all employés of the Government who are engaged in any branch of mechanics or at common labor."

Mr. Johnson said:

"We have had various amendments offered here with the view of increasing the salaries and pay of everybody connected with the Government, save the man that labors and produces. The man who wears the dinge of the shop or the dust of the field upon his garments seems to be but little thought of or cared for in this House, except on occasions when the Government needs taxes. When the Government needs men to fight its battles, then it calls on this class of persons; but when money is to be voted out of the Treasury, without stint or measure, then they are but little regarded. I should like to know why the men that work in your navy yards, and forge your anchors, and build your ships—men who wield the broad-axe, chisel, and hammer, not only five hours in the day, but ten hours, at one dollar and fifty cents to two dollars per day—should not have twenty per cent. added to their wages also.   They have not the time, after working ten hours a day—like others who are not employed five—to visit this hall and besiege members of Congress with importunities to increase their pay.   They have to work, almost from the rising to the going down of the sun, whilst others in the employment of the Government get much larger wages, although their expenses of living are not more than those who labor in your workshops. Go, for instance, to your armory.   Who proposes to increase the pay of the men who are engaged in preparing the implements of war to defend your country in its hour of need?   When provisions rise, when bread and meat advance in price, and it is almost impossible for the mechanic to support his family, do we hear these eloquent appeals in behalf of *him*, his wife and children?"

During the long political controversy on the subject of the tariff which agitated the country whilst Mr. Johnson was in Congress, he was the uniform opponent of the high protective policy, through a system of discriminating duties, where such discrimination was made with an especial view to protection.   The reader, to enable himself to understand the true source, the real groundwork, of his objection to the high protective policy, must read his speeches on the subject.   These show that his opposition arose from no sectional prejudices or narrow-minded views in regard to any branch of industry.   It had its origin in the vigilant jealousy of his nature of every thing tending to monopolies ; of all legislation looking to special benefits for any peculiar class ; of all efforts to advance the interests of the *few* in disregard of the welfare of the many. Mr. Johnson seems to have been governed, in his public life, by a political philosophy, so to speak, which has shaped and directed his course upon all questions.   This political philosophy is based on the idea that our Government and institutions were made by the people, to be administered by the people, and for the common good and general welfare of the people; that these institutions, in their recognition of the principle of equality, and in extending to all equal advantages and privileges in the great race of advancement to station, wealth, honor, and reputation, had done enough for industry, energy, enterprise, morality, and worth, *in common*, without departing from their constitutional mission in conferring special favors on any special pursuit or any particular section. Here, then, was the cause of his dislike of special protection to special interests or sections. Being a mechanic himself, and accustomed to labor from his boyhood, he could not but look favorably on the manufacturing establishments, which are great hives of industry and mechanical labor. Being remarkable for his pride of country, in comparison with other countries, he was naturally disposed to look favorably on any industrial enterprise that promised to make his country independent of others in procuring a supply of the necessaries of life. Whilst, therefore, he did not object to, but the rather rejoiced at, any aid which manufacturing industry might receive incidentally from the imposition of duties necessary to support the Government, yet he never could allow his views of *special* benefit to prevail over his conviction of duty to the *general* good.

This question of a protective tariff is not likely to agitate the public mind in this country again, in our day at least. And Mr. Johnson's position is referred to here, first, because it is necessary to an explanation of his political course, and, in the second place, it is due to him, and to the cause of truth, that any attempt that may be made to misrepresent or prejudice him in the public mind, shall be met and exposed by a statement of *facts*. To succeed in any attempt to misrepresent Mr. Johnson, is to impair his usefulness. To impair his usefulness, at this important juncture of our affairs, is to strike a blow at the country.

In giving extracts from Mr. Johnson's speeches in Congress, the author has not selected those passages which exhibit most intellectual ability and argumentative power. To judge of the intellect, the oratorical talent, and logical force of a speech, the whole speech should be read. In order to enable the reader to get a proper conception of Mr. Johnson's powers as a parliamentary debater, an additional volume or volumes would be necessary to contain his most important speeches. The object of the author in this volume is to present to the reading public that information, now eagerly sought for, that will enable them to judge correctly of Mr. Johnson's views and settled opinions as to the nature and theory of our Government, the proper policy to be pursued in its administration, the philosophical principles that underlie our free institutions, and the great national mission we have, as a people, to accomplish. The author's purpose is to afford instruction concerning Mr. Johnson, that the people of the country may know him as he is; that they may judge him fairly and impartially.

In these extracts from his speeches the author has also had an eye to what may give the reader an insight into his private character, his sentiments and feelings, as a private man. The author is not one of those who believe that talent howsoever great, intellect howsoever profound, learning howsoever deep, alone constitute fitness for high station. Great and necessary as these qualities are, yet, without the virtues of the heart, unless accompanied with high moral virtues, they are what the Apostle describes faith to be when unaccompanied by charity: they are as "sounding brass and a tinkling cymbal." Whether Pope was correct in applying the illustration to that great man, Lord Bacon, or not, yet history teaches us that it is not impossible to see the same individual take rank among—

"The wisest, brightest, meanest of mankind."

Mr. Johnson's speeches show forth the qualities of his heart as strikingly as they do those of his head. There is an open-hearted candor and freedom from all prevarication as to his views, which denote political honesty and truthfulness without mistake. No one can read his productions without seeing that he possesses that rare virtue, gratitude. Whenever he alludes to the people who have honored and elevated him, his language evidently comes swelling up from a heart full of feeling and thankfulness. His sympathy for suffering—for honest poverty—for struggling adversity—as evinced in his speeches, state papers, etc., is unmistakable. Whenever he alludes to such subjects, his language is free from all studied ornament, but gushes forth in a full tide of feeling. His allusions to " home "— to the quiet domestic joys of private life—plainly show that he appreciates, to their utmost extent, the duties enjoined by the domestic relations, and that he regards true enjoyment and happiness only to be found around the family hearth-stone. His devotion to tried and trusted friends proves beyond controversy the sincerity and fidelity of his nature. It is doubtful whether there has been any great man in our political history, whose character and opinions, intellectually, morally, and socially, can be more fairly and correctly judged of by a stranger who knew nothing of him before, than those of Andrew Johnson may be by a perusal of his productions. When he speaks or writes on any subject, he leaves no doubt whatever as to what his position is.

Mr. Johnson's great favorite measure, the " Homestead

Bill," did not finally become the law of the land till May, 1862, a short time after he had left his seat in the Senate to enter upon the duties of Military Governor of Tennessee. The historical fact cannot be lost sight of, that Andrew Johnson was the author and father of this great public boon. In every pioneer cabin throughout our vast Western domain the name of Andrew Johnson will be spoken of with gratitude and affection for a century to come. Thousands, who might have otherwise been houseless and homeless, will talk to their children of the man who for fifteen long years labored to secure *a home* to the poor and the unfortunate. Thousands, who might otherwise have been left to the evils of vagrancy and dissipation in our cities and towns, will bless the name of him who opened the way for them to a home of plenty and comfort in the far distant West. The impulse given to emigration and settlement by this beneficent measure will rapidly people our vast empire territory. Churches, academies, and court-houses will speedily, as if by magic, make their appearance, where, but for the zeal and perseverance of Andrew Johnson, the buffalo would have roamed, and the Indian pursued his game for a generation to come. Rivers will soon waft the echo of a thousand whistling engines, where, but for Andrew Johnson's labors, the solitude of nature would have remained undisturbed, save by the scream of water-fowl, or the growl of the panther. The mansions of comfort, elegance, and hospitality, will soon open their doors to the wayfarer, where, but for Andrew Johnson's benevolence, he would have been shelterless against the inclemency of the weather and the sky. "The cattle of a thousand hills" will soon be browsing on green pastures, where, but for Andrew Johnson, the footprints of a domestic animal would have been unseen for many a long year.

Thousands upon thousands of children and children's children, for centuries will bless the name of the man to whom they are indebted for their lots being cast in that land of plenty and beauty which stretches far, far away to the base of the Rocky Mountains, and up their lovely valleys and defiles to where the eagle that is perched in view may take a look either down on the eastern plains, or on the streams that flow on the west to the bosom of the Pacific. In contemplating the time when that immense domain, extending from Minnesota, Iowa, Kansas, and the Indian Territory, to the Pacific, shall be inhabited by forty or fifty millions of population, the mind is lost in wonder and admiration. The history of this people will commence with the Homestead Law of Andrew Johnson. He unlocked and opened wide the gate through which the pioneer and the emigrant commenced their journey westward in search of *a home*. Lift the curtain that conceals the future, and contemplate the scene fifty years hence. Behold a thousand grandsires under their cottage verandas on a Sabbath evening, reading to the numerous family offspring from the old family Bible, with comfort and contentment smiling around, and then relating to them that they owe their blessings (under the Providence of God) to the benevolent forecast and labors of ANDREW JOHNSON, who lived on the east of the great Father of Waters, when they—the narrators—were young men, poor, and without a home.

In thousands of school-houses the pupils will read from primary books how the settlement and improvement of that country has converted a wilderness into comfortable and happy *homes*, owing to the philanthropy and perseverance of ANDREW JOHNSON, whose name should be cherished by them as a pattern for their imitation. In a thousand churches the ministers of God, in detailing to their hearers the blessings for which they should feel grateful, will refer to ANDREW JOHNSON as the instrument through whom Almighty goodness has vouchsafed to them that great inheritance of prosperity and happiness. There will, in the far distant West, for ages to come—

> "Each running stream, each flowing river,
> Roll mingled with his name forever."

Mr. Johnson's decided opposition to the "Know-Nothing" or "American" movement has been before alluded to. It is not the purpose of the author of this memoir to discuss the merits of the question of "Americanism." It had its day, and has disappeared, in all probability, forever. It was one of those questions on which patriotic and good men might well differ honestly, according to the stand-point from which they viewed it. Mr. Johnson's speeches on the subject bear the impress of earnest and conscientious opposition to the movement. He regarded the tide of foreign emigration to our country as one of the great elements of our national power and prosperity. He considered it the true policy, on the part of the American people, to foster this emigration rather than to discourage it. Hence he considered any course calculated to retard the speedy absorption of the emigrant element into the body politic as calculated to arrest our national progress. There were very few foreigners and Roman Catholics in the mountain region of East Tennessee. This affords the strongest evidence of Mr. Johnson's honesty and sincerity. He could not be accused of pandering to any feeling in favor of foreigners and Roman Catholics in order to obtain votes. In a speech he delivered at Greenville, Tenn., in 1851, in reply to his competitor, L. C. Haynes, the last time he was a candidate for the House of Representatives of the United States

Congress, he used the following eloquent language in reference to foreigners:

"When looking across the water to the starving, oppressed, and down-trodden condition of the inhabitants of the Emerald Isle, it is not in my nature, when the poor Irishman leaves his own country and seeks this as the home of the oppressed and the asylum of the exile, to meet him on the sea-shore and forbid his entrance. When I look across to Germany, I see the population is dense, subsistence dear, money scarce, and wages for labor low. If the German, on comparing the nature and character of his own Government with ours, should determine to take his wife and children and embark in some ship bound for our ports, and after many weeks of peril, anxiety, and contest with the waves of the ocean, he succeeds in reaching our shore, who, that claims to be an American, would meet him there and bid him stay away, with up-braidings that he was a foreigner? In such case I imagine I can see the honest German pause, and draw from his pocket a small volume, written by Weems, giving an account of the incidents of the Revolution. I think I can see him turning to that page, describing the battle of Camden, in which the brave old German De Kalb fought, receiving eleven wounds, and testing his devotion to freedom by offering up his life in its cause. I think I see him point to the grave which contains the hero's bones, and then, in an emphatic manner, ask if he might not be permitted to enjoy a country beneath whose soil the brave and noble De Kalb sleeps in peace. Suppose I look to France—versatile and revolutionary France—whose history, since 1792, has been one of revolution and blood. I there see a sensitive and animated Frenchman whose very soul longs for liberty, and whose every impulse is that of chivalry—I see him becoming sick of his own ever-changing France, looking up to the flag of his own country and meditating upon the institutions of his native land—then stretching his vision across the water, fixing it upon our own glorious Stars and Stripes—then contemplating and analyzing our beautiful and complex form of government—and finally resolving to cast his destiny in our midst. The tempest and the wave are at length overcome, and he finds himself moored in an American harbor. I ask if there is a man in this assembly, who has a spark of patriotism abiding in his bosom, or one impulse of philanthropy in his heart, that would meet him at the shore and bid him return to his native land. Would my competitor, in all the fury and zeal of his opposition to foreigners, meet him on the beach, sword in hand, to drive him back into the waves, and merely because he was a foreigner? I think I can see the poor Frenchman sternly looking my competitor in the face and exclaiming, Stay thy hand; suspend the blow; then opening the history of the Revolution, pointing to the page describing the battle of Brandywine, in which his countryman Lafayette was wounded; then to the surrender of Cornwallis at Yorktown which brought peace and independence: I think I can hear the Frenchman asking, in the name of freedom and of Lafayette's sacrifices, if he could not be permitted to enter the country and live beneath the protecting branches of the tree of liberty, planted by Washington, and watered with Lafayette's blood. For myself, I can say it is not in my nature to drive him from our shore; but I would say to him, Come and be our brother; take up your abode with us under the tree of liberty and be happy, worshipping Almighty God according to the dictates of your own conscience."

Mr. Johnson was equally decided in his opposition to that feature in the "American" organization by which its members bound themselves not to vote for Roman Catholics for any political station. He has always considered religious freedom as the twin-sister of civil liberty, and never would tolerate any thing that he thought was likely to compromise or impair either. This subject was incidentally introduced in a debate in the Twenty-eighth Congress. Mr. Johnson, in alluding to it, said:

"I do not appear here to defend the Roman Catholic religion. There are but few Catholics in my region, and there are prejudices existing against them. But I protest against the doctrine here advanced by the gentleman from North Carolina. The Catholics of this country are entitled to the full exercise of all the rights secured to them by the Constitution of the United States—that of worshipping God in the manner dictated by their own consciences. They, in common with all other denominations of Christians, have the right to sit under their own vines and fig-trees, and no one can rightfully interfere with them. This country is not prepared to establish an inquisition to try and punish men for their religious beliefs ; and those who assail any religious sect in this country will find a majority of the people arrayed against them. I desire to know of the gentleman from North Carolina what he meant by the use of the language I have just read from his speech. Does he mean that there is to be a spirit of persecution aroused in this country which is to sweep away any one of the religious denominations that now prevail among us? Are the ten thousand temples that have been erected, based upon the sufferings and atonement of a crucified Saviour, with their glittering spires wasting themselves in the heavens, all to topple and fall, crushed and buried beneath the storms and ravages of a party excitement? Is man to be set upon man, and, in the name of God, to lift his hand against the throat of his fellow? Is the land that gave a brother birth to be watered with a brother's blood? Are the bloodhounds of persecution and proscription to be let loose upon foreigners and Catholics because of their party affiliations in the late contest ? "

The author of this memoir repeats—it is not his purpose to discuss the tenets and doctrines of the " American " movement, which swept over the country like an avalanche in 1853–'54. The object of the author is to show that Mr. Johnson was honest and conscientious in his course. He met the issue with that boldness and manliness for which he is remarkable ; and Tennessee was the first Whig State where the tide in favor of " Americanism " was arrested and rolled backward. No work, claiming to be a biography of Mr. Johnson, could consistently ignore his course on this question. If an effort is to be made by faction to destroy his usefulness, and to thwart him in his great effort to restore peace and concord to a distracted country; if he finds himself compelled to appeal to the conservatism, the nationality, and patriotism of *the people*, against the wiles and machinations of politicians; it is right and proper that the foreign and Roman Catholic element of our population should know who stood forward as their friend and defender, when to do so involved the hazard of political destruction.

It is due to the cause of truth and justice to say, however, that there was one element in the " American party " which might, and probably would have, to some extent moderated Mr. Johnson's opposition to it, if he had been more thoroughly informed as to its principles and objects. But it was a secret organization, and the element referred to was not incorporated into it until some considerable time after its inauguration and after it had gained some of its most important triumphs in local elections. We refer to the third or " Union degree," as it was called. According to the ritual of the Order, there were originally but two degrees in it—one designed for the purification of the ballot-box, the other to check corruption in the dispensing of Government patronage and the appointments to office. When this " American party " met in " General Grand Council " at Cincinnati, in 1854, another degree was added to the organization, called the " Union degree." Its author and originator was Hon. Kenneth Rayner, of North Carolina. He introduced it, sustained it zealously by argument, and successfully carried it through. He insisted that the growing sentiment of disunion threatened more of danger to the country than all the other evils which it was the object of the Order to guard against, and that it was his object to erect a barrier to the further progress of this dangerous heresy both North and South.

As a compliment to Mr. Rayner, he was selected by the Council to confer this degree on the members composing it. And then and there he did confer it. So that, as stated by Mr. Rayner in his lately published letter to Dr. Elder, he is, no doubt, the first man in this country who ever administered an oath to any one binding the recipient to maintain and defend the Union against all assaults from any and every quarter under the same pledge given by our fathers in support of the Declaration of Independence—that of "life, fortune, and sacred honor."

On motion of the author of this degree, it was declared and ordained that the organization should be known and recognized by its members as the "Order of the American Union." With the outside world they went by the name of "Know-Nothings." This oath, to maintain and defend the Union, was taken by more than a million of men.

The next year, 1855, the General Grand Council met in Philadelphia. But the serpent of slavery agitation had crept within its folds and demoralized it. Violent and extreme men were there from the North, resolved to convert the Order into an antislavery party. Violent and extreme men from the South were there, resolved to convert it into a slavery-propagandist party. The sessions of the Council were daily marked with scenes of turbulence, strife, and disorder. Mr. Rayner, and those who concurred with him, resisted, with all the might and power they possessed, the interpolation on the Order of any thing touching slavery, either *pro* or *con*. He begged and entreated his Southern brethren to avoid all allusion to the question of slavery. He warned them that the incorporation of a proslavery plank in their platform would result in the destruction of the American Order—that the continued agitation of the subject would ultimately destroy slavery, and in all probability the Union also, which they had sworn to sustain.

But all in vain. The proslavery element succeeded in passing a provision in regard to the protection of slavery in the territories. A large portion of the Northern members seceded from the Council, and from that time the days of the " American party " were numbered. They made a dying struggle in the effort to elect Mr. Fillmore to the Presidency, in 1856, with the aid of the remnant of the old Whig party, but it ended in failure. The Order abolished all secrecy in its operations, released all its members from their obligations according to the conditions of their initiation—that every one entering the Order should be honorably discharged therefrom whenever he might conscientiously ask for it—and thus the American party ceased to exist. It may be that Mr. Johnson was not thoroughly informed of the strong Union element in the American Order, or, if he was, he probably thought that the other provisions of it were fraught with mischief and evil far outweighing the benefits promised by the Union feature referred to. One thing is certain: he was sincere, honest, and patriotic in his opposition to the " American " organization. No one who ever heard him discuss the question could doubt for a moment his earnest and abiding conviction that it was, in the main, likely to entail evils on the country, and that it was his duty to resist its further progress.

In speaking of Mr. Johnson's relations and opposition to the American party as a part of his past political history, the author felt it due to the many noble and patriotic men throughout the country who were members of that party, to say what is here said.

CHAPTER IX.

In 1860, the elements of combustion which had been so long smouldering, began to kindle into a blaze. In this year culminated those schemes of mischief which had been brewing for thirty years. The conspiracy to destroy the Government and sever the Union, which had been carefully but secretly nursed and fostered ever since 1831, now showed its brazen front, and in defiant tones proclaimed its wicked and nefarious designs. The Democratic party, which had hitherto withstood the disruptive force of slavery agitation, now yielded to the pressure, and was split asunder. Their convention to nominate a candidate for the Presidency, which met in Charleston, S. C., after a week's bickering and discord, being unable to agree, adjourned to meet in Baltimore at a future day. During the interval, the conspirators plied their work with zeal, and on the reassembling at Baltimore, all they did was to consummate the breach, and render it irreparable. The Democratic party was split into two factions, one nominating Douglas, the other nominating Breckinridge. The

Republican party, which had been suddenly improvised only four years before, by an outburst of public opinion throughout the North, in consequence of the repeal of the Missouri Compromise, the Kansas outrage, and the Dred Scott decision, nominated Mr. Lincoln. Mr. Lincoln was elected by a plurality vote. The plans of the conspirators had thus far worked according to their wishes. They had labored for a pretext for dissolving the Union, and they now seized on that pretext, and urged it in justification of their course. South Carolina passed the ordinance of secession in December, without her members of Congress going on to Washington to take their seats. The States further south followed in quick succession. From time to time the Senators from the Southern States took formal leave of the Senate, on going home to aid the work of disunion, of war, and of blood. Andrew Johnson saw what was coming. He saw that Union which he loved so well, and to which he had declared his purpose to adhere to the end, was in danger of destruction, and with it the hopes of freedom throughout the world. He saw a people, bound together by so many endearing ties and associations, about to engage in deadly conflict. No one was misled or deceived as to his course. He had from the outset declared his determination never to enter on the wild crusade of secession and disunion. He concluded to make an appeal to his Southern brethren, and to expose the fallacy and absurdity of secession. He spoke for two days, on the 18th and 19th of December, 1860. In his speech delivered on that occasion, he went into an historical review of the constitutional relations between the States and the General Government, and exhibited a research and information in regard to our political history not surpassed by any man of his day. It is one of those speeches of ability, eloquence, and philosophical argument that will, for years to come, constitute a text-book for the political student. It is a pity to mutilate the speech, by giving extracts from it only, but the limits of this memoir will not admit of giving it entire. The object in giving the copious quotations here inserted is, to enable the reader to appreciate the deep sincerity, earnestness, and conviction of Mr. Johnson in the entertainment of his views, and his anxiety to save the Union and avoid bloodshed, if possible. He said:

"I know that the inquiry may be made, How is a State to have redress? There is but one way, and that is expressed by the people of Tennessee. You have entered into this compact; it was mutual; it was reciprocal; and you of your own volition have no right to withdraw and break the contract without the consent of the other parties. What remedy, then, has the State? It has a remedy that remains and abides with every people upon the face of the earth: when grievances are without a remedy, or without redress, when oppression becomes intolerable, they have the great inherent right of revolution, and that is all there is of it.

"Sir, if this doctrine of secession is to be carried out upon the mere whim of a State, this Government is at an end. I am as much opposed to a strong, or what may be called by some a consolidated Government, as it is possible for a man to be; but while I am greatly opposed to that, I want a Government strong enough to preserve its own existence; that will not fall to pieces by its own weight, or whenever a little dissatisfaction takes place in one of its members. If the States have the right to secede at will and pleasure, for real or imaginary evils or oppressions, I repeat again, this Government is at an end; it is not stronger than a rope of sand; its own weight will tumble it to pieces, and it cannot exist. Notwithstanding this doctrine may suit some who are engaged in this perilous and impending crisis that is now upon us, duty to my country, duty to my State, and duty to my kind, require me to avow a doctrine that I believe will result in the preservation of the Government, and to repudiate one that I believe will result in its overthrow, and the consequent disasters to the people of the United States.

"If a State can secede at will and pleasure, and this doctrine is maintained, why, I ask, on the other hand, and as Mr. Madison argues in one of his letters, cannot a majority of the States combine and reject a State out of the Confederacy? Have a majority of these States, under the compact that they have made with each other, the right to combine and reject any one of the States from the Confederacy? They have no such right; the compact is reciprocal. It was ratified without reservation or condition, and it was ratified '*in toto* and forever;' such is the language of James Madison; and there is but one way to get out of it without the consent of the parties, and that is by revolution.

"I know that some touch the subject with trembling and fear. They say, Here is a State that, perhaps by this time, has seceded, or if not, she is on the road to secession, and we must touch this subject very delicately; and that if the State secedes, conceding the power of the Constitution to her to secede, you must talk very delicately upon the subject of coercion. I do not believe the Federal Government has the power to coerce a State; for by the eleventh amendment of the Constitution of the United States it is expressly provided that you cannot even put one of the States of this Confederacy before one of the courts of the country as a party. As a State, the Federal Government has no power to coerce it; but it is a member of the compact to which it agreed in common with the other States, and this Government has the right to pass laws and to enforce those laws upon individuals within the limits of each State. While the one proposition is clear, the other is equally so. This Government can, by the Constitution of the country and by the laws enacted in conformity with the Constitution, operate upon individuals, and has the right and the power, not to coerce a State, but to enforce and execute the law upon individuals within the limits of a State.

"I know that the term, 'to coerce a State,' is used in an *ad captandum* manner. It is a sovereignty that is to be crushed! How is a State in the Union? What is her connection with it?

All the connection she has with the other States is that which is agreed upon in the compact between the States. I do not know whether you may consider it in the Union or out of the Union, or whether you simply consider it a connection or a disconnection with the other States; but to the extent that a State nullifies or sets aside any law or any provision of the Constitution, to that extent it has dissolved its connection, and no more.

" I do not think it necessary, in order to preserve this Union, or to keep a State within its sphere, that the Congress of the United States should have the power to coerce a State. All that is necessary is for the Government to have the power to execute and to carry out all the powers conferred upon it by the Constitution, whether they apply to the State or otherwise. This, I think, the Government clearly has the power to do; and so long as the Government executes all the laws in good faith, denying the right of a State constitutionally to secede, so long the State is in the Union and subject to all the provisions of the Constitution and the laws passed in conformity with it. For example: the power is conferred on the Federal Government to carry the mails through the several States; to establish post-offices and post-roads; the power is conferred on the Federal Government to establish courts in the respective States; the power is conferred on the General Government to lay and collect taxes in the several States, and so on. The various powers are enumerated, and each and every one of these powers the Federal Government has the constitutional authority to execute within the limits of the States. It is not an invasion of a State for the Federal Government to execute its laws, to take care of its public property, and to enforce the collection of its revenue; but if, in the execution of the laws, if, in the enforcement of the Constitution, it meets with resistance, it is the duty of the Government, and it has the authority, to put down resistance, and effectually to execute the laws as contemplated by the Constitution of the country. If it were not even expressed in the Constitution, the power to preserve itself and maintain its authority would be possessed by the Federal Government from the very existence of the Government itself, upon the great principle that it must have the power to preserve its own existence. But we find that, in plain and express terms, this authority is delegated. The very powers that Mr. Jefferson pointed out as being wanting in the old Government, under the Articles of Confederation, are granted by the Constitution of the United States to the present Government by express delegation. Congress has the power to lay and collect taxes; Congress has the power to pass laws to restore fugitives from labor escaping from one State into another; Congress has the power to establish post-offices and post-roads; Congress has the power to establish courts in the different States; and having these powers, it has the authority to do every thing necessary to sustain the collection of the revenue, the enforcement of the judicial system, and the carrying of the mails. Because Congress, having the power, undertakes to execute its laws, it will not do to say that the Government is placed in the position of an aggressor. Not so. It is only acting within the scope of the Constitution, and in compliance with its delegated powers. But a State that resists the exercise of those powers becomes the aggressor, and places itself in a rebellious or nullifying attitude. It is the duty of this Government to execute its laws in good faith. When the Federal Government shall fail to execute all the laws that are made in strict conformity with the Constitution, if our sister States shall pass laws violative of that Constitution, and obstructing the laws of Congress passed in conformity with it, then, and not till then, will this Government have failed to accomplish the great objects of its creation. Then it will be at an end, and all the parties to the compact will be released.

" Having travelled thus far, the question arises, In what sense are we to construe the Constitution of the United States? I assume, what is assumed in one of Mr. Madison's letters, that the Constitution was formed for perpetuity; that it never was intended to be broken up. It was commenced, it is true, as an experiment; but the founders of the Constitution intended that this experiment should go on and on and on; and by way of making it perpetual, they provided for its amendment. They provided that this instrument could be amended and improved, from time to time, as the changing circumstances, as the changing pursuits, as the changing notions of men might require; but they made no provision whatever for its destruction. The old Articles of Confederation were formed for the purpose of making 'a perpetual union.' In 1787, when the Convention concluded their deliberations and adopted the Constitution, what do they say in the very preamble of that Constitution? Having in their mind the idea that was shadowed forth in the old Articles of Confederation, that the Union was to be perpetual, they say, at the commencement, that it is to make 'a more perfect union' than the Union under the old Articles of Confederation, which they called 'perpetual.'

"We find General Washington executing the law, in 1795, against a portion of the citizens of Pennsylvania who rebelled; and, I repeat the question, where is the difference between executing the law upon a part and upon the whole? Suppose the whole of Pennsylvania had rebelled and resisted the excise law; had refused to pay taxes on distilleries: was it not as competent and as constitutional for General Washington to have executed the law against the whole as against a part? Is there any difference? Governmental affairs must be practical as well as our own domestic affairs. You may make nice metaphysical distinctions between the practical operations of Government and its theory; you may refine upon what is a State, and point out a difference between a State and a portion of a State; but what is it when you reduce it to practical operation and square it by common sense?

"In 1832 resistance was interposed to laws of the United States in another State. An ordinance was passed by South Carolina, assuming to act as a sovereign State, to nullify a law of the United States. In 1833 the distinguished man who filled the Executive chair, who now lies in his silent grave, loved and respected for his virtue, his honor, his integrity, his patriotism, his undoubted courage, and his devotion to his kind, with an eye single to the promotion of his country's best interests, issued the proclamation, extracts from which I have already presented. He was sworn to support the Constitution, and to see that the laws were faithfully executed; and he fulfilled the obligation. He took all the steps necessary to secure the execution of the law, and he would have executed it by the power of the Government if the point of time had arrived when it was necessary to resort to power.

" Have we no authority or power to execute the laws in the State of South Carolina as well as in Vermont and Pennsylvania? I think we have. As I before said, although a State may, by an ordinance, or by a resolve, or by an act of any other kind, declare that they absolve their citizens from all allegiance to this Government, it does not release them from the compact. The compact is reciprocal; and they, in coming into it, undertook to perform certain duties and abide by the laws made in conformity with the compact. Now, sir, what is the Government to do in South Carolina? If South Carolina undertake to drive the Federal courts out of that State, yet the Federal Government has the right to hold those courts there. She may attempt to exclude the mails, yet the Federal Government has the right to establish post-offices and post-roads, and to carry the mails there. She may resist the collection of revenue at Charleston, or any other point that the Government has provided for its collection; but the Government has the right to collect it and to enforce the law. She may undertake to take possession of the property belonging to the Government which was originally ceded by the State, but the Federal Government has the right to provide the means for retaining possession of that property. If she makes an advance either to dispossess the Government of that which it has purchased, or to resist the execution of the revenue laws, or of our judicial system, or the carrying of the mails, or the exercise of any other power conferred on the Federal Government, she puts herself in the wrong, and it will be the duty of the Government to see that the laws are faithfully executed.

" But it is declared and assumed that, if a State secedes, she is no longer a member of the Union, and that, therefore, the laws and the Constitution of the United States are no longer operative within her limits, and she is not guilty if she violates them. This is a matter of opinion. I have tried to show, from the origin of the Government down to the present time, what this doctrine of secession is, and there is but one concurring and unerring conclusion reached by all the great and distinguished men of the country. Madison, who is called the Father of the Constitution, denies the doctrine. Washington, who was the Father of his Country, denies the doctrine. Jefferson, Jackson, Clay, and Webster, all deny the doctrine; and yet all at once it is discovered and ascertained that a State, of its own volition, can go out of this Confederacy without regard to consequences, without regard to the injury and woe that may be inflicted on the remaining members from the act!

"Suppose this doctrine to be true, Mr. President, that a State can withdraw from this Confederacy; and suppose South Carolina has seceded, and is now out of the Confederacy: in what an attitude does she place herself? There might be circumstances under which the States ratifying the compact might tolerate the secession of a State, she taking the consequences of the act. But there might be other circumstances under which the States could not allow one to secede. Why do I say so? Some suppose—and it is a well-founded supposition—that by the secession of a State all the remaining States might be involved in disastrous consequences; they might be involved in war; and by the secession of one State, the existence of the remaining States might be involved. Then, without regard to the Constitution, dare the other States permit one to secede when it endangers and involves all the remaining States? The question arises in this connection, whether the States are in a condition to tolerate or will tolerate the secession of South Carolina. That is a matter to be determined by the circumstances; that is a matter to be determined by the emergency; that is a matter to be determined when it comes up. It is a question which must be left open to be determined by the surrounding circumstances when the occasion arises.

"But conceding, for argument's sake, the doctrine of secession, and admitting that the State of South Carolina is now upon your coast a foreign power, absolved from all connection with the Federal Government, out of the Union: what then? There was a doctrine inculcated in 1823, by Mr. Monroe, that this Government, keeping in view the safety of the people and the existence of our institutions, would permit no European power to plant any more colonies on this continent.　Now, suppose that South Carolina is outside of the Confederacy, and this Government is in possession of the fact that she is forming an alliance with a foreign power—with France, with England, with Russia, with Austria, or with all of the principal powers of Europe; that there is to be a great naval station established there; an immense rendezvous for their army, with a view to ulterior objects, with a view of making advances upon the rest of these States: let me ask the Senate, let me ask the country, if they dare permit it?　Under and in compliance with the great law of self-preservation, we dare not let her do it; and if she were a sovereign power to-day, outside of the Confederacy, and was forming an alliance that we deemed inimical to our institutions and the existence of our Government, we should have a right to conquer and hold her as a province—a term which is so much used with scorn.

"We are told that certain States will go out and tear this accursed Constitution into fragments, and drag the pillars of this mighty edifice down upon us, and involve us all in one common ruin.　Will the border States submit to such a threat?　No.　If they do not come into the movement, the pillars of this stupendous fabric of human freedom and greatness and goodness are to be pulled down, and all will be involved in one common ruin. Such is the threatening language used.　'You shall come into our Confederacy, or we will coerce you to the emancipation of your slaves.'　That is the language which is held toward us.

"There are many ideas afloat about this threatened dissolution, and it is time to speak out.　The question arises in reference to the protection and preservation of the institution of slavery, whether dissolution is a remedy or will give to it protection.　I avow here, to-day, that if I were an abolitionist, and wanted to accomplish the overthrow and abolition of the institution of slavery in the Southern States, the first step that I would take would be to break the bonds of this Union, and dissolve this

Government. I believe the continuance of slavery depends upon the preservation of this Union, and a compliance with all the guaranties of the Constitution. I believe an interference with it will break up the Union; and I believe a dissolution of the Union will, in the end, though it may be some time to come, overthrow the institution of slavery. Hence we find so many in the North who desire the dissolution of these States as the most certain and direct and effectual means of overthrowing the institution of slavery.

"What protection would it be to us to dissolve this Union? What protection would it be to us to convert this nation into two hostile powers, the one warring with the other? Whose property is at stake? Whose interest is endangered? Is it not the property of the border States? Suppose Canada were moved down upon our border, and the two separated sections, then different nations, were hostile: what would the institution of slavery be worth on the border? Every man who has common sense will see that the institution would take up its march and retreat, as certainly and as unerringly as general laws can operate. Yes, it would commence to retreat the very moment this Government was converted into hostile powers, and you made the line between the slaveholding and non-slaveholding States the line of division.

"Then, what remedy do we get for the institution of slavery? Must we keep up a standing army? Must we keep up forts bristling with arms along the whole border? This is a question to be considered, one that involves the future; and no step should be taken without mature reflection. Before this Union is dissolved and broken up, we in Tennessee, as one of the slave States, want to be consulted; we want to know what protection we are to have; whether we are simply to be made outposts and guards to protect the property of others, at the same time that we sacrifice and lose our own. We want to understand this question.

"Again: if there is one division of the States, will there not be more than one? I heard a Senator say the other day that he would rather see this Government separated into thirty-three fractional parts than to see it consolidated; but when you once begin to divide, when the first division is made, who can tell when the next will be made? When these States are all turned loose, and a different condition of things is presented, with complex and abstruse interests to be considered and weighed and understood, what combinations may take place no one can tell. I am opposed to the consolidation of Government, and I am as much for the reserved rights of States as any one; but, rather than see this Union divided into thirty-three petty Governments, with a little prince in one, a potentate in another, a little aristocracy in a third, a little democracy in a fourth, and a republic somewhere else; a citizen not being able to pass from one State to another without a passport or a commission from his Government; with quarrelling and warring amongst the little petty powers, which would result in anarchy; I would rather see this Government to-day—I proclaim it here in my place—converted into a consolidated Government. It would be better for the American people; it would be better for our kind; it would be better for humanity; better for Christianity; better for all that tends to elevate and ennoble man, than breaking up this splendid, this magnificent, this stupendous fabric of human government, the most perfect that the world ever saw, and which has succeeded thus far without a parallel in the history of the world.

"Here, in the centre of the Republic, is the seat of Government, which was founded by Washington, and bears his immortal name. Who dare appropriate it exclusively? It is within the borders of the States I have enumerated, in whose limits are found the graves of Washington, of Jackson, of Polk, of Clay. From them is it supposed that we will be torn away? No, sir; we will cherish these endearing associations with the hope, if this Republic shall be broken, that we may speak words of peace and reconciliation to a distracted, a divided, I may add, a maddened people. Angry waves may be lashed into fury on the one hand; on the other blustering winds may rage; but we stand immovable upon our basis, as on our own native mountains—presenting their craggy brows, their unexplored caverns, their summits 'rock-ribbed and as ancient as the sun '—we stand speaking peace, association, and concert, to a distracted Republic.

" Notwithstanding we want to occupy the position of a breakwater between the Northern and the Southern extremes, and bring all together if we can, I tell our Northern friends that the constitutional guaranties must be carried out; for the time may come when, after we have exhausted all honorable and fair means, if this Government still fails to execute the laws, and protect us in our rights, it will be at an end. Gentlemen of the North need. not deceive themselves in that particular; but we intend to act in the Union and under the Constitution, and not out of it. We do not intend that you shall drive us out of this house that was reared by the hands of our fathers. It is our house. It is the constitutional house. We have a right here; and because you come forward and violate the ordinances of this house, I do not intend to go out; and if you persist in the violation of the ordinances of the house, we intend to eject you from the building and retain the possession ourselves. We want, if we can, to stay the heated, and I am compelled to say, according to my judgment, the rash and precipitate action of some of our Southern friends, that indicates red-hot madness. I want to say to those in the North, comply with the Constitution and preserve its guaranties, and in so doing save this glorious Union and all that pertains to it. I intend to stand by the Constitution as it is, insisting upon a compliance with all its guaranties. I intend to stand by it as the sheet-anchor of the Government; and I trust and hope, though it seems to be now in the very vortex of ruin, though it seems to be running between Charybdis and Scylla, the rock on the one hand and the whirlpool on the other, that it will be preserved, and will remain a beacon to guide, and an example to be imitated by all the nations of the earth. Yes, I intend to hold on to it as the chief ark of our safety, as the palladium of our civil and our religious liberty. I intend to cling to it as the shipwrecked mariner clings to the last plank, when the night and the tempest close around him. It is the last hope of human freedom. Although denounced as an experiment by some who want to see a constitutional monarchy, it has been a successful experiment. I trust and I hope it will be continued; that this great work may go on.

"Why should we go out of the Union? Have we any thing to fear? What are we alarmed about? We say that you of the North have violated the Constitution; that you have trampled under foot its guaranties; but we intend to go to you in a proper way, and ask you to redress the wrong, and to comply with the Constitution. We believe the time will come when you will do it, and we do not intend to break up the Government until the fact is ascertained that you will not do it. Where is the grievance, where is the complaint that presses on our sister, South Carolina, now? Is it that she wants to carry slavery into the Territories—that she wants protection to slavery there? How long has it been since, upon this very floor, her own Senators voted that it was not necessary to make a statute now for the protection of slavery in the Territories? No longer ago than the last session. Is that a good reason? They declared, in the resolutions adopted by the Senate, that when it was necessary they had the power to do it; but that it was not necessary then. Are you going out for a grievance that has not occurred, and which your own Senators then said had not occurred? Is it because you want to carry slaves to the Territories? You were told that you had all the protection needed; that the courts had decided in your behalf, under the Constitution; and that, under the decisions of the courts, the law must be executed.

"We do not think that we have just cause for going out of the Union now. We have just cause of complaint; but we are for remaining in the Union and fighting the battle like men. We do not intend to be cowardly, and turn our backs on our own camps. We intend to stay and fight the battle here upon this consecrated ground. Why should we retreat? Because Mr. Lincoln has been elected President of the United States? Is this any cause why we should retreat? Does not every man, Senator or otherwise, know that if Mr. Breckinridge had been elected, we should not be to-day for dissolving the

Union? Then what is the issue? It is because we have not got our man. If we had got our man, we should not have been for breaking up the Union; but as Mr. Lincoln is elected, we are for breaking up the Union! I say no. Let us show ourselves men, and men of courage.

"How has Mr. Lincoln been elected, and how have Mr. Breckinridge and Mr. Douglas been defeated? By the votes of the American people, cast according to the Constitution and the forms of law, though it has been upon a sectional issue. It is not the first time in our history that two candidates have been elected from the same section of country. General Jackson and Mr. Calhoun were elected on the same ticket; but nobody considered that cause of dissolution. They were from the South. While I oppose the sectional spirit that has produced the election of Lincoln and Hamlin, yet it has been done according to the Constitution and according to the forms of law. I believe we have the power in our own hands, and I am not willing to shrink from the responsibility of exercising that power.

"How has Lincoln been elected, and upon what basis does he stand? A minority President by nearly a million votes; but had the election taken place upon the plan proposed in my amendment of the Constitution, by districts, he would have been this day defeated. But it has been done according to the Constitution and according to law. I am for abiding by the Constitution; and in abiding by it I want to maintain and retain my place here and put down Mr. Lincoln and drive back his advances upon Southern institutions, if he designs to make any. Have we not got the brakes in our hands? Have we not got the power? We have. Let South Carolina send her Senators back; let all the Senators come; and on the 4th of March next we shall have a majority of six in this body against him. The successful sectional candidate, who is in a minority of a million, or nearly so, on the popular vote, cannot make his Cabinet on the 4th of March next unless the Senate will permit him.

"Am I to be so great a coward as to retreat from duty? I will stand here and meet the encroachments upon the institutions of

6

my country at the threshold; and as a man, as one that loves my country and my constituents, I will stand here and resist all encroachments and advances. Here is the place to stand. Shall I desert the citadel, and let the enemy come in and take possession? No. Can Mr. Lincoln send a foreign minister, or even a consul, abroad, unless he receives the sanction of the Senate? Can he appoint a postmaster whose salary is over a thousand dollars a year, without the consent of the Senate? Shall we desert our posts, shrink from our responsibilities, and permit Mr. Lincoln to come with his cohorts, as we consider them, from the North, to carry off every thing? Are we so cowardly that now that we are defeated, not conquered, we shall do this? Yes, we are defeated according to the forms of law and the Constitution; but the real victory is ours—the moral force is with us. Are we going to desert that noble and that patriotic band who have stood by us at the North? who have stood by us upon principle? who have stood by us upon the Constitution? They stood by us and fought the battle upon principle; and now that we have been defeated, not conquered, are we to turn our backs upon them and leave them to their fate? I, for one, will not. I intend to stand by them. How many votes did we get in the North? We got more votes in the North against Lincoln than the entire Southern States cast. Are they not able and faithful allies? They are; and now, on account of this temporary defeat, are we to turn our backs upon them and leave them to their fate, as they have fallen for us in former controversies?

"We find, when all the North is summed up, that Mr. Lincoln's majority there is only about two hundred thousand on the popular vote; and when that is added to the other vote cast throughout the Union, he stands to-day in a minority of nearly a million votes. What, then, is necessary to be done? To stand to our posts like men, and act upon principle; stand for the country; and in four years from this day, Lincoln and his administration will be turned out, the worst-defeated and broken-down party that ever came into power. It is an inevitable result from the combination of elements that now exist. What cause, then, is there to break up the Union?   What reason is there for deserting our posts and destroying this greatest and best Government that was ever spoken into existence?

"I voted against him; I spoke against him; I spent my money to defeat him: but still I love my country; I love the Constitution; I intend to insist upon its guaranties.   There, and there alone, I intend to plant myself, with the confident hope and belief that if the Union remains together, in less than four years the now triumphant party will be overthrown.

"I have an abiding faith, I have an unshaken confidence in man's capability to govern himself.   I will not give up this Government that is now called an experiment, which some are prepared to abandon, for a constitutional monarchy.   No; I intend to stand by it, and I entreat every man throughout the nation who is a patriot, and who has seen, and is compelled to admit, the success of this great experiment, to come forward, not in heat, not in fanaticism, not in haste, not in precipitancy, but in deliberation, in full view of all that is before us, in the spirit of brotherly love and fraternal affection, and rally around the altar of our common country, and lay the Constitution upon it as our last libation, and swear by our God, and all that is sacred and holy, that the Constitution shall be saved, and the Union preserved.   Yes, in the language of the departed Jackson, let us exclaim that the Union, 'the Federal Union, it must be preserved.'

"Mr. President, I have said much more than I anticipated when I commenced; and I have said more now (though external appearances seem different) than I have strength or health to say; but if there is any effort of mine that would preserve this Government till there is time to think, till there is time to consider, even if it cannot be preserved any longer; if that end could be secured by making a sacrifice of my existence and offering up my blood, I would be willing to consent to it.   Let us pause in this mad career; let us hesitate; let us consider well what we are doing before we make a movement.   I believe that, to a certain extent, dissolution is going to take place.   I say to the North, You ought to come up in the spirit which should characterize and control the

North on this question; and you ought to give those indications in good faith that will approach what the South demands. It will be no sacrifice on your part. It is no suppliancy on ours, but simply a demand of right. What concession is there in doing right? Then, come forward. We have it in our power—yes, this Congress here to-day has it in its power to save this Union, even after South Carolina has gone out. Will they not do it? You can do it. Who is willing to take the dreadful alternative without making an honorable effort to save this Government? This Congress has it in its power to-day to arrest this thing, at least for a season, until there is time to consider about it, until we can act discreetly and prudently, and I believe arrest it altogether.

"Shall we give all this up to the Vandals and the Goths? Shall we shrink from our duty, and desert the Government as a sinking ship, or shall we stand by it? I, for one, will stand here until the high behest of my constituents demands me to desert my post; and instead of laying hold of the columns of this fabric and pulling it down, though I may not be much of a prop, I will stand with my shoulder supporting the edifice as long as human effort can do it. Then, cannot we agree? We can, if we will, and come together and save the country. Then, let us stand by the Constitution; and in preserving the Constitution we shall save the Union; and in saving the Union, we save this, the greatest Government on earth."

CHAPTER X.

On the 5th and 6th of February, 1861, Mr. Johnson
again addressed the Senate for two days, still further ex-
posing the heresy of secession, and proving from the record
that the present disunion movement was the consummation of a plan that had been conspiring and maturing for a
great many years. This great speech, equal in power,
analysis, and argument to the previous one, was the continuation of the same laborious effort to save the Union
and avert war. No one, on reading the speech, can fail to
discover the deep-seated sorrow and agony of his soul at
contemplating the death of the Union and the horrors of
civil war. He foretold the evils and disasters that would
inevitably follow. He distinctly announced to his Southern brethren in the Senate that he would not follow them
out of the Union—that he was resolved to adhere to the
Union, to the Government of our fathers, and to the flag
of his country, and to abide their destiny. He said:

"I have been uniformly opposed to the doctrine of secession,
or of nullification, which is rather a hermaphrodite, but approxi-

mates to the doctrine of secession. I repeat, that I then viewed it as a heresy and as an element which, if maintained, would result in the destruction of this Government. I maintain the same position to-day. I then opposed the doctrine of secession as a political heresy, which, if sanctioned and sustained as a fundamental principle of this Government, will result in its overthrow and destruction ; for, as we have seen already, a few of the States are crumbling and falling off.

"I oppose this heresy for another reason ; not only as being destructive of the existing Government, but as being destructive of all future confederacies that may be established in consequence of a disruption of the present one ; and I availed myself of the former occasion on which I spoke, to enter my protest against it, and to do something to extinguish a political heresy that ought never to be incorporated upon this or any other Government which may be subsequently established. I look upon it as the prolific mother of political sin; as a fundamental error; as a heresy that is intolerable in contrast with the existence of the Government itself. I look upon it as being productive of anarchy; and anarchy is the next step to despotism. The developments that we have recently seen in carrying this doctrine into practice, I think, admonish us that this will be the result.

"In the acquisition of Louisiana there was another very important acquisition. We acquired the exclusive and entire control of the navigation of the Mississippi River. We find that Louisiana, in her ordinance of secession, makes the negative declaration that she has the control of the navigation of that great stream, by stating that the navigation of the river shall be free to those States that remain on friendly terms with her, with the proviso that moderate contributions are to be levied to defray such expenses as they may deem expedient from time to time. That is the substance of it. Sir, look at the facts. All the States, through their Federal Government, treated for Louisiana. The treaty was made. All the States, by the contribution of their money, paid for Louisiana and the navigation of the Mississippi River. Where, and from what source, does Louisiana now derive the power or the authority to secede from this Union and set up exclusive control of the navigation of that great stream which is owned by all the States, which was paid for by the money of all the States, and upon whose borders the blood of many citizens of the States has been shed?

"This is one of the aggrieved, the oppressed States! Mr. President, is it not apparent that these grievances and oppressions are mere pretences? A large portion of the South (and that portion of it I am willing stand by to the very last extremity) believe that aggressions have been made upon them by the other States, in reference to the institution of slavery. A large portion of the South believe that something ought to be done in the shape of what has been offered by the distinguished Senator from Kentucky, or something very similar. They think and feel that that ought to be done. But, sir, there is another portion who do not care for those propositions to bring about reconciliation, but who, on the contrary, have been afraid and alarmed that something would be done to reconcile and satisfy the public mind, before this diabolical work of secession could be consummated. Yes, sir, they have been afraid, and the occasion has been used to justify and carry out a doctrine into practice, which is not only the destruction of this Government, but which will be the destruction of all other governments that may be originated, embracing the same principle. Why not, then, meet it like men? We know there is a portion of the South who are for secession, who are for breaking up this Government, without regard to slavery or any thing else, as I shall show before I have done.

"The Senator from Louisiana yesterday seemed to be very serious in regard to the practical operation of the doctrine of secession. I felt sorry myself, somewhat. I am always reluctant to part with a gentleman with whom I have been associated, and nothing had transpired to disturb between us those courteous relations which should always exist between persons associated on this floor. I thought the scene was pretty well got up, and was acted out admirably. The plot was executed to the very letter. You would have thought that his people in Louisiana were borne down and seriously oppressed by remaining in this Union of States.

Now, I have an extract before me, from a speech delivered by that gentleman since the election of Abraham Lincoln, while the distinguished Senator was on the western slope of the Rocky Mountains, at the city of San Francisco. He was called upon to make an address; and I will read an extract from it, which I find in the New York 'Times,' the editors of which paper said they had the speech before them; and I have consulted a gentleman here who was in California at the time, and he tells me that the report is correct. In that speech—after the Senator had spoken some time with his accustomed eloquence—he uttered this language:

'Those who prate of, and strive to dissolve this glorious Confederacy of States, are like those silly savages who let fly their arrows at the sun in the vain hope of piercing it. And still the sun rolls on, unheeding, in its eternal pathway, shedding light and animation upon all the world.'

"Even after Lincoln was elected, the Senator from Louisiana is reported to have said, in the State of California, and in the city of San Francisco, that this great Union could not be destroyed. Those great and intolerable oppressions, of which we have since heard from him, did not seem to be flitting across his vision and playing upon his mind with that vividness and clearness which were displayed here yesterday. He said, in California, that this great Union would go on in its course, notwithstanding the puny efforts of the silly savages that were letting fly their arrows with the prospect of piercing it. What has changed the Senator's mind on coming from that side of the continent to this? What light has broken in upon him? Has he been struck on his way, like Paul, when he was journeying from Tarsus to Damascus?

"Since that speech was made, since the Senator has traversed from California to this point, the grievances, the oppressions of Louisiana, have become so great that she is justified in going out of the Union, taking into her possession the custom-house, the mint, the navigation of the Mississippi River, the forts, and arsenals. Where are we? 'Oh, consistency, thou art a jewel, much to be admired, but rarely to be found.'

"Mr. President, I never do things by halves. I am against this doctrine entirely. I commenced making war upon it—a war for the Constitution and the Union—and I intend to sink or swim upon it.   [Applause in the galleries.]

"The Senator from Virginia says a State has the right to secede from the Union, and that it is a right resulting from the nature of the compact; but Mr. Jefferson said that even under the old Articles of Confederation, no State had a right to refuse obedience to the Confederacy, and that there was a right to enforce its compliance:

'Congress would probably exercise long patience before they would recur to force; but if the case ultimately required it, they would use that recurrence. Should this case ever arise, they will probably coerce by a naval force, as being more easy, less dangerous to liberty, and less likely to produce bloodshed.'—*Jefferson's Works*, vol. ix., p. 291.

"When was this? I have stated that it was under the old Articles of Confederation, when there was no power to compel a State even to contribute her proportion of the revenues; but in that view of the case, Mr. Jefferson said that the injured party had a right to enforce compliance with the compact from the offending State, and that this was a right deducible from the laws of Nature.   The present Constitution was afterwards formed; and to avoid this difficulty in raising revenue, the power was conferred upon the Congress of the United States 'to lay and collect taxes, duties, imposts, and excises,' and the Constitution created a direct relation between the citizen and the Federal Government in that matter, and to that extent that relation is just as direct and complete between the Federal Government and the citizen as is the relation between the State and the citizen in other matters. Hence we find that, by an amendment to the Constitution of the United States, the citizen cannot even make a State a party to a suit, and bring her into the Federal courts.   They wanted to avoid the difficulty of coercing a State, and the Constitution conferred on the Federal Government the power to operate directly upon the citizen, instead of operating on the States.   It being the right of the Government to enforce obedience from the citizen in those matters of which it has jurisdiction, the question comes up as to the exercise of this right.   It may not always be expedient.

It must depend upon discretion, as was eloquently said by the Senator from Kentucky [Mr. Crittenden] on one occasion. It is a matter of discretion, even as Mr. Jefferson laid it down before this provision existed in the Constitution, before the Government had power to collect its revenue as it now has. I know that when, on a former occasion, I undertook to show, as I thought I did show, clearly and distinctly, the difference between the existence and the exercise of this power, words were put into my mouth that I did not utter, and positions answered which I had never assumed. It was said that I took the bold ground of coercing a State. I expressly disclaimed it. I stated, in my speech, that, by the Constitution, we could not put a State into court; but I said there were certain relations created by the Constitution between the Federal Government and the citizen, and that we could enforce those laws against the citizen.

"When the Fugitive Slave law was executed in the city of Boston, by the aid of military force, was that understood to be coercing a State, or was it simply understood to be an enforcement of the law upon those who, it was assumed, had violated it? In this same decision the Supreme Court declare that the Fugitive Slave law, in all its details, is constitutional, and therefore should be enforced. Who is prepared to say that the decision of the Court shall not be carried out? Who is prepared to say that the Fugitive Slave law shall not be enforced? Do you coerce a State when you simply enforce the law? If one man robs the mail and you seek to arrest him, and he resists, and you employ force, do you call that coercion? If a man counterfeits your coin, and is arrested and convicted, and punishment is resisted, cannot you execute the law? It is true that sometimes so many may become infected with disobedience, outrages and violations of law may be participated in by so many, that they get beyond the control of the ordinary operations of law; the disaffection may swell to such proportions as to be too great for the Government to control; and then it becomes a matter of discretion, not a matter of constitutional right.

"Now, sir, what is treason? The Constitution of the United

States defines it, and narrows it down to a very small compass. The Constitution declares that ' treason against the United States shall consist only in levying war against them, or in adhering to their enemies, giving them aid and comfort.' Who are levying war upon the United States? Who are adhering to the enemies of the United States, giving them aid and comfort? Does it require a man to take the lantern of Diogenes, and make a diligent search to find those who have been engaged in levying war against the United States? Will it require any very great research or observation to discover those who have been adhering to those who were making war against the United States, and giving them aid and comfort? If there are any such in the United States they ought to be punished according to law and the Constitution. [Applause in the galleries, which was suppressed by the presiding officer, Mr. Fitch, in the chair.] Mr. Ritchie, speaking for the Old Dominion, used language that was unmistakable, that treason should be punished, springing out of the hotbed of the Hartford Convention. It was all right to talk about treason then; it was all right to punish traitors in that direction. For myself, I care not whether treason be committed North or South; he that is guilty of treason is entitled to a traitor's fate.

"We see that there is a design with some to break up this Government without reference to the slavery question; and the slavery question is by them made a pretence for destroying this Union. They have at length passed their ordinance of secession; they assume to be out of the Union; they declare that they are no longer a member of the Confederacy. Now what are the other States called upon to do? Are the other States called upon to make South Carolina an example? Are those slave States who believe that freemen should govern and that freemen can take care of slave property, to be ' precipitated into a revolution ' by following the example of South Carolina? Will they do it? What protection, what security will Tennessee, will Kentucky, will Virginia, will Maryland, or any other State, receive from South Carolina by following her example? What protection can she give them? On the contrary, she indulges in a threat toward them—a threat that if they do not imitate her example and come into a new confederacy upon her terms, they are to be put under the ban, and their slave property to be subjected to restraint and restriction. What protection can South Carolina give Tennessee? Any? None upon the face of the earth.

"Some of the men who are engaged in the work of disruption and dissolution, want Tennessee and Kentucky and Virginia to furnish them with men and money in the event of their becoming engaged in a war for the conquest of Mexico. The Tennesseeans and Kentuckians and Virginians are very desirable when their men and their money are wanted; but what protection does South Carolina give Tennessee? If negro property is endangered in Tennessee, we have to defend it and pay for it—not South Carolina, that has been an apple of discord in this Confederacy from my earliest recollection down to the present time, complaining of every thing, satisfied with nothing. I do not intend to be invidious, but I have sometimes thought that it would be a comfort if Massachusetts and South Carolina could be chained together as the Siamese twins, separated from the continent, and taken out to some remote and secluded part of the ocean, and there fast anchored, to be washed by the waves, and to be cooled by the winds; and after they had been kept there a sufficient length of time, the people of the United States might entertain the proposition of taking them back. [Laughter.] They seem to have been the source of dissatisfaction pretty much ever since they were in the Confederacy; and some experiment of this sort, I think, would operate beneficially upon them; but as they are here, we must try to do the best we can with them.

"I march down upon South Carolina! Did I propose any such thing? No. War is not the natural element in my mind; and, as I stated in that speech, my thoughts were turned on peace, and not on war. I want no strife. I want no war. In the language of a denomination that is numerous in the country, I may say I hate war and love peace. I belong to the peace party. I thought, when I was making that speech, that I was holding out the olive-branch of peace. I wanted to give quiet and reconciliation to a distracted and excited country. That was the object I had in view. War, I repeat, is not the natural element of my mind. I would rather wear upon my garments the tinge of the shop and the dust of the field, as badges of the pursuits of peace, than the gaudy epaulette upon my shoulder, or a sword dangling by my side, with its glittering scabbard, the insignia of strife, of war, of blood, of carnage; sometimes of honorable and glorious war. But, sir, I would rather see the people of the United States at war with any other power upon the habitable globe, than to be at war with each other. If blood must be shed, let it not be shed by the people of these States, the one contending against the other.

"Mr. President, the Senator, in the sentence I have quoted, assumes that South Carolina, for instance, had the right to secede; and he assumes, also, that South Carolina can obtain that out of the Union which she has failed to obtain in it. Let us raise the inquiry here: What is it, since she entered into this Confederacy of States, that South Carolina has desired or asked at the hands of the Federal Government, or demanded upon constitutional ground, that she has not obtained? What great wrong, what great injury, has been inflicted upon South Carolina by her continuance in this Union of States? I know it is very easy, and even Senators have fallen into the habit of it, to repeat some phrases almost as a chorus to a song; such as 'if we cannot get our rights in the Union, we will go out of the Union and obtain those rights; that we are for the equality of the States in the Union, and if we cannot get it we will go out of the Union,' I suppose to bring about that equality. What is the point of controversy in the public mind at this time? Let us look at the question as it is. We know that the issue which has been before the country to a very great extent, and which, in fact, has recently occupied the consideration of the public, is the territorial question. It is said that South Carolina has been refused her rights in the Union, with reference to that territorial question, and therefore she is going out of the Union to obtain that which she cannot get in it.

"But let us take the fact as it is. South Carolina, it is said, wanted protection in the Territories. I have shown that she said, herself, that further protection was not needed; but if it should be needed, then Congress should give it. But South Carolina—the kingdom of South Carolina—in the plenitude of her power, and upon her own volition, without consultation with the other States of this Confederacy, has gone out of the Union, or assumed to go out. The next inquiry is: What does South Carolina now get, in the language of the distinguished Senator from Oregon, out of the Union that she did not get in the Union? Is there a man in South Carolina to-day who wants to carry a single slave into any Territory that we have got in the United States that is now unoccupied by slave property? I am almost ready to hazard the assertion that there is not one. If he had not the power and the right to carry his slave property into a Territory while in the Union, has he obtained that right now by going out of the Union? Has any thing been obtained by violating the Constitution of the United States, by withdrawing from the sisterhood of States, that could not have been obtained in it? Can South Carolina, now, any more conveniently and practically carry slavery into the Territories, than she could before she went out of the Union? Then what has she obtained? What has she got, even upon the doctrine laid down by the distinguished Senator from Oregon?

"But it is argued, striding over the Constitution and violating that comity and faith which should exist amongst the States composing this Confederacy, that she had a right to secede; she had a right to carry slaves into the Territories; and therefore, she will secede and go out of the Union. This reasoning on the part of South Carolina is about as sound as that of the madman, who assumed that he had dominion over the beasts of the forest, and therefore that he had a right to shear a wolf. His friends remonstrated with him, and, admitting his right to do so, inquired of him if he had considered the danger and difficulty of the attempt. 'No,' said the madman, 'I have not considered that; that is no part of my consideration; man has the dominion over the beasts of the forest, and therefore he has a right to shear a wolf; and as I have a right to do so, I will exercise it.' His friends still remonstrated and expostulated, and asked him, not only 'Have you considered the danger, the difficulty, and the consequences resulting from such an attempt;' but, 'What will the shearing be worth?' 'But,' he replied, 'I have the right, and therefore I will shear a wolf.' South Carolina has the right, according to the doctrine of the seceders and disunionists of this country, to go out of the Union, and therefore she will go out of the Union.

"And what, Mr. President, has South Carolina gained by going out? It has been just about as profitable an operation as the shearing of the wolf by the madman. Can she now carry slaves into the Territories? Does she even get any division of the Territories? None; she has lost all that. Does she establish a right? No; but by the exercise of this abstract right, as contended for by secessionists, what has she got? Oppression, taxation, a reign of terror over her people, as the result of their rashness in the exercise of this assumed right. In what condition are her people now? They have gone out of the Union to obtain their rights, to maintain their liberty, to get that out of the Union which they could not get in it! While they were in the Union, they were not taxed a million and some six or seven or eight hundred thousand dollars in addition to their usual expenditures, to sustain standing armies and to meet other expenditures which are incurred by separation. But still she has the right to tax her people; she has the right to institute a reign of terror; she has the right to exclude her people from the ballot-box; and she has exercised the right, and these are the consequences. She has got her rights! She has gone out of the Union to be free, and has introduced a galling system of tyranny. She has gone out of the Union to be relieved from taxes, and has increased the burdens upon her people fourfold. All this is in the exercise of her right!

"Sir, let us look at the contest through which we are passing, and consider what South Carolina, and the other States who have undertaken to secede from the Confederacy, have gained. What is the great difficulty which has existed in the public mind? We know that, practically, the territorial question is settled. Then what is the cause for breaking up this great Union of States?

Has the Union or the Constitution encroached upon the rights of South Carolina or any other State? Has this glorious Union, that was inaugurated by the adoption of the Constitution, which was framed by the patriots and sages of the Revolution, harmed South Carolina or any other State? No; it has offended none; it has protected all. What is the difficulty? We have some bad men in the South—the truth I will speak—and we have some bad men in the North, who want to dissolve this Union in order to gratify their unhallowed ambition. And what do we find here upon this floor and upon the floor of the other House of Congress? Words of crimination and recrimination are heard. Bad men North say provoking things in reference to the institutions of the South, and bad men and bad-tempered men of the South say provoking and insulting things in return; and so goes on a war of crimination and recrimination in reference to the two sections of the country, and the institutions peculiar to each. They become enraged and insulted, and then they are denunciatory of each other; and what is the result? The abolitionists, and those who entertain their sentiments, abuse men of the South, and men of the South abuse them in return. They do not fight each other; but they both become offended and enraged. One is dissatisfied with the other; one is insulted by the other; and then, to seek revenge, to gratify themselves, they both agree to make war upon the Union that never offended or injured either. Is this right? What has this Union done? Why should these contending parties make war upon it because they have insulted and aggrieved each other? This glorious Union, that was spoken into existence by the fathers of the country, must be made war upon to gratify these animosities. Shall we, because we have said bitter things of each other which have been offensive, turn upon the Government, and seek its destruction?

"I have already asked what is to be gained by the breaking up of this Confederacy. An appeal is made to the border slave-holding States to unite in what is commonly styled the Gulf Confederacy. If there is to be a division of this republic, I would rather see the line run anywhere than between the slaveholding and the non-slaveholding States, and the division made on account of a hostility, on the one hand, to the institution of slavery, and a preference for it, on the other; for wherever that line is drawn, it is the line of civil war; it is the line at which the overthrow of slavery begins; the line from which it commences to recede. Let me ask the border States, if that state of things should occur, who is to protect them in the enjoyment of their slave property? Will South Carolina, that has gone madly out, protect them? Will Mississippi and Alabama and Louisiana, still further down toward the Gulf? Will they come to our rescue, and protect us? Shall we partake of their frenzy, adopt the mistaken policy into which they have fallen, and begin the work of the destruction of the institution in which we are equally interested with them? I have already said that I believe the dissolution of this Union will be the commencement of the overthrow and destruction of the institution of slavery. In a Northern Confederacy, or in a Southern Confederacy, or in a middle Confederacy, the border slaveholding States will have to take care of that particular species of property by their own strength, and by whatever influence they may exert in the organization in which they may be placed. The Gulf States cannot, they will not, protect us. We shall have to protect ourselves, and perchance to protect them. As I remarked yesterday, my own opinion is, that the great desire to embrace the border States, as they are called, in this particular and exclusive Southern Confederacy, which it is proposed to get up, is not that they want us there out of pure good will, but they want us there as a matter of interest; so that if they are involved in war, in making acquisitions of territory still further south, or war growing out of any other cause, they may have a *corps de reserve*, they may have a power behind, that can furnish them men and money—men that have the hearts and the souls to fight and meet an enemy, come from what quarter he may.

"What have we to gain by that? The fact that two taken from four leaves but two remaining, is not clearer to my mind than it is that the dissolution of the Union is the beginning of the destruction of slavery; and that if a division be accomplished, as some desire, directly between the slaveholding and the non-slave-holding States, the work will be commenced most effectually.

"I have been told, and I have heard it repeated, that this Union is gone. It has been said in this chamber that it is in the cold sweat of death; that, in fact, it is really dead, and merely lying in state waiting for the funeral obsequies to be performed. If this be so, and the war that has been made upon me in consequence of advocating the Constitution and the Union is to result in my overthrow and in my destruction; and that flag, that glorious flag, the emblem of the Union, which was borne by Washington through a seven years' struggle, shall be struck from the Capitol and trailed in the dust—when this Union is interred, I want no more honorable winding-sheet than that brave old flag, and no more glorious grave than to be interred in the tomb of the Union. [Applause in the galleries.] For it I have stood; for it I will continue to stand, I care not whence the blows come; and some will find, before this thing is over, that while there are blows to be given, there will be blows to receive; and that, while others can thrust, there are some who can parry. They will find that it is a game that two can play at. God preserve my country from the desolation that is threatening her, from treason and traitors!

<blockquote>
' Is there not some chosen curse,
Some hidden thunder in the stores of heaven,
Red with uncommon wrath, to blast the man
Who owes his greatness to his country's ruin!'
</blockquote>

[Applause in the galleries.]

"In conclusion, Mr. President, I make an appeal to the conservative men of all parties. You see the posture of public affairs; you see the condition of the country; you see along the line of battle the various points of conflict; you see the struggle which the Union men have to maintain in many of the States. You ought to know and feel what is necessary to sustain those who, in their hearts, desire the preservation of this Union of States. Will you sit with stoic indifference, and see those who are willing to stand by the Constitution and uphold the pillars of the Government, driven away by the raging surges that are now sweeping over some portions of the country? As conservative men, as patriots, as men who desire the preservation of this great, this good, this unparalleled Government, I ask you to save the country; or let the propositions be submitted to the people, that the heart of the nation may respond to them. I have an abiding confidence in the intelligence, the patriotism, and the integrity of the great mass of the people; and I feel in my own heart that, if this subject could be got before them, they would settle the question, and the Union of these States would be preserved." [Applause in the galleries.]

If ever there was presented an instance of high moral sublimity, it was in the case of Andrew Johnson, the only man in the Senate, from the eleven States lying south of Maryland and Kentucky and Missouri, who stood up and battled for the Union, unawed by the odium and the obloquy, the frowns and denunciations, which he knew would be visited upon him. And what was more, he saw his own State, Tennessee, that he loved so well, was to be drifted from her moorings on this tide of disunion. How bitter must have been his reflections, when he saw that people, who had so often honored and sustained him, yielding to the moral pestilence which swept over the South! He warned them, he plead with them, he besought them, but he would not accompany them in their onslaught on that Government and Union which was the gift of their fathers, which was purchased by their valor, reared by their wisdom, and cemented with their blood. He knew, however, there was a band of heroes and patriots, amid Tennessee's eastern mountains, on whom he might rely. There, like Tell in the mountains of Switzerland, when pursued by the Austrian tyrant, he raised his country's standard, and amid the gorges and fastnesses of her mountains he kept the flag of the Union flying.

Mr. Lincoln had been regularly elected President of

the United States, according to the forms and requirements of the Constitution and the laws. Mr. Johnson
had warmly supported Mr. Breckinridge, but having been
fairly beaten in the election, he was in favor of acquies-
cing in the popular decision. He was unwilling for history
to record the fact that he favored disunion, because he
and his party had been defeated in an election. It was
not because of any sympathy he felt for the antislavery
sentiment of the North (as has been falsely intimated) that
he was for quietly submitting to Mr. Lincoln's election.
The record proves this. For in December, 1860, he
warmly supported and vigorously urged additional guaranties for the institution of slavery, in a series of resolutions which were referred to the Committee of Thirteen.
He was as anxious to avoid a collision as he was to preserve the Union. He ardently supported the Crittenden
compromise measures, and taunted the secession members
of the Senate with their loss, in their refusing to vote,
when by their votes they might have secured the passage
of those compromises. The compromise having failed, and
many of the Southern States having " seceded," Mr. Johnson saw that a conflict was inevitable. He saw that old
party issues were dead—that old party relations were thus
obliterated ; and that henceforth the only issue was Union
and disunion. In his speech in February, referred to, he
said: " I am for preserving the Union ; and if it is to be
done on constitutional terms, I am ready to *stand by any
and every man, without asking his antecedents,* or fearing
what may take place hereafter."

It was charged against Mr. Johnson, that he had been
induced to adhere to the Government because of hatred
and dislike to certain leading Southern men, and from a
desire to wreak his vengeance on certain political and
personal enemies in Tennessee. The record proves this

to have been a foul slander. Even after the war had fairly commenced, and blood been shed, Mr. Johnson, so far from wishing the war to be waged to extremity—so far from desiring it to be carried on with cruelty and ferocity, actually insisted on its being conducted within the bounds of moderation, and to be confined to the sole purpose of "defending and maintaining the supremacy of the Constitution, and the preservation of the Union." So important is it considered to the vindication of Mr. Johnson's consistency, and freedom from all personal bitterness in his course, that a resolution offered by him in the Senate on the 26th July, 1861, is here given:

"*Resolved*, That the present deplorable civil war has been forced upon the country by the disunionists of the Southern States, now in revolt against the constitutional Government, and in arms around the Capitol; that in this national emergency, Congress, banishing all feeling of mere passion or resentment, will recollect only its duty to the whole country; that this war is not prosecuted on our part in any spirit of oppression, nor for any purpose of conquest or subjugation, nor for the purpose of authorizing or interfering with the rights or established institutions of those States; but to defend and maintain the supremacy of the Constitution and all laws made in pursuance thereof, and to preserve the Union, with all the dignity, equality, and rights of the several States unimpaired; and that, as soon as these objects are accomplished, the war ought to cease."

This resolution was passed, by a vote of 30 to 5.

CHAPTER XI.

On the 27th of July, 1861, Mr. Johnson delivered a very able speech on the joint resolution to confirm and make valid certain acts of President Lincoln for "suppressing insurrection," etc. In his course on this question, he acted on the same practical principles of common sense by which he is uniformly guided in cases of difficulty. He refused to meet any issues of technicality tendered to him, where the real question was the salvation of the Government itself. The philosophy of the speech seemed to consist in this: that the Constitution having imposed on the President the duty to see the laws faithfully executed, some latitude of discretion must be allowed him, where there is no precedent to govern, and when the purpose is to save the Constitution from destruction; that the most liberal construction of the Constitution must be tolerated, where the object is to preserve it from ruin; that there was no violation of the oath to support the Constitution, where the great leading paramount object

CHAPTER XVII.

On the score of slavery, there is nothing which Mr. Johnson has to take back—nothing for which either he or his friends can reproach themselves. As long as slavery had a constitutional and legal existence, as long as the slave-owners of the South had a right of property in their slaves, Mr. Johnson never failed to defend and maintain the institution itself, and those who had rights under it, when he considered them unfairly or untruthfully attacked. What does this prove? That he is no bigot, no one-idea man on the subject of slavery. In fact, taking his whole course on the question of slavery into consideration, does it not give him an additional claim to the confidence and esteem of the people of the country? It shows that in his public action he has not been moved by partiality *for*, or by prejudice *against* slavery and slave-owners. Ever ready to defend both if wrongfully attacked, as long as they were under the protection of the laws, yet willing and earnest in eradicating slavery from the land as soon as he saw its further

11

toleration was inconsistent with the preservation of peace and harmony between the two sections—no man ever gave higher evidence of enlarged statesmanship and patriotism than Mr. Johnson has on this very question of slavery. The record proves that in his conduct, in his adaptation to the force of the circumstances surrounding him, he has lifted himself high above the influences of passion, of prejudice, of sectional spite, and has squared his course according to the impulses of duty—not of duty to a section, but to the whole country—not to the protection of one interest, but to all the diversified interests of this great and powerful Republic.

Mr. Johnson's peculiar position on this question of slavery renders him the very man under whose administration the institution of slavery should die out and disappear. As already said, his present views are known not to be the result of prejudice or sectional ill will, but from the conviction that the further existence of slavery was *impossible*. How much better that a man of known moderation of character and opinions should be intrusted with the settlement of all the delicate and complicated questions growing out of the changed relations of the two races! Mr. Johnson stands as a connecting link between the North and the South. He knows the African character; he knows the difficulties the future is likely to present; he knows how and to what extent slavery, as an institution, is responsible for the war just terminated. In reference to this last point—the responsibility of slavery and slave-owners in bringing on the war—there are facts and considerations connected with it not generally understood, and, where understood, not always duly weighed and considered. As Mr. Johnson's course in the arrangement and settlement of the details of this system of emancipation may very much be modified or influenced by his knowl-

was to conform to its spirit, in order to maintain and defend its integrity and its very life. He said:

"I agree with the Senator from Kentucky, that there was a design—a deliberate determination—to change the nature and character of our Government. Yes, sir, it has been the design for a long time. All the talk about slavery and compromise has been but a pretext. We had a long disquisition, and a very feeling one, from the Senator from Kentucky. He became pathetic in the hopelessness of compromises. Did not the Senator from California [Mr. Latham] the other day show unmistakably that it was not compromise they wanted? I will add, that compromise was the thing they most feared; and their great effort was to get out of Congress before any compromise could be made. At first, their cry was peaceable secession and reconstruction. They talked not of compromise; and, I repeat, their greatest dread and fear was, that something would be agreed upon; that their last and only pretext would be swept from under them, and that they would stand before the country naked and exposed.

"The Senator from California pointed out to you a number of them who stood here and did not vote for certain propositions, and those propositions were lost. What was the action before the Committee of Thirteen? Why did not that committee agree? Some of the most ultra men from the North were members of that committee, and they proposed to amend the Constitution so as to provide that Congress in the future never should interfere with the subject of slavery. The committee failed to agree, and some of its members at once telegraphed to their States that they must go out of the Union at once. But after all that transpired in the early part of the session, what was done? We know what the argument has been; in times gone by I have met it; I have heard it again and again. It has been said that one great object was, first to abolish slavery in the District of Columbia and the slave trade between the States, as a kind of initiative measure; next, to exclude it from the Territories; and when the free States were three-fourths of all the States, so as to have power to change the Constitution, they would amend the Constitution so as to give

Congress power to legislate upon the subject of slavery in the States, and expel it from the States in which it is now. Has not that been the argument? Now, how does the matter stand? At the last session of Congress seven States withdrew—it may be said that eight withdrew—reducing the remaining slave States down to one-fourth of the whole number of States. Now we have reached the point at which the charge has been made, that whenever the free States constituted a majority in the Congress of the United States, sufficient to amend the Constitution, they would so amend it as to legislate upon the institution of slavery within the States, and that the institution of slavery would be overthrown. This has been the argument; it has been repeated again and again; and hence the great struggle about the Territories. The argument was, we wanted to prevent the creation of free States; we did not want to be reduced down to that point where, under the sixth article of the Constitution, three-fourths could amend the Constitution so as to exclude slavery from the States. This has been the great point; this has been the rampart; this has been the very point to which it has been urged that the free States wanted to pass. Now, how does the fact stand? Let us ' render unto Cæsar the things that are Cæsar's.' We reached, at the last session, just the point where we were in the power of the free States; and then what was done? Instead of an amendment to the Constitution of the United States conferring power upon Congress to legislate upon the subject of slavery, what was done? This joint resolution was passed by a two-thirds majority in each House:

' *Resolved by the Senate and House of Representatives of the United States of America in Congress assembled,* That the following article be proposed to the Legislatures of the several States, as an amendment to the Constitution of the United States, which, when ratified by three-fourths of said Legislatures, shall be valid, to all intents and purposes, as part of the said Constitution, viz .

' ART. 13. No amendment shall be made to the Constitution which shall authorize or give to Congress the power to abolish, or interfere, within any State, with the domestic institutions thereof, including that of persons held to service or labor by the laws of said State.'

" Is not that very conclusive? Here is an amendment to the

Constitution of the United States to make the Constitution una-
mendable upon that subject, as it is upon some other subjects;
that Congress, in the future, should have no power to legislate on
the subject of slavery within the States.   Talk about 'compromise,'
and about the settlement of this question; how can you settle it
more substantially?   How can you get a guaranty that is more
binding than an amendment to the Constitution, which is una-
mendable, that Congress, in the future, shall not even legislate on
the subject?   This places the institution of slavery in the States
entirely beyond the control of Congress.   Why have not the Legislatures that talk about 'reconstruction' and 'compromise' and
'guaranties,' taken up this amendment to the Constitution and
adopted it?   Some States have adopted it.   How many Southern
States have done so?   Take my own State, for instance.   Instead
of accepting guaranties protecting them in all future time against
the legislation of Congress on the subject of slavery, they undertake to pass ordinances violating the Constitution of the country,
and taking the State out of the Union and into the Southern Confederacy.   It is evident to me that with many the talk about compromise and the settlement of this question is mere pretext, especially with those who understand the question.

"All the compromise that I have to make is the compromise
of the Constitution of the United States.   It is one of the best
compromises that can be made.   We lived under it from 1789
down to the 20th of December, 1860, when South Carolina undertook to go out of the Union.   We prospered; we advanced in
wealth, in commerce, in agriculture, in trade, in manufactures, in
all the arts and sciences, and in religion, more than any people
upon the face of God's earth had ever done before in the same
time.   What better compromise do you want?   You lived under
it until you got to be a great and prosperous people.   It was made
by our fathers, and cemented by their blood.   When you talk to
me about compromise, I hold up to you the Constitution under
which you derived all your greatness, and which was made by the
fathers of your country.   It will protect you in all your rights.

"But it is said that we had better divide the country and make a treaty and restore peace. If, under the Constitution which was framed by Washington and Madison and the patriots of the Revolution, we cannot live as brothers, as we have in times gone by, I ask can we live quietly under a treaty, separated as enemies? The same causes will exist; our geographical and physical position will remain just the same. Suppose you make a treaty of peace and division: if the same causes of irritation, if the same causes of division continue to exist, and we cannot live as brothers in fraternity under the Constitution made by our fathers, and as friends in the same Government, how can we live in peace as aliens and enemies under a treaty? It cannot be done; it is impracticable.

"I say it is the paramount duty of this Government to assert its power and maintain its integrity. I say it is the duty of this Government to protect those States, or the loyal citizens of those States, in the enjoyment of a republican form of government; for we have seen one continued system of usurpation carried on, from one end of these Southern States to the other, disregarding the popular judgment; disregarding the popular will; setting at defiance the judgment of the people; disregarding their rights; paying no attention to their State constitutions in any sense whatever. We are bound, under the Constitution, to protect those States and their citizens. We are bound to guarantee to them a republican form of government; it is our duty to do it. If we have got no Government, let the delusion be dispelled; let the dream pass away; and let the people of the United States, and the nations of the earth, know at once that we have no Government. If we have a Government, based on the intelligence and virtue of the American people, let that great fact be now established, and once established, this Government will be on a more enduring and permanent basis than it ever was before. I still have confidence in the integrity, the virtue, the intelligence, and the patriotism of the great mass of the people; and so believing, I intend to stand by the Government of my fathers to the last extremity.

"Is the mere defeat of one man, and the election of another, according to the forms of law and the Constitution, sufficient cause to break up this Government? No; it is not sufficient cause. Do we not know, too, that if all the seceding Senators had stood here as faithful sentinels, representing the interests of their States, they had it in their power to check any advance that might be made by the incoming administration? I showed these facts, and enumerated them at the last session. They were shown here the other day. On the 4th of March, when President Lincoln was inaugurated, we had a majority of six upon this floor in opposition to his administration. Where, then, is there even a pretext for breaking up the Government upon the idea that he would have encroached upon our rights? Does not the nation know that even Mr. Lincoln could not have made his Cabinet without the consent of the majority of the Senate? Do we not know that he could not even have sent a minister abroad without the majority of the Senate confirming the nomination? Do we not know that if any minister whom he sent abroad should make a treaty inimical to the institutions of the South, that treaty could not have been ratified without a majority of two-thirds of the Senate?

" With all these facts staring them in the face, where is the pretence for breaking up this Government? Is it not clear that there has been a fixed purpose, a settled design to break up the Government and change the nature and character and whole genius of the Government itself? Does it not prove conclusively, as there was no cause, that they simply selected it as an occasion that was favorable to excite the prejudices of the South, and thereby enable them to break up this Government and establish a Southern Confederacy.

" Then when we get at it, what is the real cause? If Mr. Davis had been elected President of the United States, it would have been a very nice thing; he would have respected the judgment of the people, and no doubt his confidence in their capacity for self-government would have been increased; but it so happened that he was not elected. They thought proper to elect somebody else, according to law and the Constitution. Then, as all parties had done heretofore, it was the duty of the whole people to acquiesce; if he made a good President, sustain him; if he became a bad one, condemn him; if he violated the law and the Constitution, impeach him. We had our remedy under the Constitution and in the Union.

"What is the real cause? Disappointed ambition; an unhallowed ambition. Certain men could not wait any longer, and they seized this occasion to do what they had been wanting to do for a long time—break up the Government. If they could not rule a large country, they thought they might rule a small one. Hence one of the prime movers in the Senate ceased to be a Senator, and passed out to be President of the Southern Confederacy. Another, that was bold enough on this floor to proclaim himself a rebel, retired as a Senator, and became secretary of state. All perfectly disinterested, no ambition about it! Another, Mr. Benjamin, of Louisiana—one that understands something about the idea of dividing garments; who belongs to that tribe that parted the garments of our Saviour, and for his vesture cast lots—went out of this body and was made attorney-general, to show his patriotism and disinterestedness—nothing else! Mr. Slidell, disinterested altogether, is to go as minister to France. I might enumerate many such instances. This is all patriotism, pure disinterestedness! Do we not see where it all ends? Disappointed, impatient, unhallowed ambition. There has been no cause for breaking up this Government, there have been no rights denied, no privileges trampled upon under the Constitution and Union, that might not have been remedied more effectually in the Union than outside of it.

"What rights are to be attained outside of the Union? The seceders have violated the Constitution, trampled it under foot; and what is their condition now? Upon the abstract idea that they had a right to secede, they have gone out; and what is the consequence? Oppression, taxation, blood, and civil war. They reasoned upon the principle of a madman, who happened to discover somehow that man had dominion over the beasts of the forest; and because he had, he said he had a right to shear a wolf. A friend remonstrated with him, and asked him if he had considered the danger and the difficulty of the attempt to shear a wolf; and after the shearing was over, what would it be worth?

' Oh no,' said he, in the midst of his frenzy and madness, ' I have a right to shear a wolf, and therefore I will shear a wolf.' Yes, they have sheared the wolf, and what has come ? They have gone out of the Union; and, I repeat again, they have got taxes, usurpations, blood, and civil war.

" Since I left my home, having only one way to leave the State through two or three passes coming out through Cumberland Gap, I have been advised that they had even sent their armies to blockade these passes in the mountains, as they say, to prevent Johnson from returning with arms and munitions to place in the hands of the people to vindicate their rights, repel invasion, and put down domestic insurrection and rebellion. Yes, sir, there they stand in arms, environing a population of three hundred and twenty-five thousand loyal, brave, patriotic, and unsubdued people ; but yet powerless, and not in a condition to vindicate their rights. Hence I come to the Government, and I do not ask it as a suppliant, but I demand it as a constitutional right, that you give us protection, give us arms and munitions ; and if they cannot be got there in any other way, to take them there with an invading army, and deliver the people from the oppression to which they are now subjected. We claim to be the State. The other divisions may have seceded and gone off; and if this Government will stand by and permit those portions of the State to go off, and not enforce the laws and protect the loyal citizens there, we cannot help it; but we still claim to be the State, and if two-thirds have fallen off, or have been sunk by an earthquake, it does not change our relation to this Government. If the Government will let them go, and not give us protection, the fault is not ours ; but if you will give us protection, we intend to stand as a State, as a part of this Confederacy, holding to the flag that was borne by Washington through a seven years' struggle for independence and separation from the mother country. We demand it according to law ; we demand it upon the guaranties of the Constitution. You are bound to guarantee to us a republican form of government, and we ask it as a constitutional right. We do not ask you to interfere as a party, as your feelings or prejudices may be one way or another in reference to the parties of the country; but we ask you to interfere as a Government according to the Constitution. Of course we want your sympathy, and your regard, and your respect; but we ask your interference on constitutional grounds.

"The amendments to the Constitution, which constitute the bill of rights, declare that 'a well-regulated militia being necessary to the security of a free State, the right of the people to keep and bear arms shall not be infringed.' Our people are denied this right secured to them in their own constitution and the Constitution of the United States; yet we hear no complaints here of violations of the Constitution in this respect. We ask the Government to interpose to secure us this constitutional right. We want the passes in our mountains opened, we want deliverance and protection for a downtrodden and oppressed people who are struggling for their independence without arms. If we had had ten thousand stand of arms and ammunition when the contest commenced, we should have asked no further assistance. We have not got them. We are a rural people; we have villages and small towns—no large cities. Our population is homogeneous, industrious, frugal, brave, independent; but harmless and powerless, and rode over by usurpers. You may be too late in coming to our relief; or you may not come at all, though I do not doubt that you will come; they may trample us under foot; they may convert our plains into graveyards, and the caves of our mountains into sepulchres; but they will never take us out of this Union, or make us a land of slaves—no, never. We intend to stand as firm as adamant, and as unyielding as our own majestic mountains that surround us. Yes, we will profit by their example, resting immovably upon their basis. We will stand as long as we can; and if we are overpowered, and liberty shall be driven from the land, we intend before she departs, to take the flag of our country, with a stalwart arm, and a patriotic heart, and an honest tread, and place it upon the summit of the loftiest and most majestic mountain. We intend to plant it there, and leave it, to indicate to the inquirer who may come in after times, the spot where the Goddess of Liberty lingered and wept for the last time, before she took her flight from a people once prosperous, free, and happy.

We ask the Government to come to our aid. We love the Constitution as made by our fathers. We have confidence in the integrity and capacity of the people to govern themselves. We have lived entertaining these opinions; we intend to die entertaining them. The battle has commenced, The President has placed it upon the true ground. It is an issue on the one hand for the people's Government, and its overthrow on the other. We have commenced the battle of freedom. It is freedom's cause. We are resisting usurpation and oppression. We will triumph; we must triumph. Right is with us. A great and fundamental principle of right, that lies at the foundation of all things, is with us. We may meet with impediments, and may meet with disasters, and here and there a defeat; but ultimately freedom's cause must triumph, for—

> ' Freedom's battle once begun,
> Bequeathed from bleeding sire to son,
> Though baffled oft, is ever won.'

"Yes, we must triumph. Though sometimes I cannot see my way clear in matters of this kind, as in matters of religion, when my facts give out, when my reason fails me, I draw largely upon my faith. My faith is strong, based on the eternal principles of right, that a thing so monstrously wrong as this rebellion is, cannot triumph. Can we submit to it? Can bleeding justice submit to it? Is the Senate, are the American people, prepared to give up the graves of Washington and Jackson, to be encircled and governed and controlled by a combination of traitors and rebels? I say let the battle go on—it is freedom's cause—until the Stars and Stripes (God bless them!) shall again be unfurled upon every cross-road and from every house-top throughout the Confederacy, North and South. Let the Union be reinstated; let the law be enforced; let the Constitution be supreme.

"If the Congress of the United States were to give up the tombs of Washington and Jackson, we should have rising up in our midst another Peter the Hermit, in a much more righteous cause—for ours is true, while his was a delusion—who would appeal to the American people and point to the tombs of Washington and Jackson, in the possession of those who are worse than the infidel and the Turk who held the Holy Sepulchre. I believe the American people would start of their own accord, when appealed to, to redeem the graves of Washington and Jackson and Jefferson, and all the other patriots who are lying within the limits of the Southern Confederacy. I do not believe they would stop the march, until again the flag of this Union would be placed over the graves of those distinguished men. There will be an uprising. Do not talk about Republicans now; do not talk about Democrats now; do not talk about Whigs or Americans now; talk about your country and the Constitution and the Union. Save that; preserve the integrity of the Government; once more place it erect among the nations of the earth; and then if we want to divide about questions that may arise in our midst, we have a Government to divide in.

"I know it has been said that the object of this war is to make war on Southern institutions. I have been in free States and I have been in slave States, and I thank God that, so far as I have been, there has been one universal disclaimer of any such purpose. It is a war upon no section; it is a war upon no peculiar institution; but it is a war for the integrity of the Government, for the Constitution, and the supremacy of the laws. That is what the nation understands by it.

"I have already detained the Senate much longer than I intended when I rose, and I shall conclude in a few words more. Although the Government has met with a little reverse within a short distance of this city, no one should be discouraged and no heart should be dismayed. It ought only to prove the necessity of bringing forth and exerting still more vigorously the power of the Government in maintenance of the Constitution and the laws. Let the energies of the Government be redoubled, and let it go on with this war—not a war upon sections, not a war upon peculiar institutions anywhere; but let the Constitution and the Union be its frontispiece, and the supremacy and enforcement of

the laws its watchword.   Then it can, it will, go on triumphantly.
We must succeed.   This Government must not, cannot fail.
Though your flag may have trailed in the dust; though a retrograde movement may have been made; though the banner of our
country may have been sullied, let it still be borne onward; and
if, for the prosecution of this war in behalf of the Government
and the Constitution, it is necessary to cleanse and purify that
banner, I say let it be baptized in fire from the sun and bathed in
a nation's blood!   The nation must be redeemed; it must be triumphant.   The Constitution—which is based upon principles im
mutable, and upon which rest the rights of man and the hopes
and expectations of those who love freedom throughout the civilized world—must be maintained."

CHAPTER XII.

On his return home, from attending an extra session, in September, 1861, Mr. Johnson was frequently called on to address the people in Ohio and Kentucky and other places. He aroused and encouraged the Union men to stand firm, and did much toward organizing and strengthening the Union feeling wherever he went.

In the winter of 1862, the Federal forces having captured Forts Henry and Donelson, on the advance of General Buell the Confederate forces were compelled to abandon Nashville. Thus Tennessee was in a great degree recovered to the authority of the United States. Mr. Lincoln therefore appointed Mr. Johnson Military Governor of Tennessee. Mr. Johnson left his seat in the Senate, to enter upon the duties of his office, in March, 1862. He was received with enthusiasm by the Union men of Nashville on his arrival there; and on being serenaded, delivered to them a cheering and consoling address. In a few days afterwards he issued an " Appeal to the People " of Tennessee. It is a State paper of great merit, written in fine style, in good temper, and possessing unusual clearness and force. The following extracts exhibit the spirit that pervades it:

"The State government has disappeared. The executive has abdicated; the judiciary is in abeyance. The great ship of State, freighted with its precious cargo of human interests and human hopes, its sails all set, and its glorious old flag unfurled, has been suddenly abandoned by its officers and mutinous crew, and left to float at the mercy of the winds, and to be plundered by every rover upon the deep.

"In such a lamentable crisis, the Government of the United States could not be unmindful of its high constitutional obligation to guarantee to every State in this Union a republican form of government, an obligation which every State has a direct and immediate interest in having observed toward every other State, and from which, by no action on the part of the people in any State, can the Federal Government be absolved. A republican form of government, in consonance with the Constitution of the United States, is one of the fundamental conditions of our political existence, by which every part of the country is alike bound, and from which no part can escape.

"To the people themselves, the protection of the Government is extended. All their rights will be duly respected, and their wrongs redressed, when made known. Those who, through the dark and dreary night of the rebellion, have maintained their allegiance to the Federal Government, will be honored. The erring and misguided will be welcomed on their return. And while it may become necessary, in vindicating the violated majesty of the law, and in reasserting its imperial sway, to punish intelligent and conscious treason in high places, no merely retaliatory or vindictive policy will be adopted. To those especially who, in a private, unofficial capacity, have assumed an attitude of hostility to the Government, a full and complete amnesty for all past acts and declarations is offered, upon the one condition of their again yielding themselves peaceful citizens to the just supremany of the laws."

It is admitted that President Johnson's rule, whilst acting as Military Governor, was stringent, and in many instances apparently severe. But no other course was left him. Dire necessity forced it on him. Nothing but a positive, decided, and unequivocal line of conduct would have answered the requirements of the occasion. There was a larger Union element in Tennessee than in any other State that had formally resorted to disunion. Not only was the State at war with the Government of the United States, but the people of the State—the loyal and disloyal —were at war with each other. Scenes of violence, of outrage, rapine, and plunder were constantly being perpetrated. The civil law was in abeyance. Lawless force controlled every thing. Governor Johnson saw it was utterly useless to rely on the slow process of legal proceedings where anarchy prevailed. From the force of necessity he was compelled to act the part of a dictator in order to save the State from wreck and ruin. He saw the wound from which the community was suffering required the actual cautery, and he applied it without hesitation. Being appointed Military Governor for the purpose of saving the Union, of course he was bound to protect Union men. He ordered the mayor and council of Nashville to take the oath of allegiance to the United States, and, on their refusal, they were incarcerated. He placed the press under restraint against the utterance of treasonable and seditious language. He issued his proclamation, declaring that whenever a Union man was maltreated by the lawless bands engaged in the rebellion that were ravaging the country, five or more of the sympathizers with the rebellion, living in the neighborhood, should be arrested, and dealt with as the nature of the case might require ; and where the property of loyal citizens was taken or destroyed, remuneration should be made to them from the property of those favoring the rebellion. In some instances he arrested and imprisoned judges, to prevent them from any judicial interference with his executive functions.

These were disagreeable and painful duties Governor Johnson had to perform, but force and arbitrary will being the only instruments available for the protection of life, liberty, or property, no other course was left to him. If he had hesitated or temporized, he would have been swept away into the abyss of that social chaos that then prevailed. His boldness, firmness, and self-reliance sustained him in this hour of trial. He knew if he faltered, he would be lost. He resolved that, if fall he must, he would fall in the discharge of his duty.

For several months during the year 1862, Nashville was in a very precarious and alarming condition. The Confederate army having invaded Kentucky, and cut off the communications with the North by destroying the railroads, Nashville was left isolated for the time being. Provisions became very scarce, prices were very high, and great want and suffering prevailed. Governor Johnson never displayed his manliness, his force of character, and his capacity for managing men more strikingly than at this time. Whilst many were in despair, his courage never forsook him. He was determined to stay in Nashville, and to die there, if need be, rather than desert his post. He went everywhere, he saw every thing. He congratulated the bold, he cheered the despondent, he exhorted the wavering, and he warned the suspicious. He saw in suffering and distress the families of many who had left the city, either to secure their persons or to join the rebel army. As a humane man, he felt for them in their distress. He did not, from a feeling of vengeance, leave them to die of hunger. But he issued a peremptory order, assessing the sympathizers with the rebellion in Nashville (who were able to pay it) a certain amount per head, to be distributed by the judge of the county court among the destitute families of such persons above mentioned.

In the fall of 1862, General Buell, having reached Nashville, and being then chief in command, proposed to evacuate the city. Governor Johnson would not hear to this. He was indignant at the thought of giving up this stronghold after having held it so long and at such great sacrifice. He saw that the abandonment of Nashville would be the virtual surrender of Tennessee to the rebel arms. He requested of Mr. Lincoln the removal of General Buell. General Buell was removed, and under the command of General Negley the attack upon the city was repulsed. Governor Johnson, though no military man, took a deep interest in every thing going on. It was on this occasion that he made the celebrated remark, "I am no military man, but the first one who talks of surrendering I will shoot!" In October of this year (1862) Governor Johnson's family rejoined him in Nashville from the eastern part of the State, after a very disagreeable and perilous journey, beset with trials and dangers from guerrillas and roving bands of lawless men.

In the spring and again in the fall of 1863, Governor Johnson visited Washington, to confer with President Lincoln as to the proper mode and manner of reorganizing the State government of Tennessee so as to enable her to resume her rightful position in the Union. The rebel forces having been driven from nearly every part of the State, the people began to rise up and give free expression to their Union sentiments. Mass conventions were held in various places, many of which Governor Johnson attended, and addressed the people. He encouraged them to persevere, pledging himself to stand by and sustain them, and to abide their fate. The following extracts from an address of Governor Johnson will explain what was then his view in regard to the status of Tennessee and the course proper to be pursued in restoring her to her place in the Union:

"Tennessee is not out of the Union, never has been, and never will be out. The bonds of the Constitution and the Federal power will always prevent that. This Government is perpetual; provision is made for reforming the Government and amending the Constitution, and admitting States into the Union—not for letting them out of it.

"Whenever you desire, in good faith, to restore civil authority, you can do so, and a proclamation for an election will be issued as speedily as it is practicable to hold one. One by one all the agencies of your State government will be put in motion. A Legislature will be elected; judges will be appointed temporarily until you can elect them at the polls; and so of sheriffs, county court judges, justices, and other officers, until the way is fairly open for the people and all the parts of civil government resume their ordinary functions. This is no nice, intricate, metaphysical question. It is a plain, common-sense matter, and there is nothing in the way but obstinacy."

On the 26th of January, 1864, Governor Johnson issued his proclamation for an election in the State, preparatory to the reorganization of the State government. On the 6th of June, at the nominating convention in Baltimore, Governor Johnson was unanimously nominated for Vice-President on the ticket with Mr. Lincoln, who was nominated for President. When the news reached Nashville, it was received with great demonstrations of joy and enthusiasm. An immense meeting of the people was called, which was addressed by Governor Johnson. In the course of his remarks he said:

"While society is in this disordered state, and we are seeking security, let us fix the foundations of our Government on principles of eternal justice, which will endure for all time. There are those in our midst who are for perpetuating the institution of slavery. Let me say to you, Tennesseans, an men from the Northern States, that slavery is dead. It was not murdered by me. I told you long ago what the result would be if you endeavored to go out of the Union to save slavery; and that the result would be bloodshed, rapine, devastated fields, plundered villages and cities; and therefore I urged you to remain in the Union. In trying to save slavery you killed it, and lost your own freedom. As Macbeth said to Banquo's bloody ghost—

> 'Never shake thy gory locks at me;
> Thou canst not say I did it.'"

In a letter to Hon. William Dennison, chairman of the committee, etc., accepting the nomination for the Vice-Presidency, Governor Johnson said:

" The authority of the Government is supreme, and will admit of no rivalry. No institution can rise above it, whether it be slavery or any organized power. In our happy form of government all must be subordinate to the will of the people, when reflected through the Constitution and laws made pursuant thereto —State or Federal. This great principle lies at the foundation of every Government, and cannot be disregarded without the destruction of the Government itself.

" In accepting the nomination I might here close, but I cannot forego the opportunity of saying to my old friends of the Democratic party *proper*, with whom I have so long and pleasantly been associated, that the hour has now come when that great party can justly vindicate its devotion to true democratic policy and measures of expediency. The war is a war of great principles. It involves the supremacy and life of the Government itself. If the rebellion triumphs, free government—North and South—fails. If, on the other hand, the Government is successful, as I do not doubt, its destiny is fixed, its basis permanent and enduring, and its career of honor and glory just begun. In a great contest like this, for the existence of free government, the path of duty is patriotism and principle. Minor considerations and questions of administrative policy should give way to the higher duty *of first preserving the Government*, and then there will be time enough to wrangle over the men and measures pertaining to its administration."

The result of the Presidential election of 1864 is well known to the reader. Lincoln and Johnson received the votes of every State that voted in the election except New Jersey, Kentucky, and Delaware. On the 4th March, 1865, Mr. Johnson was duly qualified as Vice-President, and took his seat, as presiding officer of the Senate. The war was now speedily approaching a termination. When the news reached Washington of the taking of Richmond and Petersburg by the Federal army, there was great rejoicing. The friends of the Union were wild with delight. Mr. Johnson made a speech on the occasion to the vast concourse that called on him. It was a speech of great power and eloquence, teeming with the most patriotic sentiments, and national and conservative in tone and temper. The following extracts are given from this speech :—

" My friends, in what has the great strength of this Government consisted? Has it been in one-man power? Has it been in some autocrat, or in some one man, who held absolute government? No! I thank God I have it in my power to proclaim the great truth, that this Government has derived its strength from the American people. They have issued the edict; they have exercised the power that has resulted in the overthrow of the rebellion; and there is not another Government upon the face of the earth that could have withstood the shock.

" In the language of another, let that old flag rise higher and higher, until it meets the sun in his coming, and let the parting day linger to play upon its folds. It is the flag of your country; it is your flag, it is my flag, and it bids defiance to all the nations of the earth, and the encroachments of all the powers combined. It is not my intention to make any imprudent remarks or allusions; but the hour will come when those nations that exhibited toward us such insolence and improper interference, in the midst of our adversity, and, as they supposed, of our weakness, will learn that this is a Government of the people, possessing power enough to make itself felt and respected."

General Lee surrendered his entire army to General Grant on April 9, 1865. This was everywhere throughout the country, North and South, considered as a virtual termination of the war. General Johnston, at the head of the odds and ends of the Western rebel army, with Hoke's division, which had united with him at Goldsboro', was then flying before Sherman's army. Johnston's could hardly be called an army. Thoroughly demoralized by desertion and despondency, and numbering not more than 20,000 men of all arms, it passed through Raleigh, North Carolina, only a few hours in advance of Sherman's splendid army of 120,000 men. It was now only a question of time as to when Johnston must surrender. The whole country was wild with joy at the idea of a termination of the terrible and bloody war which had scourged the country with such maddening fury. On the night of the 14th April, only five days after Lee's surrender, when the population of the nation were enthusiastic with joy, President Lincoln was murdered by an assassin at Ford's Theatre in Washington. As the news was telegraphed with lightning speed all over the country, the entire population was momentarily struck dumb with horror. The consternation at the South was scarcely less striking than at the North. The guilty authors and leaders of the rebellion dreaded a terrible outburst of vengeance, on the part of the Federal army; and the innocent friends of the Union who had been dragged into the conflict against their wishes, were not only indignant and astounded at the savage and inhuman act, but they feared that in the common ruin they would be confounded with the former. Fortunately for the people of Raleigh, then occupied by General Sherman, propositions of negotiation for a surrender of his army having been sent by General Johnston, then lying near Hillsboro', had reached Raleigh just before the news of President Lincoln's death reached that place. There was great excitement among the troops, but by timely precaution on the part of the officers, order and discipline were preserved. A few days thereafter General Johnston surrendered, and thus, like Jonah's gourd, died this war as suddenly as it had been precipitately and causelessly inaugurated.

The grief of the people at the sad fate of President Lincoln, was profound and unaffected. With the people of the North, he was a decided favorite. They not only esteemed and respected him personally for his private virtues; but he had so managed public affairs, considering the great difficulties he had to contend with, as to have acquired their confidence and regard as a statesman. Among the Southern people even (except the more malignant), he was considered to be a man of kindly and generous impulses, free from all bitter and revengeful feelings toward them, and exceedingly anxious for the restoration of peace and harmony. Meetings were held all over the South, expressing sorrow and deep regret at his death, and denouncing his assassination as a most atrocious and diabolical act.

No stronger evidence can be afforded of the strength, the systematic arrangement and adaptation to circumstances, of our Government and its institutions, than was presented in the regular routine of the exercise of executive power on the death of Mr. Lincoln. Great as was the outburst of grief which followed, yet the behests of duty were not forgotten. Mr. Johnson was immediately waited on at his private lodgings, by the Hon. James Speed, Attorney-General, with a formal communication from Messrs. McCulloch, Stanton, Welles, Dennison, and Usher, members of Mr. Lincoln's cabinet, informing him (Mr. Johnson) of the sad event, and stating that " the emergency of the Government demanded that he should immediately qualify and enter upon the duties of President of the United States." Mr. Johnson designated ten o'clock as the hour, and his private apartments at the Kirkwood House as the place, where he would take the oath of office. At the appointed time and place, without any formal parade or ceremony, but quietly and unostentatiously, in a manner suitable to the occasion, the oath of office was administered to him. The short and suitable address he made on the occasion is here given entire :

" Gentlemen, I must be permitted to say that I have been almost overwhelmed by the announcement of the sad event which has so recently occurred. I feel incompetent to perform duties so important and responsible as those which have been so unexpectedly thrown upon me. As to an indication of any policy which may be pursued by me in the administration of the Government, I have to say that that must be left for development, as the administration progresses. The message or declaration must be made by the acts as they transpire. The only assurance that I can now give of the future, is by reference to the past. The course which I have taken in the past, in connection with this rebellion, must be regarded as a guaranty for the future. My past public life, which has been long and laborious, has been founded, as I in good conscience believe, upon a great principle of right, which lies at the basis of all things. The best energies of my life have been spent in endeavoring to establish and perpetuate the blessings of free government; and I believe that the Government, in passing through its present trials, will settle down upon principles consonant with popular rights, more permanent and enduring than heretofore. I must be permitted to say, if I understood the feelings of my own heart, I have long labored to ameliorate and alleviate the condition of the great mass of the American people. Toil, and an honest advocacy of the great principles of free government, have been my lot. The duties have been mine—the consequences are God's. This has been the foundation of my political creed. I feel that in the end the Government will triumph, and that these great principles will be permanently established.

"In conclusion, gentlemen, let me say that I want your encouragement and countenance. I shall ask, and rely, upon you and others, in carrying the Government through its present perils. I feel, in making this request, that it will be heartily responded to by you and all other patriots and lovers of the rights and interests of a free people."

Mr. Seward, Secretary of State, was not able to sign the communication from the Cabinet in regard to Mr. Lincoln's death, nor to be present at the administration of the oath to President Johnson. On the same night on which Mr. Lincoln was assassinated, another accomplice in the murder attacked Mr. Seward when confined to his bed by illness, and inflicted several severe wounds on his face and neck with a dagger or large knife. It was feared, for some time, that the wounds would prove fatal; but fortunately for the country he recovered, after much suffering.

Mr. Johnson was now President of the United States. Through the will of the people and the providence of God, he had reached the highest pinnacle of human station and power. He was not insensible of the importance of the duties devolving on him, or of the heavy responsibility incurred thereby. On the 20th of April, the British minister, Sir Frederick W. H. Bruce, presented his credentials, and in doing so, delivered a short and appropriate address to President Johnson, expressing a wish " to conciliate those relations of comity and good understanding which have so long and so happily existed between the two kindred nations of the United States and Great Britain," etc. President Johnson's reply is one of the finest specimens of composition. It is terse, forcible, and to the point. Its sentiments are in good taste, and appropriate to such an occasion. This was a new field for Mr. Johnson, and rather a trying one for a plain, unpretending man, but little acquainted with the usages of diplomatic etiquette. But, as on every other field on which he had been tried, he proved himself fully competent for the work before him. President Johnson's reply is here given in full:

"SIR FREDERICK W. H. BRUCE : The very cordial and friendly sentiments which you have expressed, on the part of her Britannic Majesty, give me great pleasure. Great Britain and the United States, by the extended and various forms of commerce between them, the contiguity of portions of their possessions, and the similarity of their language and laws, are drawn into constant and intimate intercourse. At the same time they are, from the same causes, exposed to frequent occasions of misunderstanding, only to be averted by mutual forbearance. So eagerly are the people of the two countries engaged, throughout almost the whole world, in the pursuit of similar commercial enterprises, accompanied by natural rivalries and jealousies, that, at first sight, it would almost seem that the two Governments must be enemies, or at best cold and calculating friends. So devoted are the two nations throughout all their domain, and even in their most remote territory and colonial possessions, to the principles of civil rights and constitutional liberty, that, on the other hand, the superficial observer might erroneously count upon a continued concert of action and sympathy amounting to an alliance between them. Each is charged with the development of the progress of the human race, and each in its sphere is subject to the difficulties and trials not participated in by the other. The interests of civilization and of humanity require that the two should be friends. I have always known and accounted as a fact, honorable to both countries, that the Queen of England is a sincere and honest well-wisher of the

United States. I have been equally frank and explicit in the opinion that the friendship of the United States toward Great Britain is enjoined by all considerations of interest and of sentiment affecting the character of both. You will, therefore, be accepted as a minister friendly and well-disposed to the maintenance of peace and the honor of both countries. You will find myself and all my associates acting in accordance with the same enlightened policy and consistent sentiments; and so I am sure that it will not occur in your case that either yourself or this Government will ever have cause to regret that such an important relationship existed at such a crisis."

During the same month, in a reply to a large number of loyal Southern men who had formally called on President Johnson, he concluded in the following patriotic and feeling language:

"I can give no greater assurance regarding the settlement of this question than that I intend to discharge my duty, and in that way which shall, at the earliest possible hour, bring back peace to our distracted country. And I hope the time is not far distant when our people can all return to their homes and firesides, and resume their various avocations."

President Johnson's course thus far, and what it may be hereafter, will belong to history. Thus far his friends have cause to congratulate him, and to congratulate themselves that he has so successfully grappled with difficulties. Many questions have arisen in regard to his plan of reconstructing the Union and of restoring harmony, on which public opinion is somewhat divided. So great is the confidence of the people of all sections that his wish and purpose are to *do right*, that there seems to be a general disposition to judge of his course with impartiality and justice.

It is now proposed to take a review of President Johnson's character as developed by his past life, and then to pass in further review his measures and policy as thus far demonstrated. The author must be pardoned for indulging in such reflections as naturally suggest themselves to the mind in contemplating the life and character of this remarkable man, which constitute a record of what energy, determination, and self-reliance, when sustained by honest, upright, and patriotic intentions, can accomplish in defiance of obstacles that would, at first, seem insurmountable.

CHAPTER XIII.

How strange is life! How contrary to all human calculations are the developments produced by time! What interesting reflections are superinduced by comparing the past and its improbabilities with the present and its realities! What opposite incidents are here afforded for a pictorial representation of human life! Contemplate Andrew Johnson when, at the age of nineteen, he was a journeyman tailor in Greeneville, Tennessee. Whilst his hands were busily engaged on his daily labor, his mind was not idle. Although his intellect had not been enlarged and expanded by education in early life, yet he felt the restless strivings of those aspirations upward with which Nature had endowed him. He felt that he had a mission higher than that of merely passing quietly and unknown through life—that he had something more to do—that he owed something more to his fellow-men than to pass his hours of recess from labor in looking out on the beautiful scenery and inhaling the bracing air of his mountain home. He had recourse to books, as have had so many other great

8

men who were deprived of the advantages of education in early life. He devoted to reading all the time he could spare from his hours of regular labor. He soon made himself acquainted with the political history of his country, and the nature and character of those issues of governmental policy which divided public opinion. His reading and acquisition of knowledge did not stop there. He enlarged the scope of his information, and brightened and improved his intellectual powers, by a course of miscellaneous reading. Let any one read his speeches in Congress from and after 1843, when he was not more than thirty-five years old, and see how laborious and extensive his reading must have been in the course of a few years. It is really wonderful that any man could have acquired such a fund of information—such a correct and accurate knowledge of the idiom and grammatical structure of the English language by his own unaided efforts in so short a time. His speeches do not exhibit merely the strong and forcible thoughts of a vigorous mind expressed in rough and uncouth style, but they show a correct knowledge of the rules of grammar and the philosophy of language. There is a terseness, a directness, a vigor about his style not to be mistaken, and he frequently rises to eloquence of the highest order when treating of subjects on which he feels deeply.

But we are anticipating. With Andrew Johnson, as with all other men of a high order of native intellect, he felt and knew his latent powers. Let others say what they may about the modesty, the distrust, the diffidence of genius, we insist that there never yet was a man of high intellectual power that did not feel and understand the strivings and struggles of the divine principle within him. Genius may be distrustful and diffident, but it is not diffident and distrustful of itself. It often feels the agony of seeing itself neglected and scouted when deprived of the adventitious aids of wealth and friends and social position. It often feels wounded and sore at witnessing others, far less gifted intellectually and morally, elevated to honors and distinctions over its own head. Sometimes it shrinks back within itself, and despairing of ever being appreciated, it sinks down into imbecility, or rushes into dissipation and ruin. It is where native genius is allied to sound practical sense—where native intellect calls to its aid application and study—where a consciousness of mental vigor is allied to a confidence that a proper appreciation of worth and talent and virtue may be secured by perseverance and untiring labor—that great characters are formed, and great men developed, and great historic names are eliminated.

Andrew Johnson's life and character prove beyond controversy the truth of our position. To deny him genius of a high order, after reflecting on the mere *facts* to which we have alluded, would be absurd. As is almost uniformly the case with men of genius who have had to struggle with hardship in early life, he is a sensitive man, and therefore rather retiring than obtrusive in his character. In speaking of him as a sensitive man, we do not mean that kind of morbid sensibility which usually unfits a man for the practical duties of life, and which tends, if not counteracted, to sullenness and misanthropy. We mean simply that kind of sensibility which is another name for self-respect, and which always accompanies strong feelings and a warm heart. Andrew Johnson would be more than human if he could erase from his memory, and obliterate the impress of, the thousand reflections and associations of his past life arising from his struggles with adversity in his early days; the bitter opposition and persecution even that he has had to encounter in his political career; the denunciation, abuse, and vilification that have been poured out on his head by disunionists and conspirators in the last four years. Every man is to himself a microcosm—a little world. This little world is made up of the impressions, the thoughts, the feelings, the reflections, the experiences of his life. All and each of these stamp upon the character the impress of their own peculiar influences, without our being conscious how, when, or where the impression was made. It is from the crucible in which all these ingredients are commingled that *character* is elaborated.

Andrew Johnson was thrown on the wide world in early life without wealth, without education, without friends, among the great and influential, with nothing but his strong mind and physical vigor, and his own good name for industry, honesty, and sobriety to aid him in his outset on the journey of life. For some years the ascent of the hill of life must have been to him a difficult and toilsome task. But he was not appalled by the undertaking. As has been said before, his life affords a study for the contemplation of the philosopher and the statesman too. Let the mind dwell for a moment on Andrew Johnson in 1826 and the same Andrew Johnson in 1865. In 1826 he finally left the place of his nativity, turned his back upon the humble roof under which he was born, bade adieu to the grave of his father, whose death left him an orphan—and whose memory is more dear to him now, in his day of prosperity and power, because of his humble but honest life—took an affectionate leave of his more distant relatives and the companions of his youthful sports and amusements, and, with a swelling heart and eyes bedewed with tears, he started on his pilgrimage beyond the Blue Mountains of the West. He was then a youth, only seventeen or eighteen years of age. But the same self-reliance, the same energy of character, the same inflexible determination of purpose, which have since enabled him to triumph over so many obstacles, then braced his nerves and fortified his aching heart for the trials and hardships before him.

Contemplate the same Andrew Johnson now. Forty years after he left his birthplace, uncertain as to where the current of destiny would waft him, he now occupies a position the highest known under our Government, and surpassing, in point of honor and in the magnitude of the powers exercised under it, any throne, principality, or power among the nations of the earth. His accession to this position was not the mere result of accident, as might be urged by some. The influences which prevailed in his nomination for the Vice-Presidency on the ticket with Mr. Lincoln were with special reference to the contingency of Mr. Lincoln's death. The facts have been lately set forth in a publication in the "New York Herald" by one who was evidently a member of the nominating convention. The great State of New York agreed to yield her supposed preference for one of her own favorite sons in favor of Mr. Johnson. In fact, there was a peculiar identity in the position occupied by Mr. Johnson which could not be disregarded. His nomination seemed to be considered as a foregone conclusion—as a thing eminently proper to be done—as something that could scarcely be avoided. And it was done with special reference to the contingency of Mr. Lincoln's death. His nomination was a voluntary tribute of popular feeling throughout the whole country to the great and unrivalled services which Mr. Johnson had rendered to the cause of the Union. No such influences as usually prevail in such nominations operated in the nomination of Mr. Johnson. It was not done with the view or expectation of securing to the ticket the vote of Tennessee. That was known to be an impossible thing. No electioneering appliances were necessary to secure his nomination. It was his general, well-known popularity throughout the Union, together with the peculiar prominence of his position as that of the Hercules who had struck the hydra of Disunion such a deadly blow on its own soil and at its own home; it was this which caused public opinion to concentrate on him *with a rush*, as it were, as *the very man* that the country would need in case of Mr. Lincoln's death.

But to return. The reader has been asked to contemplate Andrew Johnson, when he left the place of his nativity about 1826, in contradistinction to his position in 1865. What must have been his reflections, when wending his weary way on his lonely journey westward, when passing the splendid mansions, and witnessing the gay equipages of the wealthy and the great, and then contrasted with them his own friendless condition? Not that he envied them the possession of wealth and affluence, which he did not possess. No, his soul was too big for that. But still how could he but reflect on the apparent whims and caprices of Fortune, which frequently enabled bloated ignorance and vicious arrogance to roll in wealth, surrounded with all the appliances that could minister to physical pleasures, whilst the son of genius, whose bosom was swelling with the impulses of an ennobling ambition for usefulness and fame, had no other home but the arch of heaven, no other fortune than what was contained in the small pack on his back! After crossing the Blue Mountains, the very sight of which is so well calculated to elevate the conceptions, and to enlarge and purify the sentiments, or looking around him, with an empty purse, for employment in his mechanical calling, looked upon probably with distrust, as an itinerant wayfarer, how dark and forbidding must have appeared the road of life which he had to tread! Yet he did not despair. He did not drown reflection in the bowl of intoxication; he did not fly from thought to the haunts of dissipation, as so many youths of genius have done. His own stern self-reliance, his own determination of purpose, his energy of character sustained him against all the trials of adversity.

A trial on the part of his first employers was all that was necessary to secure to him their confidence and regard. The conviction of his laborious habits, attention to duty, moral and upright deportment, truthfulness and reliability under any trust confided to him, afforded by the test of experience, were worth more to him than thousands of mere formal paper recommendations, so easily obtained, and usually of such little worth. In the humble but respectable calling which he followed, he soon exhibited the same determination to excel which has marked his career in every other relation of life. He was not satisfied with plodding along the dull and beaten track of mediocrity. He added to the respectability and usefulness of his calling as a laboring man, by his promptness, his urbanity, and politeness, his strict probity and undeviating attention to business. His advancement and progress, both socially and pecuniarily, were upward and onward all the time. Those who knew and observed Mr. Johnson whilst he pursued his mechanical calling as a tailor in Greeneville, Tennessee, concur in their statements as to his social habits and character. He always preserved his self-respect as a man and a gentleman, and he always exacted and commanded it from others. He never cringed to the high, the wealthy, and the great. At the same time he never indulged or exhibited any sullen, morose, or envious feelings toward those who were more fortunate than himself in the possession of wealth or of station. Whilst he never would brook any airs of superiority assumed by those who presumed on their wealth or high social position, he was ever kind, genial, and social toward them when they observed toward him the respect and consideration due to an equal and a gentleman.

Contemplate Mr. Johnson at a later period of his life, when, in the full vigor of manhood, his knowledge had been extended, and his information enlarged by reading and reflection. Behold him in his neat and comfortable but unpretending house in Greeneville, busily engaged in his daily labor, his wife attending to her domestic cares, and his children playing and prattling around him. These were the days of struggling conflict in his mind, between the cares and anxieties of domestic life, and the strivings of that consciousness of powers within him unappreciated by the world. What must have been his reflections when he saw honors and promotion heaped on others whom he knew to be immeasurably his inferiors? Or when occasionally giving a few hours of relaxation to a visit to the hustings, what must he have thought on his return homeward, of the political morals of the times, when he saw personal abuse and vilification resorted to in the place of argument; when he saw bickerings and wrangling instead of calm discussion of great principles, and the honest and unsophisticated masses of the people used by aspiring politicians as mere counters in playing the game of deception, instead of being regarded as rational beings, with minds to think and hearts to feel? Let the mind's eye follow him still further to the time when, unable any longer to resist the promptings of his own bosom, he resolved to take an active part in political affairs, and to " cast his bread upon the waters." Contemplate him when about to make his first speech. What must have been his anxiety of mind, between his aspirations to be useful in his day and generation, and his misgivings lest he should not be able to convey in suitable language the convictions which he felt so strongly? The great British orator, Erskine, in describing his sensations when making his first speech, in his first case at the bar, said he was at first alarmed by the sound of his own voice; but that he was assured with confidence as the idea occurred to him that he felt his little children pulling at the skirts of his garment, and saying to him, "Now, father, now is the time to give us bread." We may well imagine Andrew Johnson's sensations to have been very much of the same character when he first heard the sound of his own voice, in commencing his first speech. Probably his feelings were much more acute on the occasion than Erskine's were. Erskine, though poor, yet belonged to a great and noble family. He had had, in early life, the advantages of education and the highest social position. Johnson may not have imagined he heard his children reminding him of "bread," for his industry and economy had provided for that. But well might he have imagined he heard them reminding him that then was the time to lay the foundation of a reputation and fame far more to be prized by them than wealth, than lands and stocks, and flocks and herds. It can easily be imagined how many winks and witticisms were indulged in, at the idea that the tailor-boy, who had come there a few years before in search of employment in his calling, should now aspire to ventilate his lucubrations for the benefit of the public. It can also be further imagined how blank soon became the countenances of these witlings, and how brightened up the faces of the few friends who had never doubted, as soon as they perceived his clear and pointed and forcible style; heard him grappling with arguments, and, in a new and peculiar method of reasoning and illustration, elucidating questions which had become trite and threadbare. Mr. Johnson had bided his time, and in his first effort his friends had an earnest of success.

Again, in turning over the leaves of this pictorial book of human life, on one page behold the youthful wife, her face beaming with anxious pride, as she witnesses the rapid proficiency of her pupil, while she unfolds and explains to him the elements of learning. Behold the young husband snatching a few hours from the routine of his daily occupation, or at night, when the labors of the day are over, with face intent on the volume before him, receiving instruction or explanation of the rudiments of learning, from her who was to him not only the affectionate partner of his joys and sorrows, but his instructor and adviser in acquiring knowledge. Turn over another page and behold this same couple, no longer in their neat and comfortable, but unpretending home in Tennessee, but transferred to " the White House " in Washington! And what a transfer! A transfer from the peaceful and quiet joys of domestic happiness, to the busy, and exciting, and momentous cares of a nation's life. Behold this same wife, whom time has changed from the youthful bride to the staid and dignified matron. Behold her in meditation, as she moves through the gorgeous apartments of the extensive mansion—thinking of her distant and loved home in the bosom of the Tennessee mountains—reflecting on the vanity of earthly honors, compared with the joys and endearments of the domestic home and fireside—and yet her heart swelling with the pride of affection for him who has reached the pinnacle of earthly power, honor, and renown.

Behold him who was once the pupil spoken of, now, instead of poring over the elementary text-books, perusing grave State-papers affecting the destinies of his country— or treaties involving the relations of empires; or in his moments of relaxation from business, consulting the works of the master-minds of the world, upon the science of government, or the still more abstruse questions of national trade, commerce, etc. Andrew Johnson seems to have taken advice of the poet, in reference to his acquisition of learning, untoward and forbidding as were the auspices under which he commenced *to learn*. He did not stop at a " little learning," which the poet pronounces to be " dangerous," but his literary productions, his speeches, State-papers etc., show that he rested not till he had " drunk deep " at the Pierian fountain.

It is a well-established fact in the history of human nature, confirmed by observation in every one's experience, that a man exhibits the same traits of character in every relation of life in which he may be placed. If he is devoid of truth as a private man, no dependence can be placed on his promises and professions when he is elevated to high political station. If he is deceitful and dissembling in private life, he will prove to be a trickster and an intriguer as a public man. If he is indolent and lethargic in his own private affairs, he will neglect his public duties when intrusted with power. If he has been in the habit of cheating and defrauding his neighbors in small matters, he will pervert any official position he may hold to his own private ends and interests. If he is particularly selfish in his private relations, he will sacrifice the public good to his own personal wishes and feelings. If he is morose and churlish in his social habits, he will prove to be wanting in civility, courtesy, and politeness in the discharge of his public duties. If he is loose, reckless, and extravagant in the management of his own private affairs, he will exhibit the same disregard of the public interest in the performance of official duty. And so, in regard to the whole catalogue of vices and infirmities to which man is liable.

Let President Johnson be tried by all these tests; and he will pass through the alembic unscathed, and will come out like pure gold, leaving scarcely a trace of dross behind.

As to his high regard for, and uniform observance of truthfulness, he has ever been regarded as a striking example by those who have been brought in contact with him. And so in regard to his public life, and the discharge of his official duties. Whatever he says in reference to his views on any subject, no one ever questions. Wherever he announces his policy on any measure, everybody regards it as his fixed conviction and definitive conclusion. Whenever he promises any thing, no one doubts about the fulfilment of his word. This character for reliability, this strict adherence to his declarations and professions, are the result of that religious regard for truth which he has observed through life. Even during the most heated and exciting periods of party conflict in Tennessee, the opponents of Mr. Johnson, no matter whatever else they might say against him, never accused him of *falsehood* against his adversary. He never descended to the low habit, so common in heated party contests, of resorting to, nor of encouraging his friends to circulate false accusations and personal slanders against his competitor. He always relied upon the truth and strength of the principles he professed, and the measures he advocated ; and left to smaller men and to more ignoble characters the petty and contemptible calling of falsehood and slander. Truthfulness is a virtue which political life is not well calculated to foster and strengthen, and cannot be *acquired*, unless based on principle. It must, in order to its uniform and systematic observance, be the fruit of a tree planted in early life. It must depend on habits of training in youth, followed up by practical observance, until it becomes incorporated into the character, as a condition of its existence. Truth has ever been regarded by the great and the good of every age and country, and by the great Author and founders of the Christian creed, as the groundwork of moral duty. The saying of the Spartan king who declared that *truth* was the first thing a child should be taught to speak, has immortalized his name forever. "To speak the truth" was, by the ancient Persians, placed in the category of the manly pursuits of "shooting with the bow," and the "management of the horse," to be taught to the Persian youth. President Johnson's character for uncompromising devotion to truth, is one of the brightest legacies he can leave to his children, proud as they may be of him in other respects. He may be pointed to as a model for imitation to the rising generation—as an example of how the seeds of virtue sown in early life may ultimately produce a full and plentiful harvest—and as a striking instance that the uniform practice and cultivation of a high moral duty, although long unappreciated, yet in the end enjoys its reward in the approbation and esteem of a great and just people.

As to deceitfulness and dissembling—the second in the category of human infirmities adverted to by way of illustration—this is probably the last charge that his enemies would ever think of preferring against him. Those who knew him in boyhood, speak of the promptness, the positiveness, the candor, and open-heartedness of his nature and disposition. His opinions he never concealed; he never prevaricated in regard to his course. He has exhibited the same trait of character from that day to this. Whether as an apprentice-boy in Raleigh, or as conducting a business of his own in Tennessee—whether canvassing before the people, or as discussing some great question in the House of Representatives—whether in discharging the embarrassing duties of Provisional Governor of Tennessee, or of the still more responsible position of

President of the United States—candor and sincerity have marked his course. There is no double dealing in his conduct. There has ever been a directness, a straightforwardness about his course, that has left no one in doubt as to his position. We will venture to say that no one was ever deceived in Andrew Johnson, in the private relations of life, who once regarded him as a friend. His friendships, though slow in being formed, were sincere and lasting when once entertained. It is this confidence in his sincerity, and freedom from every thing like dissimulation, that causes his personal friends to feel such strong attachment for him. When a candidate before the people, in discussing great questions of national policy, he never tried to dodge the issues presented. He marched boldly up to his work, and debated questions on their true merits. He never resorted to those tricks of the demagogue, of trying to pervert and misrepresent the views of his opponent, but met his positions fairly and squarely. In the trying and embarrassing position as Provisional or Military Governor of Tennessee, no one was at a loss to understand him. His speeches, his proclamations, his State-papers, were not of the Janus-faced order. What he said he meant, and what he meant he said. It is his dislike of all equivocation and prevarication that now gives confidence to the people of the country, North and South. The public have faith in his sincerity. They do not fear that he will dissemble or cloak his opinions under any false or specious pretences, or that he will mislead them by any jargon of words. There has probably been no man in latter times who has filled so many high and distinguished positions, and who has been uniformly so successful, who has been so free from all the arts and appliances of trickery and intrigue. These political vices have been the bane of our country in modern days. They have distempered and corrupted the political morals of our people. Andrew Johnson never was an intriguer. It was the people, and not the politicians, who have promoted and elevated him. He never was an especial favorite of the politicians. His bold, open, and manly course on all questions has set at defiance the professional politicians. He never relied on their schemes and machinations, in order to obtain political promotion; nor have they been able to alienate from him the affections of the people. It is to be hoped the reign of political trickery and intrigue is at an end for eight years at least. The country needs reformation in this respect, and Andrew Johnson is the man to crush the head of this political viper.

How stands President Johnson in regard to the third in the list of infirmities alluded to? Have indolence and lethargy marked his private life, so as to excite any fears, in that regard, as to the performance of his public duties? By no means. The history of his life is a record of untiring industry and energy. His very appearance shows that he is endowed by Nature with great capacity for labor. Regular training and constant employment have strengthened and fortified his natural aptitude for work. It is doubtful whether there is any man in this country whose life has been one constant employment in labor, both physical and mental, more so than that of Andrew Johnson. Inured to labor from early boyhood, work has become the normal condition of his life. For many years he labored physically by day, and mentally by night. In Congress, instead of spending his time as a mere holiday, he took a lively and active interest in the great questions of the day. Whilst he participated in the debates on great and exciting questions, his ambition seems to have aimed at usefulness rather than display. In his political canvasses in Tennessee, his opponents can bear witness to his energy and perseverance, which have ever been important elements in his success. His labors as President of the United States are said to be Herculean. Feeling as he does the responsibility which rests upon him, knowing as he does that the hopes and expectations of the people are directed to him, appreciating as he does the vast, the unprecedented importance of the great questions involved in reorganizing and reconstructing the Union, and re-solved to do his duty at all hazards, there is such a multi-plicity of business requiring his attention, that it must tax his physical endurance to its utmost capacity. No ordina-ry frame, no lethargic mind could stand it. Fortunate it is for Mr. Johnson that a life of toil had inured him to such habits of labor; fortunate it is for the country that it has *such a man* for President at this juncture.

Can President Johnson pass the ordeal of the fourth case suggested? Was his reputation for fair dealing and honesty in private life such as to assure the pub lic that he will be free from selfishness, and will not administer the Government with a view to his personal benefit? On this score his friends can challenge for him the most searching investigation. Those who knew him as a boy, say he was a fair, honest, and generous youth; always ready to share with his companions any little deli-cacy he might have, and to incur his share of any self-sac-rifice that had to be met. Those who knew him in mid-dle life, bear testimony to the fact that he was a scrupu-lously honest man in all the transactions of life; that so far from being a sharper or a cheat in his ordinary deal-ings, he was generous and confiding in his intercourse with all; much more apt to be *imposed* on by, than to impose on others. If the position be correct, that the same man will exhibit the same character in private and in public life, then we have a guaranty in Mr. Johnson's past life that he will administer the high functions of his distinguished station, not with reference to selfish ends, but with an eye single to the public good. As has been already said, Mr. Johnson has never relied for support and for success on the professional politicians. He has relied on the people, and therefore we have cause to hope he will continue to study the interests of the people and the general interest of the whole country. The bestowal of office on unworthy men, and the prostitution of executive patronage to the attainment of selfish aims and objects, has been one of the causes of political demoralization in our country. This is admitted by all men, of all political shades and complexions. President Johnson knows the people have confidence in him. He knows, also, that the people have sagacity and judgment to perceive who are their true friends. As heretofore, he will not rely on the intrigues of cliques and factions for support and aid in the discharge of his onerous duties; but he will rely on the great body of the people to sustain him *against* any intrigue or factious opposition that disappointed, envious, or ambitious politicians may inaugurate against his administration.

It cannot be denied that the immense public debt incurred by the war, together with the constantly increasing expenditures of the Government, will require a most rigid economy, and the strictest supervision in the administration of our finances, for years to come. As the ocean is made of drops, so the sum total of our annual expenditure is made up of the thousands of small items that are charges on the Treasury. If it was our misfortune at this time that the Chief Executive of the United States was a man of reckless and extravagant character in regard to the expenditure of money—if he was a man careless as to the amount of our annual appropriations, and indifferent as to the means of the Government for meeting them—well might

we all feel alarmed as to the future, and in regard to the
financial crash which many wise and prudent men consider as not only probable but as inevitable. But Andrew
Johnson happens to be President. Judging from his conduct in past life, in the management of his own private affairs, we have an assurance that economy and frugality
will be observed, as far as his influence and power may prevail, in our public appropriations, and the way and man-
'ner in which the money is expended. The wants and ne-
cessities of early life taught Mr. Johnson the value of
money. The habits of his early and more mature manhood taught him the necessity of economy in his domestic
affairs. To his everlasting praise be it said, he managed
to support a large and growing family by his labor, and
to provide something for comforts (beyond which he never
aspired) and for the education of his children besides. He
never went in debt, except temporarily, and under circumstances where he saw the probability of meeting his
engagement when due. Extravagance beyond his means
he always avoided. He regulated his expenses according
to his income. In his domestic economy, as in the practical details of his mechanical pursuit, he " cut his garment
according to the cloth." Judging from the management
of his private affairs in his past life—his rigid economy,
his punctuality in meeting his engagements—the country
may feel assured, as it does feel assured, that President
Johnson will discourage every thing like extravagance in
our public expenditures, will repress plunder and peculation of the public funds, and husband all our resources,
with a view of extricating us from our present difficulties, to the utmost extent of his power.

CHAPTER XIV.

It is not very often that moral and physical bravery are eminently illustrated in the same individual. There are some men who will never surrender a principle—who would brave any danger, or incur any sacrifice, in the maintenance and defence of their convictions of duty—who would die the death of martyrs rather than abandon their views of duty—who are yet physically timid and unresisting. They would submit to a personal indignity, without resistance or complaint, whilst they would never compromise a sense of moral duty even under the rack or at the stake. Again, there are men who would brook personal hazard—who would endure any privation—who would confront death itself, in the resentment of a private grievance, upon a mere punctilio of personal honor—yet who cannot even hazard the odium of popular censure, and who shrink appalled at the responsibility of their course on public affairs before the tribunal of public opinion. Strange that it is so, but it is no more strange than true. President Johnson presents a striking instance where both these qualities are united in the same person. It is well understood throughout Tennessee—the theatre of his political conflicts —that he is a man of true personal courage. The best evidence he has given of it has been, not by being frequently engaged in quarrels and difficulties, but by keeping out of them. Slow to anger, and rather hard to arouse, he knows how to exercise forbearance rather than compromise his character for peacefulness. But when he discovers unmistakably a purpose to insult or browbeat him, his resentments are sudden and unequivocal. And yet, for mere quarrelling, for an indulgence in abusive language, he has no taste. When forced to meet a personal issue, he hurls his defiance in the language of bold and manly daring, and leaves his adversary to his own reflections. It is his well-understood character, in this respect, that has saved him from many a personal difficulty. A readiness *to fight* is not a character to be coveted or admired by the virtuous and the good. When possessed by man, it is possessed in common with the brutes. It is not in any such sense as this that allusion is made to Mr. Johnson's readiness to vindicate his self-respect when unjustly assailed. It is alluded to as that readiness to repel outrage and oppression which experience proves to be unavoidable in a public man—first, to secure himself against imposition from others, and secondly, to acquire and preserve the confidence and respect of the masses.

But it is especially in reference to his moral courage that Mr. Johnson's character excites pride and pleasure. This noble virtue of moral courage has been honored and celebrated by the great and good of all ages and countries as one of the noblest traits of human character. It is this which consoles the good man under affliction—which sustains the great man who has commanded success when under adverse fortune—which enables the conscientious man to brave the reproaches of public opinion rather than neglect the high behests of duty. It seems to be based on an innate conviction of the demands of truth and justice, and a firm reliance that a sacred regard for the moral obligations of life will ultimately obtain its reward in the consciousness of an honest discharge of duty, although it should fail to receive the plaudits of the multitude for the present or the approbation of posterity in the future. This virtue of moral bravery Mr. Johnson possesses in a most eminent degree. What we have said of the incidents of his past life proves this beyond controversy. There never was an occasion where a man was called on for the exercise of a greater degree of moral courage than by Andrew Johnson as Military Governor of Tennessee. Much as he loved the State which had so often and so highly honored him—indissolubly as he knew to be connected his own future fame and personal happiness with the fate of Tennessee—at a time too when the probabilities were that Tennessee would be forever detached from the Union with the other Southern States—yet he never wavered for a moment in regard to his course. At a time when the furor of secession swept over the South, prostrating whole States and communities, hundreds and thousands of the best Union men in the South became paralyzed, as it were, and gave up all as lost. But not so Andrew Johnson. Whilst others quailed before the storm and lost their self-possession, he kept cool and composed. He stood as firm and unshaken as a sea-girt rock, defying the floods of abuse and the tempests of faction. He would not follow his State in her reckless course, and he would not desert her. He resolved to remain with her, and save her if possible, even at the most extreme personal hazard. He appealed to, and rallied under his country's flag, the mountain-boys that had so often cheered him onward to triumph and to fame.

Owing mainly to his exertions, as will be admitted by all, Tennessee was the first of the recreant States that was won back to the national arms, not however until her soil had been drenched in blood, from Memphis to Chattanooga.

Mr. Johnson, from the first, planted himself on the position that Tennessee had never been out of the Union—that all the wiles of disunionists and secessionists could not get her out. He could not fail to see, however, that, owing to the operation of the disunion movement in her borders, her position was an anomalous one; that in regard to her social internal condition, during the year or two that a disunion *régime* had borne sway, a disintegration of her political and social elements had taken place; and the difficulty was, how to readjust and reaccommodate her to the new state of affairs. Here, again, Mr. Johnson's coolness, firmness, and self-possession did not desert him. He had no precedents to guide him; he had to find his way to the object of his pursuit through darkness and difficulty. He was resolved to restore the normal relations between the State and the General Government as soon as possible. Neither the Constitution nor statute had provided for any such contingency. A great outcry was raised against him about usurping unconstitutional and unauthorized powers. But he felt that the saving the Constitution was a much more important matter than the *manner* of saving it. He brushed away at once the cobwebs and technicalities of the letter in order to save the spirit of the Constitution. Like the old lawyer, Maynard, at the great English Revolution of 1688, he took the ground that questions affecting the highest interests of the commonwealth were not to be decided by verbal cavils and by scraps of law French and law Latin. Macaulay informs us that on the bill declaring the convention (which had been elected on the mere *invitation* of the Prince of Orange, without the issuing any royal writ for the purpose) to be a Parliament, great excitement and clamor were indulged in. While some members were insisting on a rigid adherence to ancient forms and customs, and others were quoting black-letter precedents for guidance, Maynard, the greatest lawyer of his time, arose, and scornfully thrust aside as frivolous and out of place all that black-letter learning which some men, far less versed in such matters than himself, had introduced into the discussion.

"We are," he said, "this day out of the beaten path; if, therefore, we are determined to move only in that path, we cannot move at all. A man in a revolution, resolving to do nothing which is not strictly according to established form, resembles a man who has lost himself in the wilderness, and who stands crying, 'Where is the king's highway? I will walk nowhere but on the King's highway.' In a wilderness, a man should take the track which will carry him home. In a revolution, we must have recourse to the highest law, the safety of the State."

Maynard's practical common-sense view was adopted, and thus was the great English Revolution of 1688 consummated, and the rights and liberties of the citizen placed on an impregnable basis. This was done, not by adhering to ancient forms, but by disregarding them. Governor Johnson found himself in the same situation, when trying to inaugurate and install a loyal State Government in Tennessee. He is beset with the same difficulties in his efforts to reaccommodate all the seceding States, *as members of the Union*, to the status in which the war left them. It requires no ordinary amount of moral courage to face the clamor and misrepresentation, and in many instances the honest misconception entertained toward him, in the accomplishment of his work. But yet he knows that duty requires it, and he shrinks not from its performance. He has a great and commendable work to accomplish, and he is sometimes compelled to disregard old landmarks, under the pressure of *necessity*. True, *necessity* is the "tyrant's plea," as well as the plea of the practical and conscientious man, who finds himself environed with difficulties, without precedents to guide or experience to confirm him. Therefore all arguments founded on "necessity," should be closely weighed and strictly examined. Time, and it will require no long time either, is all that is necessary to vindicate President Johnson's course. Let those who, from one section, condemn him for going too far, and let those who, from another section, blame him for not going far enough, let them wait awhile, until the practical working of his system shall have tested its wisdom. This is all he asks, or his friends ask for him. They are willing to risk his reputation on the developments of the future, and the calm and unbiased judgment, a just and appreciative people may pass on his course as a whole. President Johnson's policy is the result of *a system* elaborated and matured in his own mind. His course should not be hastily judged from isolated and detached acts. No man is entirely free from error. It is the general tenor of his life which stamps the character of every man for goodness as an upright and moral man, or for patriotism as a lover of his country. Without some degree of charity and forbearance, on the part of his fellow-men, for error of judgment and human infirmity, who can pass the ordeal of a criticism that judges and condemns according to the standard of perfection? One thing is certain: President Johnson will not be *driven* from his course by outcry and clamor. Whilst ever willing to listen to the advice of friends, and to respect and pay due regard to the calm and reflective appeals of public opinion, yet he never can be shaken in his purposes, or deterred from following the path of duty, by the intrigues of the factious or the denunciations of the envious.

There is, perhaps, no State in the Union where party spirit has been more fierce and unsparing, and where party contests have been marked by more personal bitterness, than Tennessee. Their political conflicts have usually been marked by personal rancor and denunciation. Many instances have occurred in Mr. Johnson's political canvasses, where he has been warned and threatened that he would not be allowed to speak at certain times and places, or if he did speak, that he would not be allowed to indulge in the same train of remarks he had used on other specified occasions. But Andrew Johnson never quailed before such notifications as these. He never failed to meet his appointments, unless indisposition or the elements rendered it impossible. Whenever he ascended the stand, and calmly surveyed the crowd, his eye sparkling from subdued excitement, and his lips compressed with struggling emotion, his friends looked up with a confident assurance that their champion would that day bear away the laurel-wreath, whilst his political enemies felt that they were again destined to gnaw the file of disappointment.

When Andrew Johnson first directed his attention to political affairs, and began to feel an interest in the result of party contests, he decided in favor of the Democratic party, and continued to be an earnest, active, and unwavering Democrat down to the time of the disruption of the Democratic party, by the breaking up of the Charleston Convention in 1856. His democracy is peculiar in its character. It is necessary that his speeches, messages, proclamations, etc., should be carefully read and studied, in order to a proper appreciation and understanding of his democracy. He is not merely a Democrat in the ordinary *party* sense of the term. His democracy does not consist in a blind and bigoted devotion to the dogmas and measures of policy of the democratic creed, but to the philosophy of democratic principles, as constituting the groundwork of republican institutions. It cannot be fairly denied that the Democratic party is the only *positive representative* * party (except, perhaps, the old Federal party) which has existed in our country. The other parties, the Whig, the National Republican, the American, etc., have been parties of *negation*, of opposition to what

---

* The author here begs leave to explain, lest he may be misunderstood. In speaking of democracy and the democratic element in our institutions, he does not mean to speak of it as expounded in party creeds, or embodied in democratic organizations, as such, by name. By no means. In the shiftings and mutations of parties, in order to the attainment of temporary triumph, it has frequently happened that rival parties occupy positions not only in regard to governmental policy, but to fundamental principles, the very reverse of those suggested by their party names. And in such cases the names belonging to one party or the other, through the appliances of party machinery and confidence in their leaders, are led to do things directly in opposition to their professions and party designation. Hence it was that in the long and fierce conflicts between the Democratic and Whig parties in times past, the Democratic party was sometimes found contending for measures in direct contravention of pure democratic principles, and in support of official prerogative and power, whilst the Whig party was found maintaining the former and resisting the latter. Still, it was in the name of democracy and of democratic principles, that the Democratic party was so long able to sustain themselves in power. And on those occasions on which the Whig party succeeded in electing a President, they triumphed by appealing to the people, in the name of the great democratic element which pervades our institutions, and by persuading the masses that the Democratic party had deserted and proven false to the faith of the Democratic fathers. The meaning of the author is, that, *in the main*, the parties opposed to the Democratic party were parties of *negation*—of opposition to the maladministration of those in power. Parties in opposition have frequently occupied a *positive* position, and contended for *positive* and practical results, yet it has been only by appealing to the great democratic sentiment, and arousing the great democratic heart of the nation, that they have ever been able to oust the Democratic party from power. The author has felt called on to make this explanation, lest he might be considered as endorsing and sustaining the Democratic party as it existed heretofore, whilst, so far as this memoir is concerned, he ignores all *party*, both past and present.

they regarded as the corruptions and excesses of democracy. Hence it is, when occasionally triumphing over the Democratic party, they have accomplished their mission, and have usually become disintegrated, having no vital positiveness of character to sustain them. Not so with the Democratic party. It was the embodied representative of the popular element in its organization, its progress, and development under our system of government. It was this philosophy of democracy, consisting of the ever-living principle of guarding the rights and privileges *of the people* against encroachment from every quarter, that Andrew Johnson has been the active and zealous champion of, all his days. The mere party cries of the day, the mere issues of " banks," " tariffs," " internal improvements," etc., were of small moment with him, compared to the rights of the people under the Constitution, and the uncompromising defence and support of those rights when threatened. Every thing tending to special prerogative and exclusive privilege to a class, or to a corporate few, has always found in him a stern opponent.

Mr. Johnson has been charged with being a demagogue by those who have felt the force of his popular eloquence, and were unable to combat it. But in this regard he has been treated unjustly. The term " demagogue " in its true generic sense (a leader of the *populace*, as contradistinguished from the *people*) cannot be fairly applied to one whose theatre of operations has been among a rural people and a virtuous community, as was the case with Mr. Johnson. It is admitted that he is a great stickler for the rights of the masses. He has ever been popular with them, and they regard him as their friend. He has ever been ready to sound the approach of danger to their rights and their interests, and to warn them in time of the schemes of those who were preparing to injure them. But if a public man's opinions are to be judged of by his recorded speeches and productions, then may Mr. Johnson defy the taunts of the malignant in this regard. In his appeals to the people—in his defence of the rights of the people, he speaks of " *the people* " as the great mass of the community, of every position and relation, politically and socially. He does not mean a class; nor does he mean the poor and the ignorant exclusively, where they might happen to constitute a majority. When he contends for the rights of the people, by *the people* he means the great mass composing the body politic ; when he warns them against encroachment on their rights, he means encroachment, not on the part of the wealthy and intelligent classes, as unjustly insinuated by some, but he means to warn them against any and all, even of and among themselves, who may attempt by unfair legislation, or intrigue and deception in the administration of the law, to obtain special privileges for themselves at the neglect or sacrifice of popular rights.

It is not to be wondered at that Andrew Johnson should feel a strong attachment and regard for that great middle class, so to speak, which constitutes the large majority of our population. From that class he sprang ; from it his early friendships and associations were formed ; by it he has been promoted and honored. He knows—what is an unquestioned fact—that in that is to be found more of sincerity, honesty, purity, hospitality, unselfish patriotism, in fact of nearly all the manly virtues, than in any other class. No one has studied more closely, or more thoroughly comprehends the peculiar traits, the wishes, the sympathies of the great mass of the people, than Mr. Johnson. This constitutes one of the principal elements of his success with them, when a candidate for any station whatever. The people have most thorough confidence in him—in his sincerity, his political honesty, his great regard for popular rights. They regard him as one of themselves. Hence it is they are ever ready to resent any injury done him, as a wrong offered to themselves; and they feel that, in honoring and elevating him, they are simply doing justice to themselves. There probably never was a stronger attachment, a more unreserved confidence, existing between representative and constituent, than that between Mr. Johnson and the people of his district, when he represented them in Congress; or than that between him and the great mass of his constituency, when he was Governor of Tennessee. There was something morally beautiful in the relations of confidence and esteem existing between them; in the cordial greeting with which they always met him when he returned among them; and in the proud confidence with which they always spoke of him as *their* representative or *their* Governor. The appellation of " Andy," which they applied to him, was a term of endearment rather than of familiarity.

Mr. Johnson has been unjustly charged by some as being a cold, heartless man. There never was a greater mistake. The world is so apt, however, to be mistaken in this regard, that it is not so much to be wondered at that Mr. Johnson's character should be misconceived as to the trait of character alluded to. How often it happens, in almost every one's experience, that those whom we once looked on as cold and callous, have been found, on knowing them well, to have warm and ardent temperaments, and tender and feeling hearts! In fact, does it not accord with our experience, that those whom we have found to be the most generous and confiding, those whom we have come to regard as our most trusty and devoted friends, we first considered as being distant, cold, and destitute of heart? It may be that those who do not know Mr. Johnson well, may consider him a cold and unfeeling man. As has been already said of him, he is not a man of forward and demonstrative character. Friendships, personal attachments, esteem and respect for private worth, are governed by the same laws that pervade the moral and physical world alike. When of quick growth and suddenly contracted, they are apt to be short-lived in their duration. When of slow growth, and based on convictions that bear the tests of time and the trials of adversity, they are likely to endure to the end. Ask any one who ever regarded Andrew Johnson as his friend, if the latter ever capriciously deserted or neglected him in his day of adversity. He will reply, Never. Ask those who know him well, if they ever saw him turn a cold, deaf ear to the appeals of distress, or if they ever saw him look with a careless and unfeeling eye on a picture of suffering and sorrow. They will tell you, Never. So far from it, they will assure you that sympathy for the sorrows of others is a prominent trait of his character. They will tell you that the enlarged benevolence of his nature does not vent itself in mere declamatory professions, but in acts, and deeds, and efforts to relieve the sorrows of others, to the extent of his power. It has been related to the author by one who knows Mr. Johnson well, and who has observed much of his course under trying and embarrassing circumstances, that he has know him when Governor of Tennessee to refuse pardon to those who had been convicted of capital and other heavy offences, again and again; that he has known him on such occasions to stand firm and unmoved by the appeals of friends and the entreaties of written petitions, on the ground that, as a general rule, he was opposed to the interposition of executive clemency where, after a fair trial, a man was convicted by the unbiased judgment of twelve unprejudiced men. Yet, says our informant, in cases where the wife, or daughter, or mother of such culprit has suddenly and unexpectedly gained access to his person, and has beset him, amid tears and sobs, for the pardon of the convict, he has known Mr. Johnson to yield to such appeals, as if urged by a power he could not resist, to quickly snatch up a pen, sign the pardon, and seek relief from his feelings by pacing up and down the room. Can such a man as that have any other than a tender and feeling heart—a man so stern, so unyielding in every thing involving a discharge of official duty, and yet touched, overcome at the sight of a wife or mother in tears and affliction on account of those they loved?

There is one point of view in which Andrew Johnson's character has passed the ordeal of *trial*, in such a way as to secure for it the impress of true greatness. It strikes forcibly all who have observed him, that his elevation to the summit of power and of honor has wrought no change in his character or his bearing. He is the same plain, unpretending, unaffected man he has always been. There is in his manner an entire absence of that bloated importance, that false and affected dignity, which are so apt to spoil many men suddenly elevated to high station, who may even be rightly disposed and well-meaning in other respects. He wears his honors with a meekness and quiet native dignity, which shows he fully appreciates the influences which prevailed in his elevation. He seems to thoroughly understand his position. He knows that he was placed in power with a view to benefit the public interests, and to subserve the public good; and not for the mere purpose of gratifying private ambition or ministering to private pride. To be sure, there is honor conferred, the highest conceivable honor in being elected to such a position; but the honor consists in *being thought* worthy of and able to discharge such responsible duties, and in filling such an honorable station.   This Mr. Johnson seems to fully comprehend.   He labors incessantly.   So arduous are his labors that he has left scarcely any time to devote to the social relations of life.   Kind and affable to his friends, civil and polite to strangers, he seems to forget the eminence of his station in his anxiety to do justice to all.   Those who seek his presence go away with the conviction that his chief employment is the public service, his chief aim the public welfare.   Of course, like other men, he has his personal friends, who are admitted to a closer degree of confidence than others are ; but he has no back-stairs approach to his presence ; no cabal or clique who monopolize his favors or his counsels ; no train-band of retainers who are to cater to his wishes in hunting up enemies to punish, or friends to reward.

There is another peculiarity in Mr. Johnson which strikes forcibly all who come in contact with him, and which must be regarded as a most admirable trait in a man invested with great executive and administrative functions. He leaves no one at a loss to understand his meaning and his purposes on any given subject.   He speaks in no Delphic oracles.   He talks directly and to the point.   He evidently does not believe in the saying attributed to Richelieu, that the great usefulness of language consists in enabling us to conceal our thoughts.   He has not one set of opinions for one section of the country, and another set of opinions for another section, as has so often been the case with the aspiring politicians of our country.   It is doubtful whether there has been any American statesman, in the last fifty years at least, whose opinions have been more clearly and unmistakably understood than Andrew Johnson's.   His judgment may or may not be correct, his views may or may not be popular ; but one thing is certain, there will never be any mistake as to what his decision or opinions may be on any given question. He always expresses them so boldly, clearly, and unequivocally, that politicians cannot distort or pervert them in such a way as to mislead the popular mind. This proceeds not only from the innate honesty and sincerity of his nature, which abhors dissimulation, but from his entire confidence in the people. His candid and undisguised course is not only the result of *principle*, but honesty he regards as the best *policy*, in order to insure permanent success, whether in private or public life.

In conversation Mr. Johnson never affects brilliancy. He never in social intercourse attempts to lead, and still less to monopolize conversation. He is a good listener; and yet he is fond of intellectual, lively, and instructive conversation. When conversing on subjects on which he entertains strong and decided convictions, he warms up; and on such occasions strikes every one with his forcible, decided, and ardent style. It has been said that he rarely indulges in hilarity. The general tone and cast of his character seems to incline to seriousness. His countenance when at rest denotes deep thought. This is no doubt the result of the incidents and associations of his past life. So much of his early life was passed in reflection in " providing for his own household," at the time that he was preparing himself by study and observation for usefulness in the public service, that reflection and contemplation seem to have become the natural habits of his life. And yet it is said by those who know him most intimately, that when, in the hours of relaxation from the cares and duties of his station, he abandons himself to recreation, he is bright and joyous, playful and amusing with his children, and minute in his attention to his domestic pursuits.

There never was a more striking example offered of an

enlarged benevolence, a freedom from all unkind feelings for past differences of opinion, and fitness and capacity for statesmanship in rallying all good and true men under the same conservative flag, than that now exhibited by Mr. Johnson. Although a man of decidedly strong party proclivities in past times, yet he ignores all past differences of opinion growing out of party affiliations, in the bestowal of official patronage, and in the selection of his political advisers in his present laborious efforts to readjust and reconstruct the relations between the North and the South, between the States and the General Government. Although a Democrat of the straitest sect of the Jackson school in former days, he now neither knows nor cares what may have been a man's party affiliations or political status in the past, provided he is now *right* on the great absorbing question of the times. He regards all the political issues of times gone by as merged in the important effort to restore and preserve the Union in its integrity and purity. He considers mere issues of governmental *policy*, when contrasted with the salvation of the Government itself, as bubbles floating on the surface, compared to the great deep on which the ark of our national unity and glory is riding in safety. It is a well-authenticated fact that, though always opposed to Mr. Clay's policy, yet he pays a high compliment to the old line Henry Clay Whigs by expressing his willingness to trust them, upon the ground that generally they are good and true Union men. In the bestowal of pardons under his amnesty proclamation, he is equally magnanimous. With the exception probably of the "original secessionists," whom he regards—and rightfully, too—as sympathizing and affiliating with the organized conspiracy to destroy the Union, he is disposed to extend his clemency and forbearance to all those who under the *duress of necessity* were driven to follow their States in their wild and mad course toward disunion, provided they had been good Union men before, and regretted a state of things they were unable to resist. For the " original secessionists "—those who had systematically labored to bring about disunion, who had resisted all attempts to inaugurate measures for peace, and who had clamorously denounced every man who talked in favor of stopping the war, and who had by threats and vilification kept up a reign of terror in the South—for that class of men, Andrew Johnson cannot be supposed to have much sympathy in their sufferings, nor much indulgence for their political sins. They are the ones who have brought ruin and devastation on their country, who have draped almost every household in mourning, and caused so many hearts to bleed for the fate of the slain. Let these men carry out their boastful threats, to die rather than to submit to Northern domination, by making martyrs of themselves now that they have brought themselves and their country to a state of humiliation compared to which their situation before the war was the brightness of Elysium compared to the darkness of Hades. Would it be surprising if Mr. Johnson were found willing to leave these men, or the most prominent part of them at least, to that martyrdom for which they professed themselves to be prepared, rather than longer submit to the only practical grievance of which they could complain, viz., that a runaway negro occasionally escaped from one of the northern border slave States. It is certain if these men are willing, in their applications for pardon, to abide by the conditions laid down in Pope's " Universal Prayer "—

> "That mercy I to others show,
> That mercy show to me "—

then their chance for pardon will be slim indeed. They showed no mercy to those who warned them of the consequences of their folly. Those who said they were unwilling to fight against a Union they loved, were replied to by "conscription" acts; those who complained of disunion as an evil they were unwilling to encounter, were answered with "repeals of the *habeas corpus*," "impressments," "tithing acts," etc.

Mr. Johnson's peculiar aptitude, at the present time, for the position he occupies, is his *moderation*. Not that moderation, as supposed by some, consists in a want of firmness and decision. The contrary is rather the case. Ultraism on any question is usually the result of temper or of passion. With a right-minded and a right-hearted man, moderation is generally superinduced by reflection and calm consideration. No man, acting under the influence of temper or the impulses of passion, is calculated to mature and carry out great measures of public policy which are to endure for ages. It will not be denied that a four years' war, one of the most bloody on record, and waged with an unsparing ferocity on both sides, which it is sad to dwell on, has left a great amount of ill-feeling and resentment with both parties, which it will require years to finally obliterate. It must also be admitted that it is the interest of both parties, constituting as they do integral portions of one great country, that the recollection of past injuries should give way to kind feelings, and that for angry resentments and sectional animosities should be substituted a brotherhood of common interests and common historical associations. The sooner this takes place the better for both separately, the better for the honor, prosperity, and happiness of the nation as a whole, and the better for the cause of free government throughout the world. Very much depends upon who wields the chief executive power of the Government as to when and how this desirable state of things is to be consummated. Inasmuch as the present

is an anomalous state of things, without precedent to guide
—where the Constitution has, from very necessity, *to be bent*,
as it were, to prevent its being broken—where the interests, the opinions, the feelings, the prejudices even, of
both sections should be duly weighed and considered—
where new questions are likely to be constantly arising,
growing out of the complications of the times—it must
strike every one how vastly important it is that the President should be a man of great vigor of mind, of unshaken
firmness, of unswerving justice, of patience, of forbearance, of *moderation*. Fortunately for the country, it may
be claimed for Mr. Johnson that he comes as near, or
nearer, to this standard of fitness as any other man in the
country.

Born and reared in the South, his social sympathies and
associations must strongly attach him to that region. It
contains the ashes of his parents. There the destiny of his
children has been cast, and there they will probably live
and die. There he was born and reared. There was the
theatre of his early struggles against poverty, and of his
triumph over adverse fortune. The people of the South
had honored and elevated him. There he expects to return
and make his home and find a grave, when wearied " with
the storms of State " he may seek repose for the evening
of his days in the quiet and peaceful pursuits of domestic
life. How, then, can any Southern man distrust him, as not
having kindly feelings for the Southern people, as not
being ready and willing to do them ample justice ?

On the other hand, can any reasonable and reflecting
Northern man suspect him of an unwillingness to do
justice to the views and feelings of the Northern people ?
Such an insinuation, after the sacrifices he has made,
would be not only injustice, but ingratitude. In the late
bloody issue between the two sections, from a sense of duty

he united his destiny with the North, or rather with the General Government, which consisted almost exclusively of the Northern element. He encountered obloquy, defamation, proscription, on the part of his own section, and placed at hazard his life even, if success had attended the Southern arms. Northern people did him the honor to place him in a position through which he constitutionally fills his present exalted station. By Northern votes he was elected. Can it therefore be supposed, for a moment, that he is insensible of the honor and confidence reposed in him by the people of the North, or that he is likely to disregard their wishes or their views of policy? Has he not shown a sensitive respect for the feelings of the North in retaining, as his confidential advisers, the Cabinet of Mr. Lincoln? Has he not proven that he has not the least consideration or compromise for Southern disunionists and secessionists, by adding five additional classes to those who seek the benefit of the amnesty proclamation, in addition to the eight classes enumerated in Mr. Lincoln's proclamation? Does he not, in this, show a determination to thoroughly sift the chaff from the wheat in the reorganization of the Government, which ought to be satisfactory to the most ultra Northern man?

It is very probable—in fact, the evidences of it are already beginning to appear—that Andrew Johnson will not suit the extreme men of either section. Those at the South who wish to see the authors and agents of the disunion movement placed on the same footing with those who resisted it in the readjustment of our difficulties, will probably denounce him as a heartless tyrant, who is disposed to obliterate the last vestige of the rights of the States. Those at the North who wish to see the Southern States reduced to mere territorial appendages, thus confounding the innocent and the loyal with the wicked and rebellious, and who wish to see another " bloody assizes " inaugurated, where some brutal Jeffreys may satiate his thirst for slaughter, may denounce Mr. Johnson as a faithless renegade who has sympathy and compassion for Southern traitors. All this only proves his peculiar fitness for the office which he fills. There is something of the moral sublime in the attitude of a man who, making *duty* his polar star, stands firm and unshaken like a mighty breakwater resisting the storms and tides of faction and violence from the one side or the other, and whose only reply to their denunciation and injustice is, that he is determined to save them, and their country *for* them, even against themselves.

So far as are concerned the old party issues before the war, based on differences of opinion as to the proper policy to be observed in the administration of the Government, they are gone forever. They have been buried in the graves of those who fell in the contest during the late carnival of blood.

CHAPTER XV.

It must be readily seen and admitted, on all hands,
that President Johnson has a troublesome and laborious
task before him.   His way is beset with difficulties of no
ordinary magnitude.   The onerous duties of his station
require a combination of qualities and of virtues that
rarely fall to the lot of one and the same man.   Talent of
the highest order will be necessary in grappling with the
many new issues likely to be developed by the new order
of things.   Patriotism of the most enlarged national
character will be requisite in nicely balancing the conflicting opinions and jarring views of policy in the two sections.   Firmness of the most unbending nature will be
called for in resisting the importunities of the violent, the
earnest entreaties of the unfortunate, the schemes of the
selfish, and the clamors of the censorious.   The most pa-
tient and untiring labor will be indispensable in performing
the duties which will be forced on the Executive by the
complications of the times.   The most rigid virtue and
most scrupulous honesty will be demanded in the selection

of proper agents to administer the Government in its new relations, and in the management of those immense financial resources compared with which the wealth of Crœsus sinks into insignificance. Added to these, will be needed a vast fund of *common sense* and of sound *practical* judgment in adapting his action to the variety of circumstances under which he may be called on to exercise his functions. He cannot lay down any iron rule, any Medo-Persian law, for his guidance, except so far as a conformity to the abstract principles of truth and justice are concerned. Neither can he cut himself loose from, and disregard entirely, all rule and system in his administrative policy. Plutarch, in his life of Solon, lays it down that " our judgment of actions should be formed according to the respective times and postures of affairs. An able politician, to manage all for the best, varies his conduct as the present occasion requires; often quits a part to save the whole: and by yielding in small matters, secures advantages in those of greater moment."

It has been said that old party issues are dead. So they are. As to whether we shall have a revenue tariff or a protective tariff—and if for protection, whether that shall be direct or incidental—is a question not likely to be mooted for the next generation. Our enormous debt creates such a demand for money, that a revenue tariff *now* must be sufficiently protective to answer the wishes of the most ultra advocates of protection. As to whether one national bank or the sub-treasury system is preferable, that may be regarded as an obsolete question since we have several hundred " national banks " in operation. As to land distribution, by common consent the lands are wanted for other purposes. As to the improvement of harbors and rivers, we shall hear no more of States or representatives refusing to receive appropriations for their respective sections on the ground of unconstitutionality or State pride forbidding it.

But issues of greater moment, and far more exciting in their character, are now being mooted—not involving the system of governmental policy to be pursued under the Government, after the proper relations are adjusted, and the conflicting views harmonized between the two sections, but involving the very questions of *how* these very questions *are to be* adjusted—*how* these conflicting views are to be harmonized.   The first question which presented itself— which met Mr. Johnson at the threshold—was this : What is the *status*, what the relations, occupied by the seceding States toward the National Government ?   Were they ever out of the Union, or have they all the time remained *in* the Union ?   The adoption of a decided position on that question was necessary, on Mr. Johnson's part, as a rule for his governance in the exercise of his official functions toward restoring the normal relations of the two sections, and between the seceding States and the General Government.   He could not avoid a decision of the question, for upon that decision depended the course of action he would be called on to adopt.   He decided—or rather he persisted in the opinion which he had maintained from the first—that the States had never been out of the Union. In this decision he was clearly right, and it must be regarded as a very fortunate thing for both sections and for the Government, as a whole, that he did make that decision.

Under the Constitution of the United States, formed and adopted by representatives of the people of all the States, the laws of the General Government act directly on the citizen—not in his character as a citizen of the State, but in his character of a citizen of the United States. This relation can be changed only by peaceable agreement among the parties, in the mode pointed out in the instrument, or forcibly by arms. An assemblage of delegates calling itself a "convention" in a State, may, by resolution or "ordinance," say such State is out of the Union, but that does not make it so. The General Government, in the enforcement of its acts, looks only to the Constitution, which declares itself and all laws and treaties passed in pursuance thereof, to be "*the supreme law of the land.*" It therefore looks to the citizen only in case of resistance to the execution of the laws, it ignores all causes or motives inducing or sanctioning such resistance. That was the *rationale* of Mr. Lincoln's call for troops, and of the marching of armies to the South. It was not to "coerce States," as absurdly charged by some, but it was to remove the obstruction offered by individuals to the execution of the laws. It was not the adoption of the Declaration of Independence in 1776, that effected the separation of the colonies from the British crown. It was the making good that declaration by force of arms. Suppose the colonies, instead of succeeding, had been reduced to subjection ; would they not have been remanded to their original status as it was before the war began? Would they not have been entitled to claim all the privileges to which they were entitled under the British constitution and laws before the struggle commenced? Those who contend that the ordinances of secession took the States out of the Union, *proprio vigore*, yield the whole question as to the constitutionality or legality of secession. If an ordinance of secession can take a State out of the Union, then of course the laws of the Union are no longer operative in that State; and the waging of war against such State could not be defended on the ground of enforcing the laws. It could be defended only on the ground of *punishing* such State for an unwillingness to longer remain under the same Government, with the coercing power. The argument seems to be un-answerable. If the passing an ordinance of secession by a State really operates to effect secession, it must be because there is nothing in the Constitution of the United States to forbid it. That would convert the Government into a mere league that may be terminated at the mere will and pleasure of the parties to it. Here extremes meet. The ultra-radical element in the North and the extreme "State-rights" element in the South concur in the opinion that the States that passed ordinances of secession, are out of the pale of the Union. The former are forced to occupy that ground, in order to secure a stand-point from which they may gratify a feeling of vengeance. To do so, they must first deprive the offending States of all protection under the Constitution. The latter occupy the same ground, either from the delusion that first hurried them into their wicked crusade against the Union, or because *they* wish to secure a stand-point from which they may contend that, not having been in the Union, they are not amenable to the law of treason under it. Although both are equally wrong in their conclusions, yet there is more of consistency and plausibility in the course of the latter than of the former. For, if the seceding States have been out of the Union, their people are no more amenable to the laws of the Union, no more subject to punishment for their violation, than if they lived in France or Spain.

In what an awkward position do those who contend that the seceding States are out of the Union, place Mr. Johnson! How could he represent Tennessee in the Congress of the United States, if Tennessee was out of the Union? Mr. Johnson was, at the time of his nomination, had been for nearly forty years, and still is, a citizen of Tennessee. How could he have been nominated and elected constitutionally, if he was a foreigner? For a foreigner to the United States he must have been, if Tennessee was not in the Union. Is it to be supposed for a moment that Mr. Johnson will stultify, disfranchise, denationalize himself, by admitting that Tennessee, by any mere dictum of a body of her citizens assembled, could discharge him from his allegiance to the Union? Can it be supposed, after all the sacrifices he has made, and the obloquy he has submitted to for four long years, on account of his filial reverence and devotion to the Union, that he will now yield this invaluable birthright—his patrimony in this inheritance of national honor and glory? This he would do, by admitting that for four years he has been an *outsider*—that he was allowed to hold a seat in the Senate, and complimented with the nomination for the Vice-Presidency, by a sort of strained perversion of the Constitution.

It has been said it was a fortunate thing for the South that Mr. Johnson had taken the position he has done on this question. And so it is. If the insurgent States have been out of the Union, on the restoration of peace they have no right under it, they are not under the protecting ægis of the Constitution. Their only hope on being conquered, or surrendering at discretion without the stipulation of any conditions in a treaty of peace, was in the clemency of the conqueror. They are in the condition of every people or nation who, having submitted a dispute to the arbitrament of the sword, were finally subjugated and compelled to yield without terms. They can claim no rights but the rights of humanity, and magnanimity to a fallen foe. This would leave the Southern States at the mercy of the conquerors. Their condition would be much more unfortunate than that of the weakest State in Europe under similar circumstances. For in Europe there is among the ruling Powers a jealousy of national safety, and of self-protection, which preserves a " balance of power " a sort of undefinable moral force, which will not allow one Power to conquer and absorb another that is weaker, except at the hazard of a war with all the Powers combined. On the North American continent there is no such "balance of power." One colossal power—the United States—in its relations to other Governments and nations, knows no restraint upon its will but its own discretion. No Power or combination of Powers in other regions of the globe will dare gainsay its wishes or the exercise of its authority on this continent.

But if it be true, as assumed by Mr. Johnson, that the seceding States have never been out of the Union, then they are entitled to all the guaranties of the Constitution. If members of the Union, as States at all, they *must*, according to the express provision of the Constitution, possess and enjoy all the rights, privileges, immunities, and advantages of the other States. In arranging their systems of internal domestic policy, they are subject to no other inhibitions than those to be found in the Constitution. The other States, in no matter how large a majority, cannot impinge upon their rights in this regard, without at the same time subjecting themselves to the same conditions. The idea which has been already advanced in certain quarters, but which it is to be hoped does not prevail except to a very limited extent, viz., that of holding the conquered States as colonial dependencies under military sway, is likely to meet with an insuperable obstacle in President Johnson's firmness and decision of character. The unconstitutionality of such a course has been commented on. But even if there were no constitutional difficulty, on the score of policy such a course would be very objectionable. It would be in direct contravention of all those professions of devotion for, and appeals in favor of the Union and the flag, by which the national heart was warmed up, and which sent hundreds of thousands from the North to encounter the perils of war. Their graves are scattered from Gettysburg to the Rio Grande ; and it would be desecrating their memories to pervert the noble object of "*restoring* the Union," for which they fell, into the gratification of sectional hatred and vengeance. Those who fought for the flag, fought for the preservation of it in its entirety, and not for the purpose of obliterating twelve stars from its galaxy. President Johnson considers himself —and very properly so—President of the *whole* United States. A sense of self-respect, as well as of public duty, will not allow him to see any portion of that area over which his official functions extend, converted from a fertile field into a barren desert.

It has been said it was fortunate for the North, too, that Mr. Johnson entertains the views which he does on this subject. This is easy of demonstration. The sooner the Southern States are restored to their original position in the Union, the sooner will their industrial resources be developed, and an impetus given to enterprise and improvement. The sooner military rule gives way to civil law, and the Southern States are left to the entire and exclusive management of their own internal affairs, and to a free and equal participation in the national councils, the sooner will despondency give way to hope, and the people wake up to an appreciation of their true condition, and adapt themselves to the circumstances by which they are surrounded. The sooner harmony and good feeling are restored between the two sections, the sooner will the products of the South seek the markets of the North ; the sooner will manufacturers of foreign imports of the North find a market in the South. The pursuits of the South being almost exclusively agricultural, of course the manufacturers of the North find it greatly to their interest to preserve such an extensive and profitable market. The shipping and commercial interests of the North must be greatly interested in the carrying-trade both ways, not only between the North and the South, but between this country and the markets of the world. The capitalists and other moneyed interests of the North are deeply interested in promoting the prosperity and developing the resources of the South. It is mainly by the exportation of Southern products that the foreign importations in our country are paid for; thus equalizing the balance of trade, and preventing the exportation of specie from our country.

Perhaps it may be said that this will continue to be the case, as heretofore, no matter what *status* may be enforced on the Southern States. By no means. Is it to be supposed that the Southern people are so unlike the balance of mankind, that they will not feel the sting of what they would regard as an indignity put on them, not because of its necessity, but merely to gratify a feeling of vindictiveness? True, they are thoroughly subdued, so far as further physical resistance is concerned; but it is not reasonable to suppose that they are so free from the impulses of human nature as not to resist the indignity in the only way in their power. In the first place, their spirits would be so crushed, that industry and energy would make but slow progress for years and years to come. They would feel but little concern for a country in whose honor, prosperity, and glory they had no share, or in a Government which they felt only through its power and oppression. Men who feel that they are free, prosperous, and happy citizens of a free, prosperous, and happy country, can *work* with a will and an alacrity unknown to those who constantly feel the gallings of the yoke of bondage, even if the promptings of want and of self-interest should stimulate to labor, and the substitution of white for black labor should, as predicted by some, vastly increase the wealth and power of the Southern States—may we not suppose, that looking on the people of the North as their oppressors, they would avoid all possible contact with them, and encourage a direct trade between their own ports and foreign markets? Interest and sound policy would suggest such a system of direct trade, anyhow. If getting rid of slavery is likely to arouse the Southern people to an appreciation of their best interests, is it the part of wisdom for the North to discourage instead of fostering that system of commercial intercourse under which both sections have heretofore prospered? It certainly behooves the North, not only from a spirit of magnanimity, but through the dictates of policy, to do nothing now to exasperate the people of the South, merely to gratify feelings of unkindness, and to exult insultingly over a fallen foe.

It is important and necessary to the interests of the entire country in a *national* point of view, that harmony should be restored between the two sections as soon as possible. The Scripture maxim of a "house divided against itself" is as applicable in the national and political as in the private and moral world. The only rivalry that should exist among the different parts of the same country is, which can do most in advancing the common interest, power, and prosperity of the whole. This must be the result, no matter how intent each part may be in pursuing its own interest, provided it abstains from all interference or encroachment upon the rights and privileges of the other parts. President Johnson's *nationality* of character is likely to prove a great blessing to his country. It proves him to be *the* man, of all others, for the requirements of the times—the man of destiny, as it were. He has seen enough of strife—not only of the strife of arms, but the strife of words and of feelings. He wishes to see his country not only prosperous and powerful, but united and happy.

There is another question which is beginning to be mooted, and which, from the outgivings of the newspaper press, it is to be feared may become an element in the formation of new parties. The question alluded to is that of suffrage by the emancipated blacks. This subject is unwisely and prematurely thrust forward as an element of mischief, calculated to mar the prospects of an amicable arrangement of past differences, and to keep alive unpleasant associations. Heaven knows we had enough of the negro for the last four years. The South went to war on the abstract theory of slavery in the Territories, and like the dog in the fable, by clutching at the shadow lost the substance. The great mass of the Southern people have made up their minds to abide the issue. They are willing to leave the solving of the problem, in its details, to the operation of time. But the sudden introduction of the question of the political status of the freedmen can do no good, and it may do much harm. Neither the Northern nor the Southern mind has sufficiently quieted down from its effervescent condition, to take a calm and fair view of the subject. Let the white race of the South have time to acquiesce gracefully in the loss of such an immense amount of property. Let the black race have time to adjust themselves to the great change already taken place in their condition. And let the people of the North be content for the present with their victory and their triumph. As to whether it may be advisable for the Southern States hereafter to extend the privilege of voting to the colored race, when they shall have become sufficiently enlightened and improved to appreciate the importance of civil and political rights, that is another question. It is a question on which it is not deemed proper now to express any opinion. As to the merits of the question, in the abstract, whether the Southern States should extend to the blacks the right of suffrage, Mr. Johnson has not committed himself, by expressing an opinion one way or the other. In this he exhibits his usual sagacity and statesmanship. He says it is a question for the States themselves. In this he is clearly right, and his well-known firmness affords the best guaranty that neither frowns nor threats, neither coaxing nor censure, can drive him from his position. As to exacting from the Southern people that they shall conform to the result of the issue tendered by themselves, those who know any thing of his character know that he will not falter. But as to requiring from some States conditions not imposed on all of them, in that is involved a principle of official duty which he cannot ignore or disregard—a principle of constitutional law which appeals to his judgment, and of simple fair play and justice, which appeals to his feelings as a man. And where *duty* is concerned, Andrew Johnson is not to be found swerving in the hour of trial.

There must be too much conservatism, too high a sense of justice among the people of the North, to attempt to *enforce* on the Southern States a change in their constitutions, so as to provide for the black race to vote in elections. Upon what ground can such an argument be based? It is true the doctrine of "State-rights" has been perverted to such wicked purposes as to cast odium and ridicule upon the very name. But still *there is* such a thing. It is not to be found in the constitutions of the States, nor in the crotchets of Southern politicians. It is to be found in the Constitution of the United States. That Constitution recognizes a perfect equality of political rights among all the States. It goes further. It expressly recognizes the rights of the States to regulate the qualification for suffrage within their borders, by making the right to vote for President depend upon the State regulation as to the qualification to vote for a member of the lower house of the Legislature in such State. The case is so plain, that there is no ground for argument. To state the proposition to any one who has ever read the Constitution, is to prove it. An argument in favor of the General Government imposing on the States the constitutional qualification for suffrage within their borders, would be an argument in favor of violating the Constitution. As that argument would necessarily have to be based on the propriety or impracticability of disregarding the obligations of an oath, that being a question of ethics, would be out of place here.

Connecticut has lately voted on the question of extending the right of suffrage to her colored men, through a change in her constitution. Are not the people of Connecticut willing that Tennessee should have the same right of deciding that question for herself that she (Connecticut) has lately exercised? Just think of it, that Virginia, that surrendered the vast Northwest Territory, out of which so many great and flourishing States have been formed, and that, too, on the condition that slavery should be forever excluded therefrom, should now be told by Ohio, Indiana, Illinois, etc. (her own children), " 'Tis true we do not allow black men to vote in our States, but as for you, you must allow it, and you *shall* allow it, otherwise you shall remain in a territorial condition, and not come into the Union at all!" The gallant and magnanimous people of the Northwest will never be guilty of such political impiety and injustice as this.

It does not require any very extraordinary amount of sagacity to perceive why this question has been thus inopportunely introduced, and is being agitated at this time. No one can be imposed on by the pretence that it originates in a feeling of kindness for the negro. If it grew out of a feeling of charity of that kind, that charity would "begin at home" in an effort to make the provision apply to all the States. Besides, if the black man should be entitled to vote, he should be entitled to be voted for. And here is the secret of the movement. The votes of the colored race are not wanted for their operation *at home*, but with reference to their influence elsewhere. The movement is a political one—the ends aimed at are political. If Mr. Johnson had taken ground in favor of imposing on the Southern States this provision in their constitutions in favor of negro suffrage, it is doubtful whether we should have heard of the agitation of the question in the quarter from whence it comes. No Northern man can suspect Mr. Johnson of having any sympathies or affiliations with slavery as it formerly prevailed. So far from it, he was among the very first to proclaim that slavery had brought on the war. And at a time when many Northern politicians, who now oppose Mr. Johnson's policy, evaded the question, or touched it very gingerly, he took a decided stand in favor of holding the South up to the consequences of the issue they had provoked.

CHAPTER XVI.

THERE is one question on which, to a superficial observer who had not taken the pains to inform himself of the facts, President Johnson's course might appear somewhat inconsistent and vacillating. The question alluded to is that of slavery. A thorough investigation of his course on this subject will show that he has been governed by the same high regard for *principle* which has actuated him throughout his life. During his entire Congressional career of fourteen years, he was the ardent, earnest, bold, and consistent advocate of the constitutional rights of the Southern people and the Southern States to their slave property. No man in the South had more uniformly and more ably and energetically battled for the rights and interests of the South on this subject than he had. As long as the institution of slavery involved the rights of property, under the protection of the Constitu tion and subordinate to it, he sustained and defended it. Those mischievous agitators at the North who advocated disunion as a means of disconnecting themselves with slavery, met with no favor from him. His denunciations of them were unsparing. As long as he could do so, consistently with his loyalty to the Constitution and the Union, he maintained the rights of the Southern people to their slave property. He heartily coöperated with the efforts of the true friends of the Union in the "Peace Congress" of March, 1861, in trying to harmonize the two sections. Even after the war had commenced, as heretofore explained, he introduced a resolution declaring the war should be waged for the preservation of the Union only, and should be confined to that result. But when every effort at peace and conciliation had been made, and had failed—when he saw that the disunionists had made the institution of slavery the instrument for combating and destroying the Union—when he saw the issue fairly joined, and that either the Union or slavery must yield in the struggle—he did not hesitate. He gave up slavery to the fate which the disunionists had brought upon it. It was just as he had predicted. He had again and again warned the people, and their representatives, of the South, that in their mad attempts to sever the Union they would destroy slavery. He had also warned them that he would not unite with them in their fight for slavery outside the Union —that its only protection was under the guaranties of the Constitution—and that, whenever they threw away this shield of protection, slavery as an institution must perish. So that Mr. Johnson did not deceive or mislead any one. So far from it, he had most unequivocally declared, on many occasions, that he intended to adhere to the Constitution and the Union at all hazards.

Mr. Johnson had been an attentive observer of the political movements of the times. He saw that the secession operations of the Southern States were the consummation of a fixed purpose and of a deep-laid conspiracy to destroy the Union, that had been organized for thirty years. A brief review of the acts and doings of the conspirators, from 1831 to 1861, clearly establishes this charge.

The nullification ordinance of South Carolina, in 1832, although passed under a pretended unwillingness to destroy the Union, was arranged with a special view to that result. The public mind in that State had been educated to believe that nullification was a peaceful remedy under the Constitution—that under its operation the people of that State would be rid of an odious and oppressive law, without incurring the danger of war. Her leading men knew—they could not help knowing—that General Jackson would resort to *force* in executing the laws, and that thereby, as they supposed, the other Southern States would, from the sympathy of a common interest and a common locality, take part with her in case of a conflict. From the demonstrations of public sentiment in these other Southern States, however, the leaders in South Carolina saw plainly that they would not take part with her, but would leave her to her fate. Then it was that South Carolina backed down from her position of nullification under the fortunate pretext of the tariff compromise of 1832. It has been perfectly apparent to the whole country, from that day to this, that South Carolina was discontented, moody, and churlish. The speeches of her prominent men teemed with the most glowing accounts of what the South would be as an independent country, separated from· the North—that the interests of the two sections were diverse and conflicting—that the South was oppressed and impoverished by the connection—and dwelling upon its prosperity, wealth, and future greatness, if allowed to develop her resources freed from the depressing influences of the Union.

Shortly after the nullification movement commenced in 1832, a new system of political ethics, on the question of slavery, began to be agitated throughout the South. The doctrine of the early fathers of the Republic, concurred in by nearly all the leading statesmen of the South, had been that slavery, as a mere institution considered in the abstract, had been an evil to the white race, wherever it existed. Washington, and all the early Presidents, had taken this view of the subject, and had spoken hopefully of a time in the future when the Southern States would, of their own accord, make provision for the discontinuance of slavery. Here was the true, the strong, the impregnable basis, on which to have rested the institution—viz., that slavery was an existent fact, entailed on the present generation by the cupidity, first of British, and afterwards of Northern commercial enterprise ; that the Southern people were not to blame for it—that it was their misfortune, but not their fault. Slavery had ever presented difficulty and trouble to Southern statesmen. They had, scarcely without an exception, admitted its evils, and regretted its existence. The framers of the Constitution of the United States had had to grapple with the difficulty ; and in fixing the relations between the General Government and the States on this subject, they probably placed slavery on the most secure and satisfactory basis possible under the circumstances. The framers of the Constitution of the United States left slavery where they found it—as a local institution, to be regulated by the local law where it existed ; and if an evil, an evil to be remedied and modified by the white race among whom it prevailed. Down to 1832, the public sentiment of the whole country, North and South, sustained the true constitutional and conservative view of the question of slavery. The people of the North, with a few very inconsiderable exceptions, were for leaving the South undisturbed on the subject, where slavery existed by the local law. The people of the South, with equally few exceptions, simply asked to be let alone and to be allowed to deal with what they admitted to be an evil to them, without asking or wishing to extend the institution of slavery among any other people who did not desire it, or where the laws of Nature would not carry it. After the abortive attempt at nullification in 1832, the leaders and agitators, who had been foiled in that movement, started the idea of " uniting the South," as they termed it. Knowing the sensitiveness of the Southern people on the subject of slavery—that although they regarded slavery as an evil to themselves, yet they would brook no interference with it where it existed, by those who had no concern with it—they concluded to raise the " cry " of slavery agitation. They allowed a handful of crazy fanatics at the North to force them into a false position. They met the issue tendered them by Garrison and his few co-laborers, who insisted that slavery was a great social, moral, and political evil, by taking the opposite ground that it was a moral, social, and political blessing.

Here was the origin of slavery propagandism, on the part of the ultra men of the South. Having assumed the position that slavery was a blessing, they easily persuaded themselves into the belief that it was their duty to extend it wherever it could be forced, not only because it was right of itself, but for the purpose of gaining additional political strength for its maintenance and support. The authors and leaders of the nullification movement had indignantly disclaimed all idea or purpose of disunion, although it would seem that every rational man must have perceived that nullification, to be effective, must have led either to disunion or civil war. But with the sentiment of slavery propagandism marched that of disunion, side by side. From the position that slavery was a blessing, was rapidly developed the idea that a confederation of slaveholding States exclusively would be the very perfection of all government. For years this idea was promulgated by a portion of the Southern press, and the ultra men in Congress from the South. The happiness, prosperity, wealth, and greatness of the South were dwelt upon and depicted in the most glowing colors, as certain in the future, in case that section could be disconnected from the North, and be left to develop its powers and resources by itself, and in accordance with its own system of policy. For years these ideas made but slow progress among the masses of the Southern people. Love of the Union was a deep-seated sentiment in their minds and hearts. But the leaders made up in zeal, ability, concert of action, and determination of purpose for what they lacked through paucity of numbers. Although public opinion was sound and conservative, it offered no open resistance to the agitators. Men rarely interpose any practical opposition to the spread of heretical and false ideas, as long as they themselves are not directly injured thereby. Then, again, the fear of denunciation, the dread of being charged with a want of fealty to the South, deterred thousands from making open resistance to the spread of slavery propagandist disunion sentiments. They remained quiescent, rather than enter into a conflict with the self-constituted organs of public opinion. Thus it was that nine-tenths of the Southern people were opposed to the repeal of the Missouri Compromise, and the attempt to force slavery on the people of Kansas against their wishes, and yet they remained quiet, and acquiesced, rather than incur the charge of disloyalty to their section, on the part of the agitators, few as these latter were, comparatively, in numbers.

The South committed a great error, proved woefully blind to its own interests, when it allowed a few active zealots, who claimed to be the organs of public opinion, to tender the issue that slavery was a blessing to the white race among whom it existed, and to fight the battle from that stand-point. The position was an erroneous one, and could not stand the test of argument and investigation. Slavery never was a blessing to the white race; instead thereof, it was an evil. The advancement and propagation of this idea did violence to the feelings of the Northern people. It drove off or neutralized thousands of the strongest and staunchest friends and defenders which the South had theretofore had in the North. The South was secure in all its rights under the Constitution, and in that sense of justice prevailing throughout the civilized world, which recognized the Southern people as not responsible for the existence of slavery among them; and if an evil, an evil for which they alone could provide the remedy in their own way and at their own time. The right policy of the South was a defensive policy. As long as it acted on that policy, it was safe and secure. But when it changed that policy and adopted an aggressive one, it lost the prestige of its invincibility. It strengthened its enemies, and it weakened and discouraged its friends at the North. The course pursued by the Southern people on this subject of slavery was like that of a general who, with an army far inferior in numbers to that of his adversary, yet has it posted behind intrenchments that are impregnable, but who, instead of remaining on the defensive, voluntarily leaves his strong position, for the purpose of attacking the enemy from a weak and indefensible point, where he is cut off and destroyed by overwhelming odds. The cause which the Southern people put forward as a pretext for disunion (the election of Mr. Lincoln), was the result of their own aggressive policy. But for the repeal of the Missouri Compromise and the effort to force the Lecompton Constitution on the people of Kansas, Mr. Lincoln would never have been elected President. The Southern people were warned again and again of the dreadful consequences that would result from the attempt to dissolve the Union. They were warned and entreated, not only by their friends and sympathizers in the North, but by many of the truest and most patriotic of their own sons, and by none more earnestly and pathetically than by Andrew Johnson. Mr. Johnson cannot be charged with having deceived or misled any one. Whilst his previous record shows that he had ever been a most earnest and zealous advocate of the rights of the South, he had always declared that he would fight the battle nowhere but in the Union, and under the Constitution. He had often said in Congress, that slavery could not be preserved in the South, except in the Union, and under the guaranties of the Constitution. And he had often given notice that when the suicidal attempt should be made, to resort to a dissolution of the Union, as a means of maintaining slavery, he should be found battling for the preservation of the Union.

After the failure of the nullification movement in 1832, there commenced being held a series of " Commercial Conventions " at different points in the South, Montgomery, Richmond, Charleston, Memphis, etc., the pretended object of which was to advance the commercial interests and develop the commercial resources of the South. It so happened that the South Carolina politicians generally took the lead in these conventions. But no one could be at a loss to understand their real purpose, who read the speeches made, and the resolutions passed, and the comments of the press, advocating these assemblages. The destruction of Southern commerce, and the depression of the pecuniary interests of the South, growing out of the monopolizing extortions of the North, constituted the leading idea in their proceedings. The evident design was to indoctrinate the public mind of the South with feelings of dislike to the Union, and to prepare it for a separation from the North. Still the leaders did not dare to openly avow their purposes; and the people, seeing that no practical good resulted from these " Commercial Conventions," they died out.

Soon after the failure of the nullification project, Mr. Calhoun made that celebrated remark, " that the tariff having failed to unite the South, the question of slavery was the only one left by which the entire South could be united." That was the secret of the great unanimity which prevailed in South Carolina. It was the only State in the Union where no party divisions existed. All party organizations were merged in the paramount organization against the Union. The orators and presses of South Carolina, seconded by those in other States who affiliated with them, commenced their concerted plan of slavery agitation, and holding forth " *secession* " as the great sovereign remedy for the grievances under which the South labored. This slavery agitation went on, increasing in intensity year after year. In 1856 Fremont obtained a very large vote for the Presidency, Buchanan having received so small a majority over him as to warrant the belief that if the canvass had lasted a month longer, he (Fremont) would have been elected. The secessionists then thought their time had come. They made their preparations accordingly for carrying out their long-cherished project of dissolving the Union. They held a convention in Nashville, Tennessee, which enunciated the strongest disunion sentiments. But the disunionists were divided as to the manner of proceeding. Some were in favor of immediate independent State action; others were known as " coöperationists," being those who were in favor of all the Southern States (or the " Cotton States " at least) going out together. But public opinion in the cotton States even was not yet prepared for disunion, either by "coöperation" or by separate State action. As for the latter, South Carolina declared against it in a special election of members of a convention, ordered with a view to consider of the propriety of secession. South Carolina and her co-workers in the other States having failed to "precipitate the cotton States into revolution," there was a lull for a while. Mr. Buchanan was President. The secessionists bent all their efforts toward securing the selection of a cabinet favorable to their views, and of enlisting the Administration in the support of a series of measures favorable to the furtherance of their projects. They saw how the Northern mind had been maddened and provoked in the heavy vote cast for Fremont, and the sudden rise and great strength of the "Republican" party, in consequence of the slavery propagandist policy of the secessionists and disunionists. The great object was to obtain a *pretext* for disunion—to get an excuse for doing what was predetermined on. They saw that their principal difficulty lay in the strength and moral power of the Democratic party. They saw that the Democratic party was the only organization of a national character which had been strong enough to resist the disruptive force of slavery agitation. They had arranged for having the nominating convention of that party, to be held in 1860, to meet in Charleston, South Carolina, an inconvenient point, that as much outside pressure as possible might be brought to bear upon it.

It met there accordingly, under ominous signs and outgivings of dissension and failure. The secession presses and politicians had anticipated its action with predictions of discord, and threats as to the result, unless they could obtain such guaranties for slavery as they required. They saw plainly that Douglas was the only candidate spoken of who could unite a majority in favor of his nomination. True, Douglas was objectionable to the conservative Union men of the Democratic party, because of his agency in repealing the Missouri Compromise; but yet, from a desire for peace and harmony and the safety of the Union, they were willing to compromise on him. His connection with the Missouri Compromise repeal was no objection with the secessionists. In fact, he had supported that measure with a view of conciliating them. But yet they would not sustain his nomination, because they knew that, if nominated, his election would follow, and thus the pretext for disunion would be lost to them. After a protracted session of wrangling and squabbling— the breach widening every day—the convention adjourned, to meet at a future day in Baltimore. On meeting at the latter place, the final rupture of the Democratic party was consummated. Those who recollect the events and tone of feeling of that day, well remember the strange and anomalous state of things that then prevailed. The secession presses were jubilant with joy. They predicted the defeat of the Democratic party; they predicted the election of the "Republican" candidate. They expressed their delight at the conviction that the South would thus be united, and that it would never submit to the election of a sectional candidate, forced on them by sectional votes and influences. On the other hand, the true friends of the Union were filled with sadness and dismay; strange to say, those of them belonging to the old Whig party were pained and distressed at the disruption of the Democratic party. Much as they had differed with that party on questions of governmental policy, they yet believed as long as the integrity of that party was preserved that the Union was safe. The result of the election is well known. Mr. Lincoln was elected by the electoral college, though by a minority of 200,000 votes in the Northern States, his popular vote being that much less than the combined vote of Douglas and Bell and Breckinridge. And taking the entire vote of the whole Union, including the Southern States, Mr. Lincoln was in a minority of nearly a million of votes. The disunionists, therefore, could not complain that the people of the country, not even of the North, had, in the election of Mr. Lincoln, shown any fixed purpose of interfering with their constitutional rights of property in the institution of slavery. In looking at the political complexion of the two houses of Congress, it was evident the South had nothing to fear of any encroachments on their rights. Taking in the estimate the entire Southern members, the Republican party was in a minority in the House of Representatives, leaving the election of Speaker and the appointment of the committees under the control of the Opposition. In the Senate, by the same estimate, Mr. Lincoln was in a minority of six votes, thus leaving the confirmation of all executive appointments, the ratification of treaties, and the control of legislation, in the hands of the Opposition. The same was the case with the Judiciary. The Dred Scott decision had shown the temper and feeling of the Supreme Court, clearly indicating that that tribunal was ultra Southern in its views, and stood ready to arrest the execution of any law that might involve an interference with the constitutional rights or privileges of the Southern people. Mr. Lincoln himself, in divers declarations before his election, and in his inaugural speech, declared his fixed purpose not to encroach upon the rights of the South, but to observe strict justice and a spirit of conciliation toward all sections alike. He had been fully committed for years against any interference by the General Government with slavery in the States where it existed. Every department of the Government was virtually pledged against any disturbance of slavery in the States. In all the Territories, the status of slavery had been fixed by the Kansas-Nebraska Act, leaving it to the people to decide the question of slavery for themselves, on making their constitutions, preparatory to their admission into the Union as States; so that slavery never was better protected, and all points of interference with it better guarded against, than at the time of Mr. Lincoln's election.

But with the secessionists and disunionists all this availed nothing, as " Mordecai sat at the king's gate." Mr. Lincoln was elected President. His election had been in great measure procured by the very men who now urged it as a pretext for destroying the Union. And yet how was the news of his election received at the South ? One would have supposed that those who regarded his election as a great misfortune to the Southern people, as foreboding calamity and usurpation of unwarranted power, would have received the news with sorrow and sadness. Such was not the case with the organized disunionists. In Charleston, South Carolina, and at other points which had been for years hot-beds of secession, the news of the Republican triumph was greeted with open demonstrations of rejoicing. It was the consummation of a purpose for which they had schemed and plotted. It precipitated the crisis they had been long laboring to bring about. True, there was a large class in the South, the great majority in fact, who did receive the news with misgiving and dread. That was the true loyal Union men. Not that they were alarmed at the idea of any serious encroachment on their rights on the part of Mr. Lincoln. They knew that he stood pledged against any interference with the rights of the Southern slave property. They knew that in Congress and in the Supreme Court there was a majority ready to interpose against any disturbance of their constitutional rights on that subject. But they knew further that the disunion and secession element in the South was thoroughly organized; that it was strong and powerful, and fatally bent on mischief. They dreaded the consequences. No better evidence can be afforded of the feelings and sentiments of any class of men at a period of agitation and excitement, than the declarations of the representative men, and presses that are their organs, of such class. They generally follow, and reflect, the views of the class they belong to, instead of leading them. By way of showing that it was the predetermined purpose of a certain class of men at the South to destroy the Union, without reference to any danger to slavery, or of any postive grievance under which the South labored, reference is here made to some of the surface-indications (to use the language of the miners) contemporary with the secession ordinances of the winter of 1860–'61. Governor Gist, in his message to the Legislature of South Carolina in 1860, said :

" All hope of concerted action by a Southern Convention being lost, there is but one course left for South Carolina to pursue, consistent with her honor, interest, and safety; and that is, to look neither to the right nor the left, but go straight forward to the consummation of her purpose. It is too late to receive propositions for a conference, and the State would be wanting in self-respect, after having deliberately decided on her own course, to entertain any proposition looking to a continuance of the present Union."

Let it be recollected that this message was written before Mr. Lincoln was inaugurated—before his cabinet was announced. Therefore he could not have then attempted any encroachment of which complaint could be made; and he speaks of secession as the " consummation of her *purpose*." It is evident that no sort of concession or compromise could have satisfied him; for he says the States would be wanting in self-respect to entertain *any* proposition looking to a continuance of the Union.

About the same time, Mr. Keitt, in a speech in Columbia, said:

"South Carolina, single and alone, was bound to go out of this accursed Union. Mr. Buchanan was pledged to secession, and he meant to hold him to it. Take your destinies in your own hands, and shatter this accursed Union. South Carolina could do it alone. But if she could not, she could at least throw her arms around the pillars of the Constitution, and involve all the States in a common ruin."

The account goes on to say that Mr. Keitt was greatly applauded throughout his address, which proves that the sentiments of the audience were in accord with those of the speaker. Here, then, we see that at the capital of South Carolina, the prevailing sentiment was "rule or ruin"— that the determination of that people was either to force the other Southern States to go with them, or to drag them all down to one common destruction.

In the South Carolina Convention, in December, 1860, Mr. Gregg said:

"If we undertake to set forth all the causes, do we not dishonor the memory of the statesmen of South Carolina, now departed, who commenced forty years ago a war against the tariff and against internal improvements, saying nothing against the United States Bank and other measures which may now be regarded as obsolete?"

Mr. Rhett said:

"The secession of South Carolina is not an event of a day. It is not any thing produced by Mr. Lincoln's election, or by the non-execution of the fugitive slave law. It has been a matter which has been gathering head for thirty years."

About the same time the Augusta (Georgia) "Chronicle

and Sentinel," in a labored editorial, and the " Columbus (Georgia) Times " in a communication, took ground that not only the Union, but our republican system of government, had proven a failure; and intimating that our only recourse was to a monarchy. The "Montgomery Daily Advertiser" said:

"Has it been a precipitate revolution? It has not. With coolness and deliberation, the subject has been thought of for forty years; for ten years it has been the all-absorbing theme in political circles. From Maine to Mexico, all the different phases and forms of the question have been presented to the people, until nothing else was thought of, nothing else spoken of, and nothing else taught in many of the political schools."

The pretence was put forward by disunionists at the South, that the Southern States resorted to secession because the propositions of the " Peace Conference " and the Crittenden Compromise afterwards having failed to receive the sanction of Congress, they saw they were to be left to the mercy of a " Black Republican " majority. Now let us examine into the fallacy of this pretext. South Carolina did not send her Senators to Congress in December, 1860, at all. Instead of going on to aid in defending the rights of the South, and in procuring a peaceful compromise of the pending troubles, the South Carolina Senators stayed at home, knowing as they well did that the secession of that State was already determined on, and which, in fact, took place only two or three weeks later. So that, so far as South Carolina is concerned, she is estopped from urging any such excuse as the failure by Congress to pass any thing looking to the further guaranty of Southern rights. But Congress proceeded to act, nevertheless. A proposition passed the Senate by an almost unanimous vote (only three or four voting against it) to so amend the Constitution as to forever prohibit any interference by Congress with slavery in the

States. It had previously passed the House of Representatives by the requisite two-thirds majority. Mr. Crittenden had offered his compromise, the passage of which would no doubt have arrested secession in the other States, by taking from them all decent pretext for disunion. It was well known that the moral effect upon the public mind would have been so great that the conspirators would have been unable to carry the people with them. When this compromise of Mr. Crittenden was under consideration, Mr. Clark, of New Hampshire, offered an amendment, calculated to embarrass and in fact to destroy the force and efficacy of the proposition. On a vote taken a few moments before, fifty-five Senators had voted, showing there was that number present in the hall. On the vote on the Clark amendment, there were only 48 Senators voting—the vote standing yeas 25, nays 23. Six Senators sat in their seats and refused to vote ; and thus the Crittenden Compromise was lost. Those refusing to vote were Messrs. Benjamin and Slidell of Louisiana, Messrs. Hemphill and Wigfall of Texas, Mr. Iverson of Georgia, and Mr. Johnson of Arkansas. President Johnson, then a member of the Senate, who had a seat near Mr. Benjamin, said to him : "Mr. Benjamin, why do you not vote ? Why not save this proposition, and see if we cannot bring the country to it ?" Mr. Benjamin replied abruptly, saying he "would control his own action without consulting him (Mr. Johnson) or anybody else." Mr. Johnson rejoined with some feeling—"Vote, and show yourself an honest man." Here, six Southern Senators refused to vote, when they could have defeated the Clark amendment, and saved the Crittenden Compromise by four majority, if they had voted.

At a later period, Mr. Cameron, of Pennslyvania, moved to reconsider the vote—the vote *was* reconsidered, and when finally the Crittenden propositions were submitted on the second day of March, the Southern States having nearly all seceded, and their Senators left their places, they were lost by only one majority—the vote being yeas 19, nays 20. Not only so, but after most of the Southern Senators had abandoned their seats in the Senate, Congress passed bills for the organization of three new Territories—Dakota, Nevada, and Colorado; and in each act it was provided that these Territorial Legislatures should have no power to legislate so as to impair the right to *private property*, nor lay any tax discriminating against one description of property in favor of another. Not a word was said upon the subject of slavery. These three Territories, as thus organized, embraced every foot of territory the United States held on the continent. The Supreme Court having decided that the Constitution protected slavery as *property* in the Territories, slavery as an institution was thus guarded and secured as strongly and efficiently as it could be, by the action of the General Government, so far as the Territories were concerned, and its failure to receive the strongest constitutional guaranties in the States was owing to the refusal of Southern Senators to vote. And yet in the face of all this—strange and incredible as it may now appear—the secession and disunion agitators raised the cry throughout the South, that the South having failed to obtain guaranties for the preservation of their rights, were forced into disunion as the only means left of saving them from " Black Republican " tyranny and oppression. There never was a more apt illustration of the fable of the wolf and the lamb. The disunion conspirators having resolved upon a rupture at all hazards, resorted to a pretence as false and unreasonable as that of the wolf when he charged that the lamb, though at a point lower down the stream, muddied the waters where he (the wolf) was drinking.

Here is proof positive, from the record, that slavery might not only have been saved to the South, but put beyond the reach of danger—peace and harmony restored between the two sections, and war and bloodshed averted —but for the recklessness and madness of Southern men. The responsibility for all the horrors, sufferings, and disasters that have since befallen the country, rests upon those men who might have prevented them and would not, and those who concurred with them instigated and encouraged them in their work of ruin. Contrast the course of Andrew Johnson with that of these men. After they had deserted the post of duty, he still held on, pleading, and laboring, and doing all he could to preserve peace, to secure the rights of the South, and to prevent a resort to arms. He continued to struggle for the interests of the South, and to save that fair and sunny land from the miseries he foresaw and foretold would result from an attempt to dismember the Union, whilst its own chosen champions deserted its cause.

edge of the facts and considerations alluded to, it is thought by the author to be eminently proper to offer to the reader some suggestions on the subject.

It has been generally supposed—or rather, it has been assumed—that the slave-owners of the South were the main agitators of the subject of slavery; that they have been the main disturbers of the peace and quiet of the country, so far as slavery is concerned; that they have mooted the question in elections, and that their influence on public men has instigated the latter to excitement and violence in regard to that institution. At the North this opinion prevails almost exclusively. At the South but little effort has been made to remove the erroneous conclusion. So far as the fate of slavery as an institution is concerned, it makes but little difference who is to blame; still, the truth of history should be vindicated. Let justice be done. The slave-owners have lost several thousand millions of dollars' worth of property. In this they have paid the penalty of their shortcomings; let them not be blamed for that of which they are innocent. It is in the very nature of property, of invested capital, to shrink from agitation. What it wishes is peace, quiet;— to avoid rather than to seek public notoriety and discussion. It may be asserted, as a fact that would stand the test of the most rigid scrutiny, that *a very large majority* of the slaveholders of the South have deprecated the continued agitation of the subject of slavery. They have regarded it with dread and misgiving, as likely to end in disaster to their interests. Paradoxical as the opinion may seem to some, yet it may be safely expressed, that if the question could have been left to the whole body of Southern slaveholders, neither secession, nor the agitating measures which culminated in secession, ever would have taken place.

How, then, it may be asked, was the excitement and agitation about slavery kept up in the South? The answer is easy. It was the *politicians* who did it. For many years past, in almost every election of any importance, the main issue between the opposing candidates was, who was the best Southern man ; who would most ably and zealously contend for the institution of slavery ; who hated abolition and abolitionists the hardest, and would resist them most strenuously. It might perhaps be asked, what interest had the great mass of the non-slave-owners in an issue of that sort—why wage it before them, but that they might be reached through the influence the slaveholders had over them? Here, again, is another mistake. The non-slave-owners had no sort of sympathy with the slave-owners, and the protection of their property *as such*. The masses not owning slaves, so far from looking on the owners of slaves with kindness and favor, were rather disposed to regard them with disfavor and distrust, unless they otherwise considered them as kindly and benevolent men, and for other reasons rather than those connected with slavery, as entitled to their confidence. The *rationale* of the matter is this : The masses of the non-slaveholding population of the South were more violent in their opposition to " *abolition* " and " *abolitionists* " than were the slave-owners themselves. They had in their minds a fixed and definite meaning attached to the word " abolitionist." They regarded it as meaning one who was " in favor of setting free all the negroes in the country, to remain there among themselves, and to have all the rights and privileges of, and be on an equality with, the poor white men." Thus it was a question of caste, of social position, of personal pride, in regard to which, above all other things in the world, human nature is most sensitive. Consequently, for a candidate for popular favor in the South to be "doubted" on the question of slavery, was to be "damned." It was a very common thing to see a man owning hundreds of slaves charged with being unsound on the question of slavery by men who did not own any at all. Moderation on this subject was fatal to any public man in the South. The slaveholder who might, from a sense of policy and of self-interest, wish to sink all such issues, soon found himself denounced as a sympathizer with "abolition." It was this everlasting agitation of the negro question which demoralized the hustings all over the South, and which had produced a pestiferous brood of demagogues that had become the very scourge of society. The parrot-cry of "unsoundness" on the slavery question was heard on the approach of every election throughout the Southern States; not by those who were deeply interested in slave property, and against those who had afforded cause for suspicion, but very frequently by those who did not care a rush for the negro one way or the other except so far as they could use him to mount to power. The charge of "*unsoundness*" on the question of slavery was like that of "*incivism*" during the French Revolution, almost invariably resorted to as the promptest method of killing off a political enemy. In fact, so long had the public mind shuddered before this cry of "unsoundness," etc., that when the great issue of secession was precipitated upon them, many of the best Union men in the South were paralyzed, as it were, by the reign of terror which prevailed.

As to the correctness of the view here presented—that the politicians, and not the slaveholders, as a class, were the real agitators in the South—the author is sustained not only by his own observations of Southern society, Southern politics, and Southern character, but by the concurrent opinion of many of the most reliable and observant men in the Southern States. The author feels that it is not only due to the truth of history that these facts should be duly weighed and considered, but is due to a proper appreciation of President Johnson's course in dealing with the details of readjustment and reconstruction. President Johnson understands this matter. No one knows better than he does that many of the large slaveholders of the South were among the best and truest Union men to be found. Hence it is, that in the exercise of the pardoning power, he has shown no disposition to assume that, because the applicant was a slaveholder, therefore he was a disunionist. He has exhibited no animosity to slaveholders *as a class*. He judges of them as he does of all other classes of the population, and in all sections of the country, in the exercise of the pardoning power, in the distribution of official patronage, and in the bestowal of his confidence. He judges of all men, of the reliability of their characters, and of their fitness for public trust, by the uniform tenor of their lives, and their deportment and bearing in times of difficulty and danger.

There are other considerations touching the precipitation of the war which belong to the history of the times, and which should not be passed over in a biographical memoir of President Johnson. And for this reason: No one can judge fairly and impartially of President Johnson's course unless he takes into consideration the circumstances attending the inauguration of the conflict, and the incidents calculated to modify on the one hand, or to exaggerate on the other, the conduct of those who may have been implicated. In regard to secession and disunion, and those who may have countenanced and recognized the authorities under the same, the population of the South may be divided into three classes, or rather be regarded under three aspects. First, there is the great majority class, consisting of the indifferent—men whose impulses were in favor of the Union and the continuation of the old order of things, but who, not mingling in political conflicts generally, and being of plastic dispositions, allowed themselves to drift on a current which they had no agency in setting in motion. These men, quietly and unsuspectingly engaged in their domestic pursuits, were engineered out of the Union without their knowing how or why. In resuming their original position in the Union, they do not hesitate to express their pride and pleasure in at last reaching a port of safety, after having been buffeted on the waves of anxiety and trouble for four years past.

Of the balance of the Southern population, a very large majority, except perhaps in South Carolina, were Union men. They had stood firmly, and resisted the efforts of the organized secessionists for years. They had never failed at previous periods of agitation and excitement, when this question was made the issue, to carry the elections in their States under the Union banner. The conventions in the first seceding States were hurriedly called at a time when the public mind was excited, agitated, and confused. The feeling was a pervading one that danger and trouble impended over the country—that the ship was amid the breakers, while the sky above was rent with storms—that something must be done—that a convention, to be composed of the wisest and best men in the State, should be convened. This feeling, which prevailed in nearly all the Southern States, was not so much a feeling of destructiveness as of conservatism. Those who voted for members of conventions did not regard it as a foregone conclusion that the convention was to secede. The probability is that, in most cases, they had no definite opinion as to what the final result would be. They hoped for the preservation of the Union, and the restoration of peace and harmony.   They were willing to trust the convention to do the best that was possible under the circumstances, supposing, no doubt, that the acts of such bodies would be finally submitted to the people for ratification or rejection. While this state of things was going on—while the elements of strife were commingling and assuming shape and form— the eyes of the people of the respective States were turned alternately from their own capitals to Washington, and from Washington to their own capitals again.   Mr. Buchanan was then President.   The people of the South had a kind and friendly feeling toward him.   He was regarded as being favorable to them and to their interests.   The whole country looked on anxiously to see what would be his action.   He did nothing.   At that time a kind admonition, a warning, a firm and decided position on his part, might have arrested the evil and averted the war.   At all events, an admonition or warning from him would have been listened to and considered.   A decided stand on his part, based on a declaration of intent to do his duty, would have induced the South to pause and consider, and probably to desist.

But nothing could be heard from him, except croaking over the difficulties of his situation, and his crotchets about his want of power to " coerce a State."   He allows one member of his Cabinet (Floyd) to distribute arms and munitions throughout the South, in anticipation of a conflict. He allows another member of his Cabinet (Thompson) to go as a commissioner from Mississippi on a secession crusade to the convention of North Carolina, and then return and assume his Cabinet position.   He allowed national steamers endeavoring to communicate with Fort Sumter, under official orders, to be twice fired on without noticing it.   What was the effect of all this?   The Government of the United States insulted and set at defiance, and the chief executive of the nation admitting he was powerless !

The public mind of the South being in a condition of ferment, not conducive to very sound reason or to logical deduction, jumped to the conclusion that the Government of the Union was effete—that it had " played out "—that disintegration of the elements composing it had taken place. Although this conclusion was not a rational one, yet under the circumstances it is not at all strange that it should have been arrived at. And in this, as an historical event not to be lost sight of, is to be found a vast palliation of the course of many of the best and most consistent Union men in the Southern States. They deplored Buchanan's criminal shortcomings; they were startled thereat; they had hoped that by firmness on his part, in meeting promptly the issue tendered by the disunionists, the friends of the Union and of peace might have interposed, and brought about a restoration of harmony. But when they saw month after month expire—when they saw State after State secede—when they saw armies raising, and all the appliances of war preparing, and no effort made, not a finger raised by the Government in vindication of its honor, their hearts sank in despair. As the question presented itself to them, the Government of the Union had abdicated its powers, and, in admitting its inability to extend protection to its friends, had thereby absolved them from allegiance to its authority. This conclusion, it is again repeated, was not a reasonable one. They should have recollected that James Buchanan was not the Government, but only the temporary custodian of its executive powers; and that a refusal by him to discharge his duty, could not absolve his successor from *his* constitutional obligations. But, to repeat, it is not remarkable that the Union men of the South should have been affected as they were. They were sad, mortified, crushed at witnessing, as it looked to them, the Union dying.

In this way is to be accounted for the position occupied by many of the true Union men of the South. Let no one condemn them who has never had to pass through a similar ordeal. And it was no time for a man to stand still and wait for the subsiding of the storm, that he might then duly consider what was best to be done. So sudden and violent was the shock of the conflicting elements, that every man had to seek for safety in one position or another. Many of the most conscientious Union men of the South yielded temporarily, like the traveller before the *simoom* of the desert, to the violence of a storm they could not resist. Many of them, as members of State conventions, voted for ordinances of separation from the Union. This, not because they did not reverence and love the Union, for they had fought its battles for years. Not that they were secessionists, for they had resisted secession as a fallacy and a cheat. But believing, from the causes mentioned, that the Union had died from mere inanition, their purpose was to save from the wreck all that was left, and to adapt their States to the condition in which circumstances beyond their control had placed them.

If Mr. Buchanan had exerted the powers of the Government in opposition to disunion, and had appealed to the Union element of the South, he would have met a response of approval. He might have enlisted a Union feeling strong enough to have counteracted the disunion movement in many of the Southern States. The South had voted for Buchanan. The Southern people regarded him as having kindly feelings for them and for their interests. An attempt on his part to execute the laws would have been regarded with due allowance, as involving what he considered a discharge of duty. Mr. Lincoln had no such *prestige*. When he came into power, and called by proclamation for troops to put down the rebellion, those whose minds had yielded to the delusion that the Union had died out from inability to enforce its authority, could not, all of a sudden, realize the fact that the call for troops was the act of a Government that instead of being dead, had only been asleep, and, being waked up, was resolved to vindicate its power and authority. Mr. Lincoln had been elected by Northern votes exclusively, without having received an electoral vote in the South. His call for troops struck the Southern people as the threat of a foreign power thirsting for vengeance, rather than as the constituted authority of their own Government preparing to sustain the national honor and to defend the national flag. The author does not hereby mean to intimate that such an erroneous view was at all justifiable. But he thinks the truth of history should be vindicated, and that those who were true Union men at heart should have all due charity and forbearance extended to them, on account of the bewilderment of mind they labored under at the time. Ultimately the issue of battle was joined between the two sections. Blood began to flow in torrents. The Union men in the South looked on aghast, panic-stricken, and powerless. The original secessionists and conspirators had been working unremittingly and in earnest. They had perfected their organization and inaugurated a reign of terror. The Union men saw, when it was too late, that they were no longer " masters of the situation." They saw that they had allowed the favorable moment for effecting a counter-revolution to escape. They saw that any movement or declaration in favor of peace and restoration, was at the risk of personal injury, even the hazard of life itself. No other recourse was left them but to watch and wait, and bide their time.

The people of the North, those who were distant from the theatre of operations, cannot understand or appreciate the difficulties and trials which beset the Union men of the South. At the North it cost nothing to be a friend of the Union. All the impulses of personal safety and personal interest, as well as of patriotic duty, induced the people of that section to support the Government and the Union. In the South it required the highest effort of moral courage for a Union man to simply keep quiet, pursue his private and domestic occupations, and abstain from all participation in public and political affairs. It is no answer to this to say that if the Union element so greatly preponderated, as assumed by the author, then why did not the Union men organize, and by concert of action get up a counter-revolution, and sweep the disunionists from power? The causes of that moral paralysis that rendered them powerless *at first*, have been explained. Afterwards, when they waked up to a sense of their real condition, it was too late. Every reader of history knows how difficult it has always been to expel despotism from power, when once installed under the forms of law, and in possession of the *insignia* of authority; more especially where *terror* is the agent by which public action is controlled. When Nero fiddled over the burning of Rome, which he had set on fire, there were probably not ten men in the empire who did not wish him dead; yet no one was ready to strike the blow. When Robespierre was sending victims to the scaffold by hundreds every day, and drenching the streets of Paris in blood, ninety-nine hundredths of the people of France would willingly have plunged a dagger in his heart; yet he continued his work of slaughter until those who had been his compeers in villany sickened at his merciless butchery. There are two reasons for this, depending on the sameness of human nature in all times and in all countries: one is, that the public mind may be so shocked and astounded as to become paralyzed and impotent for every efficient action, and thus manhood is unnerved, as it were, for the time being; another is, that whilst every man may be ready to strike, yet he is afraid to whisper it to his neighbor. No man better understood this seeming inconsistency in man's nature than that great master of the human heart, Shakspeare. Observe with what delicate caution he makes Brutus and Cassius approach each other, in the celebrated dialogue between them. Although bosom friends, yet how warily and ingeniously each tries to worm out of the other his opinions and feelings in regard to the mighty events then in progress of development! It is possible, and even probable, that but for some *incidental* conversation between the two chief conspirators, such as that hypothecated by the great dramatist, Cæsar might have lived and died in the possession of absolute power, as the master of his country.

No man in the country understands all this better— perhaps no one understands it as well—than President Johnson. He knows what it cost to a Union man to stand up firmly to his principles and his duty, even in Tennessee, where he, by his commanding influence, through the great confidence reposed in him, was enabled to rally and organize the Union element for efficient action. He knows the tenor of that ban of public opinion—factious though it was—to which Union men were subjected. He knows how, sick and sad at heart, they sought privacy and obscurity in the retirement of private life, and even there were not allowed to find it. He knows how their hearts were wrung with anguish when they saw the sons of Revolutionary sires imbruing their hands in each other's blood, and hecatombs of victims daily sacrificed to the Moloch of civil strife. He knows how, like the sturdy old Romans in the days of their country's ruin, they wept over the degeneracy of the times. His acquaintance with all the facts, his own personal experience, enabled him to do justice to these men. Is it to be expected—can the most embittered Northern man expect—that Mr. Johnson should place in the same category all the people of the South, without regard to their position in the crisis spoken of? Is it to be expected that he should indulge a feeling of prejudice against the entire South, as a section, because wicked men in the South there planned and perpetrated their deeds of mischief? Such prejudice, such injustice, are equally inconsistent with his character for fair dealing and strict justice, and with the duties of his high and noble mission.

As to the original secessionists, who plotted and planned disunion; who had been for years intriguing to bring it about; who aided in, or rejoiced at, the disruption of the Charleston Convention in 1860; who rejoiced at the election of Mr. Lincoln, as affording a pretext for the consummation of their nefarious designs; who wished to throw obstructions in the way of the "Peace Congress," that met in Washington in March, 1861, and who rejoiced at its failure to avert a collision; who hearkened on the dogs of war toward the shedding of blood; who were in favor of precipitating the conflict by firing on Fort Sumter; who, to the last, would not tolerate the idea of peace, except on terms to be dictated, as a condition precedent, by the South; who denounced, as a traitor or an imbecile, every one who expressed a wish to see terminated this carnival of blood—language contains no terms of reproach too odious to apply to them. The history of the human race scarcely presents a parallel to such madness, such infatuation, such crime. If they were to pass a thousand years of the most virtuous and repentant lives, they could not atone for the evil and mischief they have done. For these men President Johnson has but little sympathy. He knows how much trouble they have occasioned him—how much trouble they have brought on the country. The most ultra Northern man may not distrust him in this regard. If he studiously withholds from them his personal confidence and official patronage, it will not be for the purpose of gratifying his personal prejudice, but because he knows the public interests will not be safe in their hands.

There is one point of view in which the public mind of the South, to a considerable extent, labors under a delusion—a delusion from which reflection ought easily to awaken it. Many men who arrive hastily at conclusions, or reasoning from the mere surface of things, assume that the present troubles and difficulties of the Southern people have originated in their being conquered and reduced to obedience by the United States Government—or by the North, as it seems to strike them—and the occupation of their territory by military force. As President Johnson has no wish to inflict unnecessary pain or annoyance on the people of the South, as harshness and cruelty form no part of his character, justice and truth require that the facts should be presented in their true light. Again, many men in the South who are conscientious, who deprecated the war, and who are anxious to see law and order reestablished, and the old order of things restored, feel that the terms imposed in the proclamation and in the reorganization of the State governments, are the cause of the present disordered and deranged condition of affairs, the prostration of business, etc. This is a great mistake. It is not the way in which the war was terminated, nor is it the terms and conditions on which the relations between the States and the General Government are to be restored, that have ruined and impoverished the South. It was the four years of war that did it. The great resources of the wealth of the South consisted in her annual production of three hundred millions of dollars' worth of cotton, tobacco, rice, sugar, naval stores, etc., which were exported to the markets of the world. For the last four years these resources have been cut off, and her energies have been directed toward raising a supply of provisions for the armies. Here, then, twelve hundred millions of dollars of productive wealth, instead of contributing to her prosperity, comfort, and improvement, have been lost forever. This was done by the war which the South commenced. Thousands and hundreds of thousands of her laborers, instead of contributing to her national wealth, went to the armies, and instead of being producers they have been consumers. The war did this. Owing to the factitious demands for specie by blockade-runners, refugees from the country, etc., the high price paid for it caused it all to leave the country. There are hardly any of the banks in the South able to redeem their circulation, their assets consisting of millions of worthless "Confederate" paper. And thus the currency of the South is destroyed. This was the effect of the war, and not of the terms of peace. What has suspended the operations of the colleges and academies of the South, thus arresting the education of the young? It was the war that did it. Where is the commercial name of the South? It has all disappeared in the casualties of war—not a tug-boat was left. What reduced all the railroads of the South to such a state of dilapidation? It was the war that has filled the South with sadness and sorrow, and covered the land with the drapery of mourning? Why is it that throughout that once smiling and happy region thousands of "Rachels are weeping for their children, and refusing to be comforted because they are not"? What has deprived the South of its intellectual and social wealth, in hurrying to their graves her young men, who were the hope and promise of the succeeding generation ? It was the war that wrought these calamities to the country, and not the hard terms imposed by the conquering power.

Even in regard to slavery, although the final status of that institution was not definitely decided till the war was at an end, yet the Southern people well knew when they began the war that the existence or non-existence of slavery was involved in the issue. They proclaimed and affected to believe—and urged that as a reason for secession—that it was the fixed and determined purpose of the North to destroy slavery in the South. If they were in earnest, if honest in their professed belief, that even without war the North was bent on abolition throughout the South, then of course they could expect no other result if they failed in the struggle. Mr. Lincoln, in his proclamation of 1862, tendered to the South the issue of either the restoration of the Union before the first of January, 1863, or a definitive abolition of slavery on that day if they persisted in their course. The South *did* persist ; the definitive abolition of slavery was proclaimed on that day, and from that time to the end of the war the South understood that slavery was to live or die as one side or the other prevailed in the contest. So that the immense loss of slave property by the Southern people, as well as their other disasters, may be attributed to the war, and not to the terms of peace and the conditions of reorganization. The South was ruined before General Lee surrendered. The present moral incubus that now depresses their feelings and energies, the stagnation of all kinds of business arising from the want of a currency—that leaves no field for enterprise and industry—the poverty incident to a transition state, in the substitution of one system of labor for another—all these are the consequences of a bloody civil war commenced by the South, and pertinaciously continued till her resources were exhausted.

CHAPTER XVIII.

THE people of the Southern States evidently feel aggrieved and deeply wounded at the continued occupation of their territory by the national troops. A little reflection ought to convince them that their feelings on this score are unreasonable. If they suppose that this is done for the purpose of mortifying and depressing them, by keeping the evidences of their subjugation constantly before their eyes, they judge President Johnson unfairly. He has no such cruelty in his disposition. His object is to benefit the South rather than to injure it. Let Southern men reflect for a moment. Is it to be supposed that after a four years' bloody war, waged by the South with a desperation almost unparalleled, that the ferment and excitement should suddenly cease altogether, and that perfect order, quiet, and decorum should as suddenly take their place? Such is not our experience with the subsidence of storms, whether physical or moral. Is it not much more reasonable to suppose that for a while at least there should be local disturbances and spasmodic cases of violence and disorder? Is it not for the interest of the Southern people themselves that a sufficient military force should be kept among them to protect them from the lawlessness and violence of their own disorderly population, whether of one color or the other? It is true, that quiet and order do prevail in the South, to an extent almost incredible, considering the nature of the contest just terminated. But this is contrary to, and not in accordance with, what might have been reasonably expected. President Johnson will keep garrisons in the South no longer than he may consider the interests of the country—and the interests of the South, too—may require it. On the score of economy alone, it is desirable to dispense with them as soon as possible. Let not the Southern people think hard of Mr. Johnson for the discharge of an unpleasant duty imposed on him by the inevitable force of circumstances beyond his control. The discharge of this duty on his part originated from no capricious purpose to exercise tyrannical powers. It proceeded from the consequences of the war itself. In the performance of this duty he will abstain from every thing in his power that is calculated to wound the sensitiveness of the Southern people. He will observe every delicacy toward them compatible with the high behests of duty.

That portion of President Johnson's public conduct which has given rise to most agitation and discussion, and which has perhaps caused more dissatisfaction than any other, is his decision that the public acts and doings under the semblance of State authority, since such State passed an ordinance of secession, are null and void. It cannot be denied that many fair-minded, conservative, loyal friends of the Union regard this decision of Mr. Johnson as harsh and unnecessary, as destructive of every vestige of the rights of the States, and as setting a precedent which may be destructive of civil liberty. A calm and deliberate examination of this question is all that is necessary to convince the public mind that, in this course, President Johnson has been actuated by a sincere wish to save public liberty and republican institutions, instead of destroying or impairing them.

Mr. Johnson, in coming to the conclusion he did on this question, found himself surrounded with difficulties of no ordinary magnitude. The social and political elements were in a state of discord and confusion. The old landmarks were broken down. To proceed along the beaten track of "the king's highway" was impossible. Mr. Johnson had already decided the preliminary question that the insurgent States had never been out of the Union. Still he could not ignore the fact that the normal relations between the General Government and the States had become deranged and complicated. The question was, *How* were the States to be accommodated to their original status in the Union—*how* were their disturbed relations to the General Government to be readjusted, so as to give the least possible shock to our republican institutions? President Johnson had no precedent to guide him. The restoration, or rather the reconstruction, of the Union was the polar star by whose guidance he was directed. That was the goal to which his course was aimed. The work had to be done. The responsibility had to be met. He knew and he felt that "where there is a will there is a way." He did not flinch from the task before him. Relying on his consciousness of a sense of duty, and on the honesty and justice of his countrymen, and poised and sustained by that energy and self-dependence which are the leading traits of his character, he met the question boldly and manfully. With a rigid adherence to *the spirit of the Constitution*, and reasoning from the principles of analogy, he resolved to work out the problem in such a way as to subserve the two great paramount objects of guaranteeing to each State a republican form of government, and of securing *to the people* all their rights and privileges as recognized by the Constitution.

The view Mr. Johnson took was this: that the great mass of the people composing the body politic in a State had never been out of the Union; that they had never been absolved from their allegiance to it, nor had they deprived themselves of its protection, except so far as individuals may have forfeited it by their own conduct; that the Federal Constitution was "the supreme law of the land" within the States, so regarded and recognized by them; that the State governments cannot legally exist, *as such*, except under the Constitution of the United States as the supreme law; that any action by those professing to be the constituted organs of such State, if in disregard, or under repudiation, of such supreme law, was thereby vitiated, and deprived of validity. What the States did, under and in pursuance of their ordinances of secession, they did in their professed characters as foreign powers—foreign so far as the United States and its Constitution are concerned. To admit the legality of their acts while the war was pending, would be to admit that they were out of the Union, because these very acts were based on the consideration that they were members of another and a hostile confederation. Once assume the position that the seceding States were still in the Union, and it necessarily results, as a corollary to that conclusion, that any action of theirs, based on an assumption that they were out of the Union, must be null and void. The integrity and preservation of the State governments against insurrection and invasion are guaranteed by the Federal Constitution. This includes the protection of their functionaries in the discharge of their duties and the execution of their laws relating to their own internal and domestic regulations. Now, would it not involve an absurdity to suppose that the General Government might be called on, and that if called on, it would be bound to interpose in enforcing obedience to the official action of a State Governor, elected as Governor of a State that was a member of a foreign and hostile government?   The same absurdity would be involved in the General Government being called on to enforce obedience to a State law, where such law was passed by those who were arrayed in hostility to the General Government, and intended to subserve the interests of a community foreign and hostile in its relations.   How can those who affect to speak in the name and by the authority of a State government, claim the protection or recognition of the Federal Government, when they were elected to the places which they profess to fill, as owing no allegiance to the said Federal Government?   How can laws passed by a State affecting to be out of the Union, ask for recognition by the Union?

This argument applies to all questions involving *political* relations and *political* consequences.   It is no answer to it to say that, if carried out to its logical consequences, it would unhinge and disarrange all the relations of life by invalidating all official acts involving mere administrative functions in the details of internal police.   Not at all.   The laws in force in every State, at and before the date of its secession ordinance, make ample provision for all mere private rights.   And the law, in its many judicial decisions, provides for all such cases, and protects all such rights against injury.

Assuming that the insurgent States have never been out of the Union, and following the necessary inference therefrom, that while in a state of insurrection all political actions of those claiming to be the organs of such States were null and void, the next question which arises is, *How* are the States to be gotten into a position where they can conform to their original relations and exercise and enjoy all their original rights and privileges as members of the Union? The object to be attained is plain enough. The manner to be observed is plain enough. But the agents to put the machinery in operation are wanting. Who is to give the impetus, who is to exert the motive power, in commencing the work? The call for an assemblage of the Legislature by one calling himself Governor, who was elected as Governor of a State foreign to the Union, would be a mere *brutum fulmen*. The call of a convention by such Legislature, when assembled, would be equally inoperative. And yet there is the Constitution of the United States declaring that to each State shall be " guaranteed a republican form of government," and also declaring it the duty of the President to see that " the laws are faithfully executed." President Johnson takes a cool and calm survey of the field of operations. He discovers the difficulties of the situation. He sees there is *work to be done*, and instead of shirking it, he marches up boldly and confronts it. Jackson-like, he "takes the responsibility."

This the author considers to be the explanation of President Johnson's course in the premises. He appoints " Provisional Governors " for the States that he regards as having no legal Governors. Here the first and greatest difficulty is removed. From the same law of necessity, the Provisional Governors are instructed to appoint subordinate State officers, and thus was put in operation the machinery necessary for the reorganization of the State governments and the readjustment of the Union. The system has thus far worked smoothly, harmoniously, and successfully. The people have adapted themselves to it with great readiness and facility. The election of members of Congress, and the admission of those members to their seats, will consummate the work. Thus far, the result has proven Mr. Johnson's wisdom and sagacity. Having risked any odium that might have attached to a failure of his system, he will be entitled to, as he will surely receive, the thanks and the plaudits of the country, North and South, and East and West, for having so soon and so efficiently calmed the strife of sections, and healed the wounds, to a very considerable extent, caused by an unnatural and unfortunate conflict.

There is one subject on which the public mind to some extent is greatly in error, and on which truth and justice require it should be put right. The error consists in this, that the exercise of the *pardoning* power, under the terms of the amnesty proclamation, is not only a tyrannical proceeding, merely for the gratification of private malice and personal vanity, but that it is a usurpation of unconstitutional power. It is surprising that many intelligent and thoughtful men should have fallen into this error, who regard the conditions of pardon as a degradation to which they are compelled to submit under duress, as it were. Let us examine this question. The Constitution of the United States declares, in the the third section of the fourth article:

"Treason against the United States shall consist only in levying war against them, or in adhering to their enemies, giving them aid and comfort."

Consequently, any one who may have "given aid and comfort" to the "Confederate" government, or any of its authorities, or to the military forces of the same, have subjected themselves to the charge of treason, and to a liability to the penalties thereon imposed. The laws of war, as they originally existed, have been so softened by the progress of Christian civilization, that in this age the wholesale punishment of entire communities for the crime of rebellion is no longer known. Therefore, in the event of an unsuccessful rebellion, a general amnesty is usually granted to the great mass of the people who may have been implicated, reserving from its operation such cases as the sovereign power may select in its discretion. As to the right and the policy on the part of the sovereign power of reserving the prominent and leading men in such rebellion for trial and punishment, on conviction, the laws of civilized nations still recognize their existence.

The public law of Christendom on this subject is laid down by Vattel in great detail. This standard authority in the " laws of nations " says :

" When the evil " of popular commotion " spreads—when it infects the majority of the inhabitants of a city or province, and gains such strength that even the sovereign himself is no longer obeyed—it is usual more particularly to distinguish such a disorder by the name of *insurrection.*" * * * " But what conduct shall the sovereign observe towards the insurgents ? I answer, in general, such conduct as shall at the same time be most consonant to justice and the most salutary to the State." * * * " Subjects who rise against their prince without cause, deserve severe punishment. Yet even in this case, on account of the number of the delinquents, clemency becomes a duty in the sovereign. Shall he depopulate a city or desolate a province in order to punish her rebellion ? Any punishment, however just in itself, which embraces too great a number of persons, becomes an act of downright cruelty." * * * " When a party is formed in a State, who no longer obey the sovereign, and are possessed of sufficient strength to oppose him—or when, in a republic, the nation is divided into two opposite factions, and both sides take up arms, this is called a *civil war.*" * * * " The sovereign never fails to bestow the appellation of *rebels* on all such of his subjects as openly resist him ; but when the latter have acquired sufficient strength to give him effectual opposition, and to oblige him to carry on the war against them according to the established

12

rules, he must necessarily submit to the use of the term "civil war." * * * "Those two parties" to a civil war "therefore must necessarily be considered as thenceforward constituting, at least for a time, two separate bodies, two distinct societies. Though one of the parties may have been to blame in breaking the unity of the State, and resisting lawful authority, they are not the less divided in fact." * * * "This being the case, it is very evident that the common laws of war—those maxims of humanity, moderation, and honor, which we have already detailed in the course of this work—ought to be observed by both parties in every civil war." * * * "When the sovereign has subdued the opposite party, and reduced them to submit and sue for peace, he may except from the amnesty the authors of the disturbance—the heads of the party; he may bring them to a legal trial, and punish them if they be found guilty. He may act in this manner particularly on occasion of those disturbances in which the interests of the people are not so much the object in view as the private aims of some powerful individual, and which rather deserve the appellation of *revolt* than of *civil war*."

President Johnson is acting on this well-recognized principle of public law, and no one can charge him with any exhibition of harshness or cruelty in its exercise. He issues his proclamation of general amnesty to the great mass of the people of the Southern States, including ninety-nine hundredths of them, upon the simple condition of their taking an oath of allegiance to the United States. Upon a compliance with this condition, they are *ipso facto* remanded to all their privileges and rights of citizenship, and exempted from the penalties of treason, confiscation, etc. Can any reasonably object to this condition of "*pardon*," if it is his purpose to demean himself as a peaceable and loyal citizen of the Union for the future? If he does not so intend, then ought he to expect to have the rights and privileges pertaining to such citizenship? It is true, President Johnson has excepted thirteen classes of persons from the benefit of the amnesty, even on the compliance with the condition of the proposed oath. This does not apply to more than one-hundredth part of the male population, and it is in accordance with the usage of other governments that have had formidable rebellions to contend with. But on what ground can these last complain of any special grievance? Their exception from the provisions of the general amnesty is the penalty they have to pay for their prominence and influence. They are in no worse condition than they would be if no such proclamation had ever been issued. They seem to think that it is the President's proclamation that subjects them to the charge and penalty of treason. Not at all. It is the Constitution of the United States that does that. Suppose they fail to avail themselves of the condition proposed, and refuse to ask for special pardon? They are just where they were. The proclamation and the terms offered therein make their case no worse.

The tender of pardon by President Johnson, on certain conditions, is no mere capricious exercise of power on his part. It is an act of clemency offered to all; it is an invitation, on his part, to all to return to the great brotherhood of citizenship, and to aid in restoring themselves and their States to their original position in the Union. Some object to the term " pardon " as grating to the feelings of a proud and sensitive people, as implying the forgiveness by a master of a recreant slave. They forget that Mr. Johnson does not do this as a mere personal exercise of power, not through any assumed or implied prerogative of executive authority. It is as the organ of the Government that he does it, under express constitutional provision. The term " pardon," which he uses in his proclamation, is not a word arbitrarily selected by himself, but it is the technical language of the Constitution itself. The second section of the second article of the Constitution declares that the President, among his other powers mentioned, "shall have power to grant reprieves and *pardons* for offences against the United States, except in cases of impeachment."

If Mr. Johnson wished to gratify his mere personal vanity in the exercise of power, he would prefer to wait till after trial and conviction in each separate case, that he might pardon or punish in accordance with his likes or his dislikes ; but from sheer clemency, and for the sake of convenience and comfort to those implicated, he is willing to shield them not only from punishment but from trial, in case they afford evidence of loyalty for the future. As to his power in this regard, there is no doubt on that score. The Supreme Court of the United States has decided that the President may pardon as well before trial and conviction as afterwards, and that he may also grant a conditional pardon. (See 7 Peters' Rep. 161 ; 5 Howard's Rep. 368 ; and 18 Howard 307.)

In regard to this question, as to most others in which President Johnson's views have been discussed, he occupies the same position of moderation. Ultra and inconsiderate men at the South complain of his harshness and severity. The same class of men at the North blame him for his leniency and forbearance to " rebels." His course is a difficult one. It is between Scylla and Charybdis. But while he is at the helm, the country has confidence that the ship of State will make the perilous passage in safety. All he asks is that the crew and passengers will keep cool and calm, and that they will render the aid in their power at the proper time.

It has been remarked by a very distinguished man, that the highest honor and praise that could be bestowed on Washington consisted in the fact that his life could not be properly written without its being, at the same time, the best history of the Revolutionary War. That is true—so intimately identified was Washington with all the great leading incidents of the war, and so great was the influence of his character in conducting it and bringing it to a successful termination. To a certain extent, the same may be said of Mr. Johnson, so far as the great conflict just terminated is concerned. Looking at the war in its political aspects, to those influences which turned the tide of the conflict in Tennessee, that proved fatal to the cause of disunion, and to the historical results involved in the adjustment of the controversy, no man has played a more important part—no man has marked more strongly the impress of his character and genius on the events of the times, and the direction imparted to industrial and social progress under the new order of things. In some respects the war just ended is much more important in its consequences than was the war of the Revolution. The latter involved political results and national relations to an extent perhaps that no war ever did before. By evolving a new set of ideas, it effected greater changes in other countries than it did at home. But it did not at all deflect the regular current of civilization on this continent. The war just brought to an end involves a great social, industrial, and financial upheaval, that may affect the character of the civilization of the age.

Andrew Johnson's name and status in history are indissolubly connected with the moral results of this great struggle. It was remarked to the author, a short time ago, by a very shrewd and observant man, who has a morbid fondness for historical reading—" Andrew Johnson," said he, " occupies a position more interesting, and likely to exercise on the public opinion of the age and on the national complications of the times a greater influence than any man living, not excepting the Emperor of the French. His cannot be an ordinary, commonplace destiny. If he has the ability to retain that mastership of the situation which he now holds, he will go down to posterity either as one of the greatest men that ever lived, or as one of the greatest *failures* recorded in history." It was this very idea of the important position occupied by Mr. Johnson—important in its power, in its influence, and in the results to be eliminated from his policy—that first induced the author to attempt this biographical memoir. The author felt so deeply convinced of the importance of correct impressions being made, and correct views entertained by the public *now*, before faction, or prejudice, or personal ambition should have perverted the public judgment or poisoned the public mind in regard to Mr. Johnson's position and character, that he has been induced to undertake what he regrets abler pens have not done. The object of the author has been truth, justice, fair play, not so much on Mr. Johnson's account as for the sake of the country. Mr. Johnson is an historical character. The labors and duties now devolving on him are too high, too intimately connected with the country's interests, for weal or woe, to be regarded as party questions, or as involving party results. It is as important that the public should fairly understand what really and truly are Mr. Johnson's position, his views, his purposes, his character, as that Mr. Johnson should be right himself in these particulars.

The interests and sympathies of all civilized countries are so interlocked, through the agency of commerce, that any event seriously affecting the industrial wealth and resources of any *very productive* country, is felt throughout Christendom. Like a pebble dropped in the water, the ripple of the wave is felt to the furthest shore. The Southern States are a very productive country. In regard to the future of the South, as yet all is doubt and uncertainty. Among her wisest and calmest men opinions are variant and conflicting. *Some* are hopeful and buoyant in reference to the future. They think they already see the dawning of a brighter day. According to their view, an immense immigration will set in to the South of the hardy and enterprising laborers from the North and from Europe, who will improve and cultivate the lands to their highest capacity of production; that capital by the million will rapidly seek investment in developing the immense mining and manufacturing resources of the Southern States; that our rivers and sounds will soon be whitened with the sails of commerce, and joy, gladness, and prosperity pervade the whole land; that the black race will from the force of natural laws soon disappear, and leave an unencumbered field for the energy and enterprise of the white race. *Others*, again, can see nothing in the future to cheer, but every thing to depress and dishearten. They regard the idea of immigration of laborers, and the investment of capital in the South, as utterly Utopian, so long as millions of blacks, without any regularly organized system of employment, are prowling over the country; that these blacks will not work, and, when pinched with hunger, they will in roving bands subsist by violence and plunder; that a physical conflict between the two races is inevitable—that this conflict will continue till one obtains the mastery by the extermination of the other; that the fertile fields of the South will grow up in briers, and go to waste and ruin; that for years to come, the South will raise no surplus products, to bring money into the country, as the basis of a currency; that all the population who are able will leave the country, and thus deprive it of what little wealth and energy it has left. In other words, that the South is so thoroughly crushed, impoverished, and broken-spirited, that its future is shrouded in the very blackness of despair.

Probably the truth may lie between these two views; but as one or the other is nearer to realization, will be the effect produced by the solving of the problem, upon the interests and destiny first of the North, and 'then' of the commercial nations of the earth. It may perhaps be said, the North can get along without the aid of the South any way. So it can, if by "getting along" is meant retaining its geographical position on the map, and the working and trading and living and dying of its population. But it is absurd to contend that the North is not very deeply interested in the welfare and prosperity of the South. The "report on commerce and navigation," annually issued by the Treasury Department, shows the importance of Southern prosperity to the North. The devotion of the Southern people to agriculture exclusively, not only leaves an open and uncontested field for the commerce and manufactures of the North, but the South furnishes to the North the elements for sustaining its commerce, and the raw material for its manufactures; and then, again, a market for the manufactured articles. But the importance of the South to the North does not stop here. Every country, no matter how diversified in interests or vast in extent, is in its commercial relations with other countries a unit. Thus it is that the two hundred and fifty to three hundred millions of annual products from the South, like the gold of California, answer the purposes and wants of the North in paying for its importations from abroad, and preserving the "balance of trade," as if grown in New York or New England.

Suppose the view entertained by a portion of the Southern people—first alluded to—should turn out to be the correct one. Suppose the South relieved of the incubus caused by the presence of the black population. Suppose the infusion of the enterprise and industry of an immigrant white population in developing our agricultural, manufacturing, and mining resources. Suppose the South to spring forward, like an invigorated giant, in the race of industry and improvement. Suppose the hum of myriads of spindles and the click of thousands of anvils to be commingled with the roar of her waterfalls. Suppose her stagnant marshes drained, her gullied fields levelled over, the pursuits of agriculture varied so as to meet the tastes and habits of all, every variety of soil adapted to its own peculiar production, and neat and handsome cottages of the white laborer substituted for the squalid huts of the slave. Suppose her railroads taxed to their utmost capacity in carrying off for the markets of the world her surplus products. Every additional dollar thus added to the wealth of the South, in a corresponding degree adds to the wealth, the power, and the influence of the North. The North has too far the start, the established routine of a century past too firmly fixed, for the South ever to become her competitor in manufacturing, commercial, or financial power. The wealth of the latter must be auxiliary to that of the former. If the bright and hopeful view of the future of the South be the correct one, then the South will continue to pour into the lap of the North teeming millions of wealth. And as the North increases in material and pecuniary power, in proportion will be her moral influence on the ideas and civilization of the age, all over the world. It has been said that the thermometer of the monetary and commercial power of the globe hangs up in the London Exchange. If the problem presented for solution by the late war is worked out favorably for the South, it will not be many years before this thermometer will be suspended in the exchange in Wall Street, New York.

Suppose, on the other hand, the views of those who can see nothing in the future of the South but clouds and darkness, be correct. Suppose the production of her great staples, cotton, tobacco, etc., at an end—not exceeding a few hundred thousand bags of the former, and a few thousand hogsheads of the latter, grown on their uplands by white labor; with no capital to embark in manufacturing and mining pursuits, and no surplus products, from the sale of which to bring money in the country. Suppose immigration and capital from abroad to avoid the South, as heretofore, because of the presence of three or four millions of blacks. What is to become of the millions of Northern capital invested in the commercial pursuits of the coast carrying-trade both ways, and to a very great extent in the carrying-trade both ways across the ocean? Where are the manufacturers of the North to find a market for their shoes, blankets, hats, and the thousands of other articles for which the South afforded them a market? To whom are the pork-dealers and the stock-raisers of the Northwest to sell the products of their industry? How are Northern merchants to pay for their importations from abroad? how prevent the " balance of trade " against them from keeping their country drained of gold? If the fears and misgivings of those who look on the dark side of the picture—so far as the South is concerned—should be realized, the reaction *must* prove ruinous to Northern interests. It is inevitable, just as sure as effect follows cause.

In that event the North would lose its *prestige* among the nations; and in this commercial and trafficking age the loss of material and monetary influence would involve the loss of moral influence. The war has proven the fallacy of the Southern dogma that " cotton is king." But to the extent that there ever was any semblance of truth in it, its crown was worn by Northern heads, its sceptre wielded by Northern hands. Cotton did more to promote the prosperity and power of the North than of the South. If the dark view for the South be the correct one, whilst Great Britain would have her colonies all over the world to glean cotton from, the North would get from the South hardly enough to supply her own manufacturing wants. Nations that have occupied prominent positions in the world—especially if they be youthful nations—cannot stand still. They must advance or retrograde. The influence and power any country may exercise is generally in proportion to the *dread* other countries feel of a conflict with them. This *dread* grows out of the commercial and monetary power more than their material strength, in this age. The loss of this commercial and monetary power by the United States, would not only detract from our present commanding position, but it would destroy, to a great extent, the progress of American ideas and American civilization.

The object of the author in this apparent digression has been to show that the North and the South are integral portions of a great country, and that each has its own proper mission in developing and advancing our national character and national prosperity; that they are necessary to each other, and that either in attempting to destroy the other would be striking itself a blow; that if the connection of the two sections was made to preserve it, their cordial feeling and harmony ought not now to be prevented by the indulgence of unkind and bitter feelings; that the recollection of past injuries on one side or the other, and the unpleasant associations connected with the contest, ought to be buried in one common effort to advance the joint interests of both.

CHAPTER XIX.

Mr. Johnson has just fairly gotten under way, with the first term of his administration. He will certainly be President for three years to come, if he lives. He is managing these delicate and complicated questions, growing out of the late conflict between the two sections, and the changed relations of the two races, with consummate ability and tact. He is giving satisfaction to the moderate and conservative men of both sections of the country. He continues to gain popularity, and to " win golden opinions " daily in all parts of the country. As to the future, as to whom the people of this country shall call on to stand at the helm of the ship of State in 1868, that is a matter which Mr. Johnson and his friends would prefer not to have mooted at present. They prefer to leave it to the developments of time. There are difficulties enough to encounter in the adjustment of pending troubles, without thrusting in this ill-timed subject of future elections. Mr. Johnson and his friends would deprecate, and would prefer to avoid, any discussion in regard to the election to the next Presidential term. They would prefer to leave that to the great tribunal of public opinion, which will decide on it at the proper time. Still it is not to be expected that they should look with unconcern upon the inception of a movement designed to *control* the decision of future elections, without reference to the judgment which the great Public may pass upon Mr. Johnson's administration from 1865 to 1869. Mr. Johnson neither expects nor desires to see any party organization, with a view to the continuation of himself in power. All he asks is to be let alone, that he may calmly and quietly work out the great problem now in a course of solution. So far as he is himself concerned, he is willing to leave his conduct of affairs to be passed on *by the people* at the proper time. And he has too much confidence in the people to question the justness of their decision.

In a free and popular Government such as ours, it requires a rare combination of virtues to make a great and *successful* statesman. In the use of the term " successful," is not meant the mere triumph or prosperous issue of any isolated project or undertaking. What is meant is *success* in the general advancement of the country's true interests, and the general promotion of the public good. Strong intellect, sterling honesty, and enlarged patriotism are indispensable to the achievement of success, in the sense alluded to, but they alone are not sufficient. No man can administer a government ably and successfully who does not fully enter into the spirit and theory of that government, and who does not believe in, confide in, admire and respect it. Camillus and Cincinnatus would never have been heard of in history, if they had lived in the time of Nero or Commodus. Richelieu would have been out of place in the cabinet of William III. of England; Washington would have made but a sorry minister under the Czar of Russia. Ours is a Government *of the people*, acting not directly, it is true, but still no less efficiently, through their chosen representatives. Toward a successful administration of a Government like ours, it is requisite that he who is intrusted with the chief executive power, should realize and thoroughly comprehend this truth as the basis of our institutions. But further still, he should believe in his head and feel in his heart that it is the best system of government that could possibly be devised for our people and country. He should admire and respect it, as best designed to promote our national character and prosperity; as best calculated to secure the great blessings of national independence and civil liberty. If he doubts in this regard, he is out of place when intrusted with the administration of high and executive powers, or with the consideration of high legislative functions.

A man may have capacity sufficient for the discharge of any public duties devolving upon the station which he occupies. If, however, he really believes that popular government is a fallacy—in case he is an honest and conscientious man, he will shrink and retire from all active interference with public affairs, and from all official positions under the Government. This we frequently see to be the case, and in this way we may account for some of the ablest and best men in the country abstaining from all political affairs. If a man believes that ours was never designed by its founders to be a Government of the people; that the fathers in forming it, whilst presenting the semblance of popular government, yet so provided, through the machinery of representative system, that the people should be amused with the *forms* whilst the politicians should be possessed of the substance of power—how could such a man, when intrusted with official authority, be any thing other than an intriguer and hypocrite? On the other hand, suppose the case of a man who believes that ours *is* a Government of the people, designed to be such by its authors—a Government in which the will of the people should control, direct, and regulate the action of those intrusted with the exercise of power (within the limits of the Constitution, of course). But yet he thinks that, in this, the fathers made a mistake—that the great mass of the people have neither intelligence nor virtue sufficient, to judge understandingly or conscientiously on questions of public policy. If such a man be honest, he will not take any pride or pleasure in serving those who cannot appreciate his labors or his sacrifices, or who will not do him justice in his efforts to serve them. All the inducements of a laudable ambition to struggle for fame cannot exist with a man who feels that those from whom he may look for his reward, are not actuated by the high considerations of virtue that he is. Hence it is, that the man entertaining such views of the people—that they are neither sufficiently intelligent nor virtuous to control the action of the Government—when in public life, becomes a *demagogue* in the most odious sense of that term. Having no faith in their intelligence, he never tries to inform or explain to the people, except with a view to mislead and deceive. Having no faith in their honesty, he appeals not to the better but to the worse impulses of their natures.

There is a very mistaken idea generally prevailing on this subject, viz., as to what constitutes a demagogue. Most persons seem to think a demagogue means one who really admires, respects, honors, and loves the great mass of the people. This is a great mistake. The real demagogue scorns and despises the people. Having no respect for them as rational beings, and treating them as ignorant brutes, he never appeals to their judgments, or to their reason. Having no regard for them, as being actuated by principle, and considering them as mere counters, with which ambition is to play out its game of selfishness, he never appeals to their conscientiousness, considering honesty to be a virtue which they do not possess. Thus it is, as all antiquity proves, that the demagogue, when once firmly seated in power, becomes the most cruel and unfeeling of tyrants. It is no answer to this to say that the fact of the masses being deceived and misled by demagogues goes to prove that they are ignorant and easily duped through their feelings. Not at all. Experience proves that men of intelligence are as apt to be deceived and imposed on by the arts and schemes of the designing, as are ignorant men. Liability to be influenced through the feelings, instead of the judgment, is not confined to any class. It is one of the weak points in human nature, common to all men. Let Mr. Johnson be subjected to these tests of requirement, in the qualities necessary to form a great statesman, and neither he nor his friends need fear the result. There is no man in the Union who has a stronger record on this point than he has. Examine his past history, read his speeches, messages, etc., and he will ever be found the same ardent and enthusiastic admirer of our popular form of Government, and free and republican Constitution. He will be found the same earnest and uncompromising advocate of the rights and privileges of the people, with the same jealous determination to defend and support them against all and every encroachment. "Free government, and the rights of a free people," seems to have been the very key-note of his political life. In speaking of "the people" in this connection, no *class* of the population is meant. It is meant in the same sense in which the term "the people" is used in the Constitution—the great body politic, in which resides the source of all power.

At the State elections which took place in the fall of 1865 throughout the Northern and Northwestern States, the Republicans triumphed by increased majorities in nearly every State. It is very difficult to see or to understand the nature of the issues involved in these elections. The intensity and earnestness with which the struggle was maintained only prove how men will continue to contend and disagree, merely on the associations of past differences, long after all practical issues have disappeared. The Democratic party had organized under their old name, and under the leadership of many of their former prominent men. Judging from the tone of the press and the proceedings of public meetings, if there was any latent issue involved, it was that of more of forbearance and kindliness of feeling on the part of the Democratic party toward the Southern States and people—more of readiness and anxiety to see them restored to the Union with all their former rights and privileges; and, on the other hand, more of distrust and misgiving on the part of the Republicans, on the ground that the Southern people were not thoroughly subdued, and willing to submit to the domination and supremacy of the Federal Government. The Republican party, as represented in the present Congress, may be regarded as consisting of two sections—the one, which by common acceptation has received the name of " Radicals," under the leadership of Mr. Chase; and the other, which claims to be *the* Republican party, of which Mr. Seward may be regarded as the type and representative. And yet all three of these parties, if so they can be called—Democrats, Radicals, and Republicans—claim to be friends and supporters of President Johnson. It is a little remarkable that the Democrats and Republicans, whilst contending against each other with great intensity for local power within their respective States, yet both endorsed President Johnson and his policy in their party conventions, and pledged themselves to his support. This must show the strong hold which the leaders of these parties know Mr. Johnson has upon the affections of the people at large. And never in the course of his eventful life has he shown himself more of a statesman, more self-poised and self-reliant, than in the attitude he now occupies between the contending parties. He belongs, strictly speaking, to neither. He refuses to identify himself with the partisan objects or purposes either may be trying to accomplish for the future. He seems thoroughly to understand his position as a great popular tribune in these times of commotion and trouble—and to know what the people of this country expect at his hands. He seems to fully appreciate his duty and his mission—the restoring and readjusting the disturbed relations of a mighty confederacy, and of avoiding all party complications likely to mar that result. He cannot and he will not forget that he is the President of the nation, and not the head or the instrument of a party. In a country where rival parties exist, it is very difficult for any man intrusted with high functions to maintain an independent position between them without affiliating with either, and yet preserve his influence and power so as to control and direct the current of political events. History shows but few such men. Andrew Johnson is one of them.

The Democratic party have no exclusive claims on President Johnson, either on the score of consistency or of gratitude. Although a Democrat in his antecedents, yet, by the irretrievable force of circumstances, he was forced into association with the Republican party in 1861. Mr. Buchanan, as the organ of the Democratic party, had

placed that party in a false position before the country.
By his inertness and imbecility in refusing to exert the
national supremacy, when State after State raised the flag
of disunion, he placed the Democratic party in the attitude
of being willing to tolerate, if not of directly assenting to,
the validity of secession. The Republican party, on coming into power in 1861, by the prompt alacrity with which
they voted men and money, and the determination they
exhibited to maintain the authority of the Government,
thereby secured to themselves the strength and influence
in the public mind of being regarded as the Union party.
Mr. Johnson, true to his previous professions, warnings,
and declarations, followed the impulses of *duty*, regardless
of all previous party affiliations. He regarded the salvation of the Union as paramount to all partisan or selfish
considerations; and in taking his position in the Union
ranks, he did not care or inquire what position in party
warfare his comrades either on the right or the left had
occupied before. The Republicans nominated and elected
him. The Democrats, in the main, voted against him.
The latter, therefore, cannot charge Mr. Johnson with
having in anywise misled them, or with being ungrateful
for confidence reposed.

On the other hand, the Republicans, it is true, nominated and elected him. But it was not because he was a
Republican. It was because of his incalculable services
in fighting the battle for the Union. It was because of his
well-known strength and power in Tennessee. No one
will deny that it was owing to his influence and exertions,
that East Tennessee stood firm in defence of the Union, and
that that State furnished some thirty thousand men to the
Union army. It may safely be asserted that no one man
throughout the entire country did as much effective service
in the cause of the Union as Andrew Johnson. On the

score of favors conferred, therefore, if any one should be disposed to rest the matter on no higher grounds, the Republican party owes as much to President Johnson as he owes to them. They nominated him with the full knowledge that he had been a lifelong Democrat of the Jackson school. They did not require of him that he should disavow any of the principles or professions of his former political life. They well knew that although he had always been a firm, decided, and consistent Union man, yet at the same time that he had on many occasions, in the most emphatic manner, declared himself as opposed to *consolidation*, and in favor of maintaining the dignity and integrity of the States. Neither, therefore, has the Republican party any exclusive claims on President Johnson in a party point of view. No more than the Democrats, can they charge him with having misled or deceived them. He is a Republican to the extent of an unwavering determination to maintain the Union. There is no reason, however, for supposing that he has repudiated the long-cherished and well-known principles of his political life, except so far as he may be compelled by circumstances to modify them in adapting his action to the changed condition of affairs.

The Republicans must not expect President Johnson to merge the identity of his position, as the great arbiter between struggling parties and conflicting opinions, as the magnanimous ruler of a great people, into that of the mere partisan. They must not expect him to lend himself to measures of bitter and unsparing resentment against the Southern States, contrary to all the professions and principles of his past life, and in contravention of that paternal regard which, as the Chief Executive of the Republic, he entertains for every part and parcel of the entire Union. No one suffered more personally; no one incurred greater sacrifices; no one has greater cause for re-sentful feelings against secessionists and disunionists, than President Johnson. If he can afford to forget and to for-give, if he can ignore the troubles, the horrors, and the wrongs of the past in his great anxiety to promote harmony between sections, and national prosperity in the future, with what show of justice can those who incurred no per-sonal sacrifice, who were distant from the scene of opera-tions, and are therefore the less qualified to judge of the mitigating circumstances and considerations of the late ter-rible conflict, charge Mr. Johnson with undue sympathy for those who were the authors of the late troubles?

Although the record of President Johnson's past life proves him to be a man of unyielding firmness of purpose when acting on his conscientious convictions of duty, yet the charge of impracticable stubbornness cannot with jus-tice be urged against him. He puts forward no claims to a dictatorship, great as are the powers with which he has been invested. His course, since the Northern elections in the fall of 1865, shows that he considers himself as the organ of public opinion, and the exponent of the popular will, where the violation of no great cardinal principle is involved. It cannot be denied that the unanimity with which the Republicans triumphed at the last State elec-tions, has induced them to make additional demands and requirements of the Southern States, in order to the final readjustment of their relations with the Federal Govern-ment, so as to secure to them all the rights and privileges of the other States. Previous to those elections, it was understood throughout the country that President John-son's system of reconstruction, as prescribed to the Provis-ional Governors appointed by himself, contained all the requirements necessary of the insurgent States, and that they were perfectly satisfactory to all parties at the North.

All parties had endorsed and approved this policy in their conventions and their platforms. Nothing was then said of requiring of the Southern States that they should by their own conventions abolish slavery; that they should ratify the amendment of the Federal Constitution, forever forbidding slavery in the United States; and that they should repudiate the debts of the respective States, contracted in the prosecution of the war. After the elections referred to, the Republican party put forth these additional requirements, as conditions precedent to the Southern States being admitted to a full participation of their rights in the National Legislature, by the admission of their members in Congress.

President Johnson did not throw himself in hostility to the Republican party, in regard to these additional requirements of the Southern States. He acted as a wise and prudent statesman should have done. Of unshaken firmness where *principle* is involved, he is conciliatory and accommodating where mere expediency is concerned. The views and sentiments of the Republican party, as expressed through the ballot-box, he felt himself bound to regard as the will of the controlling power in the nation. The Republican policy largely predominated in the National Legislature. An issue between the Executive and Legislative Departments of the Government would have added to the difficulties already existing, and which Mr. Johnson was so anxious to remove, and would have hindered and delayed the work of readjustment which he was laboring to accomplish. He would have destroyed his usefulness to both sections by allowing himself to be drawn into a conflict with Congress. His position was too important a one, his duties too high, the accomplishment of his mission fraught with consequences too vast to allow of his merging his character as a great national umpire into that of a *partisan* on the one side or the other. As the friend of both sections, as the only practicable connecting link between them, anxious to bring them in harmonious connection, he frankly informed the authorities of the Southern States what was required of them by the controlling public sentiment of the North. This controlling power was a *fact* which he could not ignore or disregard. As to what may have been his own individual opinions in regard to the interpolations of these additional requirements of the Southern people, nothing is positively known. Nor is it at all material, so far as his consistency or patriotism is concerned. If he would have preferred that these additional demands should not have been made of the Southern States, then it shows that he appreciated the power and influence of the Republican party. It shows his unwillingness to break with them. It shows his anxiety to cultivate harmony, and concert with them in carrying out the great work of reconstruction on which he is engaged. It shows that where mere expediency is concerned, he is willing to yield, for the sake of peace, and to secure the accomplishment of great and important results. It shows that he regards himself as the constitutional President of a great Republic, and not as a despot whose will should be the law. On the other hand, if there are any in the South who are disposed to censure President Johnson, and to complain of his course as arbitrary and tyrannical, then they judge him unfairly and ungenerously.

Mr. Johnson knew that slavery was dead and gone forever, independently of any action on the part of the Southern States. He knew that by yielding with calmness and dignity to what was their inevitable destiny, the Southern people would acquire great moral strength—that they would thus occupy a vantage ground from which they might enforce their claims for speedy admission to all their constitutional rights in the Union. He knew that they would thus falsify the charge that they still entertained sentiments of bitter hostility to the Government, and that they still cherished rebellious feelings against it. It was in the spirit of friendly advice, and not of heartless dictation, that he communicated to the Southern States the additional guaranties they were required to afford that slavery should no longer be a bone of contention between the two sections, nor further disturb their harmonious relations. In reference to the debts contracted by the individual States in the prosecution of the war, he acted in concurrence with the views of a majority in probably every Southern State. The war had wrecked the fortunes of nearly all men in the South, Union men and secessionists alike. He could see no just cause why those who had invested in State securities should be so much more highly favored than those who had invested in " Confederate States " securities, when both had been issued for the prosecution of a war which had spread ruin and desolation over the land. Besides, he knew that a very large portion of the people of the South were opposed to the war, both in its origin and its reckless continuation, and that it was only under duress that they had submitted to its burdens and its exactions. He thought it hard and cruel that these men, in addition to their heavy losses, should be further taxed to pay the expenses of a war which in their hearts they condemned. It is true, the hopes held out to the Southern States, of a speedy admission to all their rights and privileges in the Union as the result of a compliance on their part with the additional requirements mentioned, have not yet been fulfilled. But the fault is not President Johnson's. He makes no secret of his earnest and anxious desire to see the Union fully restored in its integrity and its entirety. He is laboring, with all the influence and power he possesses, to produce that result. The Southern States that have acted according to his suggestions, have gained this advantage, at least—they have by their course taken away every pretext or excuse on the part of the dominant majority in Congress for longer excluding them from the halls of legislation. Let not the Southern States regret what they have done. They have gained moral power, at least. They have, moreover, strengthened Mr. Johnson's hands, in case any issue (unfortunately for the country) be *forced* on him by the dominant power in Congress, where his well-known decision and firmness may be called in requisition.

Some very ungenerous and unjust remarks about President Johnson have been indulged in by certain prominent men of the dominant party in Congress. They have been of a general character, however, not involving any specific charges against him, thus showing they were the ebullition of unfriendly feeling, without any tangible objection on which to rest. This, in connection with certain harsh and severe language by a portion of the public press, must be regarded as the premonitory symptoms of a concerted assault to be made upon him as soon as the arrangements are completed for this purpose. To what extent this disaffection to Mr. Johnson's administration may prevail, it is difficult to judge. For the good of the entire country, it is to be hoped it is confined to a faction, and that the great body of the Republican party, true to their uniform professions of anxiety for a restored Union, will repudiate those who are trying to thwart Mr. Johnson in the accomplishment of that great and patriotic object he has so much at heart. If he succeeds, peace, harmony, and prosperity will be restored to a long-distracted country. If he fails, through the machinations of wicked men, the patriot heart sinks in sadness and dismay at contemplating the bitterness, heart-burning, and alienation of feeling, which will, for ages to come, keep the North and the South as thoroughly hostile as are Russia and Poland, as Austria and Hungary. In reference to the efforts made to embarrass him, Mr. Johnson has shown himself the philosopher as well as the statesman. He has not allowed it to ruffle his temper or disturb his composure. Guided by the polar star of duty, and intent on reaching the goal of a restored and harmonious Union, he continues to move forward on the direct line of principle, relying upon the justice of his countrymen, and the impartial verdict of posterity. He refuses, and very properly, to take up any gage of battle, thrown down to him by faction, envy, or sectional bigotry. His position is such that he cannot *afford to quarrel* with anybody. It is the common lot of all men who have reached the highest eminence by their own efforts and force of character, and as the reward of merit—and who have made for themselves proud names in history—to incur the hatred of the censorious, the envious, and the malignant. It is "the rough brake that virtue must go through." The few *men of destiny* who have appeared in history, and who have been the reformers or reconstructors of the shattered institutions of their country, have been remarkable for the calmness and composure with which they have allowed the waves of faction to dash themselves to pieces harmlessly at their feet. The towering eagle must not allow himself to be diverted in his onward flight when "hawked at by mousing owls."

On the other hand, whilst President Johnson will not accept the issue of any war of factions or of parties tendered to him—yet those who calculate on intimidating him by threats, or of diverting him from the course of duty by raising hard words for arguments, will soon find out that they have mistaken their man. He will never consent to be a mere automaton President. He regards his duty as something higher, his position as more responsible than that of merely *keeping* the White House, and giving weekly *receptions;* or merely going through the routine of signing his name to acts of Congress. He will never agree to play the part of the Merovingian Kings of France, when mayors of the palace had usurped the kingly power in their own hands—nor of the Doges of Venice, when the Council of Ten had monopolized all the powers of the State. In his message to Congress in December, 1865, Mr. Johnson clearly laid down the principles on which he thought this Union should be readjusted and this Government administered. That message, taken in connection with an address to a delegation of citizens from Montana, in February last, contain the true chart of his future course, and never did there emanate from this distinguished man any thing showing a more calm, philosophical, and conscientious purpose to persist in the course of duty, than this address here alluded to ; and yet so free from arrogance, dictation, or selfishness ! In this address he refers to his previous message to Congress, and reiterates his purpose to adhere to the principles therein laid down. The following extract from this address will enable the reader to judge of the tone and temper pervading the whole of it :

"I think no one can mistake the doctrines of that message. It is very easy for persons to misrepresent it, and to make assertions that this, that, or the other had taken place, or will take place ; but I think I may be permitted to say to you on this occasion that, taking all my antecedents, going back to my advent into political life, and continuing down to the present time, the great cardinal principles set forth in that paper have been my constant and unerring guide. After having gone so far, it is impossible for me to turn and take a different direction. They will be my guide from this time onward, and those who understand them may know where I shall always be found when principle is involved.

"If I can be instrumental in restoring the Government of the United States, in restoring to their true position in the Union those States whose relations to the National Government have been for a time interrupted by one of the most gigantic rebellions that ever occurred in the world, so that we can proclaim once more that we are a united people, I shall feel that the measure of my ambition has been filled, and filled to overflowing; and at that point, if there be any who are envious and jealous of honor and position, I shall be prepared to make them as polite a bow as I know how, and thank them to take the place I have occupied, for my mission will have been fulfilled.

"In saying this in the performance of my duty, and in response to the encouragement you have given me, I feel that I am in a condition not to be arrogant, not to feel imperious or supercilious. I feel that I can afford to do right, and so feeling, God being willing, I intend to do right, and so far as in me lies I intend to administer this Government upon the principles that lie at the foundation of it.

"I can inform all aspirants, who are trying to form their combinations for the future, who want to make one organization for one purpose, and another for another, that they are not in my way; I am not a candidate for any position, and hence I repeat I can afford to do right, and, being in that condition, I will do right. I make this announcement for the purpose of letting all know that my work is to restore the Government—not to make combinations with any reference to any future candidacy for the Presidency of the United States. I have reached the utmost round; my race is run; so far as that is concerned, my object is to perform my duty, and that I will endeavor to do."

He has, at a still later period, given additional evidence of his devotion to long-cherished principles, and of his determination of character and of purpose. On February 10, 1866, a delegation of gentlemen, specially selected by the Legislature of Virginia, formally called on him to present certain resolutions of that body, expressive of their confidence in him, and in his wish and intention to do justice to the Southern people. In reply to an address by Mr. Baldwin, President Johnson spoke at some length. He took occasion to give a more detailed exposition of his views and purposes than he had done before. He alludes to the unmistakable intention of certain ultraists at the North to thwart and embarrass him in carrying out his plan of reconstruction, and to change and revolutionize the character of the Government; first, by perverting the meaning and intent of certain provisions of the Constitution—and secondly, by interpolating additional amendments in that instrument, utterly at variance with its general spirit and design. That factious disposition to force a quarrel on, and bring about a rupture with Mr. Johnson— the outcroppings of which have been heretofore hinted at in this work—has now disclosed itself too plainly to be mistaken. President Johnson, no doubt, feels that to attempt to ignore this combination against him, would be a useless affectation. In his reply to the Virginia delegation, he alludes to it in plain and pointed terms. He does it in perfect calmness, and free from all temper and personal resentment. He does not treat it as a wrong to himself, but to the people of the country—the whole country, North and South—whose constitutional rights he feels himself bound to protect. In his response alluded to, he used the following language:

" ' No taxation without representation ' was one of the principles which carried us through the Revolution. This great principle will hold good yet; and if we but perform our duty, if we but comply with the spirit of the resolutions presented to me to-day, the American people will maintain and sustain the great doctrines upon which the Government was inaugurated. It can be done, and it will be done ; and I think that if the effort be fairly and fully made, with forbearance and with prudence, and with discretion and wisdom, the end is not very far distant.

"I shall continue in the same line of policy which I have pursued from the commencement of the rebellion to the present period.   My efforts have been to preserve the Union of the States. I never, for a single moment, entertained the opinion that a State could withdraw from the Union of its own will.   That attempt was made.   It has failed.   I continue to pursue the same line of policy which has been my constant guide.   I was against dissolution.   Dissolution was attempted—it has failed—and now I cannot take the position that a State which attempted to secede is out of the Union, when I contended all the time that it could not go out, and that it has never been out.   I cannot be forced into that position.   Hence, when the States and their people shall have complied with the requirements of the Government, I shall be in favor of their resuming their former relations to this Government in all respects.

"I do not intend to say any thing personal, but you know as well as I do that at the beginning, and indeed before the beginning of the recent gigantic struggle between the different sections of the country, there were extreme men South, and there were extreme men North.   I might make use of a homely figure (which is sometimes as good as any other, even in the illustration of great and important questions), and say that it has been hammer at one end of the line and anvil at the other ; and this great Government, the best the world ever saw, was kept upon the anvil and hammered before the rebellion, and it has been hammered since the rebellion ; and there seems to be a disposition to continue the hammering until the Government shall be destroyed.   I have opposed that system always, and I oppose it now.

"The Government, in the assertion of its powers, and in the maintenance of the principles of the Constitution, has taken hold of one extreme, and with the strong arm of physical power has put down the rebellion.   Now, as we swing around the circle of the Union with a fixed and unalterable determination to stand by it, if we find the counterpart or the duplicate of the same spirit that played to this feeling and these persons in the South, this other extreme which stands in the way must get out of it, and the Government must stand unshaken and unmoved on its basis. The Government must be preserved.

"I am gratified to find the loyal sentiment of the country developing and manifesting itself in these expressions; and now the attempt to destroy the Government has failed at one end of the line, I trust we shall go on determined to preserve the Union in its original purity against all opposers.

"I have no ambition and no object beyond the restoration of this Government. I feel that I am in a condition where I can afford to do right. The climax, the acme, the summit of my ambition, has been fully reached, yea more than reached. If now I can only arrive at a point at which these States are all restored, each having its representation in the national councils, with the Union restored so that we can once more proclaim peace and good will among the people of the United States, it will be to me a happy day. I care not what may be said in taunt or jeer, I care not what may be insinuated, but I tell you that whenever I shall have reached that point, the measure of my ambition will have been filled, and more than filled. I have no object beyond it. Oh, how proud and gratifying it would be to me to retire from this place, feeling and knowing that I had been instrumental in consummating this great end!"

CHAPTER XX.

It must be apparent, to all observing men, that President Johnson's position is a difficult and unpleasant one. He was elected by "the Republican party," as that party was constituted in 1864. He affiliated with that party, at that time, on the great and absorbing question of the day—the preservation of the Union. To carry out that object expressly, he was nominated and elected Vice-President. To consummate that purpose, not in name, but in fact and in truth, he is still anxious to continue his affiliation and coöperation with the party that elected him. He intends to remain true to his professions and his faith. If those who united with him to prevent the dismemberment of the Union, now attempt to prevent its thorough restoration—more especially after having endorsed his reconstruction policy in their party platforms—how can they, with any consistency, expect him to forget all his past professions; how can they expect him to forget the very cause and groundwork of his association with them, and abandon the accomplishment of that work which has been his leading object in all his struggles and sacrifices for the last five years? The ultra men of the North have no more right to expect him to unite with them on the ground of party association in their reckless and intemperate course, in endeavoring to prevent the restoration of the Union, than had the ultra men of the South to calculate on his following *them* in *their* wild crusade of destroying the Union, because he had been previously united with them in maintaining the constitutional rights of the South against aggression. He ignored party in 1861, to save the Union from disruption; and if necessary he will again ignore party in 1866, in order to its restoration in all its integrity.

As said before, President Johnson will not allow himself to be forced into any party ground. The work he has in hand is above all party. He will continue his onward march along the path of duty, regardless of denunciation, sneers, and taunts, from any and all quarters. His course will be directed by his convictions of duty to the rights and interests of the people, and to the people he will appeal when embarrassed by faction. An issue between the Executive and Legislative Departments of the Government would be a result greatly to be deplored. It is an issue Mr. Johnson will never seek. It is an issue he will avoid, if possible; but if forced on him, with a view of destroying his power, influence, and character, and of reducing him to a mere cipher, he will stand firm and unshaken. He is over and above all other departments of the Government, the national representative of the will and power of the people of the whole country.

President Johnson *cannot* recede. If he falters, he is lost. The *prestige* of his power and his name rests upon his character for firmness, conscientiousness, and devotion to the rights of the people. He has all the time during the war, and since the war, maintained the position that the insurgent States were not out of the Union, and that as soon as they afforded evidence of returning loyalty, they were entitled to a full restoration of all their rights in the Union—to an admission of their representatives into the national councils, and to a participation in all the national privileges and benefits. If he yields this point now, if he allows himself to be made the instrument of faction, in merely executing the orders of those who may be intent on preventing the operations of the Government, with a view to party combinations and party ends hereafter, he will become a nonentity, he will be made to be his own political self-executioner, and history will write him down as a *failure* instead of a *success*. But this will never be. He is too sagacious to be entrapped by the wiles of those who are trying to circumvent him. He is too firm to yield to their dictation. He is too conscientious and patriotic to turn back on the pathway of duty because briers and thorns may be thrown in his way.

The author by no means intends to intimate that the Republican party is either engaged in or sanctions the covert attempts now being made to undermine and destroy President Johnson's power and influence, and to reduce him to a mere *caricature* President. It is hoped and believed that when an issue is finally forced on him, the great body of that party will be found adhering to and sustaining him, true to the professions of their party platforms in endorsing his reconstruction policy, and on which the people elected their representatives in Congress. When the crisis has fully come, and the issue has to be met, it will probably be found that a comparatively few in the Republican party have by their greater zeal and clamor manufactured a sort of factitious public opinion, which they assume to be the sentiment of that entire party. Just as it was in the South in 1861, when a comparatively few men, by their stratagem, concert, combination, and energy, succeeded in imposing on the people their own disunion sentiments as the fair expression of the popular will. This they effected in a great degree by clamor, and by the charge of disloyalty to the South against every man who dared to resist their efforts. In the same way the ultraists of the North are trying, by the charge of " copperheadism," to " frighten from their propriety " the conservative Republicans who are disposed to sustain President Johnson in his great work of restoring the Union in its original spirit and object—of equal privileges and equal burdens to all the States.

But the misfortune of the South in 1861 was, that there was no Andrew Johnson at the head of affairs. If there had been, he would have saved the country from the blood and slaughter, the sorrows and sufferings, the financial troubles and cumbrous debt, of four years of civil war. Does any one doubt, if Andrew Johnson had been President in 1860–'61, instead of James Buchanan, he would have crushed disunion and secession in their origin ? Andrew Johnson *is* President now. The " extreme " men of the South were forced ultimately to succumb. And now we have the assurance of President Johnson, as enunciated by him in his reply to the Virginia delegation, that " the other extreme," in the North, " which stands in the way " of a restoration of the Union, " must get out of it, and the Government must stand unshaken and unmoved on its basis." It was the dying boast of Augustus that he found Rome built of brick, and left it built of marble. If President Johnson succeeds in the accomplishment of his great mission, his dying boast will be a much prouder one than that of Augustus. He will be able to say that he found a great and powerful republic of thirty millions of people, shaken and distracted by a bloody war of four years' duration, and left it united and harmonious, and again progressing in its onward career of prosperity, happiness, and renown.

It must strike impartial men, who are free from party bias, that President Johnson has been badly treated. At an early period after the termination of the war, he laid down his plan of reconstruction preparatory to the admission of the insurgent States into the Union, with all the rights and privileges of the other States. This plan was contained in his chart of instructions to the Provisional Governors appointed by himself. This plan was virtually approved by the people of both parties at the North, in their endorsation of Mr. Johnson in all their party platforms previous to the election. The people of the Southern States, with almost entire unanimity, conformed to this plan, under an *implied* understanding, as they supposed, that this was all that was necessary on their part in order to the acquisition of their former *status* in the Union. At this time nothing had been heard of their being required to abolish slavery by their State conventions, the ratification of the amendment of the Constitution of the United States, and of the repudiation of the debts contracted by the individual States in the prosecution of the war. President Johnson and Secretary Seward, as the organs of public opinion expressed by the dominant Republican party at the North—in the result of the fall elections of 1865 —suggested to the people of the Southern States a conformity with these additional requirements. They were conformed to with alacrity and in good faith, by the conventions of those States. In communicating these demands to the Southern States, as additional conditions precedent to their complete and entire rehabilitation in all their rights as members of the Union, the President and

Secretary acted in good faith. They were honest and sincere in advising the Southern States that it was the part of wisdom and of policy to comply with these demands. The Southern people regarded these requirements as *final and conclusive*. In complying with these suggestions on the part of the highest functionaries of the Government, under the intimation, as they supposed, that the last objection would be thus removed, they thought they had finally passed through the fiery ordeal of the consequences of resistance to the Government, followed by conquest and subjugation.

But, lo, and behold the result! The Southern people have done all that men can do in atonement for past wrong on their part. They have admitted their error in the passage of ordinances, annulling their ordinances of secession, and declaring them void *ab initio;* they have given the strongest evidence of their loyal submission to the Government; and they most earnestly request to be fully and finally restored to that Union from which they madly attempted to depart. They, no doubt, feel most keenly the disappointment and mortification to which they have been subjected. They feel that they have been misled— that where they expected generosity and forbearance, they have received neglect and scorn. But they do not blame President Johnson for this. So far from it, they seem to entertain a stronger attachment for him, and a stronger faith in his truth and justice—believing, as they do, that he, too, was misled and deceived in holding out hopes and making implied promises, which he is ready and anxious to fulfil on his part, but in which he finds himself thwarted by others. How can any sane man expect him to quietly allow himself to be made the instrument of misleading and deluding the Southern people? Not only his sense of justice, but his sense of self-respect, alike forbids his disappointing hopes resting upon implied promises on his part. To require this of him would be to ask him to forfeit his word—a thing he never has done, and will not do now. The ultraists of the North seem resolved to put President Johnson's metal to the test. When they force the issue upon him, they will find that he has not forgotten that the ashes of General Jackson rest in the soil of Tennessee. It will not require any pilgrimage to the tomb of the hero, to teach him his duty. His assailants will find that his power rests in the conservation and loyal masses of the people, North and South. These will sustain him against the schemes of faction, and will stand by him in any measures he may be compelled to adopt in consummating his great object of perfecting the Union, and placing it on a basis which will make it perpetual. As well might the fanatical sectaries of Germany, who committed such horrible excesses in the name of the Protestant faith, have required that Luther and his great compeers in the Reformation, should pervert the true principles of Protestantism, to the proscription and persecution of those who objected to their hateful and wicked course.

Since the foregoing pages of this work were written, President Johnson has returned to the Senate, where it originated, with his *veto*, the bill for the enlargement of the powers of the "Freedmen's Bureau." It would be idle for the author to attempt any argument to prove the demerits and evil consequences likely to follow the bill, in case it had become a law. The message of the President, accompanying the return of the bill, presents the argument against it in the most simplified, condensed, and unanswerable form. It confirms and strengthens his reputation as a strong and forcible writer. It rarely happens that the same man is able and fluent, both as a speaker and a writer. Such, however, is President Johnson. As a

State paper, this veto message cannot be excelled. It is in good taste, free from all temper and excitement, respectful to the Legislative Department of the Government, decided in tone, plain and easy of comprehension, and free from all *ad captandum* appeals. He could not have done otherwise than veto this bill, and yet preserve his consistency as a constitutional Executive. The approval of this bill would have been in violation of all the professions of his past life. It would have forever destroyed the *prestige* of his character and name, which rests on the conviction pervading the public mind, that he is a man who thinks for himself, and that he cannot be *driven* to violate a high sense of public duty. The great objection to this bill was not so much in its special objects designed to be accomplished, as in the consideration that it would have thoroughly effected a consolidation of the Government. It would have virtually erased all State lines, and have reduced the States to a condition even below that of corporations; for corporations have their protection under the law, and the courts to enforce the law. Even in imperial France, such an interference with municipal rights, such a usurpation of the internal domestic police regulations of the territorial departments, would be regarded as an act of unwarranted despotism. The veto message shows on its very face the deep regret Mr. Johnson felt at taking the position he has done. The blame is not his. An issue is now fairly made up, which the people must ultimately decide. It is in the name of the people and the people's rights that Mr. Johnson has vetoed this bill. It was not because the provisions of the bill were to apply to the Southern States exclusively—it was not because of any especial regard for the Southern people that he refused to approve it. It was because its passage would have established a precedent that would have enabled the General Government to monopolize any and all the powers of State legislation—which would, in fact, have revolutionized the whole principles and structure on which the Government has been administered from its foundation.

It is hoped and believed that the majority in Congress that voted for the bill do not fairly reflect the sentiments of the Republicans of the North. It is to be hoped the conservative masses of the Republican party will rally to Mr. Johnson and sustain him in his efforts to save the rights of the people and of their respective States from being absorbed by the central power. He rallied to them—and he rallied a large portion of the people of Tennessee to them —to save the Union from disruption; will they now refuse to rally to him in his endeavors to heal the wounds inflicted on the Union by a terrible war, and to remove the obstacles in the way of its harmonious reconstruction? That an effort will be made by some to read President Johnson out of the Republican organization, there is no doubt. But if the people are true to themselves—true to their professions of devotion to the Union, both before and during the war as to the object of its prosecution—true to the great principles on which the Government was founded, and on which it has been so long administered—those who may endeavor to read out President Johnson will find themselves read out, when the ballot-box shall issue its irresistible decree. Those who may suppose that he issued that veto on a calculation of political chances, and that, in case he may not be sustained by public opinion, he would hereafter regret his course as having been based on a misconception of popular feeling, know not the man. *His course has been dictated by his conviction of duty.* And even supposing it possible that, through the appliances of party machinery, the popular decision should be against him, still those who may believe that his future days

would be embittered by regret and disappointment growing out of the reflection that he had misjudged the temper
of the public mind, understand nothing of the notions and
principles by which such a man as Andrew Johnson is
actuated. Although he is a firm believer in the capacity
of man for self-government, although he has full confidence in the ultimate correct decision of the popular
judgment, yet he is no mere vane on the political house-
top, shifting with the current of every passing breeze. He
considers it the part of a great statesman to march in the
van, or at least abreast of public opinion—to aid in
pioneering the popular judgment to a correct conclusion—
and not merely to follow behind, and hurrah in its wake.

On Wednesday, 28th February, 1866, there was a very
large and enthusiastic meeting of the citizens of Washington, held for the purpose of sustaining and endorsing President Johnson, and his course in vetoing the bill alluded
to. The people, numbering thousands, marched to the
White House, to testify their admiration and respect for
him. He was called for, and he had to appear. To avoid
addressing the crowd on such an occasion, was out of the
question. He *did* address them, and in his address he
spoke in his usually bold, straightforward style. He
reiterated his determination to persevere in the discharge
of the great duties devolving on him. There was no turning or prevarication in his remarks. He repeated his unyielding purpose to adhere to the Constitution, and to
maintain and preserve, to the extent of his power, the
great principles of free government embodied in that
instrument. He announced his resolution to do his duty,
regardless of all consequences, either political or personal.
That he felt deeply, is evident from the tenor of the whole
speech. He felt deeply wronged from certain quarters;
and manly resentment under a consciousness of wrong has

ever been a trait of his character. Still he is too well-balanced in mind and disposition to even carry his resentment beyond the bounds of due self-respect and self-defence. Those who expected him to quail before denunciation, sneers, and threats, have now discovered what sort of a man they have to deal with. The responses from the people in all parts of the country, in support of Mr. Johnson's veto, and his general policy, are of the most cheering character. It shows that the masses are being aroused to the conviction that the Government is in danger of being revolutionized by faction, and that they rely on THE MAN OF THE PEOPLE—ANDREW JOHNSON—to guard and protect their rights and their liberties.

Insinuations have been made by Mr. Johnson's enemies that he had abandoned the Republican party, and was about to throw himself in the arms of the Democratic party. This is a foul and unmitigated slander. The peculiar circumstances of his position, and the peculiar character of the work he has to do, forbid his being a *mere party man*. He is very much in the situation Washington was in 1789, when he first took charge of the Government. When Washington saw his Revolutionary compatriots arrayed against each other in party conflict, he identified himself with neither, although he sympathized with the Federal party, because of his association with them in the advocacy of a *Confederate* Government of separate States; yet he never belonged to any party, in the real sense of a party man. His was the high mission of inaugurating and putting into successful operation a Union under which for seventy-one years the country was prosperous and happy. Mr. Johnson was, by the current of events, drawn into affiliation with the Republican *organization* (we prefer not to use the term *party* in connection with his name), upon the great issue of preserving the

Union from dismemberment. The stand-point of this organization was, that the Union should be maintained on its original basis and in its original character, as comprehending all the States, upon terms of perfect equality. His sympathies and affiliations must continue with the Republicans, as long as they remain true to the great principle which first brought him in affiliation with them—*the maintenance of a Union of all the States, with equal privileges and equal burdens.* If every Republican were to desert him, he would be found "solitary and alone," as he was in the Senate of the United States in 1860–'61, when he was left, the only one of all the Southern Senators, to fight the battle of the Union. Although his heart was then wrung with anguish at finding himself deserted day after day by his former political comrades, who abandoned the post of duty to rush into the vortex of revolution, yet his stout heart, his devotion to duty, his glowing patriotism, and his unerring judgment as to the result, bore him up and sustained him. It was an awful and trying crisis, but he went through it unscathed. No *small* man could have gone through such a tempest without shipwreck. When smaller men were quaking and trembling amid the din of war and the clash of arms, Andrew Johnson stood firm, erect, and undismayed. When the Government seemed to be shaken as it were by a moral earthquake, the voice of Andrew Johnson was heard above the loudest howlings of the storm, in those mighty efforts of his, from which we have given extracts, calling on his countrymen to come to the rescue.

Unjust and uncharitable insinuations have also been indulged in, that Mr. Johnson is endeavoring to build up a new party, by enlisting recruits from all other parties and factions, with a view to his reëlection as President in 1868. Louis Napoleon, in his late life of Julius Cæsar, says: "How little able are common men to judge of the motives which govern great souls!" Whether or not such a sentiment came consistently from the French Emperor, it does not matter. The remark is true. Those who thus misjudge Mr. Johnson, estimate him according to a standard of political morality by which their own movements are regulated. The history of Mr. Johnson's administration since he came into power, as well as his whole previous life, stamp with falsehood any such charge. There has been no President since the days of Monroe, who seems to have thought so little of himself in the dispensing of patronage, and the exercise of official power, as Andrew Johnson. He neither knows nor inquires what may be the personal views or party predilections of the thousands of officials in the country. Has there been any proscription for opinion's sake? None whatever. Has he required those who hold office to commit themselves to his political fortunes? Not at all. Has he not by his course risked his popularity with that party so strongly in the ascendant? Where, then, are the evidences of his trying to pervert his official influence, to further the aims of personal ambition? They exist nowhere except in the distempered brains of those who thus impugn his motives. Mr. Johnson thinks in his head, and feels in his heart, that the greatest boon he could bestow on his country, the greatest blessing he could confer on the people of this Republic, would be the restoration of harmony and concord among sections and States, and the reconstruction of the Union upon an enduring basis, preserving in their integrity the original landmarks and guaranties of freedom to the citizen, and municipal rights to localities, as we received them from our fathers. He also thinks and feels that the accomplishment of this great object would give him more enduring fame with posterity, a loftier name in history, and a brighter and richer legacy to leave to his children, than the mere possession of the Presidential office for the balance of his life. Some may say this is ambition. Yes, it is ambition, such as Washington possessed. It is the ambition to be useful in his day and time, and to leave his country great, prosperous, and happy, when he is no more.

CHAPTER XXI.

In his estimate of the character of the great men who
have adorned our country's annals, Mr. Johnson seems to
regard General Jackson, next to General Washington, as
his *beau-ideal* of a great man.   This is not to be wondered
at.   There was very much of similarity in the early history of the two men.   They were both natives of the same
State.   General Jackson's birthplace, at the time he was
born, was in what was then considered as North Carolina;
but on running the division between the two States afterwards, it fell south of the dividing line.   On leaving their
native State, both found a home in Tennessee, where they
were honored and promoted by the same people.   Both
were left orphans at an early age, with widowed mothers
to provide for.   Both were thrown on their own resources,
with no other fortune than their energy and self-reliance to
sustain them.   Both were favorites of the people, by whom
they were invariably confided in and sustained.   Both
were decidedly and unaffectedly DEMOCRATIC in their politi-

cal principles and personal feelings. But it was General Jackson's peculiar traits of character as a public man that excited the admiration and reverence which Mr. Johnson has ever felt for him. His boldness and candor in the maintenance and expression of his political opinions on all subjects—his determination of purpose amid the most trying obstacles—his self-reliance under any and all circumstances—his ardent attachment to friends—his unquailing resistance to his enemies—his strong, straightforward common sense, which carried him directly to the object to be attained, regardless of the technical difficulties of logical deduction—his love for the people, and his pride in the possession of their admiration and esteem—his freedom from all affectation of dignitied importance—these are the traits in General Jackson's character which excite Mr. Johnson's profound reverence and veneration. Whenever alluding to General Jackson, he cannot repress his feelings. In a speech delivered in the House of Representatives in 1845—not long before General Jackson's death—Mr. Johnson thus spoke of him :

" It is not necessary for me to speak of Andrew Jackson. A mere recital of his acts stamps him as one of the greatest civilians and military chieftains the world has ever produced; eulogy detracts from, instead of adding any thing to his great name; he has performed the important task assigned to him by an all-wise and inscrutable Providence. The measure of his country's glory is now full; his memory is deeply embalmed in the hearts of a grateful and prosperous people; he is now in retirement in the bosom of his adopted State, surrounded by Tennessee's native forest, enjoying the domestic sweets of his own Hermitage, there reflecting upon the varied and chequered scenes of his eventful life, which has been devoted exclusively to the promotion of his country's good. How consoling the meditation in this his very evening of life, while the lamp is sending forth its longest and brightest blaze, which is soon to sink down to rise no more, and with the consoling hope of being crowned with eternal happiness beyond the grave! I thank God that General Jackson's reputation stands above and beyond the reach of all assaults coming from pretended friends or open enemies. His history is his country's legacy; it is for the people to defend it against all such attacks; and palsied should be the tongue that dares to calumniate his great name; powerless and withered should be the hand that attempts to pluck a single gem from that brilliant chaplet that encircles his illustrious brow!"

In perusing Mr. Johnson's speeches, the reader is forcibly struck with his thorough acquaintance with the Scriptures. His quotations and apt illustrations from the Bible show a great familiarity with that book, and that his reading of it must have been systematic. His frequent and reverential allusions to an all-wise and overruling Providence show very clearly that he recognizes, in their full measure, the great essentials of religious obligation and of Christian duty. Although not a communing member of any particular church, he is known to entertain the greatest reverence for the Christian religion, and veneration for the ministers of that faith, whilst he is entirely free from any trait of bigotry or sectarianism.

There is a striking similarity between the history of every great people and the characters of great historical men. Every great people has its peculiar type of civilization—its peculiar mission to fulfil in solving the problem of human progress. Every great man, whose name and achievements are a portion of his country's history, is in a measure the representative of some great abstract principle which gives him his peculiar identity. Washington was the impersonation of a conscientious discharge of DUTY. We see that same trait in his character in every relation in which he was ever placed. He was as dutiful a subject to his king and country, before the war of the Revolution, as he was a patriot of independence after. Mr. Clay was the representative of PATRIOTISM. He judged of every question, and acted accordingly—with reference to how it would affect the honor and glory and happiness of his country. The great leading element in Mr. Webster's character was LIBERTY REGULATED BY LAW, as secured in the Constitution of the United States. Hence his idolatry for that instrument. With Andrew Johnson the great stand-point of his character is THE RIGHTS OF THE PEOPLE. His devotion, admiration, and regard for the Democratic-republican element in our institutions, is no mere affectation. Hence we see in the whole history of his life, his acts, his speeches, his State papers—all exhibit the same watchful jealousy for the *rights of the people*. He has evidently been a great reader of history, especially with a view to the investigation of those causes that have undermined and destroyed other Governments. He regards the philosophy of government as consisting in the advancement of the masses in intellect, prosperity, and happiness. He has the most unquestionable faith in the capacity of man for self-government. His faith in this respect has been strengthened by historical reading, which teaches that the constant tendency in all Governments is " the stealing of power from the many to the few; " and that the highest duty and noblest mission of the statesman is to guard and defend the rights of the people against official and representative usurpations of power.

We find the same principles pervading Mr. Johnson's construction of the Constitution. In his interpretation of that instrument, he occupies a medium ground between the rigid constructionists who chaffer over the letter of the Constitution, and those latitudinarians who would stretch its spirit so as to embrace any and every power. Whenever the rights of the people are involved on any question on which the Constitution is silent or doubtful, Mr. Johnson looks to the spirit of the instrument. And regarding, as he does, the *rights of the people* to be the great paramount object that underlies the whole framework of our social and political systems, he construes the Constitution liberally in their favor wherever these rights are involved. On the other hand, wherever there is a conflict between popular rights and official prerogative and power, he is a rigid and strict constructionist in favor of the former as against the latter. He has always claimed to be a State-rights man. But his view of State rights is different from that ordinarily entertained by the special advocates of that school. In his maintenance of State rights, he contends not for mere territorial privileges, not for the mere rights and privileges of one politically organized community as against another, but the rights of the people of such State or community against official encroachment from any other quarter.

There is a moral lesson in the study of the life and character of Andrew Johnson which is calculated and cannot fail to make a deep impression on the minds of the rising generation. Genius, as has been before remarked, is naturally distrustful and retiring. When in poverty and undeveloped by education, it needs encouragement to enable it to exert its powers. Andrew Johnson's life and history speak to genius, when tethered by poverty and obscurity, the language of cheering and of hope. Let every poor boy in the land, no matter how dark may be his prospects in early life, no matter how friendless, no matter how unlearned, think of Andrew Johnson, and never despair. He here sees an instance of a man who, by constant toil and unremitting effort, fought his way from humble obscurity to the highest position in the nation. Let him reflect that manual labor, so far from being degrading, is honorable and praiseworthy when resorted to as a means of honest independence. It is also well calculated to make him proud of, and devoted to his country, when he reflects that our Government recognizes no royal road to honor and distinction, but that, as in the Olympic games of antiquity, every one may enter the lists for distinction with equal chances for success, and that the laurel crown of the victor is awarded to merit and to worth. Let him reflect that even without early education it is never too late to begin to learn, and that the human mind, by its own exertions, may achieve wonders in science and learning when urged on and sustained by a determination to excel.

But let him reflect at the same time that toil and energy, and force of character, alone will not suffice. These, when united with the most brilliant genius, must fail of success unless accompanied with sobriety, honesty, truthfulness, justice. Here is the solution of the problem of Andrew Johnson's success. He saw that moral principle must be the basis of all exalted character and fame with posterity. Constant success has never intoxicated him (as it has many of the highest promise) with the idea that he dare disregard the high moral obligations of those private virtues mentioned. Let the youths of our country contemplate the history of Andrew Johnson, and then resolve that "onward and upward" shall be their motto. Let neglected genius, when it weeps at the want of sympathy on the part of the world; let honest poverty, when it shudders at the dark prospect of the future; let humble obscurity, when it writhes under "the oppressor's wrong" or "the proud man's contumely;" let a noble ambition to be useful as it turns with despondence from a survey of the great theatre of life, or beholding the parts filled in great measure by the unworthy and the time-serving—let all these think of Andrew Johnson, take cheer and comfort, and brace themselves up for an encounter with the obstacles of life. But let them all remember, in their noble emulation for usefulness and fame, that a high and exalted moral virtue is the very key-stone of the arch of greatness —that

> " talents angel-bright,
> If wanting worth, are shining instruments
> In false ambition's hand, to finish faults
> Illustrious, and give infamy renown."

Mr. Johnson possesses in an eminent degree one faculty which is a never-failing characteristic of greatness. That is the faculty of, insensibly as it were, and without effort, influencing, directing, and regulating the action of those with whom he is brought in contact. This mysterious mesmeric influence, which some men thus imperceptibly exercise over others, is a thing impossible to analyze or explain. But so it is. It is an unquestionable evidence of force of character. It is native, and can't be acquired. It has been described by the historians of all ages and countries as an element of greatness. Andrew Johnson never has been, and could not be, mediocre and commonplace, in any position occupied by him. In old party times, it is doubtful whether any man of his day influenced and directed the party action of those with whom he was affiliated more than he did. Whether as commissioner of the village of Greeneville, Tennessee, or as a member of the Senate of the United States, he stamped the impress of his character and influence on all those with whom he was brought in council. This trait of character he seems to have possessed from boyhood, so the author has been informed by one who received the statement as coming directly from an old companion of Mr. Johnson in his boyhood, and who is now living. He was asked if there was any thing remarkable or striking in Andrew Johnson when a boy, differently from other boys. "No," said he, "nothing particular, except this: There was a set of us apprentice-boys that generally went together, when we were not at work, and Johnson always led the crowd. I don't know how it was, but somehow or other he always had things his own way, and without any contention we all gave up to him. If he said, 'Go a-hunting,' why, all the rest of us agreed to it, and we went a-hunting. Or if he said, 'Let us go in swimming,' we all went a-swimming. And so it was with every thing else. We all gave way to him."

In his manners and bearing toward those who are brought in contact with him, President Johnson is very much the same man now that he was when in early manhood he labored for an honest living. It is not unknown to the author that it has been ungenerously and untruly charged that he was a man of morose, sullen, and unsocial disposition. That calumny had its day, and was lived down by Mr. Johnson. It came from sources personally unfriendly. He is rather a retiring man, as is almost uniformly the case with sensitive men of genius, who have been neglected in early life. Being a man of great sagacity in his judgment and estimate of human character, he observes men a little closely before admitting them to his confidence. Besides, he is a man of great dignity of character, and he must know a man well, and have known him long, before encouraging a familiarity which, when indulged too far, is apt to undermine esteem and respect. Instances no doubt have occurred where those who have maligned and flouted Mr. Johnson during the canvass, have after his triumph affected to honor the position by the proffer of respectful consideration to the man. He has rarely been deceived in such cases. In fact, sagacious men who have had much experience in public life, acquire a sort of intuitive perception, which enables them to discover who are sincerely their friends and who are not. In some such supposed instances Mr. Johnson may not have greeted his quondam calumniators with the warmth they expected, and hence the unfounded insinuations that he was a man lacking in the amenities and courtesies of life. The author has been at pains to inform himself correctly on this score. And the concurrent testimony of all who have been brought in contact with him, either officially or socially—whether his political friends or enemies, whether his personal admirers or those who felt indifferently toward him—Mr. Johnson is a man who, while he never forgets what is due to himself, never fails in the observance of that civility and politeness which is due to others. He never presumes on his official station to treat with rudeness or discourtesy those who seek his presence. To his old friends and acquaintances he is affable and cordial, to strangers he is respectful and dignified, to his political opponents civil and polite. The striking trait of his personal deportment is a plain and unostentatious manner, with a quiet dignity which commands the respect of all who approach him. There is a naturalness about him which assures the beholder at once that there is nothing artificial in his character. It is this which has secured for him that reputation for *sincerity* which he has ever had. Without being loquacious, he is fond of lively and intellectual conversation. Without being boisterous, and rarely indulging in hilarity, yet he is cheerful, and sometimes jocose. To those who object to him that he has not the artificial manners of a Chesterfield, he may well make the reply of Themistocles, who, being told that some complained of him as wanting in polish of manners, " 'Tis true," said the great Athenian, " I cannot play the lute, but I know how to make my native State great and powerful." Andrew Johnson may not know how to play the lute; it is doubtful whether he knows how to dance scientifically; but one thing is certain: he knows something about how to preserve, re-adjust, and reorganize the free and republican institutions of his country when jarred and shaken by discord and faction.

In size Mr. Johnson is of about the medium height, with a firmly-knit frame, indicating a capacity for great labor and physical endurance. His general appearance is youthful for one of his age. He might well pass for ten years younger than he is. He has a thick, full head of hair, formerly very black, now of a slight gray tinge. His eyes are black, keen, and penetrating, of a liquid appearance, and of a rather serious expression. His complexion is a natural bronze. He has a finely-formed head and well-developed forehead, denoting the reasoning and inductive faculties to a very considerable extent. His most expressive features, perhaps, are his strong massive jaw and compressed lips, indicating, as they almost invariably do, force of will and decision of character. His step is firm and elastic. His general appearance and bearing are those of a man in the vigor of life.

President Johnson has had five children, four of whom are still living. His eldest, a daughter named Martha, married Judge David T. Patterson, a gentleman of high character and fine legal attainments, residing in East Tennessee.* Mrs. Patterson, owing to Mrs. Johnson's indifferent health, presides over the domestic arrangements of the " White House," and " does the honors" with that quiet ease and refinemement of manner which bespeak her the

* For some years he was Judge of the Circuit Court, and is now one of the Senators elect to Congress from Tennessee.

accomplished lady and hospitable and kind-hearted hostess to all who call. The President's second child, a son, Dr. Charles Johnson, was killed by a fall from his horse near Nashville in April, 1863, to the great sorrow and distress of his afflicted parents. At the time of his death he held the position of surgeon of the Tenth Tennessee Infantry. Colonel Robert Johnson, his third child, is living, and is said to be a man of ability and of promise in his profession as a lawyer.

His fourth child, Mary, married Colonel Daniel Stover, who, during the late civil war, commanded the Fourth Tennessee Infantry. He died in Nashville, a refugee from his home, in December, 1864, of disease contracted in the service. His youngest child, a son, Andrew Johnson, Jr., is a lad born in 1852.

President Johnson may be regarded as the representative, the organ, the exponent of the feeling of a common interest and a common brotherhood between the two sections, struggling against the adverse influences of the late desperate conflict. He is the impersonation of American civilization and American ideas, developing, combining, and exerting their moral and material influences in such way as to extort the respect of foreign Governments, and the admiration and attachment of *the people*, who love liberty regulated by law, in every clime. His name, and his character, and his *status* with posterity, are indissolubly connected with the mighty developments now in progress. His task is a difficult and perilous one. Although the main fury of the storm has subsided, still the heavings of the mighty deep are yet heard and felt. He cannot avoid his destiny, and, fortunately for his country and for himself, he does not wish to avoid it. As is usually the case with historic characters, posterity will probably hold him responsible for the consequences to be developed from the present state of the country to an extent not warranted by strict and impartial justice. If he is to be held responsible for the future, ought the necessary powers, to enable him to contend successfully with the difficulties before him, to be unwillingly or grudgingly conferred ?   Not only the dictates of an enlarged patriotism, but the requirements of interest, both national and sectional, demand that the people of the country should yield to him their confidence and support. They should sustain him against suspicious doubts, and carping criticisms, and factious insinuations. In order to wield effectively the powers of American civilization (the author prefers to use this term of " American civilization," as contradistinguished and meaning something different from "civilization" in its ordinary sense), President Johnson must be *national* in his feelings, in his means, and in his ends. If he is *national*, he can't be *sectional*. If he should be sectional, he will live in history not as the *representative man* of the moral grandeur, material power, and recuperative energy of American civilization, but as the impersonation of a faction.

The author, in his historical reading, and his reflections on historical characters, has often dwelt on the character of Sylla. So far as intellect is concerned, he was unquestionably one of the greatest geniuses that ever lived. His life was one uniform success over obstacles and difficulties rarely equalled. As a military commander, judging from what he accomplished and what were the difficulties to be overcome, it is doubtful whether he had a superior in the long annals of his country's military greatness. As an administrative officer he was equally successful. In his estimate of men his perception was unfailing and almost intuitive. At a glance he saw in Cæsar, when a youth, the germs of his future greatness. He is said to have then remarked of Cæsar, " There are many Mariuses in that young man." And yet Sylla does not occupy in history, or in the estimate of succeeding generations, the position of one of the great representative men of Roman grandeur and power. He has not received from posterity that apotheosis awarded to many of his countrymen who were vastly his inferiors. Why is this? It is not because he is regarded as a bad man. It is true he drenched the streets of Rome in the blood of her citizens, and slaughtered his enemies without mercy. But it was at a period of mutual extermination by the factions. And Sylla is generally regarded more in the light of a man who felt that the pressure of necessity required him to make "short work" of the Marian faction, than of a man naturally malicious or fond of blood. In fact, the general tenor of his life proved him to have been a man of kindly and generous character. He was not a man of morbid ambition, nor was he a tyrant by nature, for he abdicated the supreme power when he might have held it, retired to private life, and died in comparative obscurity. The reason why he does not occupy a higher place in the estimation of posterity is this: He was the head of a faction. His position in the Social War was that of the representative and leader of the patrician against the plebeian order. If he had exhibited the same powers and performed the same exploits in behalf of *the nationality* of the people in sustaining their honor and glory, and in defending their interests, against either external or domestic foes, Sylla would have occupied as lofty a niche in the Pantheon of Roman greatness as any name in the history of that wonderful people, not excepting the great Julius himself.

President Johnson needs no such warning as that conveyed in the history of Sylla. That factions will arise from the disturbed elements of the times may well be expected. That these factions will endeavor to keep alive heart-burnings and animosities between sections, and classes, and interests, is equally certain; for strife is the element in which faction lives, the food on which it subsists. These factions will endeavor to *use* Mr. Johnson in the furtherance of their purposes, and, failing in this, they will make war on him, either open or secret. Fortunately for the country, he knows men well. His perception of human character is of no ordinary kind, and it will stand him in stead in the selection of those to whom he may intrust his confidence. His position before the country is so well defined as the representative of American nationality, and the embodiment of the political rights and moral power of *the people*, that the leaders of faction will have to encounter his iron firmness of disposition, his great shrewdness in the appreciation of character, his well-known reliance on the masses of the people, and his nationality of patriotism, in their efforts to divert him from the path of duty.

In using the term " American civilization " (a favorite one with the author) is not meant a mere progress in moral and intellectual improvement, according to its usual acceptation. A steady advancement in moral, intellectual, social, and material power, in such way as to elevate the great mass, *the people*, in the scale of virtue, prosperity, and happiness, is what is meant. We hear a great deal about the cultivation of science and art, and the high standard of civilization reached by the ancients. But when closely examined, it is found to be progress and cultivation by the few, regardless of the condition or fate of the masses. Egypt gave letters and science to many of the peoples of antiquity. But the learning of Egypt was confined to an organized priesthood, who vigilantly guarded its mysteries within an esoteric sanctuary, against intrusion from the great mass of the people, who were used as the mere instruments of despotism, and regarded as unfit for any thing but *labor*, which was considered degrading. This is not the sort of civilization for America. The ancient Greeks attained to the highest perfection in science, art, and philosophy, of all the nations of antiquity. In fact, it is doubtful whether the human intellect has ever reached as high a point of development in any other age or country. But still it was the social law of Athens that an appreciation of the beautiful in art, and the achievements of the mind in science, were the proper pursuits of the contemplative and reflective few, whilst toil and drudgery were the business of the common herd. Her earlier philosophers confined their researches and reflections mainly to natural phenomena, and the laws that govern the material world, as a mere discipline of the mind, and a means of private pleasure and enjoyment. The duty of utilizing their knowledge and discoveries, so as make them available to the common people in promoting their prosperity and enjoyment, seems not to have been a part of their system. Nor is this the sort of civilization suited to America.

Roman civilization was the embodiment of material power. This enabled them to conquer the world. The structure of their power abroad over the conquered world lasted long after the key-stone had tumbled from the arch of their citadel at home. But the elevation and prosperity of the masses of the people was not the stand-point of Roman civilization. Her government was a government of the patrician order. The tribuneship was extorted from the Senate by a revolutionary movement, but the same forms in the Government and the same social ideas continued to prevail. They were eminently oligarchic. The Senate granted the appointment of tribunes to the people, as a concession to a popular outbreak; but the tribunate itself soon came to be an element in the system of obligarchy which pervaded the social and political structure. It was the rarest thing for the behests of the "conscript Fathers" to be impeded by the interposition of the tribunes. The Government of Rome became great and powerful; but it was a Government of Patricians. Her historical characters, down to the time of the civil wars, were, in the main, of the Patrician order. The system of *clientage*, so satirized by her dramatists, shows how difficult it was for a Plebeian to reach social respectability, except by attaching himself to some man of position in the State. Nor is Roman civilization the civilization suited to America.

English civilization is but little better adapted to the wants and requirements of the American people. The civilization of the former seems to consist in making money— mere material wealth—the panecea for all political complaints; and that true philosophy consists in trying to deceive oneself, as an antidote for the prickings of conscience. British statesmanship can see nothing higher for the aspiration of the masses, than good wages, snug cottages, and the condescending notice of the great occasionally, at the hustings, or at stated festivals. That, as to political affairs or governmental concerns, that is the business of the aristocracy, either of blood or wealth. That political morality consists in keeping fleets on the coast of Africa to suppress the slave-trade; and at the same time importing *coolies* into her colonies, to undergo a bondage much more objectionable than that of African slavery. That political truth and consistency consist in contending that every people possessing a separate district, and historical nationality, should have the right to govern themselves by their own laws, and yet compelling Ireland and India to wear a yoke of bondage, not simply to live *with* them as equals, but to live *under* them as inferiors. That national honor and national propriety consisted, during the late four years' bloody war on this continent, in professing to both parties great regret at the continuation of the struggle, and at the same time encouraging both to persevere. Great Britain supposed, like the ostrich, that she was concealing her designs by hiding her head, whilst every man on either side well understood that it was her purpose to encourage both to continue the struggle till both were exhausted, that she might advance her own interests and power by the ruin of others.

French civilization is also out of place in America. In France, the Government is every thing, the people nothing. Their ideas of happiness and prosperity consist in a monopoly by France of the military glory of the age. That the people have nothing to do with the Government except to go through the forms of voting for those first selected by it. That the Government is discharging its functions, in providing for the entertainment and amusement of the people; and that the people are doing their duty in sustaining the Government in its aspirations for military glory. Alcibiades, in cutting off the tail of his favorite dog that the people of Athens might have something to amuse themselves with, and to talk about, by way of withdrawing their attention from his peculations on the treasury—foreshadowed French civilization in its present operation and influence. "Let us eat and drink, for to-morrow we die"—seems to be the philosophy of life with that strange and wonderful people.

German civilization is no better. There can be no active result-achieving civilization without patriotism. Without patriotism there is nothing to intensify effort—nothing to stimulate in the pursuit of some great national object. In Germany patriotism, after all, is a myth. The German writers are continually harping on "THE FATHER-LAND." And yet, what does that mean? With a Prussian, does it mean Prussia, or does it mean the Germanic

Confederation ? In the little principality of Reuss, does it mean the small territory contained within its limits, or does it mean something more ? Patriotism is a very jealous sentiment. It will not admit of any divided allegiance. Whether it is owing to this want of a concentrated and undivided patriotism growing out of the peculiar political arrangement of the Germanic Confederation, or whether it is owing to some peculiarity in the constitution of German character, it is difficult to tell. The Germans are probably the most intellectual people on the globe so far as mere mental power and research are concerned. And yet, so far as regards the practical application of mind to the development of the useful in promoting the comfort, well-being, and elevation of the masses, they are doing nothing. As a people they are stationary. They have no future—they have no great object to attain —no great mission to accomplish—no great status to preserve. Hence it is that the German mind is mainly directed to the investigation of the mysterious and the abstruse. The Germans are a nation of metaphysicians. Mental effort is with them employed in an investigation of the nature and properties of, and the relations between, mind and matter—in trying to unravel the tangled skein, at one end of which is Deity, and at the other is Man. Contemplation, without reference to any useful or practical end, seems to be the occupation of German mind and thought. This may, perhaps, operate as a sort of " escape-pipe " to mental activity, which, otherwise, under the fermentation of outward pressure, might vent itself in revolution and social disorder. But there is no *progress* in it —no advancement of human good. Compared with American civilization, it is like gazing at the heavenly bodies, reflecting upon their ages, their composition, and the purposes of Almighty wisdom in their creation, instead of measuring their distances, relations, and orbits for the purpose of applying the result to the practical uses of commerce, the measurement of time, and their influences on weather and the seasons.   If the powerful intellects of her Leibnitzes, her Kants, and her Fichtes, and a host of others of the same class, had been devoted to the practical and the useful in advancing the material prosperity of man, instead of groping through the labyrinths of ideology, what might they not have effected, not only for Germany, but for the whole human family.

The course of American civilization is direct and onward to the accomplishment of a mission which it has, under the dispensation of Providence, to fulfil.   Its march is along a double road, with two tracks parallel and contiguous, one of material, the other of moral advancement. The emigrant-pioneers, who first came to these shores, if they had been guided by the standard of European civilization, at the end of half a century would not have been out of hearing of the surge of the ocean.   Necessity, and the sense of duty superinduced by reflection, swept away the antiquated notions of the degradation of *labor*.   The simple rearing of houses in which to live, and the clearing of fields from which to obtain food, taught them that *labor* had to go in the van of material improvement.   The workshop went up side by side with the church, the school-house, and the court-house.   Here, then, were the elements of American civilization.   A free and untramelled religious worship under the system of voluntary association ; a system of education for the sons and daughters of all in common, so as to develop, for the common good, the intellectual resources of the coming generation ; the preservation in its purity of the common-law, that great inheritance from their Anglo-Saxon forefathers, which the latter had brought with them from the forests of Germany ; the political equality of all men, based on the principle that man is capable of governing himself, and that the object of government is the good of the *many* as contradistinguished from the *few ;* the redemption of a continent from the dominion of savage solitude, the levelling the forests, the scaling of mountains, the spanning of rivers, and the substitution for the roving savage of sixty or eighty millions of people, free, prosperous, and happy, in the enjoyment of liberty regulated by law, and of popular government administered by themselves. This is American civilization. It has already swept across the Continent, and from the shores of the Pacific it is straining its eyes westward. If we could lift the curtain that conceals the future, might we not expect to see it still "with the star of empire westward taking its way," till it passed the isles of the seas through Japan, China, and over the Himelayas, reaching the cradle of man's existence and the scene of his redemption—and still travelling in the track, and with the impetuosity of the great Gothic exodus of the long gone-by ages, finally reaching, remodelling, and adapting to the wants of the age the dilapidated systems of European civilization !

Andrew Johnson is the impersonation and representative of this American civilization. His name and his fame are identified with it. With him, so far as the past is concerned, all is secure. Let him go on and accomplish his high mission and fulfil his high destiny. The muse of history will then crown him with the chaplet of fame she is now wreathing for his brow. She will then write him down as

> " One of the few, the immortal names,
> That were not born to die."

CHAPTER XXII.

The Close of the War—An Article in the "London Quarterly Review"—Cause for Indignation at the Course of the British Government and People—It Encouraged the South to Persist—It could have Stopped the War—Proposed Mediation of the Emperor of the French—Jealousy and Alarm of Great Britain at the Growing Power of the United States—Statements of the "Review" Examined—Its Fling at President Johnson—Wishes and Hopes of the Reviewer.

Since the author commenced the task in which he has been engaged, he has read in the "London Quarterly Review" for July, 1865, an article headed, "The close of the American War." This article, though written in good temper, and exhibiting a very accurate acquaintance with the events and incidents of the war, is thoroughly *British* in its character, in its reflections as to the present, and in its hopes as to the future. Under the guise of affected moderation and impartiality, it exhibits the same jealousy and apprehension of American greatness and power, that marked the course of the British Government and people during the continuance of the war. Under all its croaking about principle, and duty, and right, the reader can easily discover that by these terms is meant what they invariably mean in the vocabulary of a British politician or pamphleteer, viz.: the promotion of British power and influence, and the control and monopoly by Great Britain of the commerce and finances of the globe. Whether viewed from a Northern,

a Southern, or a national stand-point, the article alluded
to is equally objectionable. It may be regarded as an exponent of the views and feelings of the tory party in Great
Britain. At the same time it is a defence of the party in
power (the Whigs) for their course during the war.
From the general tone of the article, it sympathizes deeply with the South; and yet, there is such an inconsistency
between the views presented in regard to the merits of
the struggle, and the course which the Government and
people of Great Britain pursued, and which the article alluded to now justifies, as plainly to prove that the sympathy for the South therein affected, is hollow-hearted and
insincere.

The people of both sections, North and South, have
equal cause to feel indignant at the course of the British
Government and people. Both sections understand it
thoroughly, and both are likely to remember it, and pon-
der on it for many years to come. From the commencement of the war and throughout its duration, the evident
hope and design of the British Government and people
was to intensify and fan the fires of the strife. The British press, and the speeches of the British members of Parliament, again and again reiterated the assertion that the
South could not be conquered, that its independence was
only a question of time. The ability of Southern generals
and the prowess of Southern armies, were praised to the
skies. The South was encouraged to persist in the struggle, was told that their cause was just and right. It was
easy to tell from the *tone* of the British press, and the
speeches of British orators, to which side fortune
seemed to incline, in the course of the war. When fortune
favored the South in the fighting of battles, or the movements of armies, the press of England—with the " London
Times " in the lead—would teem with praises of Southern

valor, and predictions of Southern success. But they always took care to wind up with the declaration that in no event could Great Britain interpose to arrest the shedding of blood, and frequently with the allusion that, in consequence of slavery in the South, they could not intervene toward building up a great power based on that institution. All that was to keep the North up to the work of putting down the disunion movement, under the assurance that they had nothing to fear or apprehend from British aid or interference in favor of the South. On the other hand, whenever the prospects of the South looked dark and gloomy, whenever Southern armies lost any great battle or any important strategic point, these same presses and orators told the South to hold on and fight to the last, that their subjugation was impossible; that a wonderful reaction in their favor was going on in the minds of the British people. And on such occasions, it invariably happened that letters affecting to be from those who had access behind the scenes, found their way sometimes from Paris to London, sometimes from both those places to this country, assuring the people of the South that diplomatic movements were going on, looking to recognition or intervention in their favor. Southern men in England were assured by the people of that country, that perseverance in the contest would surely result in ultimately bringing the British Government to the rescue. It was in one of these dark and despondent periods for the South that Earl Russell described the war as " a struggle for independence on the one side, and for empire on the other." All this was for the purpose of keeping the South well up to *its* work of fighting and contending to the last.

The British Government could have stopped the war, and brought about a friendly adjustment of our difficulties, if it had wished to do so. It will hardly be denied that national pride had much to do in preventing propositions for an amicable arrangement coming from one side or the other. A kind and friendly offer on the part of any great nation to interpose in procuring a peaceful settlement of our troubles, would no doubt have been received in a proper spirit by both parties. Each would, at least, have been willing to hear what such friendly power had to say. But an amicable and peaceful arrangement was just the very thing Great Britain did not want. That she desired a separation of the two sections, and the independence of the South, there is no doubt; but while intriguing for this secretly, she had not the manliness to avow it. If she was sincere in wishing to arrest the flow of blood and in her pretended opposition to a government based on slavery, why did she not interpose in favor of a friendly reconstruction of the Union? She knew that in making such a proposition, she had nothing to fear from the resentment of the South. It was because she knew that such restoration would only strengthen and consolidate the power of the American Union, of which she is so jealous. If she thought that the South was in the right—that it deserved independence, that it must ultimately succeed, as insisted on by the British press and British orators, why did she not, from feelings of humanity, and as the pretended friend of both parties, interpose and intercede with the North to grant Southern independence? Because she knew that such a course would anger and offend the Government of the United States.

At one time the Emperor of the French proposed to Great Britain to unite with him in a joint mediation between the North and the South. The Emperor explained his purpose to be nothing more than a friendly offer on the part of the two powers to harmonize and reconcile differences without any wish or purpose to dictate terms to

either. Knowing, as both Governments did, the temper
and determination of the Government of the United
States, they both understood by the proposed mediation
the preserving the integrity of the Union. But that was
what Great Britain wished never to see again. If she had
even stood by perfectly neutral, and looked on with calm and
stoical indifference, it would have proven her to be callous
to all the appeals of humanity, and destitute of sympathy
for suffering man, when by kind interposition she might
have ended the struggle. But, instead of looking on with
heartless unconcern, she gloated over the common dis-
tresses and sacrifices of both parties, and encouraged the
one party or the other to persist as she thought she saw
signs of flagging in either. Her course proves that she
hates the Government and people of the United States at
the same time that she fears them. She was willing
enough to see vessels of war built in her ports for the use
of the "Southern Confederacy," and munitions of war
supplied to it to any extent, as long as she could use the
pretext of laying the blame on her private citizens and her
municipal laws. She even connived at it as long as she
could covertly do so. But she did not dare to protect her
own citizens or to sustain her own laws when the United
States Government gave her to understand that it would
not be tolerated.

Great Britain has long looked on the growing power of
the United States with jealousy and alarm. She is appre-
hensive lest the spread and influence of the principles of
our free institutions may undermine the monarchical and
aristocratic foundations of her political fabric. She is
jealous of the North on account of its great commercial
power and wealth, which threaten to supplant her in the
markets of the world. She is annoyed by being dependent
on the South for cotton. Whilst railing against Southern

slavery she is encouraging a far worse system of slavery than ever prevailed in the South, by oppressing the Ryots in India and enticing coolies to her West India possessions. Her hypocrisy on this subject is enough to disgust the nations of the earth. If Great Britain had acted a noble, manly, high-toned, and Christian part in this struggle between the North and the South, she would forever have had the gratitude of both sections, and for all time would have had a fast friend in the United States. When she saw blood flowing in torrents, the fairest portions of the earth devastated, ravaged, and ruined, and sorrow and distress pervading the land, if she had been actuated by an elevated philanthropy and had offered her friendly mediation, not for the purpose of destruction but of preservation, not for the purpose of widening the breach but of healing it, what a blessing might she not have conferred, what suffering might she not have prevented? Nay, more: what an immense advantage might she not have secured to herself? To the North she would have saved hundreds of thousands of lives and thousands of millions of debt incurred. To the South she would have saved not only the same, but the devastation of their country and the humiliation of subjugation.

Great Britain has, by her selfishness, her heartlessness, and her Jesuitical hypocrisy, struck herself a blow from which she will reel and stagger for many a year to come. She has not only fastened on her manufactures exported to this country a high tariff, that will not be diminished, but under the impulse this will give to manufactures in this country, she may look out to find us competing with her in every market in the world. Instead of weakening her great rival by her attempts at dismemberment, she has made that rival far stronger and more powerful than ever. She may, possibly, by a change in our Constitution, which prohibits the imposition of any export duty, or through the machinery of an excise law, find herself compelled to pay five or six cents a pound for cotton grown in this country more than our Northern manufacturers will have to pay for it.   But above all, she has lost more than in all else in the kindly feelings and respectful consideration entertained by the people of the United States for the British Government and the British people.   She has been instrumental in converting the United States into a great military and naval power, which never dreamed of its own resources before.   Our facility for raising and maintaining armies would enable us to drive British power out of Canada in sixty days.   Our immense navy, improvised by the war, enables this Government to meet Great Britain not only on distant seas, but to sweep the British and the Irish channels whenever we feel disposed to do so.

The foregoing reflections have been superinduced by reading the article referred to in the " London Quarterly Review."

In the article alluded to, the author finds great fault with the Government of the United States because its *object* in prosecuting the war was not to destroy slavery but to save the Union.   Absurdity and inconsistency are constantly urged against Mr. Lincoln and the action of the Government, because they set out with the avowal that their object was not to interfere with slavery in the States. The reviewer says :

" It is, however, on record, to show the readiness of the Federal Congress to debar itself forever from any pretence to interfere with slavery in the States, and this whilst persons in this country were loudly asserting that it was to destroy slavery that the war was waged."

Again, speaking of President Lincoln's emancipation proclamation, the reviewer says ;

"As a matter of moral principle, nothing could be more inconsistent, for it prohibited the sin to the enemy and permitted it to the ally. It made right and wrong a matter of geographical convenience; for certain counties in Louisiana were to retain the system, whilst the rest were denied it: and more than this, it retained slavery where there was power to end it; and it pretended to sweep it away where there was no power to touch it."

Oh, yes! If the war had been waged expressly to destroy slavery in the outset, and it had thus been destroyed, all would have been right and proper! Great Britain would thus, in the opinion of the writer, have been no longer dependent on America for cotton, and the cotton manufacturers of America themselves would have to rely for a supply of the raw material elsewhere than on the Southern States. His great regard for the rights of the States, about which he discourses as flippantly as any fire-eater when it suits his purposes, disappears when the destruction of slavery is involved. With an Englishman the destruction of slavery means the destruction of the cotton-growing interest in the United States. What the writer designed as a censure of the Government of the United States is, in fact, the best defence of it. The object originally was not to interfere with slavery as it existed in the States. It was only as that necessity was developed during the prosecution of the war, that the Government felt bound to strike at the institution. It was done not from a fixed purpose in the outset, but only as a means of weakening the power and resources of the insurgent States. The writer, in speaking of the way in which the war was conducted, says:

"There was an entire absence of fixed principle or persistent action; nothing but getting along with the affairs of the day—now yielding to the pressure on this side, and now on the other; adopting no great principle without reversing it, etc., etc."

15

Yes, the Government had to adapt its action to the emergencies of the occasion; there was no precedent to govern under circumstances never contemplated by the founders of our institutions. But, after all, the course pursued resulted in success. One would suppose that as slavery was finally overthrown the writer would have been content. But then, the Union was preserved—the national life was saved—the Government was made stronger, more compacted, the better able to teach other nations their duty whenever they shall attempt to invade our rights. There is where the shoe pinches. The writer of the article says:

"No war of modern times has been urged in a spirit so bitter, so unsparing, so ungenerous. The sinking of stone-fleets, to destroy harbors, the bombarding of dwelling houses with Greek fire, the cutting of levées to inundate great districts and drown out the inhabitants, the shooting of prisoners on more than one occasion in cold blood, the official insulting of women and of clergymen, the avowed attempts to destroy by famine, the burning of mills, farm-houses, barns, the plunder of private property—these, apart from incidents of individual outrage, which ever accompany invading armies, have made memorable the names of Butler, Turchin, Pope, Sheridan, Blenker, Hunter, Milroy, McNeill, as a band of Generals, of all human beings, the least fitted to restore a fraternal Union."

Aye, and did Great Britain, with all her proud boasting of being at the head of civilization, stand quietly by with folded arms, and look on these horrible outrages on humanity, and not lift a finger to prevent them? When the Emperor of the French proposed to the Government of Great Britain a joint mediation for the purpose of procuring an amicable adjustment of the difficulties between the North and the South, why did the latter decline if her sensibilities were so shocked at the barbarities this writer speaks of? Was she *afraid* of offending the North? The writer will hardly admit that. Was she doubtful about the success of an attempt by mediation to heal the strife of the contending parties? As no harm could have resulted, ought not the effort to have been made from sheer feelings of humanity, if the people of England really believed that these atrocities were being perpetrated on the people of the South? This very writer, who assumes that these savage barbarities were being practised, yet defends and justifies his Government for holding back and making no effort for peace. He justifies this non-mediation on account of the existence of slavery in the South. He says:

"Slavery was doubtless the real cause, why the independence of the South was not recognized by the European Powers, when the great effort of the North for the capture of Richmond, made after ample preparation, and in enormous force, ended in utter failure." "Recognition would have been warranted by the facts, and by the precedent most closely in point, the separation of Belgium from its union with Holland. The step was dictated, so far as this country (Great Britain) is concerned, by the most obvious considerations of self-interest. But it was thought by those with whom the decision rested, that until forced to it by circumstances, our Government ought, on *principle*, to abstain from action. It was not permitted to weigh political advantage against what seemed to be a moral obligation. Few in America are likely to understand this."

The writer is mistaken. *Everybody* in America understands it thoroughly. What does he mean by "the most obvious considerations of self-interest," what by the "political advantage" he speaks of? What *can* he mean, but a disruption of the American Union, and a consequent weakening of American power and influence? That was the "principle" on which the British Government "abstained from action." He admits that from the "facts" and from the "precedent of Belgium," recognition even, would have been warranted. Then, according to this writer, by the laws of nations, the "Southern Confederacy" should have been recognized. And yet he prates about the "moral obligation" to abstain from action. What higher moral obligation rests on any Power that claims to lead in the van of civilization, than to boldly step forward and vindicate the laws of nations, where the facts and a precedent directly in point warranted it? But the difficulty lay in slavery! Ah, indeed! when before has it been avowed that one country observed toward another its objections under the laws of nations according to its approval or disapproval of the internal domestic institutions of the latter? Why did not Protestant Britain object to the Roman Catholicism of Belgium? Why did not highly civilized England and France object to polygamy and harem-slavery in Turkey, when they went to war with Russia in order to preserve the national integrity of the Sultan's dominions? Where was the writer's regard for "principle" and for "moral obligation" then?

The views of the writer in the "London Quarterly" are not objected to on the ground that Great Britain *should have* recognized the "Southern Confederacy;" but it is from his own stand-point that his argument is here exposed. On "principle" and on "moral obligation," Great Britain could not recognize a people who tolerated slavery! And yet she was perfectly justifiable in aiding and encouraging the insurgent States by selling to them munitions of war—in winking at the building of vessels-of-war for them in the dock-yards, as long as it could be done clandestinely—in encouraging them by their presses and orators (those in the cabinet as well as those out of it) to persevere, to fight on, that their cause was just, that theirs was the cause of independence against empire, and that they must ultimately succeed. England could not recognize the South because of slavery! Principle and moral obligation forbade it, although according to the laws of nations the South was entitled to recognition. Did principle and moral obligation forbid her proposing a friendly mediation, with a view of ending the strife, and of arresting those cruelties, outrages, and barbarities on the part of the North that this writer speaks of? She knew that such friendly mediation would probably end in putting a stop to these very horrible outrages the writer speaks of— the very thing she did not wish to see. The combatants were not sufficiently exhausted. Like the fox in the fable, watching the lion and the tiger at fight, Great Britain looked on with chuckling delight, that she might carry off the spoil when both were overcome by the contest.

With all his Jeremiads over the sufferings and wrongs of the South, the writer in the " London Quarterly " may rest assured that the people of both sections understand this matter thoroughly. And it is hard to tell which section, North or South, feels most indignant at the miserably selfish and hypocritical conduct of the British Government. If the British Government had from the first acted a candid, manly, and ingenuous part; if she had frankly told Mr. Mason from the first that, owing to slavery or any other cause, she could not from principle and moral obligation recognize the South, instead of " pattering with him in a double sense; " if she had promptly issued her proclamation declaring that she would not allow vessels-of-war to be built in her ports and dock-yards, intended for the Southern Confederacy, and warned her people against supplying the Southern States with munitions for the waging of war against a friendly power, instead of covertly winking at it; if her presses and orators had fairly and honestly told the people of the South that they had nothing to expect from the British Government or the British

people, instead of flattering, cajoling, and deceiving them
with the hope of recognition or intervention, the South
would not have persisted beyond the second campaign.
But, up to the very last, the delusion was cherished by the
South that Great Britain would interpose in her favor.
During the war, there is no doubt but great barbarities
and excesses were perpetrated on both sides, and Great
Britain is mainly responsible for it.   The Southern people
had tired of the war two years before its close.   They
would have been glad of any decent pretext to have
stopped it.   Having blundered into a difficulty through
the intrigues and conspiracy of a comparatively few
wicked men, nothing but an unwillingness, through a false
and stubborn pride, to make the proposition of a reconciliation on the basis of reconstruction, caused them to persevere in a hopeless contest.   A proffer of friendly mediation on the part of Great Britain would have removed this
objection of wounded pride, and peace might have been
secured, and those atrocities on the part of the North,
which the writer bemoans, been arrested.   The North
and the South both feel equally aggrieved by the course of
Great Britain.   If a war were to be waged against that
Power by the American Government, even to compel her
to make compensation for Northern commerce destroyed
by the ships of the " Confederate " government that were
built and fitted out in Britain, the men of the South would
feel that they had wrongs to avenge equal to those of the
North.

But the writer in question must needs have a fling at
President Johnson.   This is not to be wondered at.   The
" London Quarterly," which the writer selects, as the me-
dium of his lucubrations, is the recognized organ of the
aristocratical, divine-right-of-kings party in Great Britain.
Neither it nor its contributors can possibly understand how

it is that a man of humble birth, of plebeian origin, of little
wealth, of non-collegiate education, should be elevated to
the highest office in the gift of thirty million people.
With him and his co-workers of the "London Quarterly,"
it staggers all belief that such a man can ever be any thing
but a low and vulgar fellow. That he ever should reach
an eminence where he is the equal in social position of
dukes, earls, and lords, is monstrous, no doubt, in their estimation. Let them understand that the very object and
natural result of our free republican institutions is to elevate merit, and talent, and usefulness, from obscurity and
poverty, and make them conducive to the public good.
According to the political ethics of our institutions—

"Worth makes the man, want of it the fellow."

In speaking of the sad fate of Mr. Lincoln, this writer
says :

"That calamity is greatly increased by calling to his place one
even less fitted for it by education or knowledge, and without
the redeeming personal qualities of his predecessor. That Mr.
Johnson is a man of considerable natural ability we cannot doubt;
for without it no man could have worked his way from the condition of a journeyman tailor to the position he held at the outbreak of the war. But there are many kinds of ability, and there
is one kind which has been usually regarded in the North as by
no means beneficial to the country—that of the professional politician; the man who adopts politics as a trade to live by and
thrive by. Such was the occupation of Mr. Johnson, and it was
successful under these circumstances."

Here is a set of jingling sentences, thrown together
without consistency, without reason, without justice, without truth. The writer having first come to the determination to write down President Johnson as without worth
or fitness for his station, has assumed facts, and resorted to
arguments necessary to sustain his "foregone conclusion."

He admits Mr. Johnson's "natural ability." If he has the natural ability, and if he possesses high moral character and unexceptionable personal qualities, what is there strange or wonderful that he should have deen honored and promoted as he has been? And as to the latter—moral and private worth—his character is without stain or reproach. It has never been assailed by his enemies even in the times of highest party excitement. "But," says the writer, "there are many kinds of ability," and Mr. Johnson's ability is "that of a professional politician." It is really difficult to understand what the writer means by this term "professional politician." How can any man reach eminence in any pursuit or calling, unless it be the chief occupation and business of his life? When a prudent man wants to get his rights in a court of justice, he employs a professional lawyer. When suffering from illness, he sends for a professional physician. When a nation is to be defended, it calls for the professional soldier. When a people intrust the guardianship of their rights to an agent of their choice, if they are wise they select a professional statesman. A statesman cannot be improvised for the occasion, any more than a poet can be. It requires the experience and training of a lifetime to make a statesman. And in all free countries this training can only be attained by a long mingling and thorough acquaintance with political affairs. It is so in Britain. Are not Palmerston, and Russell, and Derby, and Gladstone, "professional politicians"? Is not the confidence which their respective followers repose in them, based on the knowledge and experience acquired by their lifetime devotion to political affairs? Look at some of the great men of our own country, whose fitness and capacity this writer will hardly question. Were not Clay and Webster professional politicians? They devoted their lives to politics. Both were of humble and obscure parentage, as well as Andrew Johnson. Both were thrown on the world poor and friendless like him. Look at Fillmore. He was a poor, uneducated boy, bound to a mechanical pursuit in early life. He reached the same elevated position now held by Andrew Johnson. He was a professional politician. Does the writer think he reached the Presidency through the " extreme prejudice and narrow education " of his constituents ?

If the writer means by " professional politician " one who " adopts politics as a trade to live and thrive by," then he is simply ignorant of the true state of affairs in this country. Of such men as those mentioned, who devote their lives to politics as a profession, nine-tenths of them die poor. But few of our retiring Presidents have saved a competency for their old age. True, there are a set of *trading* politicians in our country who *do* " live and thrive by " politics. But these men are rarely in the legislative councils. Generally, they hold no positions of responsibility to the constituent body. They are the men who work the wires and manœuvre the appliances of party machinery, who hunt around for jobs and contracts, who have a keen scent for hunting out the local offices out of which money can be made; who cluster around Washington, hunting up spurious claims, and trading off their penny-a-lining talents to those who will pay them best. But this is the very class of men who never found any favor at the hands of President Johnson. If the writer in the " London Quarterly " will read his speeches in Congress, he will find that Andrew Johnson has again and again held up this class of trading politicians to public reprobation. He has denounced them as "vampires," as " vultures gathering together over the carcass," etc. This class of men are the last to expect any favor or countenance from President Johnson.

In order to strike President Johnson, the writer in question must stigmatize his constituents, the people of Tennessee, who have so often and so long honored and sustained him. He says:

"Tennessee, one of the younger States, contains a very mixed population, and a great proportion of small farmers, who are usually men of extreme prejudice and narrow education. These, from their number, could always swamp the educated classes; and with such a constituency, no man was more likely to succeed than Andrew Johnson. With the energy necessary to go through the work, views, and habits suited to their own, and unlimited command of words, he gradually attained all the honors and emoluments their votes could confer. He was an ardent defender of slavery, and a slave-owner himself to the extent of his means," etc.

The writer is entirely ignorant on the subject upon which he is attempting to inform others. Tennessee is not one of the younger States. She is older than this century. She is regarded as one of the old States. Her population, so far from being a "very mixed one," is as homogeneous as that of any State in the Union. So far from being a new State, filling up with pioneer adventurers, she has long been furnishing emigrants for the more distant West and Southwest. So far as East Tennessee is concerned, it is admitted that there is "a great proportion of small farmers." But if this writer will visit America, and especially the mountain region of East Tennessee, he will find that those sections where this great proportion of small farmers prevails, and where the soil is fertile and the country healthy, contain the best populations on the continent. There is not probably any portion of America containing a more substantial, hardy, industrious, enterprising, and thrifty population than East Tennessee. True, there are not very many men of large fortunes there; but the great mass of the population are well to do, and live in great comfort and plenty. Real poverty is but little known there, or was not before the war. In that portion of the State the population is not mixed at all. They are the descendants of the settlers of ante-Revolutionary times. Like all mountain people, they are devoted to liberty, and very jealous of their rights. To have been so often honored and promoted by such a people—as President Johnson has been—is the highest evidence of his ability and worth—the highest compliment that could be paid to him. The same high character may, in a great degree, be awarded to the people of Tennessee generally. Tennessee is proverbial for the political intelligence of her people, and the great number of prominent and able men she has produced, more especially those noted and celebrated for their powers of popular eloquence. Mr. Johnson has met the ablest of them on many hard-fought fields, and uniformly he has been sustained. The writer says further of President Johnson:

" What judgment is to be formed by the speeches he has made so frequently since his elevation? They ring the changes on three notes—first, the boast of being a plebeian; secondly, the malediction of all traitors; thirdly, the disparagement of mercy. Was ever such a creed presented to the world? We have sought in vain for one noble sentiment, for one generous emotion, for the faintest trace of a recollection that he ruled over the sons of rebels, that his own position was the fruit of rebellion, that the first and great President he had to follow had been a traitor. When it was the business of the statesman to pour oil on the troubled waters, the cry is for vengeance, confiscation, blood."

Very prettily written, but all mere assertion, without proof. What "speeches made so frequently since his elevation" does the writer refer to? This is a covert insinuation that President Johnson has a prurient fondness for speech-making display of himself. When or where has he made any speech that he could with decency and politeness have avoided making? It has been the custom, from the origin of the Government, for the Vice-President, on his inauguration, to make a short address. When respectable delegations from entire States call on him, and offer their congratulations in a formal address, how can he without rudeness fail to respond? When the people in large numbers call to do him honor, how can he refrain from acknowledging their kind respect for him? He has *sought* no occasion to make a speech, and has spoken only where politeness and a due appreciation of respect tendered him, required it. But he " boasts of being a plebeian"! The writer is mistaken. He does not *boast* of it. He has spoken of the fact, and hard run must be the writer for objections, when he has to resort to such as this. Is it at all remarkable that, considering his untoward prospects in early life, the difficulties he had to contend with, owing to his poverty, his want of education and patronizing friends, his toils and labors in providing for a growing family, his final triumph over all obstacles, his regular promotion from a commissioner of the village of Greeneville to the Vice-Presidency, and then to the Presidency of the United States, is it at all remarkable that he should feel pride and exultation at having reached the pinnacle of honor and of station? In alluding to his plebeian origin, he did it not so much by way of glorifying himself, as of glorifying his country and institutions, which had placed him where he was, not *because* of his being a plebeian, but in despite of it. Even if he had boasted of it (which he did not), a generous heart would have excused it *under the circumstances* as a pardonable foible—much more pardonable than if he had been ashamed of it. For whom has the sensible reader most respect—for honest Old Rapid, in the play, who never could forget his early occupation, or for Young Rapid, whose constant appeal to his father after he had acquired great riches and high social position, was, " Sink the tailor dad, sink the tailor."

But the writer says he has sought in Mr. Johnson's speeches " in vain for one noble sentiment, for one generous emotion ; " that his cry is " for vengeance, confiscation, blood." Now, it must be recollected that these speeches to which the writer alludes were delivered directly upon the occurrence of Mr. Lincoln's assassination. It was at a time when the passions, and resentments, and indignation of the people were wrought up to the highest pitch of intensity. Mr. Johnson never claimed, nor did his friends claim it for him, that he was more than man ; that he was entirely free from the impulses and feelings of human nature. Mr. Lincoln was a great favorite of the Northern people, loved and respected by them. At the very moment when they were rejoicing at the consummation of the war and the return of peace, he (Mr. Lincoln) was struck down by an assassin. Who does not wonder that excitement did not go higher than it did ; that retaliation was not instantly visited upon thousands, and blood flow in torrents, under the impression of the moment that the deed *might have been* instigated by the Confederate rulers at Richmond ? No such charge is intimated or countenanced by the author ; he is only speaking of the elements of excitement and passion then prevailing, which maddened the public mind. It was during this period of excitement that these speeches were made to which the writer in the " London Quarterly " refers. But never did he speak of wholesale vengeance, confiscation, and blood. Both before and after, and during the war, he always spoke of the attempt at disunion as a conspiracy on the part of a few, and expressed his sympathy and compassion for the masses who had been deluded and misled. He expressed the opinion (and even then under the exciting circumstances mentioned) that some examples should be made of the leaders, as a warning for others in after-times. Suppose, immediately on the suppression of the last outbreak in Ireland, the monarch or the prime minister of Great Britain had been assassinated in Drury Lane Theatre in London, the assassin using language at the time to indicate that his object was to avenge Ireland; would any English minister, in making a speech in the midst of the excitement, not have been likely to throw out intimations of vengeance and blood? And would not some of the leaders of the Irish rebellion have been more likely to go toward the gibbet than toward Botany Bay?

A public man is to be judged of more by his acts and deeds than by his speeches made under circumstances of excitement almost sufficient to unhinge the judgment for the time. So far as acts go, there is no vengeance, no confiscation, and no blood, except in the case of the murderers of Mr. Lincoln. Mr. Johnson is now actively engaged in pouring oil on the troubled waters. All the preliminary movements toward restoring the insurgent States to their original positions in the Union, with all their former rights, are in progress. Mr. Johnson has already encountered opposition which threatens to become formidable on the ground of his feelings of leniency toward the people of the South. Considering the circumstances, he is proving himself to be a man of great generosity, forbearance, and forgiveness. If the writer in the "London Quarterly" knew the trials and hardships, the oppressions and persecutions, Mr. Johnson had encountered because of his devotion to the Union, he might perhaps make some allowance for any ebullition of feeling he may have exhibited. He was denounced as a traitor, pursued like a felon, his property confiscated, his wife turned out of doors, his house converted into barracks, his son-in-law imprisoned, another a refugee in the mountains, himself insulted and threatened with Lynch-law, and his very name bandied throughout the South as the synonym of villany, treason, and infamy. And yet, when under the stern law of necessity he becomes invested with powers dictatorial in their character, not a drop has he shed. The delight which he evinces at the returning loyalty of the Southern people, and the prospect of a speedy restoration of the Union, and harmony between the two sections, instead of showing him to be a bloodthirsty tyrant, proves that he has the paternal feelings of a public benefactor for the errors and delusions of a misguided people. But the writer has "sought in vain for one noble sentiment, for one generous emotion." The writer is referred to President Johnson's reply to the British minister, Sir Frederick Bruce, on presenting his credentials. It is to be found in this volume. As a specimen of fine English composition, for elevated national sentiment, for good taste and appropriateness to the occasion, it cannot be excelled. President Johnson knew what good taste, national politeness, and the propriety of the ceremony required. But lest the writer in the "London Quarterly" may suppose that Mr. Johnson has forgotten the course of Great Britain during the war, he is also referred to the following extract from a speech delivered by him to a collection of his own countrymen but a short time before, on the occasion of the announcement in Washington of General Lee's surrender :

" The hour will come when those nations that exhibited toward us such insolence and improper interference in the midst of our adversity, and as they supposed of our weakness, will learn that this is a Government of the people, possessing power enough to make itself felt and respected."

But the writer in the "London Quarterly," in the conclusion of the article in question, exposes his feelings, his wishes, and his hopes—as the postscript to a lady's letter does the thoughts uppermost in the writer's mind. He says :

"However different may be the popular feeling of the day, we regard the extent of the Union as a cause that must be fatal, in the end, to the Confederation."

"It is difficult to see how a Union that was not expected to hold good over a homogeneous part, is more likely to endure over a combination of discordant elements."

"This is the first civil war of the race on that continent. It would be difficult to find an instance of a republic whose first civil war was its last. But the terrible cost of this struggle will long be remembered; and with such experience, if it should prove that any large section of the American people again desire to exercise Mr. Lincoln's 'most valuable and most sacred right'—that of possessing a government of their own—we trust the spectacle will be exhibited which Mr. Seward once described—that of a great people rearranging its Government to common advantage, peacefully, and with the approval of the world."

Oh, yes! division, disruption, disintegration of the American Union, still dance before the mental vision of the writer. Let him not roll any such sweet morsel under his tongue. The bonds which hold this Union together are tenfold stronger than ever. The process of rearrangement and reconstruction, toward which President Johnson is bending the energies of his strong mind and energetic character, is progressing successfully and harmoniously. This reconstruction will replace the Union on the most sure and lasting foundations. Our institutions have proven themselves as possessing the element of adaptation to circumstances in an eminent degree. They may be bent, in order to fit the exigencies of historical development, but they cannot be broken. The natural reaction or rebound will adjust them to the very shape and direction designed by their founders. Our own people have just been aroused to an appreciation of the power and resources of our Government. The limits of the Union are much more likely to be extended, than to be curtailed. The ": manifest destiny" the writer in question flouts at, is no myth. There is a deep philosophy in it. It means that great moral causes are just as sure and unchangeable in their influence and progress as are those of the physical world. It means that American ideas, liberty, law, and civilization, cannot be arrested in their march by mountains, rivers, and lakes—by piles of granite or frowning battlements. Mr. Monroe, with almost prophetic foresight, prefigured it, when he significantly intimated many years since that the climate and soil of America were not adapted to the growth of monarchical institutions or the prevalence of monarchical ideas. The American Union having withstood the external pressure of foreign wars, and the conflict of foreign ideas, and having now withstood and surmounted the internal pressure of domestic violence, will henceforth march forward refreshed and reinvigorated on the accomplishment of its great mission. Poorly as the writer in the "London Quarterly" may affect to think of President Johnson, yet he and those of his co-laborers who are chafing with disappointment that they could neither disrupt the Union nor prolong the contest till it sank from exhaustion—cannot roll back the current of time, not unwrite the page of history. President Johnson will go down to posterity identified with that mighty effort which saved the life of the nation, and infused into its Constitution renewed vigor, health, and strength.

CHAPTER XXIII.

March 28, 1866.

THE telegraphic wires have flashed the news throughout the country that President Johnson has returned to the Senate, where it originated, with his objections, another important measure known by the designation of " the Civil Rights Bill."   As it is not the purpose of the author to discuss mere party politics, he does not propose to examine this question itself, or the President's veto of the same, with reference to any partisan combinations or influences growing out of it.   The President's vindication is to be found in reading the veto message.   This document, like the previous veto, is written in admirable taste and temper; its calm, argumentative, and respectful tone, must be admired by Mr. Johnson's worst enemies.   He places the issue on the high ground of a mere difference in judgment and opinion between him and the majority who voted for the measure.   Those who have thus taken issue with him, or rather who have forced the issue of these vetoes on him, seem to have forgotten that Mr. Johnson *had a record* of his previous political life of twenty years, as embodied in the proceedings of Congress, and the many State papers and public documents issued by him in the important positions he had filled. In regard to many of the great issues before the country, he was committed in principle, not as a mere politician, but as a statesman. When he was nominated for Vice-President, his views were known and understood in reference to many points embraced in the " Freedmen's Bureau Bill " and " the Civil Rights Bill," both of which he has vetoed. Those who had nominated him, and with whose political organization the events of the time connected him, had a right to count on his acquiescence, to the extent to which, under the emergencies of the occasion, he had pledged or committed himself. To that extent he is still anxious and willing to unite with them, and is acting with them in perfect good faith. That was the preservation of the Union, when the Union was in danger. Now that the danger is removed, the restoration of the Union to its original status, as near as may be, making allowance for adaptation to circumstances, is the point of junction between Mr. Johnson and the Republican party. But have the latter the right now to add to the conditions on which Mr. Johnson was nominated? They should recollect that on many occasions, in his recorded speeches, he has taken the strongest and most uncompromising grounds against centralization of power in the Federal Government. He is as strongly committed as he can be in favor of leaving to the State Governments the management and control of their domestic municipal regulations. This with him is *a principle*. How, then, can the Republicans ask of Mr. Johnson to repudiate and disregard the professions of his past life—to turn his back on principles enunciated by him in the most solemn manner?

It would be much better for the North, for the South, and for the whole country, to see perfect union and accord between the Executive and Legislative branches of the country, in the great work of restoring the Union. It is deeply to be regretted that this discord should prevail, and exactions should be required of Mr. Johnson so much at variance with the recorded opinions of his past life. Mr. Johnson is acting strictly on the defensive. It is to be hoped that the schism applies to but a fraction of the Republicans. He has a right to consistently appeal to the great body of the Republican party to sustain him upon the grounds of their original alliance. He has been true and unwavering on every point on which he and the Republicans were brought to act in concert. All his sympathies and feelings are with the original Union men, who resisted the attempts to sever the Union. It is true that, after having subdued them, and brought them to a confession of their error, he is in favor of staying the arm of persecution. The generosity of his nature here interposes, and he is disposed to be magnanimous to a crushed and stricken foe, who show a willingness to submit at discretion. But he has given no evidence of a disposition to withdraw his confidence from the Republicans, as such. He has evinced no purpose to bestow his patronage and trust the direction of his administrative policy to those who were untrue to the Union in its day of peril. If ever there was a man who has " proven his faith by his works," that man is Andrew Johnson. His sacrifices and sufferings in behalf of the Union, the dangers he encountered from those who were plotting its overthrow, must be judged of from a standard that scarcely any Northern man (secure from the privations, dangers, and difficulties he had to encounter) can present for the consideration of calm, sedate, and reflecting men. The history of his life is a standing and eloquent appeal to the reason, the reflection, the generous forbearance of the Republicans. This appeal will certainly, ere long, find a kind and just response in their bosoms.

Those who may suppose that President Johnson is inclined to flout or defy those with whom he so long and so zealously labored for the preservation of the Union—those who suppose he derives any pleasure from the unfortunate disagreement with a portion of those whom a common peril to the Government brought together—are seriously in error. Time will prove to them that they are mistaken, that they do Mr. Johnson injustice. Of course, it is impossible to *prove* what is going on in any one's mind; but, if those who suspect his motives could see and know what he has to encounter; if they could understand his mental struggles in deciding between his convictions of duty and his earnest desire to preserve the associations of a common effort in behalf of the Union; if they could thoroughly appreciate his pure and unselfish patriotism in trying to preserve *only one* party (that of the country) until the present troubles shall have passed over; if they could know, as *is the case,* and as *time will prove,* that he is not actuated with any purpose to split the true national Union party, and build up a party devoted to himself, with reference to any combinations in the future; if they could see, and understand, and appreciate these facts, as less than three short years will prove to be the case—those who now do him such great injustice in impugning his motives, would rush in haste to him, readily confess their errors of judgment, and with ardor and zeal proffer their renewed alliance in saving the Government and the Union against the danger of all mere party complications. The author has no wish to see this strife perpetuated. No friend of Andrew Johnson's, no friend of his country, can derive any pleasure from witnessing this disagreement between the Executive and Legislative departments of the Government. The associations out of which the union between Mr. Johnson and the Republicans grew, involve feelings and sacrifices of too important and historic a character to become the mere playthings of party or of faction. May not the appeal be made, as it is here made (is it too late?), to the Republicans, not to endeavor to force Mr. Johnson to gainsay and ignore the events of the past; not to force him to stultify himself by repudiating the long-cherished principles of his life? As to all his pledges in favor of preserving, restoring, and perpetuating the Union of the States, he is ready, willing, and anxious to comply with them both in letter and spirit. There is a striking analogy between the history of the French revolutionary convention and the developments of our own civil strife. Andrew Johnson and those who concurred with him, occupied a position in the United States Senate, in 1861–'62, very much like that occupied by Verginaud, Barbaroux, Brissot, and others, in the Convention in France. Andrew Johnson and those in his position never did belong to the party of "the Mountain." Even in 1862 (as heretofore noticed), more than a year after the war had been in progress, Mr. Johnson introduced resolutions in the Senate declaring that the war was being waged for the preservation of the Union, and that when that purpose was accomplished, the war should cease. Here, then, was the clearest and most unmistakable exposition of his views. His sagacity foresaw, and his purpose was to anticipate, the very evils that have since presented themselves. If he was honest, sincere, and patriotic then—and no one seems to have doubted it—if he dreaded and thought he foresaw that the violence engendered by the strife might possibly lead to a revolution in the framework and structure of the Government, after the Union had been preserved by arms, calculated to sap the very foundations of liberty; and if he sees or thinks he sees, in the consummation of those measures pressed by "the Mountain" section of the Republicans, results tending to the subversion of our Government and its liberties, is he not consistent, is he not patriotic, is he not to be commended rather than blamed, in again risking himself for the salvation of his country? It is not in anger, but in sorrow, that he again bares his breast to the storm. He confided and trusted in the people to save the free institutions of their fathers, when threatened with a terrible civil war; he confides and trusts in the same people now, to save the same institutions against the impulses of temper, of passion and resentment. Will the same people, whom his counsels and warnings led along the path of safety, and to the goal of success, fail to heed him now? To save his country, he abandoned the party affiliations of his past life, *then*—shall he be suspected and denounced for being forced, under the duress of duty, for a partial severance from those with whom circumstances impelled him to unite politically in 1860–'61? This may be his misfortune; it surely is not his fault. He has preserved his consistency; he is simply acting out what he foreshadowed years ago.

It may, perhaps, be said that the analogy of the French Convention is an unfortunate one for Mr. Johnson; that as the Girondists were overthrown by the Jacobins, so the Republicans "of the Mountain" will crush out the "Girondist" Republicans now. But the analogy does not hold good in one particular. History, with scarcely a dissenting voice, proclaims that the Girondists, with all their virtue, and patriotism, and talents, fell, through a want of moral courage. By temporizing and yielding to the extreme measures of the Jacobins, they lost their *prestige* for conservatism.

Moral courage is the great stand-point of Andrew Johnson's character. His combativeness, though defensive in its nature, is of the most firm and unyielding character. But follow out the analogy. Moderation and conservatism finally triumphed in France. With the fall of Robespierre, " the Mountain " fell in France, to rise no more. Then it was the people of France waked up to the conviction that an insignificant minority, claiming to speak the voice of the nation, had, by a factitious public opinion, ruled through terror, and in the name of liberty had been preying upon liberty itself.

The author hopes that he is not misunderstood. His purpose is to present the question analogically. In speaking of the " Jacobins," the party of " the Mountain," etc., his object is not to apply these terms to the Republicans, as such. His object is not to apply these terms to the great majority of that party in Congress who have differed with Mr. Johnson on his late vetoes. The author has no wish or intention to indulge in epithets, in denunciation, or in the suspicion of motives. He views the action of the majority as resulting from those influences of party affiliation, which frequently bias the minds of honest and conservative men, without their being aware of it. The author hopes that time and reflection, and the developments of the future, will bring the conservative portion of the majority in Congress to the conviction that they have misunderstood Mr. Johnson ; that they have misconceived his purposes and misjudged his motives, and that before a great while harmony may be restored between them ; and that the great body of the Republicans will be found rallying around him in his efforts to restore peace, concord, and prosperity to a divided and distracted country.

CONCLUSION.

THE reader will readily perceive the difficulty of preserving systematic arrangement, and of avoiding repetition, to some extent, in a work of this sort. The object of the author being to bring down the review of Mr. Johnson's political history to the very latest period, before going to press, he has been necessarily compelled to allude again and again to the same topics, as the questions treated of have assumed different phases from time to time. Instead of rewriting what has been said on any one subject, whenever any new developments on that subject have taken place, the author has concluded to let his previous comments stand, and add others as new facts and incidents were brought to pass. This work was commenced some seven or eight months before publication. In the first portion of it, many subjects are discussed which excited great interest at the time, but which no longer engross public attention. Events succeed each other so rapidly, and the public excitement shifts so quickly from one subject to another, that no dissertation could be written on the political condition of affairs, or on the life and character of any man who fills an important *rôle* in the events of the day, without its involving this very repetition, and want of systematic arrangement alluded to by the author in his preface.

16

To remedy this defect, such a work would have to be written one day and printed on the next. The writer of this memoir having no ambition of authorship to consult, has preferred to rely on the indulgence of the reader, in presenting his views in a plain, unadorned, and unsystematic method, rather than attempt any of the appliances of regular book-making.

The author has chosen to withhold his name from the public. His object was not to gratify any pride of authorship, nor was it to subserve any personal aim. If by concealing his name he has chosen to forego any personal advantage that might have otherwise accrued to him, he has also secured himself personally against the shafts of unfriendly criticism. He has nothing to retract or apologize for, as to the garb of " hero-worship " in which he has clothed his humble work. Macaulay and Carlyle have given the world examples in that respect, which place no limit to the terms of praise in which the biographer may speak of his hero, provided they are honestly entertained and truthfully expressed. The author frankly admits that he regards Andrew Johnson as *a man of destiny*, that he has a mission to accomplish, that he is the chosen instrument in the hands of a Higher Power, to carry out its inscrutable plans. When Divine Wisdom uses human agency as the means of accomplishing its purposes, it selects *great* men to effect *great* results. The gigantic war which scourged this country for four long years, with all its wonderful incidents and momentous results, was too big an affair to have happened by chance. *It had to be.* Notwithstanding the severe ordeal through which the country is now passing, yet the author has strong faith that the Government will be maintained, the Union reëstablished, and free institutions preserved. Time only can prove whether the author's faith is well founded, that Andrew

Johnson is the destined agent through whom these great ends are to be subserved. The history of his past life is confirmed by the passing events from day to day that *he will not fail.* His success will be the triumph of his country.

THE END.

THE ORIGIN OF THE LATE WAR:

TRACED FROM THE BEGINNING OF THE CONSTITUTION TO THE REVOLT OF THE SOUTHERN STATES.

By GEORGE LUNT.

1 Vol. 12mo. 491 Pages. Cloth, Price $2.50.

"In writing this book, I have endeavored to trace, in a manner which I trust will be intelligible to the general reader, the interior course of the long controversy, sometimes active and again much subdued, but never absolutely at rest, between the North and the South. It was my purpose to make known whatever the facts of the case should of themselves indicate, without any regard to party interests or prepossessions. In thus presenting a sketch of the progress of those causes which led to the Southern revolt, it will be seen that Slavery, though made an occasion, was not, in reality, the cause of the war."—*Extract from Objects of the Work.*

———

"It is one of the books needed at the present moment, and should have a very wide sale. Mr. Lunt has long been distinguished as one of our most able editors and writers. He has had opportunities for observation not surpassed by those of any other man. The result in this volume is most valuable."—*Journal of Commerce.*

"The ability of Mr. Lunt as a writer and his accuracy as a scholar prepare the reader to find it a strong, an interesting, and a valuable historical work. It is all of this. Its style is clear and compact, its array of facts irrefragable, its reasoning calm and cogent. We most cordially commend the book to thinking men of all parties as one which they will read with interest and instruction."—*Eastern Argus.*

"This book is precisely what its title imports. Although a few readers may dissent from some party views that are casually advanced, we are sure that no one can take issue with a single statement bearing upon the real question involved in the work. The book is replete with instruction, and freighted with matter for serious reflection."—*New York World.*

"This is what we want. Mr. Lunt writes well, ably, comprehensively. It is the best book on the conservative side that the country has produced."—*Boston Post.*

"A very remarkable production; we say this, not only with reference to its high literary ability, unsurpassed, we really think, by any thing that has lately been issued from the American press, but in view of the author's position and antecedent social relations."—*Philadelphia Age.*

"Mr. Lunt has searched authorities and precedents carefully, and has made a book that will be read, even if it does not command the confidence of the mass of the people."—*New York Commercial Advertiser.*

A Report of the Debates and

Proceedings in the Secret Sessions of the Conference Convention for Proposing Amendments to the Constitution of the United States, held at Washington, D. C., in February, A. D. 1861. By L. E. CHITTENDEN, one of the Delegates. Large 8vo. 626 pp. Cloth.

"The only authentic account of its proceedings."—*Indianapolis Journal.*

"It sheds floods of light upon the real causes and impulses of secession and rebellion."—*Christian Times.*

"Will be found an invaluable authority."—*New York Tribune.*

The Conflict and the Victory of

Life. Memoir of MRS. CAROLINE P. KEITH, Missionary of the Protestant Episcopal Church to India. Edited by her brother, WILLIAM C. TENNEY. "This is the victory that overcometh the world, even our faith."—*St. John.* "Thanks be to God, who giveth us the victory through our Lord Jesus Christ." —*St. Paul.* With portrait. 12mo.

"A work of real interest and instruction."—*Buffalo Courier.*

"Books like this are valuable as incentives to good, as monuments of Christian zeal, and as contributions to the practical history of the Church."—*Congregationalist.*

Sermons Preached at the Church

of St. Paul the Apostle, New York, during the year 1864. Second Edition. 18mo. 406 pp. Cloth.

"They are all stirring and vigorous, and possess more than usual merit."—*Methodist Protestant.*

"These sermons are short and practical, and admirably calculated to improve and instruct those who read them."—*Commercial Advertiser.*

The Trial. More Links of the

Daisy Chain. By the Author of "The Heir of Redclyffe." Two volumes in one. Large 12mo. 390 pp. Cloth.

"The plot is well developed; the characters are finely sketched; it is a capital novel."—*Providence Journal.*

"It is the best novel we have seen for many months."—*Montreal Gazette.*

"It is marked by all the fascinating qualities of the works that preceded it. * * * Equal to any of her former novels."—*Commercial.*

Chateau Frissac; or Home Scenes

in France. By OLIVE LOGAN, Authoress of "Photographs of
Paris Life," etc., etc. Large 12mo. Cloth.

"The vivacity and ease of her style are rarely attained in works of this kind,
and its scenes and incidents are skilfully wrought."—*Chicago Journal.*

"The story is lively and entertaining."—*Springfield Republican.*

The Management of Steel, in-

cluding Forging, Hardening, Tempering, Annealing, Shrinking,
and Expansion, also the Case-Hardening of Iron. By GEORGE
EDE, employed at the Royal Gun Factories' Department, Wool-
wich Arsenal. First American from Second London Edition.
12mo. Cloth.

"This work must be valuable to machinists and workers of Iron and Steel."
—*Portland Courier.*

"An instructive essay; it imparts a great deal of valuable information connected with the making of metal."—*Hartford Courant.*

The Clever Woman of the Fam-

ily. By the Author of "The Heir of Redclyffe," "Heartsease,"
"The Young Stepmother," etc., etc. With twelve illustrations. 8vo.

"A charming story; fresh, vigorous, and lifelike as the works of this author
always are. We are inclined to think that most readers will agree with us in
pronouncing it the best which the author has yet produced."—*Portland
Press.*

"A new story by this popular writer is always welcome. The 'Clever Wo-
man of the Family,' is one of her best; bright, sharp, and piquant."—*Hartford
Courant.*

"One of the cleverest, most genial novels of the times. It is written with
great force and fervor. The characters are sketched with great skill."—*Troy
Times.*

Too Strange Not to be True.

A Tale. By Lady GEORGIANA FULLERTON, Authoress of "Ellen
Middleton," "Ladybird," etc. Three volumes in one. With
Illustrations. 8vo.

"This work, which is by far the best of the fair and gifted Authoress, is the
most interesting book of fiction that has appeared for years."—*Cairo News.*

"It is a strange, exciting, and extremely interesting tale, well and beautifully written. It is likely to become one of the most popular novels of the
present day."—*Indianapolis Gazette.*

"A story in which truth and fiction are skilfully blended. It has quite an
air of truth, and lovers of the marvellous will find in it much that is interesting."
—*Boston Recorder.*

What I Saw on the West Coast

of South and North America, and at the Hawaiian Islands. By H. WILLIS BAXLEY, M.D. With numerous Illustrations. 8vo. 632 pp. Cloth.

"With great power of observation, much information, a rapid and graphic style, the author presents a vivid and instructive picture. He is free in his strictures, sweeping in his judgments, but his facts are unquestionable, and his motives and his standard of judgment just."—*Albany Argus.*

"His work will be found to contain a great deal of valuable information, many suggestive reflections, and much graphic and interesting descriptions."—*Portland Express.*

The Conversion of the Roman

Empire. The Boyle Lectures for the year 1864. Delivered at the Chapel Royal, Whitehall, by CHARLES MERIVALE, B.D., Rector of Lawford, Chaplain to the Speaker of the House of Commons, author of "A History of the Romans under the Empire." 8vo. 267 pp.

"No man living is better qualified to discuss the subject of this volume, and he has done it with marked ability. He has done it, moreover, in the interest of Christian truth, and manifests thorough appreciation of the spiritual nature and elements of Christianity."—*Evangelist.*

"The author is admirably qualified from his historical studies to connect theology with facts. The subject is a great one, and it is treated with candor, vigor, and abundant command of materials to bring out its salient points."—*Boston Transcript.*

Christian Ballads. By the Right

Rev. A. CLEVELAND COXE, D.D., Bishop of Western New York. Illustrated by John A. Hows. 1 vol., 8vo. 14 full page engravings, and nearly 60 head and tail pieces.

"These ballads have gained for the author an enviable distinction; this work stands almost without a rival."—*Christian Times.*

"Not alone do they breathe a beautiful religious and Christianlike spirit, there is much real and true poetry in them."—*Home Journal.*

Mount Vernon, and other Poems.

By HARVEY RICE. 12mo.

"Fresh and original in style and in thought. * * * Will be read with much satisfaction."—*Cleveland Leader.*

The Internal Revenue Laws.

Act approved June 30, 1864, as amended, and the Act amendatory thereof approved March 3, 1865. With copious marginal references, a complete Analytical Index, and Tables of Taxation. Compiled by HORACE DRESSER. 8vo.

"An indispensable book for every citizen."

"An accurate and certainly a very complete and convenient manual."—*Congregationalist.*

Speeches and Occasional Addresses.

By JOHN A. DIX. 2 vols., 8vo. With portrait. Cloth.

"This collection is designed chiefly to make those who are to come after us acquainted with the part I have borne in the national movement during a quarter of a century of extraordinary activity and excitement."—*Extract from Dedication.*

"General Dix has done a good service to American statesmanship and literature by publishing in a collected form the fruits of his ripe experience and manly sagacity."—*New York Tribune.*

The Classification of the Sciences.

To which are added Reasons for Dissenting from the Philosophy of M. COMTE. By HERBERT SPENCER, Author of "Illustrations of Universal Progress," "Education," "First Principles," "Essays: Moral, Political, and Æsthetic," and the "Principles of Psychology." 12mo.

"In a brief, but clear manner, elaborates a plan of classification."—*Hartford Courant.*

"One of the most original and deep thinkers of the age. * * * Will greatly assist all who desire to study Mental Philosophy."—*Philadelphia Press.*

Orlean Lamar, and Other Poems,

by SARAH E. KNOWLES. 12mo. Cloth.

"Not only lively and attractive with fancy, but it has the excellence of being pure, moral, and Christian."—*Religious Herald.*

Lyrical Recreations.

By SAMUEL WARD. Large 12mo. Cloth.

"There is a wealth of beauty which discovers itself the more we linger over the book."—*Journal of Commerce.*

"Its pages bear abundant evidence of taste and culture."—*Springfield Republican.*

Lyra Anglicana ; or, A Hymnal

of Sacred Poetry. Selected from the best English writers, and arranged after the order of the Apostles' Creed. By the Rev. GEORGE T. RIDER, M.A.

"As beautiful and valuable a collection of Sacred Poetry as has ever appeared."—*St. Louis Press.*

"Will be found very attractive from the warm devotional tone that pervades it."—*New York Times.*

"Much of the poetry is not found in American reprints."—*Gospel Messenger.*

Lyra Americana ; or, Verses of

Praise and Faith, from American Poets. Selected and arranged by the Rev. GEORGE T. RIDER, M.A. 12mo.

"They are collections of the most beautiful and touching poetic expressions of devotion."—*The Chronicle.*

"The collection is purely American ; the lyrics are all full of devotion and praise. Unusual taste has been evinced in the selection of the poetry."—*Troy Times.*

On Radiation. The "Rede" Lec-

ture, delivered in the Senate House before the University of Cambridge, on Tuesday, May 16, 1865, by JOHN TYNDALL, F.R.S., Professor of Natural Philosophy in the Royal Institute and in the Royal School of Mines. Author of "Heat considered as a Mode of Motion." 12mo. Cloth.

Contributions to the Geology

and the Physical Geography of Mexico, including a Geological and Topographical Map, with profiles of some of the principal mining districts. Together with a graphic description of an ascent of the volcano Popocatepetl. Edited by Baron F. W. VON EGLOFFSTEIN. Large 8vo. Illustrated. Cloth.

"The general interest excited on this continent as well as in Europe by late political events in Mexico, where a wide field for mining and land speculation is about to be opened again to foreign industry and foreign capital, has induced me to submit to the public two interesting publications of this highly favored region."—*Extract from Introduction.*

9 783337 402730